D.J. WILLIAMS

KING OF THE NIGHT

"Some say your entire life flashes before your eyes the instant before you die, but for Michael Hardeman there was only one moment—the day his son was born."

Acknowledgement

First of all, I want to thank all who have read *any* of my novels. Your encouragement and excitement for turning the page keeps my creativity flowing. And I can't wait for you to dive into this one. I'm grateful for the opportunity to share my stories with you.

To friends and family, who are too many to list. Besides, I realize the odds are high that I will miss names so you know who you are and what you mean to me. Thank you for standing alongside me on this crazy journey. With that said, I do want to give a special thanks to my wife who knows me better than anyone—and continues to guess who the characters might be in real life.

Behind the scenes, there is a team who brought this story and the world of Chase Hardeman even more alive through their insightful wisdom, engaged creativity, editing prowess, design flair, and marketing savvy. I will thank each one of you personally beyond the page. No doubt, you're the hardest workers in the room.

PROLOGUE

ATHENS, GREECE

Deep in the shallows where darkness lingered, a secret disrupted a delicate balance within the hallowed halls of freedom. Whispers in alleyways of depravity exposed shattered fragments of loyalty, tilting the scales of truth and power.

Chase Hardeman was not always a truth seeker, but he'd seen firsthand the depths those in power dove to keep their deepest secrets hidden. At times loyalty blurred the lines, bringing death at his hands. For that, he buried his shame in the graveyards of tormented souls. There was no doubt, he was a sinner, not a saint. So, how does a sinner fight in the shallows? One target at a time.

A grim silence echoed beneath a moonlit sky. Breathing steadied as he tucked the Sig Sauer (SIG) against his chest, moving stealthily through a parlor of the Vihkrov's mega-yacht. Red lasers reflected off the windows, beaming across the interior. With his wetsuit partially on, he stood motionless in a corner, aiming the silencer at a shadow. Two quick shots left the body slumped against a glass door. More shadows appeared dead ahead. No hesitation. All neutralized, inviting an eerie silence back into the night.

Nearly a year out of sight, sailing across the oceans aboard the *Midnight Moon*, left him at a crossroads. He'd sworn to never take another life, and yet death reached out from the grave. Slipping below deck, his pace quickened toward the master bedroom. Ears zoned into the slightest sound. On a nightstand, an antique clock jackhammered as the seconds passed.

Carrying an extra twenty pounds of muscle on his bones, sweat seeped down his cheeks and neck. The Stars and Stripes tattoo sleeved on his forearm disguised a crude memory. The unthinkable never should've happened, but it did. And time had never healed—it merely tormented the waking hours.

Snapping out of a downward spiral, one that left empty bottles by sunrise, Chase slipped both arms into the wetsuit, pulled it over his shoulders, and zipped it tight. From a hidden compartment beneath the king-sized bed, he grabbed a leather-bound book, ammo, a rugged hard drive, and a small dented *Speed Racer* tin box. Before returning upstairs to the parlor, he shoved all of it in a waterproof backpack knowing his actions had sent him back to a legend he'd buried in the deserts of the Middle East.

A sense of urgency washed over him as unanswered questions played on an endless loop. When his eyes caught movement, he instinctively aimed the SIG with accuracy, ready to fire, surprised at how easily he'd once again crossed the lines. He eased his index finger off the trigger as a familiar voice stopped him.

"Quiet as an anchor outside," Dax whispered.

"Everything rigged?"

"As good as it's gonna be."

Dax stood beside Chase, wearing an identical wetsuit, taking in the scene. For a moment, they stared at the lifeless bodies. A ritual done countless times as part of their covert operations under the Red Venture Group. Instincts and training returned as naturally as a Greek strolling through the Parthenon. Dax snapped photos of each intruder. With any luck, he'd track down their identities and confirm what they'd both feared. After hiding out on an oligarch's yacht, they were being hunted. Again.

"You know it'd be easier if we just dug our own graves," Dax said.

"It's not too late for you to cash in your chips and go off the grid."

Dax handed Chase a remote trigger. "Who else is gonna save your ass?"

Watching Dax limp across the parlor was a reminder of the battles waged and sacrifices made to keep each other alive. They'd said it thousands of times—while they weren't blood, they were brothers bonded by life and war. Secrets they shared, and the ghosts they fought, were one and the same.

Tonight at the Piraeus Marina, the city of Athens would be shaken by what many would believe to be a terrorist attack, leaving global intelligence agencies questioning whether it was merely retribution against Dmitry Vihkrov and the Kingpin's daughter, Elena. From the moment her eyes pierced Chase's soul, he was captured under a spell. She'd grabbed his heart like no other and more than once kept it beating in the fog of war. Nightmares. Loss. Betrayal. After Mosul, she was the one who brought him through the darkest days—which made his actions on this night indefensible. If they were ever face-to-face again, she'd know it was he who betrayed her trust.

Before stepping outside, he tucked the SIG into the waterproof backpack and slipped the remote detonator into a zippered pocket in his wetsuit. Scanning the dock and the surrounding marina, there was only one way to avoid the security cameras. He climbed overboard with Dax right behind, lowering themselves into the frigid water. Wading between the docked mega-yachts, they left no disturbance in the stillness of their wake.

Eight months had passed since she disappeared. Now death was the only way to find proof of life. Chase retrieved the trigger, and with a flip of a switch, the *Midnight Moon* exploded into a fiery inferno.

ONE

"You sure we can trust him, Chase?"

"Trust has nothing to do with it. He's one step from Bouchard."

"Which is exactly what nearly got us both killed the last time."

"We need what he has, and he wants what we do."

Less than an hour after the explosion, locals sipped wine and downed lagers at a corner taverna as news of the marina bombing spread across the city. Chase had followed the instructions and parked the Mini in an abandoned garage before heading down cobble stone streets flanked by bakeries and eclectic souvenir shops.

Blending in with the locals, they cut down a pedestrianized alley beneath bright red terraces before turning onto another stepped street where the addresses counted upward. Chase stopped outside a blue doored white house decorated with an assortment of clay flower pots. All of which were empty. He retrieved a key he'd found in the glovebox of the Mini, then hesitated to insert it into the lock. *Being on the run means wheels up by daybreak.* Surrendering to the inevitable, he inserted the key and pushed the one question at the root of it all aside.

Is she already dead?

Inside, the apartment was musty and dingy, scarcely furnished, with cracked tiled floors beneath inch thick dust. No pictures on the walls. No television. Only a single overhead bare bulb illuminated a ragged mustard sofa and folding table. It wasn't a home, it was a safe house.

Both froze as the back door creaked.

Pulling their SIGs, they positioned themselves at opposite sides of the living room, ready for whoever entered.

"You left quite a mess at the marina," a hoarse voice mumbled. Simon Adams, President Bouchard's Chief of Staff, ignored the weapons pointed at his chest as he closed the door and faced them. "Seems to be your modus operandi."

Would've been cleaner if you'd given us more warning.

"We improvised," Chase shot back. "Or else you'd be standing here alone."

"Intelligence was unreliable." Adams sized up Chase. "Any idea who they are?"

"We took a few headshots in case you needed them for the next news cycle." Dax shoved his cell in Adams' face, not bothering to hide his contempt. "Bouchard's secret war on terror."

With a steady glare, Adams bantered, "Less I know, the better."

"We're wasting time," Chase interrupted. "We're here, now what?"

"The President is in negotiations with the G10," Adams said. "But he has considered your request. I must tell you, there are reservations about what you're asking. In my opinion, it's a cluster waiting to happen that could derail his presidency."

"While we're getting punched in the nuts," Dax chimed in, "your modus operandi is to worry about the political fallout? Unbelievable."

Easy, Dax. He's a chess piece in the game.

Adams was a seasoned CIA operative, once assigned as Station Chief in Germany before Bouchard convinced him to join the Administration. As a shadow hunter, one who spied on the actors who threatened U.S. interests, he knew his way around a city after dark. But a late-night rendezvous on foreign soil as Chief of Staff without a Secret Service detail was a risk. And the fact he was standing in front of them meant there was a deal on the table.

I left Bouchard no other choice.

After what occurred in Los Angeles nearly a year earlier, Chase knew Bouchard relied heavily on Adams to not only keep the Red Venture Group (RVG) buried, but to run interference as his attempts to contact the President directly went unanswered.

"We're not asking for RVG to be operational." Chase placed the keys for the safe house and the Mini on a table. "You have my word."

Adams smirked. "Collateral damage is highly probable with the two of you."

"We'd still be winners in Vegas," Dax quipped.

"If I don't hand over what you've asked for, then what?"

"I'll go public about her disappearance," Chase answered. *And bury all of you.*

Adams pointed a crooked finger as his eyes narrowed. "If you're caught or reveal one shred of evidence that points back to the President, you'll be deemed enemies of state."

"Sounds like the deal of a century," Dax blurted. "Does

that come with Medicare?"

"And you'll have no further access to the President." Adams handed over an envelope. "Everything we have is inside."

Chase opened the envelope and removed surveillance photos of his younger self and Dax standing alongside known terrorists, many of whom were left with a bullet in their skull. And there were other photos, including snapshots of them with Dmitry and Elena Vihkrov. At first glance, the dossier not only labeled them enemies of state but also linked them to the head of the Bratva—Russian mob.

A perfect combo from a Cold War pro.

"Think of the dossier as insurance," Adams said. "And the thumb drive has the intel."

"Full disclosure," Chase replied. "We have our own package of RVG secrets."

"Then let's hope neither one of us will have to piss on the other." Adams nodded at the thumb drive. "Street camera footage and the list you requested. Names. Addresses. All RVG assets given asylum." He paused for a moment. "President Bouchard has one additional stipulation."

"Bait and switch," Dax mumbled. "Politicians are street magicians."

Chase ignored the truth spilling from Dax's lips. "What's the catch?"

"Bring Bernhardt Brandis back to U.S. soil," Adams stated. "Alive."

Growing up with a legendary politician, hall of fame auctioneer, father meant Chase had seen the art of the deal up close. It was an illusion to persuade one to believe they were getting what their hearts desired most.

During his run for the Presidency, Michael Hardeman promised in debates to change the lives of the lower and middle class, who were the backbone to America's independence, even though he knew the debts he owed to those in power.

When his run in politics was over, he stood before thousands on the auction stage, sold the most prized collector cars to the wealthiest in society, and made everyone feel as if they were getting a steal of a lifetime. But when the votes were counted and the gavel slammed, the real deal makers struck gold or smashed dirt when backed against a wall with nowhere to turn.

Bring Bernhardt Brandis back alive, and we're free to hunt the hunter.

Chase reached out his hand, ready to strike gold. "Rules of engagement are clear."

Adams snatched the keys from the table, then stepped back. "It's your funeral."

Two rounds shattered the window, ripping through the curtains. Chase dove for cover, then rolled over to see Dax ducking near the front door, eyeing the street outside.

"This is like a freakin' death coaster that never ends," Dax blurted.

"We need to move," Chase said in a lowered voice, knowing a heat signature was the only way for a sniper to get them in the crosshairs. "Ready?"

Glancing over his shoulder, adrenaline pumped harder at the sight of Adams face down on the floor. Blood oozed beneath the body across the distressed floor. Crawling on his stomach, Chase reached out and pressed his fingers against Adams' neck, hoping for a pulse. Dax stared back as Chase shook his head.

Bouchard's Chief of Staff, an ex-CIA operative and political fixer, was dead.

TWO

Crouched behind Adams' lifeless body, Chase braced for another onslaught. *Wars fought in the shadows refuse to remain buried forever.* Escaping the past aboard a corrupt oligarch's yacht sailing across the Atlantic was wishful thinking. Less than a year after the events in Los Angeles, they were back in the trenches.

"Heads or tails?" Chase asked.

Dax kept his eyes glued to the streets, as well as opposite windows and rooftops. "You know it's bad luck to call for tails."

"Tails it is then."

With his SIG tucked against his chest, Dax inched back along the wall. Even with the pronounced limp, the aftermath of the Prodigal, Chase noticed how Dax still moved with purpose. They'd kicked in doors, busted skulls, smuggled treasures, and silenced terrorists far from congressional oversight. In the fight and in life, there was no other Chase trusted more. Dax had saved his life more than once. The last time nearly killed them both.

BUZZ. BUZZ.

Chase glanced at Dax, who stared back in mirrored confu-

11

sion as the vibrating tone continued. Reaching into Adams' pocket, Chase retrieved a cell then used the Chief of Staff's thumbprint to unlock the screen.

"Thirty seconds, you'll both be dead." A woman's steadied voice cut the tension, yet the pounding in Chase's chest intensified. "Light switch inside the storage closet."

The line went dead as Chase turned back to Dax. "McIntyre."

With eyebrows raised, Dax crept backward as Chase tucked Adams' cell into his own pocket, then snatched the keys and dossier. Dax grabbed their backpacks, and both headed down a hallway, checking doors until they found the storage closet.

"You sure she's not the one shooting at us?" Dax asked.

Opening the storage closet, Chase peered inside and searched for a light switch. "If she is, then we should've picked heads."

Flipping the switch, the floor beneath shifted to reveal an iron ladder bolted to the side of an underground passageway. Chase was the first one down with Dax right behind. As the underground entrance sealed, footsteps creaked across the floor above. With a swipe of a blade, Chase sliced through electrical wiring, disabling the trigger. For a moment, they stood in blackness, inhaling the damp, cold, and musty air.

From the beginning, they'd been sworn to secrecy by the Oval Office. Each trusted Chase's father for protection while in deep cover hunting the ghosts of terror. Of course, along the way, they'd seized a few spoils of war for themselves. Call it the Hardeman retirement package hidden within the vaults of the family auction business.

For years, rumors of the Red Venture Group (RVG) circulated within intelligence circles, but the conclusion had always been that the very idea was a made-for-Hollywood myth. But after the night Michael Hardeman's life was taken from him, those chambers of conspiracy within the hallowed halls of Washington reverberated with echoes of its existence.

Chase and Dax were pawns in an endless game as patriots turned warriors, not war dogs drunk on heroics. Flashes from Fallujah, Ramada, Amarah, Hawija, Mosul, and Baghdad dissolved into faces from countless operations. Too many to count. While the nightmares faded over time, those who died wandered the graveyard of their sins.

Using their cells to illuminate the tunnel, they moved stealthily. Reaching the opposite end of the tunnel, they found a second ladder. An escape route, courtesy of a woman they'd sworn to never trust. A woman known to them only as McIntyre. She was a handler without a first name who Michael Hardeman recruited. Neither Chase nor Dax knew she existed until RVG was non-operational. She had shadowed them across the Middle East, which meant she knew where the bodies were buried. The last time Chase saw her was on a chilly night at the Griffith Observatory when she revealed the truth about the Prodigal then disappeared.

Climbing the ladder, Chase forced the manhole cover aside, then pulled himself out of the tunnel, emerging into an alley. Dax ignored the outstretched hand as he struggled to get to his feet before shoving the manhole cover back into place. Across the street, a dark sedan flashed its headlights.

"So, we're getting the band back together?" Dax grumbled.

"This isn't a reunion tour."

Ducking across the street, they slipped into the sedan. McIntyre wasted no time as she pulled away from the curb, cruising north away from Plaka District. She drove in silence while Chase eyed the side mirror. When they were far enough from the safe house, she pulled over and parked near Monastiraki Square.

"How long've you been following us?" Chase asked.

"Didn't expect to see either of you," she answered. "I've been monitoring Adams."

"What do you mean, *monitoring*?"

"Tracking his encrypted cell for calls, texts, and email." McIntyre held out her palm as Chase reluctantly handed over the Chief of Staff's cell, as well as the keys to the safe house and Mini. "My turn. Why were you meeting with him?"

Chase weighed his answer, unsure of whether to tell the truth, the whole truth and nothing but. In the backseat, Dax started downloading files from the thumb drive onto his laptop.

"We needed intelligence only Bouchard or Adams could provide on RVG."

"Leave it to the two of you to wake a sleeping dragon." McIntyre shook her head as her gaze shifted to the rearview. She dialed her cell, relayed the address of the safe house and garage, then disconnected the call. "I assume you two blew up Dmitry's yacht."

After all you've done, you think you're our handler again?

"We had no other choice," Chase replied. "Situation was fluid."

"More like reckless."

"Call it a necessary distraction."

"To do what, disappear?" She checked her watch, then the rearview again, clearly itching to move. "Monterey was a spectacle that placed you on center stage. Nothing you do will change the fact that your legends are burned."

A twinge of uneasiness struck Chase hard. "Well, we can't sit here all night then."

Fingers rifled across the keys before Dax announced, "He's in Freetown."

"We need wheels up," Chase said to McIntyre. "Can you handle it?"

"Better than you've handled this so far."

THREE

Special Agent Laney Kelley walked beneath the palm trees leading up to a glowing entrance of Union Station, perhaps the last of the great train stations. Stepping inside transported one back to the golden age of the thirties. Brass chandeliers illuminated the main lobby. Mission-styled mosaic tiles. Custom leather chairs rather than hard plastic seats. Intricately designed wood ceilings etched with handcrafted workmanship. A perfect LA homage to the legendary architect Frank Lloyd Wright.

Laney found an empty chair that faced the entrance. She pulled her jacket tight to hide a sidearm, then settled in shortly after 10 P.M. Scanning faces was second nature, something she'd been trained to do since her first week at Quantico. Travelers on Amtrak, LAX Flyaway, Greyhound, Metro, Megabus, and those glued to their screens waiting for a ride share. She thought of how this was a sign of the times, being lost in your own bubble, unaware of the world around you. Her thoughts shifted to how quickly Angelenos had fallen back into the normalcy of life less than a year after the secret keepers extinguished any ray of truth about the attack in Los Angeles.

Memories from the undercover assignment were horrific. She was left scarred in ways she had yet to fully understand. But she wasn't going to spend the next six months on a sofa pouring out her greatest fears and regrets. Still, no matter how hard she tried to get back to normal, the loss she suffered left her a bit sideways.

Weeks after the city returned to its Angeleno hustle, President Bouchard promoted Laney to Agent in Charge of the LA black site. It should've been cause for celebration, even though her superiors complained she was too young and inexperienced. She'd been an agent going on nine years and knew the chain of command stretched high above her new role. What she didn't realize when she buried the old black site near Skid Row was that her new role wasn't what she expected. Instead of chasing the Bureau's most wanted, she busied herself for months as forewoman in the construction of the new black site on the outskirts of South Pasadena. On most days, she couldn't help but wonder if it was President Bouchard's way of keeping her benched.

A text pinged: EL PUEBLO. 5 MIN.

Reading the text several times, she weighed the change in plans. She'd tried to push the operation through official channels but had been ordered to stand down. The words of her mentor, Russell Vaughn, rang in her ears.

"Your instincts are what will keep you alive or leave you bleeding in a back alley."

He was also the one who paraded her in front of the nation during a terrorist manhunt that left LA on lockdown. Ever since, she'd been itching to get back on the streets. It's where she belonged. And an informant was her best shot to locate a target who'd remained elusive from the Bureau for over a decade.

With a brisk chill in the air, Laney pulled her collar up as her breath wafted ahead of her stride. Crossing Alameda, she headed toward Father Serra Park. At this hour, the park was alive with the homeless camped out in a makeshift village. A skunked odor of cannabis and urine filled her nostrils. Ignoring the catcalls, her pace quickened through the park and across Los Angeles Street toward Olvera. Before entering the tree-canopied marketplace, where trinket shops and Mexican restaurants were locked up for the night, she turned left toward the El Pueblo Los Angeles Historical Monument.

A shadow stepped into the dimly lit plaza. Laney's fingers brushed across her jacket as she fought the urge to retrieve her weapon. A few feet away stood Eric Wright, an ex-con turned informant she'd recruited after his sister disappeared. Laney stopped a few steps away, noticing his hands shoved deep in his pockets.

"It's been three years," Wright said coldly. "You promised you'd find her."

"I've never stopped working the case." Laney peered over his shoulder into the darkness. "And I intend to keep my promise to find Michelle."

Wright's eyes shifted nervously. "Do you know the last time anyone saw her?"

"She was at a party on the Westside." Laney inched forward, knowing she needed to control the conversation. "Eric, whatever's going on, we can sort it out."

"Tonight, my sister is coming home." Tears welled up in his eyes as he pulled a Glock from his jacket before aiming it at Laney. "I'm sorry, Agent Kelley."

Laney spun around as a black SUV skidded the corner before

jumping the curb. High beams blinded her as she reached for her sidearm. Screeching to a halt, four armed men jumped out as her Glock moved between them. One of the men was dressed in a suit and tie, early forties, six-three, two-twenty. Laney noticed a partial tattoo along the right side of his neck. But it was his accent that caught her off guard.

"You've done well," the Englishman said. "Bravo."

"Where's my sister?" Wright kept the Glock pointed at Laney. "That's the deal."

"Yes, of course." The Englishman waved at one of his men. "I'm a man of my word, Mr. Wright."

A woman was pulled from the back passenger seat and shoved forward. Barely conscious. Clearly drugged. She stumbled into Wright's arms as he dropped the Glock to the ground. Seconds after a brother and sister were reunited, a bullet was lodged in each of their skulls.

"Now, it is you who are on center stage." The Englishman nodded toward the Glock, which was firmly in Laney's grasp. "Surely, you cannot shoot all of us."

Laney stared down at the bodies, stunned yet on edge, then shifted her gaze toward the Englishman as she set the Glock on the ground. He motioned for her to raise her hands. She complied, searching for a way out. She flinched as he snatched the Bureau ID from inside her jacket.

"On your knees," he ordered.

Her eyes flared as she braced herself. "You'd like that wouldn't you."

The Englishman smirked slyly. "I assure you, Mr. Brandis will not be as polite."

Laney was out of time. *Fight or flight.* She lunged forward, digging her shoulder into his ribs, knocking him off balance.

To her surprise, he restrained from firing his weapon. But her window to escape slammed shut as a jolt of electricity punched her squarely in the back, leaving her body stiff as a dead fish. She tumbled to the concrete, flopping and struggling as her muscles convulsed. Barely able to catch a breath, she rolled over wide-eyed as the Englishman pounced and straddled her body.

With one swift blow, the nightmare began.

FOUR

No words were exchanged on the forty-minute drive across the city. Keeping his sights on the side mirror, Chase was fully aware that McIntyre was the only person who had witnessed firsthand the origins of their RVG legends in the Middle East. As smugglers with cash to burn they bought stolen artifacts from terrorists to sell on the black market. With each deal, the worst in humanity were targeted and silenced. The files contained on the rugged drive tucked into his backpack were proof the RVG myth was real.

She knows my darkest tendencies, and yet we're strangers.

From the beginning, Michael Hardeman was promised protection by the President, including anonymity. But in the aftermath of the Mosul operation, RVG was dismantled, leaving Chase and Dax at the top of a dark web hit list. Months had passed since he'd slept through the night as he struggled to escape the tortured nightmares. Out of all of them, Mosul was the one that haunted him the most. In the past, he escaped in his drugs of choice—a trifecta of alcohol, cocaine, and pain killers. While memories lingered in the waking hours, his dream to leave the dead behind and carry on the family legacy remained an elusive fantasy.

At eight years old, all he wanted was to be an auctioneer. His father taught a masterclass in the arena and gave Chase the tools to navigate the halls of the rich, as well as the shadows of true power. Father and son traveled the world, closing deals with the wealthiest in society while keeping spoils of war for themselves. Standing beside his larger-than-life tornado father was a rush, even when they crossed the lines to keep their clientele satisfied and the bounty hidden.

Dreams are nothing more than impossible wishes. There's a price for what I've done—the nightmares are a death sentence to my soul.

McIntyre flashed a forged passport at a restricted entrance to Athens Airport. She handed an envelope to a security guard, then drove onto the airfield toward an exclusive area lined with private hangars far from security lines, herded economy class, and stale peanuts. Chase hadn't been on a plane after returning from Iceland. Since then, he'd searched for intelligence on McIntyre and discovered before she was their handler, she was a spook for the Agency. Her tradecraft was evident in surveillance and bugging Adams' encrypted Blackberry, helping them escape through a safe house tunnel, and how smoothly she'd gained entrance to the Athens airport. After RVG, she'd stepped across the pond, gaining a reputation within circles of power as a top broker willing to unload military weapons to America's enemies.

True patriotism isn't etched in black and white. Who am I to condemn anyone?

"It's time you start spending your Monterey bounty." McIntyre pulled up to the front of a hanger, cut off the headlights, then sent another text. "Crypto is the best form of payment."

"Who did you call about the safe house?" Chase asked.

"A trusted cleaner. With the two of you, it seems I'll need one in every city."

Doors of the hanger slid open, and the sedan rolled inside. A pilot busied himself with a pre-flight routine while McIntyre parked next to a sleek metallic silver Gulfstream.

"Chase, if this is going to work," she said, "we need to trust each other."

"Famous last words," Dax chimed in.

"Dad trusted you. That'll have to be good enough for now."

Climbing from the sedan, Chase relayed a flight destination to the pilot, then transferred a hundred grand in crypto to an untraceable account. Dax swept the sedan, wiping fingerprints and grabbing backpacks. *No time to leave without a trace.* McIntyre took their sidearms and secured them inside a hidden compartment in one of the anvil cases rolled next to the Gulfstream. They did a quick double-check before boarding, buckled in, and were wheels up before sunrise.

Ascending to thirty thousand feet, the city beneath was lost in a thick layer of clouds. Chase gripped the armrest of a plush black leather seat while the Gulfstream reached cruising altitude. A slight turbulence rattled the shiny chrome trim and shook the mahogany panels inside the cabin. *Ever since London, my chest feels like it's going to burst.* Chase breathed in deep and stared out the window as the flickering stars faded into daylight. He glanced over at Dax, who was settled in sorting through the thumb drive from Adams, and wondered how Dax managed to weather the storm after the brutal pain inflicted on him.

"Why were you shadowing him?" Chase asked McIntyre.

"A client offered information on Bouchard."

"Who's the client?"

"A hacker who developed Unicorn."

"Seriously?" Dax interrupted. "No one's ever confirmed an identity."

"And I plan to keep it that way," McIntyre replied. "He allowed me limited access to monitor Adams' Blackberry to prove what he claimed was true. But after I called you, the software disabled."

"Fail safe," Dax pointed out. "Surveillance only."

"What did your client claim to know about Bouchard?"

"To start with, DOJ is investigating what occurred in Los Angeles. Rumors within Washington are that General Abbott has agreed to a closed-door interview with the House Intelligence Committee. If the truth were brought to light, Bouchard would be impeached or worse. And there's more."

"General Abbott is an iceberg," Dax pointed out, "and Bouchard is the Titanic."

"When is this happening?" Chase pressed.

"I've monitored Adams for months. No texts. No calls. Nothing that confirms when the interview will occur."

"Maybe it's just a rumor," Dax suggested. "Washington's loaded with fake news."

"My source is extremely reliable, and Adams meeting with you is proof."

"Who would've been following him?" Chase asked.

"As Chief of Staff, he did what was necessary to keep the President out of the line of fire. Bouchard publicly brushed off the rumors regarding LA. When Adams slipped out of the hotel, that was the first sign they were trying to get ahead of it. And choosing an old Agency safe house meant Adams wanted no trace of his actions."

"How did you know about the tunnel?"

"I've used the apartment before, years ago."

"Did your client offer specifics about the information?"

"My client agreed to grant me access to Unicorn under the guise of anonymity. But what I can tell you is that the software is used covertly by numerous governments. It's possible there are those outside of our own with knowledge of Bouchard's connection to RVG." McIntyre shifted her weight and faced Chase. "Now, it's your turn."

"In Monterey, Special Agent Kelley offered us a chance to hunt a black market smuggler, Bernhardt Brandis. We turned her down. Eight months ago, she disappeared." *No need telling her about the dead hitmen at the bottom of the marina, or the dossier Adams was using as leverage.* "No ransom demands. No investigation. No KNR team. She's a ghost to the Bureau."

"Laney Kelley is the reason you met with Adams?"

"No one else we've contacted offered any insight. She doesn't have any living relatives. And to those who knew her within the Agency, it's as if she never existed." Chase leaned forward, his hands balled into fists. "I need to know if she's alive."

"My client is not the one who possesses the information on Bouchard, but I have my suspicions of who might." McIntyre held up the screen of her cell for them to see. Chase's eyes locked in on a black and white photo of Bernhardt Brandis leaving a restaurant surrounded by bodyguards. "With someone as dangerous as Brandis, you don't walk in the front door."

"Looks like we share a common target."

McIntyre leaned back in her seat and closed her eyes. "So, who are we visiting in Freetown?"

Dax glanced up from his laptop, dialed into the conversation. "Omar Youssef."

"Operation Whirlwind," she mused. "Omar won't be thrilled to see either of you."

FIVE

SEOUL, KOREA

Across the metropolitan area, express terminals bustled with citizens lost in a sea of humanity, headed for the outskirts of an alpha city with the fourth-largest economy on the planet. For those beaten down after a rigorous week, desperate to escape the packed buses and trains of rush hour, there was Myeongdong Kyoja. A local landmark where fifty years of traditions were served in bowls of piping hot rice noodles and chicken broth, with a side of dumplings. A simple dish done to perfection.

Ordering a second plate of dumplings, the Englishman blended in behind wire-rimmed glasses and a Goorin flatcap. His dark hair dyed white. Brown eyes now blue. From a corner table with a clear view of the customers, the thrill of the hunt was more than camouflage or the anticipation of the pounce. What brought the real rush was stalking in the blind. It, too, was a simple dish done to perfection.

In the months since the American was captured, Brandis escalated by hiring the Englishman to secure a dozen more trophies making the German his number one client. It seemed on the dark web, kidnap and rescue had become more lucrative than the smuggling trade. Governments paid millions to recover their assets while opposing leaders bid even higher for their enemies' secrets. Trapping each of Brandis' trophies required a unique approach. While the American was a classic snatch and grab, his next target required a lighter footprint.

The Englishman eyed a Korean gentleman a few tables over. From the dossier, the Englishman knew he had been following a genius scientist who specialized in viruses, chemical agents, and global pandemics. A man highly respected by leaders within his own country, who at one time considered him a national treasure after he rescued the nation from the H1N1 crisis. He had also spoken publicly of the UN's need to confront mainland China over the continual viruses that escaped their borders. Then he disappeared. Rumors believed the scientist was abducted by the Communist regime. Now a decade later, Dong Hyun-Ki had resurfaced as a ghost amidst the people.

After weeks of surveillance where the scientist never left his heavily guarded compound, the genius revealed his vice and was lured from his fortress.

Using a burner, the Englishman logged on to a messaging app where the profile was of a woman of European descent. Mid-thirties. Long hair draped over her shoulders. A seductive smile that drew the eye to curves in all the right places. She was way out of the scientist's league. But that was the point.

We always want what we can't have.

IM: NISHETETSU HOTEL. ROOM 407.

A few seconds later, Dong Hyun-Ki reached into his jacket and retrieved his cell. He read the message, then waved a waiter down for the bill. The Englishman finished off the last dumpling and scanned the room, knowing the scientist had not traveled alone. As if on cue, two men followed the target out of the restaurant keeping their distance but clearly shadowing him. The Englishman skipped out on the bill, pulled up the collar on his coat, and headed out into the cold night.

After a few blocks, the scientist entered the Nishetetsu Hotel.

Mastering the hunt between hunter and hunted.

A game with no rules, secret lives confronted.

A rush flowed through the Englishman's veins as he strolled across the lobby, ignoring both bodyguards who lounged near the floor-to-ceiling windows facing the street. He nodded at the front desk clerk before stepping aboard the elevator, standing next to the target. As the doors closed, he breathed in deep, inhaling the adrenaline. As the elevator ascended, he turned and smiled at the scientist, who smiled back.

Victim or victor, a scent of innocence wavers.

Hide and seek, the game shows no favors.

Stepping slightly behind the scientist, the Englishman slowly removed a syringe from an inner pocket of his coat. With precision, he leaned forward and stuck a needle into the target's neck. A fast-acting dose left the scientist struggling to keep his balance while the Englishman casually pressed a button for the roof.

Run as you may, the hunter catches his prey.

Surrender yourself, and die another day.

When the doors opened to the fourth floor, there was no one there. No European beauty. No chance at a night lost under the sheets. No chance to fulfill one's darkest fantasy. The Englishman held the target against the elevator wall as the doors closed. When they opened again, he hoisted the target over his shoulder and stepped out onto the roof. In the distance, a light in the sky approached.

SIX

PIRAEUS MARINA, ATHENS—MORNING

Elena Vihkrov strolled along the marina, her bloodshot eyes hidden behind dark sunglasses. Gazing at a partially sunken *Midnight Moon*, the charred wreckage struck more than a sentimental note.

Born along the Tegel Lake region of Berlin in 1995, she was an only child shipped off to boarding school at the age of seven. Raised on the grounds of Wicker Castle in East London, with summers spent along the California coastline of Montecito, her Cambridge education was not an escape from the family business. Rather, it was in preparation to one day rule over the Vihkrov empire.

Her mother, Olivia Bailey, an analyst for MI6 stationed in Brandenburg, provided intelligence on agency targets leading up to the 1998 Russian Flu. She predicted the devalued ruble and the financial disruption in countries throughout Europe. Elena's father, Dmitry Vihkrov, orphaned at the age of six, lived on the streets of Dagestan, where in his early teens, he was beaten into the Bratva before steadily climbing the ranks one body at a time.

An encounter at the legendary nightclub, Madame Soho, in west London sparked a love affair between Dmitry and

Olivia that rocked British intelligence throughout Europe and exposed Dmitry's enemies within the Russian mob. What began as a whirlwind romance evolved over the years into a partnership with hundreds of millions flowing through a sophisticated network of narcotics, money laundering, prostitution, as well as corporate and political espionage.

When Elena was six years old, she lost the innocence of family as she chased her father across the grounds of Wicker Castle to find her mother hanging from a tree beneath a full moon as the clock struck midnight. As time passed, Elena remembered less and less of her mother, but her love and loyalty to her father remained steadfast.

Detective Castellanos, a twenty-year veteran of the Hellenic Police Force, greeted Elena as she slipped between a gathering crowd and local media. Escorted through the barricade, she thought of the significance of the vessel's name—*Midnight Moon*.

A message to our enemies that loss is never forgotten.

"Four bodies recovered," Castellanos pointed out. "Due to the severity of the fire, it will take time for positive identification."

"I wish to see them."

"Ms. Vihkrov, may I suggest..."

"My father assured me you are the one in charge."

Castellanos glanced uneasily toward the vessel as a body bag was raised from the stern using a hydraulic hoist. "As you can see, the investigation is in a sensitive stage."

Knowing the Greek was in the midst of a contentious custody battle, Elena removed her sunglasses and locked her piercing stare on him.

"Perhaps our arrangement has run its course."

"I assure you, I am here to protect your family's interest."

"Show me the bodies."

"As you wish."

Elena followed Castellanos along the pier, ignoring the other officers and investigators. Three days earlier, Chase and Dax lounged aboard the yacht as she left to see her father in London. From the moment she received the news, her messages and texts to Chase had gone unanswered. On the return flight to Athens, the hours passed at a snail's pace, leaving her fearing the worst. As she stood over the body bags lined up in a row, she hesitated before directing Castellanos to unzip the first one.

Gazing down at a burnt corpse, a stench permeated her nostrils. Pieces of clothing were melted into the skin. A blackened face was scarred from the flames. She scanned the right forearm, searching for the Stars and Stripes tattoo.

Certainly, the fire did the damage, but is it what killed him?

"Without dental records," Castellanos said, "this victim will be hard to identify."

Ellena swallowed hard. "Let me see the others."

One by one, Castellanos unzipped the next three bags until they stood over the last one. Stone-faced, Elena knelt and studied the body closely, noticing it wasn't as badly burned as the others. He definitely wasn't Chase or Dax, but he looked familiar.

"Close the investigation." Elena slipped her sunglasses back on as she stood. "We will make arrangements to move the vessel."

"You must understand, I have only so much authority."

"Detective Castellanos, do you love your daughter?"

Leaving the detective standing at the pier dumbstruck,

Elena headed for the street with a cell pressed against her ear. Her father answered on the first ring.

"What have you found?"

"*Midnight Moon* is destroyed. Four dead."

"I am truly sorry."

"Castellanos has yet to identify them."

"Of course, then we must wait for good news."

She forced the lump in her throat back into her chest. "Half of the vessel is underwater."

"I will arrange for a barge to salvage."

"After all he has done, his enemies have never rested." Reaching the street, Elena slipped into the backseat of a waiting SUV. "If we are the reason..."

"Elena, it is not yet time to grieve. There is much to be done."

"Yes, Papa."

SEVEN

ROYAL OLYMPIC HOTEL, ATHENS

President David Bouchard stepped from the shower and toweled off his weathered, chiseled physique. Standing in front of the mirror, he looked like a Hollywood actor straight out of Central Casting.

From coast to coast, the one percent discreetly bankrolled his presidential campaign with a mounting roster of celebs, Silicon Beach tech entrepreneurs, and Wall Street moguls.

No politician in history harnessed the power and influence of X, Instagram, and Facebook, with greater tenacity. Rumors of a streaming series after his presidency circulated, leaving the world questioning whether Bouchard would run for a second term.

Publicly he stood in opposition to Washington's elite alongside his mind-reading, speech-writing sister. Together they rallied minorities and majorities to a landslide victory the first time around. It was an epic story scripted from the moment he announced his presidential run standing in the midst of the family's vineyard in Los Olivos.

Streaks of grey in his sandy blonde hair and crow's feet ridged alongside his brows framed signature emerald eyes that had lost a bit of their luster, even though he was hanging on to his late forties. Youthful exuberance and optimism aged within isolated complexity and confinement as Commander in Chief. While his approval ratings skyrocketed early in his first term, rivaling the likes of Kennedy, the last eighteen months brought a steady decline.

From the stone countertop, he grabbed his encrypted Blackberry and dialed. He hated texting, so he left a voicemail for his Chief of Staff, Simon Adams.

Dealing with a buffet of international flash points seemed endless.

Trade disputes with China were escalating with each side drawing hard lines. Russian provocation in the last election was a distant memory as the regime warred against countries beyond their borders. Iran's cries over an abandoned nuclear deal and the billions infused into their economy left many Americans protesting against Bouchard's administration. A lingering aftermath from a botched evacuation of U.S. troops from Afghanistan still stung deep—a blemish on his presidential record that could not be wiped away. And then there was the slow-burning fuse of climate change.

But he *had* brokered a peace treaty in the Middle East no one thought possible—which was being held together by a few grains of sand.

With all of the uncertainty in the world, Bouchard was sure of one thing. After the morning press conference, where world leaders paraded like peacocks then sliced like Ripper, he was headed to the vineyard. Slip on a pair of jeans and a t-shirt, dig his boots in the stirrups of his quarter horse Cheyenne, and strategize a way to turn his presidency and administration around.

Everyone wants answers, but all I want is to escape.

Shuffling across the opulent Penthouse living room, he entered a sprawling master bedroom overlooking the Temple Zeus and the Acropolis. Hanging in a closet was a perfectly tailored navy blue suit, starched white shirt, and a crimson silk tie—the armor of the most powerful leader in the free world.

After he was dressed, he stepped out from the bedroom as the Penthouse door opened. Avery entered and stood in the center of the living room holding a six-pack of Red Bull in one hand.

"Breakfast of champions." Bouchard grabbed the cans, set them on a side table, then opened one and took a long gulp. "You're a Godsend, sis."

"We all have our vices."

In her late thirties, Avery Bouchard was attractive without suggesting an imposing appearance. As a teenager, she was the lone survivor of a boating accident off the coast of Monterey that killed Bouchard's wife and kids. Guilt followed her from graduation with a Master's in Literacy to a lucrative career ghostwriting for a list of bestselling authors.

The night before Bouchard's big announcement, he asked Avery to put family first. Whether it was guilt, loyalty, or both, she placed her roster of bestselling authors on hold to become her brother's fiercest protector. While Bouchard's charisma charmed the nation, the words Avery penned defined his presidency.

"Have you spoken with Simon this morning?"

"Left him a message earlier," Bouchard answered. "Why?"

"He didn't call with notes on your speech."

"That's strange."

"I agree. I tried to reach him, but he's not answering."

"Secret Service check his room?"

"He wasn't there. Hotel security cameras showed him ducking out the service entrance last night around nine-thirty. No sign he's returned."

Bouchard finished off the Red Bull and stared through the freestanding bulletproof glass in front of the window framing the Acropolis—the Parthenon, Propylaea, Temple of Athena, Nike, Erechtheion, and the Statue of Athena Promachos. A throne to kings. A citadel. A mythical home of the Gods. From the Mycenaean Civilization to the Golden Age and beyond, the restored temples of the Acropolis endured as history embraced its legend.

Taking in the breathtaking sight, Bouchard thought of how over the centuries, wars rooted in power, religion, and freedom left bloodshed buried beneath their cornerstones.

"I never thought I'd win," Bouchard said. "I still don't feel like I belong."

"I'm not sure anyone ever gets used to being *the* President."

"I don't want to get used to it, ever."

"David, is this about General Abbott?"

"He's the tip of the iceberg. We're in a war we can't win, Avery."

"We've beaten the odds before. We'll do it again."

"If I leave at the end of my term, there's a chance the world won't tear me apart like wolves once I'm gone."

"Even the greatest in history have stood amidst the rubble of their own legacy. Adversity forced them to rebuild, to become stronger, to battle their own doubt. David, you're a battle-tested warrior who welcomes the fight, no matter if it's a world away or on our own soil. You're in this now, so there is no turning back."

Avery's words drifted in deafening silence. She squeezed Bouchard's arm. "Now, what are we going to do about finding Simon?"

EIGHT

FREETOWN, SIERRA LEONE

Walking across the tarmac into the immigration area of Lungi International Airport, Chase was aware of a developing country where third-world poverty lurked behind the veil. *Corrupt. Unstable. Unpredictable.* Once you stepped away from the tourist brochures to witness the struggles of millions, the truth of Sierra Leoneans penned a more disturbing story.

Since leaving Athens, Chase couldn't help but wonder whether news of Simon Adams had hit the global networks. If McIntyre was worth her reputation, neither Adams nor the Mini would ever be found. But the escape wasn't Copperfield or Angel. They'd left the *Midnight Moon* burning with dead aboard. They'd walked along public streets to the safe house. They'd left the car inside the private air hangar. Odds were the clues in their wake would catch up to them. Disappearing without a trace was the plan, and within a few steps, they'd know whether it worked.

Chase leaned in and whispered to Dax, "Feeling lucky?"

"Heroes first," Dax answered. "It's the price you pay, bro."

Handing over a forged passport, Chase's gaze wandered from the immigration officer to his surroundings. Once a British Royal Air Force base, the civilian airport with its plastic chairs and stale floors left an unimpressive hub decades behind most regional airports in the States.

The immigration officer glanced up from the passport. "Purpose of your visit?"

"Vacation," Chase answered. "I've always wanted to go to Bunce Island."

"Where will you be staying?"

McIntyre stepped up to the desk, offering a cordial smile. "Lumley Beach."

Holding out his hand, the officer waved for McIntyre's passport. Without flinching, she handed over an alias of her own. *No telling how many identities she uses.* Next, the officer motioned for Dax to do the same. All three waited until the officer stamped each passport, then handed them back. Heading for the exit with luggage and anvil cases, Chase breathed easier knowing they'd escaped Greece without landing on Interpol.

During the flight, Chase had searched online rather than allowing himself to sleep. He thought he'd get over the impending dread of crashing, but that seemed to haunt him still. Reading up on Sierra Leone, he ran across the words inscribed in stone at King's Gate commemorating an African city liberated from the slave trade, breaking the chains that first enslaved them on Bunce Island.

Any slave who passes through this gate is declared a free man.

To the locals and tourism board, the city signified unity, peace, and freedom. But for foreigners, Sierra Leone was better known as the epicenter for a corrupt diamond and gold trade that destabilized a government, targeted presidents, and ended in bloody revolutions.

Freedom is never free. Never. A price is always paid for those

41

who fight for change.

Heading through the exit, Dax's words left Chase questioning if he was willing to pay the price to pass through the gates a free man. He glanced at the blank screen of his cell, which had been turned off since vanishing from the marina. His thoughts shifted to Bouchard and the Vihkrovs. *Power on my cell, they'll find us, and the hunt will be over before it begins.* He slipped the cell back into his pocket, slid his shades onto the bridge of his nose, and was hit by a sweltering heat as they stepped outside.

"So, this is what hell feels like." Dax tugged at his shirt, instantly sweating. "No wonder McIntyre said Omar's gonna be pissed when he sees us. We promised him paradise, and he ended up in another desert."

McIntyre chimed in. "Not all of Sierra Leone is this way."

"Reminds me of Mosul," Dax bantered. "Except with less bullets and bombs."

Chase added to the dark humor. "Give us time."

A long line of green, red, and white taxis were parked near the curb. Behind the wheel were drivers ready to bombard the American tourists. McIntyre pointed out a silver minivan. As they approached, the driver waved from behind the windshield. Chase and Dax climbed into the backseat while McIntyre rode shotgun. The driver, late twenties, blasted the air con as the van headed away from the airport into the heart of the city.

"Mum, it is so good to see you," he said to McIntyre.

"Hard to believe it's been two years," she replied. "Chase and Dax, meet Mustapha Dollar."

"Whoa, that name is priceless," Dax quipped. "Is your nickname *Money*?"

Mustapha grinned wide. "My family and friends call me Stapha."

"So, how do you two know each other?" Chase asked.

McIntyre answered dismissively, "Stapha's family is well connected in the city."

"It is your first time in Freetown?" Stapha asked.

"It's one place I've always wanted to visit," Chase lied. "You were raised here?"

"I was born in Kangbe. Ten brothers and sisters. We live together with my mother and father on a farm about one hour drive."

"Can you tell us some stories about *Mum*?" Dax poked.

"No one wants to hear those stories," McIntyre interrupted, flashing a glare over her shoulder. "Stapha, were you able to secure what I need?"

"Not yet." The African's grin faded. "Mum, there is an issue."

As the miles ticked, Chase dozed off, feeling the failing air con suck every ounce of energy from his bones. Traveling along packed dirt roads in bumper-to-bumper traffic, the van rode the temperature needle on the verge of overheating. Concrete structures. Tin shanty storefronts. Crowds of Africans swarmed the streets, leaving the world closing in tight. Women balanced stacks of flattened cardboard boxes on their heads, while on street corners cooked corn smoldered as exhaust wafted in polluted air.

"Shave ice." Dax pointed toward a street market buzzing with locals bargaining as rhythmic island tunes played as an embedded soundtrack. "No luau for you."

"A few miles up are the hotels and casinos." McIntyre nodded in the distance where dirt roads changed to smooth tarred streets headed toward a horseshoe-shaped harbor. "Mostly ex-pats, aid workers, and foreign businessmen stay at the Hotel Barmoi or at the west end of Lumley in short-term beachfront rentals."

"No better place to search for Omar," Chase said. "Dax, what was the address?"

"Intel says he's living in the Tower Hill district, but no address."

"That would've been too easy."

"Tower Hill is an affluent area," McIntyre pointed out. "Are you going to fill me in on the plan?"

"It's a work in progress," Chase answered.

"Which means," Dax bantered, "you're on a need-to-know basis."

"You've always been Chase's interpreter." McIntyre jabbed, not bothering to hide her disapproval. "It's foolish to leave me in the dark."

"Look who's talking about being left in the dark." Chase knew Dax was referring to the RVG operations where they'd improvised, believing they were on the edge without a lifeline. "If we would've known, we could've left with a few less scars."

"I was always close."

"You were always close, my ass."

"Pissing contest is over." Chase knew when to step in to stop the bickering. It was pointless to air their dirt in front of a stranger. "Stapha, are we close?"

"Nearly there."

The van crested a hill to reveal the beauty of white sand beaches set against the majestic Sierra Lyon mountains. A two-lane road stretched along the coast. Stapha pulled up to a two-story beachfront house protected by barred windows and an iron fence with pointed spears. Chase, Dax, and McIntyre climbed out and unloaded their luggage as well as the anvil cases.

"You two settle in." McIntyre handed them a set of keys. "I'll go with Stapha to resolve our issue."

"What kind of issue?" Chase asked.

"The kind that requires a favor to Stapha's father." McIntyre glanced up at the beachfront fortress. "You may find it hard to believe, but I'm sorry for what happened in Mosul and LA. Being unable to save your father is one of my deeper regrets."

With that, she climbed into the front seat. As the van pulled back onto the street headed east, Chase and Dax disappeared behind the walls of another safe house.

NINE

Chase sat across from Akram Kasim inside the Sadoun Tower, one step closer to finding a man the U.S. government labeled the Prodigal. Kasim wore a dark suit, a one-eighty from the American flag burning jihadist in the propaganda videos. But he wasn't the head of the snake, merely one of the Prodigals followers who slithered in the sand. There was no disguising his murderous eyes, which flared when talking about attacking the West. Once Dax left the table, the two men were alone.

"How did you meet Sarina?" Kasim asked, curious.

"We introduced ourselves at the hospital."

"She believes you can be trusted, and yet she barely knows you."

"We're the best at what we do, and we're here to make a deal."

"You will go no further unless I am convinced."

"What else can we do to prove ourselves?"

Kasim pushed his chair back and stood. "Come with me."

Glancing around for Dax, who was nowhere to be found, left Chase surrounded by Kasim's men. He was escorted out of the building into a waiting SUV, leaving his cell behind on the table. Fifteen minutes later, they pulled up to the Ibna Sina Hospital, where Sarina waited near the entrance. She approached Kasim as he rolled down the backseat window.

"What is wrong?" Sarina asked.

"If you are mistaken," Kasim replied in Arabic, "Abu will kill us both."

Sarina grabbed his forearm. "You must trust the American."

Whatever happened next determined Sarina's fate, as well as Chase's next move. For months they protected their *backstop*—names, addresses, business dealings—to support their legends as black market smugglers. Chase cultivated the relationship with Sarina by offering what she desired most. Freedom. Seated in the backseat, he watched the only person who could compromise him holding the arm of one of the world's fiercest killers.

"Time is money," Chase pressed. "Are we doing this or not?"

Sarina whispered in Kasim's ear. Without another word, Kasim barked in Arabic, sending the driver peeling out in a hurry and leaving Sarina standing outside the hospital. Chase didn't fight back when Kasim pulled a hood over his head. He prepared himself for what might happen next. There was no escape, only the unknown. No one to cover his six. And with a prick in his arm, the world turned dark.

When Chase opened his eyes, there was blackness. A few seconds passed before he realized he was seated on a flimsy chair which creaked when he shifted his weight. Both hands and legs were bound. His breathing steadied, blowing back in his face as he controlled the pounding in his chest. Whatever drug flowed through his veins left a migraine pulsing into a steady hammer. The instant the hood was removed, he was left squinting at a bright spotlight on a stand inches from his face. Kasim was seated across from him, resting a gun on his thigh.

"Why does Sarina trust you?"

"We offered to help with her mother's treatment in exchange for an introduction. She said the only way to get face to face with her husband was through you."

"What do you know of Abu Haji Fatima?"

"It's no secret he's at the top of the chain. And to get close to someone that powerful, we needed to gain the trust of someone within his inner circle. Sarina was our way in, and she delivered me to you."

"We have spoken to those who have done business with you."

"I'll assume that would be Omar Youssef." Kasim didn't respond, so Chase continued. "He's the only one you'd go to since you were raised in the same village."

"You believe you are smarter than me?" Kasim tightened the grip on his weapon, then pointed the barrel inches from Chase's face. "Are you CIA?"

"We made Omar a ton of cash." Chase flexed his wrists to gauge how tight the restraints were, realizing he wasn't going anywhere. He stared into Kasim's deadpan eyes. "You don't want to be the one who costs your jihad millions. We have buyers for the Artifacts of Exile, but they won't wait around for long."

With the butt of his weapon, Kasim swung with such force that Chase's body slammed against the floor, leaving the chair smashed in pieces. Blood oozed from his nose, mouth, and cheek. Dazed, he readied himself for the next step of the interrogation.

He lost track of the days, hours, and minutes as he suffered through a barrage of questions and beatings. Kasim tortured his prisoner inside a heavily guarded house only miles from Mosul in a village known as Gogjali. Chase was injected with hallucinogens that should've blown his legend and left him in a ditch. But there was a contingency plan.

Sarina had arrived in the early evening of the first day. She was the lifeline. Injecting an antidote, which kept him in control of his senses, he answered all of the questions. It was brutal to endure, but the lies lured Kasim deeper into the trap.

Chase later learned that he had been missing for six days. He was left beaten, bloodied, and dehydrated in the desert. For hours he stumbled along a dirt road until the dust trail of a Land Rover barreled toward him. Skidding to a stop, Dax jumped out from behind the wheel and raced toward him. Chase dropped to his knees, knowing he'd not only survived but had gained access to the Prodigal.

TEN

On the second floor of the beach house, Chase changed clothes as McIntyre's apology echoed in his soul. Scars from Mosul, and other RVG operations, crisscrossed his body. A roadmap in search of greater purpose, or maybe it was the pain of selfish ambition. Impossible to decide which had been the driving force. Reaching into his backpack, he tossed the rest of his clothes onto a dresser and removed the remaining items—a time capsule from the past.

A leather-bound book taken from the Prodigal, which contained handwritten lists of covert U.S. intelligence targets. A hit list to shift the darkness toward the light. At the moment, there was only one name in the crosshairs—Bernhardt Brandis. Next to the book was a beaten and scratched portable hard drive containing the top operations they'd completed under RVG. Last, a dented *Speed Racer* tin box, purchased when he was eight from the Indianapolis Speedway gift shop. One memory of his father which would never fade. He flipped the lid and stared at bullet fragments removed from him a year earlier. Closing the tin box, he tossed it on the bed, questioning if any of it was worth it.

"You're gonna want to see this." Dax entered the room and

flipped on the television to BBC. "Press Secretary's issuing an official White House statement."

Last night, shortly after nine o'clock, Chief of Staff Simon Adams left the Royal Olympic Hotel in Athens. However, as of this afternoon, we have no knowledge of his whereabouts. We are working with the Hellenic Police Force, as well as Greek officials in partnership with our own security agencies, to ascertain the situation as this is completely out of character for Chief of Staff Adams to simply disappear. As you can imagine, we are extremely concerned about his safety and well-being. Many of us have worked closely with Simon since joining the administration, so we are hopeful this will be resolved quickly. President Bouchard is fully aware of the situation and has ordered the full resources of the United States to be available. As this is an active investigation, I will not be answering any questions at this time. Thank you."

"Do you think McIntyre's the one who pulled the trigger?"

"She knew we were on the Vihkrovs yacht," Chase answered. "She could've followed us from there."

"And she was monitoring Adams like a Communist."

"She's playing her own game, but so are we."

Dax turned off the television, then stood with arms crossed. "Why are we here?"

"Laney asked for my help, and I turned my back."

"You had good reason, Chase. But I still don't get what game we're playing, exactly."

"She's missing, and no one's searching. It's that simple."

"Why can't we leave that up to Bouchard and the Feds?"

"If they wanted her found, it would've happened by now."

"Bouchard, the Vihkrovs, and I'll bet McIntyre too, don't

care whether we live or die. Don't get me wrong, I know how you feel about Elena, but..."

"We're keeping Elena out of this for as long as possible. I owe her that much."

"Because you don't want this to blowback on her?"

"I don't want her to know the truth, not yet. Not until we are positive."

"So, keep McIntyre distracted with Omar?"

Chase nodded. "And I'll set the honey trap."

Heading downstairs, Chase and Dax unpacked the anvil cases in the center of the living room. Surveillance cameras were mounted around the exterior of the house to monitor all entry points. Laptops, microphones, and recording gear were set up as a mini command center. Accessing the laptops required McIntyre's password, so going further needed to wait until she returned.

"Show me what you found from LA," Chase said.

Dax pulled out his laptop, adding it to the other two on the table. Quietly, they watched footage of Special Agent Laney Kelley leaving Union Station, cutting between street cameras as she headed toward Olvera Street. Grainy video rolled as a dark SUV jumped the curb. Four men climbed out. *Two people shot.* Laney was struck by a man wearing a suit before being loaded into the back of the SUV. Dax opened a stack of screen captures of the kidnappers. *Nothing clear enough for a positive ID or a license plate.* Each frame captured Laney's abduction and left Chase wishing for a way to turn back the clock.

ELEVEN

Digging her toes in the sand, Laney leaned back in a lounge chair and breathed in a brisk ocean breeze. She couldn't remember the last time she'd been on a *real* vacation. After five months of specialized training at Quantico, she was amped to lead a double life for the Bureau. Her handler, Lead Agent Russell Vaughn, warned her about losing herself undercover. Then eight weeks earlier at *Tanets*, an electronic dance club in Hollywood, the operation officially began when a glass of Pinot sparked a whirlwind romance.

Walking toward her from the main resort lobby was her target.

"Sure is a beautiful day." Chase handed her a cold beer. "You know, Dax was pissed he wasn't invited."

"I'm sure he'll find a way to get into trouble without your help."

"Did I ever tell you about when he crashed a '29 Duesenberg on stage?"

"About a dozen times." Laney pulled Chase down next to her, then leaned into him. "I wish we could stop the clock and stay like this forever."

"Dad needs me to go with him to close a deal." Chase took

a long swig from his bottle. "We leave tomorrow afternoon."

"Where are you jet-setting to this time?"

"United Emirates."

"I've never been there," Laney said, excited. "Maybe I can tag along."

"You won't be allowed to go anywhere while we're working." Waves pounded offshore before rolling up the sand. "Besides, if you're going to be stuck somewhere, wouldn't you rather be here?"

Laney gazed into his eyes, battling between truth and lies. "As long as I know you'll come back for me."

"Sold," Chase shouted in his signature auctioneer voice, "to the most beautiful woman in the world."

TWELVE

Chase's voice faded as Laney blinked several times before a ceiling inside a stone-walled room came into focus.

That day was forever ago.

A shooting pain ripped through her ribs. Dirty fingers tugged at a mop of tangled hair, pulling strands away from her sunken eyes. She rolled off the cot, shuffled barefoot across a damp floor, then used her fingernail to etch another hashmark into thick moss-covered stone. Counting the hashmarks, she guessed two-hundred and fifty-eight days in solitary.

Touching her boney cheeks, an ache burned through her worn muscles. Fingers rubbed the bruises on her forearm from the needles that blurred every hour since she was taken. For so long, she'd been lost in a haze, but as she stared at the mossy wall, that haze seemed to fade.

A metal slat opened at the bottom of an iron door before a plate slid across the floor. She knew better than to move, remembering the fork she'd stabbed into the hand that lingered and the beating that followed. She waited until the slat closed, then dug barehanded into a pile of rice and beans. Inhaling like a ravaged dog, she tossed the plate aside and slumped down on the edge of a wooden cot.

No one is coming. Not now, not ever.

She flinched when the iron door clanked open, bracing herself as the Englishman appeared in the doorway. He tossed a grey sweatshirt and blue scrubs on the cot.

"Get dressed. You have a visitor."

Laney stood and turned her back, sensing his stare as she slipped out of her worn clothes into the sweatshirt and scrubs. Crossing her wrists behind her, she waited for the Englishman to secure the handcuffs.

Once she was restrained, he grabbed her arm and pulled her out of the cell. Heading down a narrow corridor, she kept her head down, taking in every detail.

Twenty steps to the turn. Eight doors. Cameras in each corner. Thirty more steps to the room he brought me to before. Nowhere to escape.

"When I get out of here," she said in a lowered voice, "I'm killing you first."

"Your stubbornness has inflicted your pain."

The Englishman unlocked the door, then nudged her inside. He removed the handcuffs, looped a chain beneath a bar bolted to a metal table, then secured her wrists again, clicking the cuffs into place.

Before leaving, he spoke to a darkened corner of the room. "Mr. Brandis requests your presence once you are finished."

Laney's eyes darted from a camera mounted to the ceiling to a shadow stepping into the dim light. Tears spilled over as she exhaled in disbelief. With those same tears dripping from her chin, she glared defiantly across the table. When she joined the Bureau, she swore an oath to hunt the Devil. Little did she know that when she went undercover in the Hardeman operation, she'd be introduced to the Devil's daughter.

"Agent Kelley," Elena said coolly. "Eight months. Still, no negotiation."

Laney's weakened voice replied, "Give me one reason to believe you."

"President Bouchard is willing to keep his secret and leave you rotting in filth." Elena's beauty was matched only by her cunning. "I am the only one here to help you."

"Does Chase know you are here?" Laney white-knuckled the restrictive metal bar bolted to the table. "Does he know what Brandis has done to me?"

"Who do you think sent me to rescue you?"

There was a time when Laney trusted Chase, but as the pain in her ribs struck, she questioned if that trust was destroyed after his father's death. When she approached him in Monterey, he'd chosen the other woman. Shifting her gaze away from Elena toward the door, she swallowed hard, feeling the saliva burning her raw throat.

"Brandis tortured me," she seethed. "But he didn't break me."

"Men act recklessly when they are threatened."

"Always the one moving the pawns."

"Kings and queens." Elena set a key on the table, just out of reach. "You have one hour to decide your fate."

Elena Vihkrov left the room without waiting for an answer. Laney clenched her fists, closed her eyes, and forced the screams from escaping. She pictured the Englishman's crooked nose, scarred jaw, tatted neck, and the bear paws that forced her into submission in the dark.

She wanted to remember every detail.

When she opened her eyes, the key seemed to shift slightly

on the table, inching further away from her.

Betray my country, or die protecting my oath.

THIRTEEN

HALF MOON ISLAND, NORTH ATLANTIC

An eighty-acre island was surrounded by a coral reef hidden beneath the surface of turquoise waters blending into an endless deep blue ocean. A white sandy beach was a natural red carpet to the Peak House perched at the highest point of a private oasis. Imported bamboo and teak roofed and framed the Thai flared estate amidst a lush forest.

Elena passed an infinity pool before climbing the steps to the main house. Greeted by burly security, she was ushered to a private staircase leading to the crow's nest. Entering an open-air living space, she was wrapped in 360-degree breathtaking views where a vibrant marmalade and royal purple sunset filled the skies.

From the crow's nest, Bernhardt Brandis overlooked the island as he worked efficiently on an elliptical. Broad-shouldered. Square jawed. Cauliflower ears. A former amateur MMA fighter from Frankfurt, he'd been associated with the Vihkrovs for years. But Elena knew better than to trust the German smuggler. She remembered the night in Stockholm when Brandis was in a drunken stupor. He forced himself on her and was left bleeding out after she plunged a bottle opener into his iliac vein.

Brandis stepped off the elliptical, grabbed a towel, and wiped the sweat from his face and arms. "Elena, always a pleasure to see you."

"Our instructions were clear," she said. "Interrogation, not torture."

"Thank you, Bernhardt. Thank you for keeping our dirty little secret from the Americans. That is what you should say to me." Brandis dropped the towel onto the floor. "You wanted it to be convincing."

"And yet she has not provided the information we need."

"If it were not for my loyalty to your father," Brandis pointed out, "she would have been sold months ago. There are many buyers who would pay top dollar."

"She is not your property to sell."

"But she would fetch one helluva price."

Elena glanced at a bank of screens mounted to the wall, each monitoring captives being held in the underground fortress. While her father had done business with Brandis in the past, being isolated on his island was a first for Elena. She stared at the prisoners, determining if the whispers of Half Moon Island's depravity were true.

"Eight months I have watched over your prize," Brandis said. "After all this time, you have decided to pay a visit. Why?"

Elena's eyes shifted from one screen to the next. "Who are the others?"

"Stay for dinner, and we will tell each other our secrets."

"Remember my bite," she said coldly. "I have kept *that* secret from my father."

"And I am grateful, but Dmitry will not approve of you flying across the Atlantic after dark. You are my guest, Elena."

It was all a game to Brandis, a way for him to be in control. But Elena wasn't one to be moved like a chess piece. "Perhaps I should leave in the morning."

"Perfect." Brandis motioned toward the balcony. "I despise eating alone."

As the last bit of sun disappeared on the horizon, the brightly colored sky dimmed until blackness left a super moon shimmering across the water. After nightfall, Half Moon Island transformed into a fortress of solitude rather than a paradise retreat.

A spread of plant-based cuisine was set on a rustic table.

Elena sat across from Brandis, who was facing the interior of the crow's nest. She noticed his attention was divided between the prize he would never have and the ones he itched to auction on the dark web. Brandis poured two glasses of *Stags Leap*, then leaned back in his chair.

"Per your instructions, we have reduced the doses. Most of my guests have betrayed their country with far less persuasion."

"Everyone has a breaking point," Elena admitted. "Even you, Bernhardt."

He toasted his glass. "Dmitry's flesh and blood, always so shrewd."

"One way or another, the American will hand over keys to Bouchard's kingdom."

"The Englishman will miss her greatly." Brandis smirked. "As will I."

The evening drifted on. Brandis finished a second bottle while Elena nursed her glass. He bragged openly about counterintelligence agencies negotiating to retrieve their prized assets. Beijing's Ministry. Aussie's SSR. Canada's SIS.

French Directorate. Germany's Federal Service. Russians Foreign Bureau. UK's SS. Israeli's Mossad. Without revealing the names of his captors, it was clear the underground prison housed a host of special operatives.

Elena grew weary of his endless rants about economic, electronic, and military espionage. He continued on to false information leaked to opposing governments, wiretapping, counter-terrorist units, and elite assassins. With any other person, she would have listened with interest, but with Brandis, the conversation only fueled his ego. She nodded every now and then to keep Brandis spilling his secrets, but her thoughts were consumed with the dead bodies at the marina.

Were any of them Chase or Dax?

Her fingers brushed against a gold compass pendant around her neck as she remembered the day Chase gave it to her in Carmel. *You'll always be able to find your true North.* She pushed her seat back. "It is late."

"I have bored you long enough," Brandis slurred. He stood and drunk-walked inside. "You will let me know in the morning what you plan to do with the American."

Elena finished off her glass and waited. Five minutes passed before she entered the crow's nest to find Brandis passed out on a sofa. She stepped over toward the monitors and watched Special Agent Laney Kelley seated in the interrogation room staring up at the camera. She'd given her an hour, but that was four hours ago. Still, the American had not made a move to indicate she was willing to cooperate.

Elena texted Detective Castellanos: ID?

Waiting for a response, she turned her attention to another monitor. An Asian man was seated on the floor with his arms wrapped around his legs. For a few moments, she watched him in silence. *BUZZ.*

A chill shot through her veins as she read Castellanos' response: ONLY ONE. VADIM ZHUKOV.

FOURTEEN

KANGBE, SIERRA LEONE

McIntyre strolled alongside Stapha's father, Maliki, down a fence line stretched nearly a square mile. As daylight faded, scattered across a grassy landscape, hundreds of cattle grazed and settled in for the night. Ripe manure wafted in the air, disguising the truth about the Dollar farm.

"You have brought an enemy to my door," Maliki said.

"Would've been easier if you'd given me the intel on Bouchard."

"Anonymity is key to Unicorn and to protecting my family. You should know that better than anyone."

"And yet this is where we find ourselves."

"Allowing you access to Simon Adams was a mistake."

McIntyre rested her elbows on the fence, digging the sole of her boot against a bottom plank. "What will it take, Maliki?"

"You are welcome to stay for dinner." Maliki turned his back and headed across the field. He called over his shoulder, "Then you must leave."

A bonfire blazed in the center of the property. Young and old gathered around a hundred-year-old tree carved and shaped into a long table. Maliki sat at the head while McIntyre found a seat further down beside Stapha. Ribeyes. Farm-grown vegetables. Bunny chow. Wine from the family vines. A meal from the land, unaffordable to most Sierra Leoneans.

"Your friends trouble my father," Stapha said in a lowered voice. "Why?"

"He wishes to forget the past." McIntyre passed a plate down the row. "Five million bought his future and your family's windfall."

"He has done what is necessary to protect us. Do you not believe he is also protecting you?"

"Who introduced Unicorn to the world?" McIntyre faced Stapha. "He owes a great debt to me and others. Now he is unwilling to offer any help in a pressing matter."

"What is it you need from him?"

"The truth, Stapha. That's all I ask."

Standing between father and son was not ideal. She'd considered leaking Maliki's identity to a contact within Interpol but stopped short, knowing he was still an asset. Loyalty was the deciding factor. She remembered when Michael Hardeman approached her, a man she'd recognized as someone in the newly elected President Bouchard's inner circle. At the time, Hardeman was looking for a coder, someone to write a program deemed illegal by NATO. She was an ex-CIA intelligence officer with expertise in Europe and Africa, but she never thought her career would pivot into becoming a handler for the Red Venture Group. Her first assignment was to recruit Mailiki Dollar. Looking back, she should've seen the pitfalls, but she had grown to trust Michael as more than a politician.

After dinner, Maliki gathered the family around the bonfire. A reddish-orange glow cast a shadow off of their faces. McIntyre stood in the background as Maliki waved several straggling grandchildren closer. Everyone waited quietly for the patriarch to weave an ancestor's tale.

"Many years ago on this land, there was a farmer who believed the power of night turned children into wild beasts. Beasts who devoured their enemies in secret. Those within his own house called him crazy, possessed by witchcraft." Maliki pointed in the distance. "It was there on the hill where his home once stood. And on this night, he was safely inside when he heard a noise." Grandchildren listened with great intent as Maliki echoed the sound of nails scratching against a door. "A voice called out to him. *I am in danger. Please open the door.* Yet the man stood frozen, afraid to open the door to this stranger."

"Sekuru," one of the children called out, "what did he do?"

"He was a good man, a righteous man, willing to help anyone in need. So, even in his fear, he was tempted to let the stranger in." Maliki made the scratching sounds again while the children watched as if seeing the scene play out before their eyes. "He stood before the door, questioning if his actions would put his family in danger. Then he *jumped* when his son entered the room." With those words, the children screamed, but Maliki continued. "Father and son grew more afraid of the noise. Looking into his eyes, the farmer told his son to be brave. Then he opened the door, and what did he see? His son, standing there looking back at him."

"Eish!" Stapha exclaimed. "Father, this is not a story for the children."

"When there is no enemy within," Maliki said pointedly, "the enemy outside cannot harm you."

McIntyre stepped back from the bonfire, receiving Maliki's message loud and clear. She strolled across the Dollar farm, hearing his voice ringing in her ears. *The enemy outside cannot harm you.* As she reached the van, Stapha caught up with her.

"Mum, I know what you have done for my family, even if he does not."

"I'm sorry, Stapha." McIntyre climbed behind the wheel. "I never should've put you in the middle."

His eyes were glossy. "Tonight, my father has questioned my loyalty."

McIntyre closed the door and turned the ignition. As the engine sputtered, she rolled down the window. "I'll pay you for the van, I promise."

He reached out and grabbed her hand. "I will not question yours."

McIntyre felt him place a thumb drive into her palm.

FIFTEEN

CASINO ABERDEEN, LUMLEY BEACH

Brightly colored neon illuminated the grand entrance as Chase slipped down the stairs to a lower level beneath the hotel lobby. Greeted by a woman dressed in a blue and pink uniform, he entered and headed straight for a cashier window. Exchanging five grand for a stack of pink gambling chips felt a little Miami Vice.

No matter where you travel, there's always a place to lose your fortune.

Slots. Blackjack. Roulette. Money counters rifled through stacks of international currency. A pit boss lurked nearby. Slender African, mid-twenties, with a stare that had seen far too many lose themselves to one more chance.

Chase's nostrils filled with the aroma of Din Tai, a Chinese restaurant connected to the casino with private dining rooms reserved for exclusive clientele. He'd been there shortly after returning from Iraq when his dad closed a deal between a billionaire and the Sierra Leone government. At the time, the client had secured legal ownership of Bunce Island in a wager with an unnamed official. Chase witnessed how anything and everything was for sale to the highest bidder. The deal was closed over a plate of Peking duck when the government paid a premium for the return of their sacred grounds, preventing it from turning into a tourist resort.

Finding an open chair at a Caribbean Stud Poker table, Chase settled in for the next hour, keeping his sights on the other gamers. He nursed a Jack and Coke, lost a few grand, then gained it back. More than once, he bet large enough for those around to notice he was a high roller. After losing half his chips in one hand, he tossed the cards and pushed back from the table. Cradling the chips like a newborn, he headed for the bar where Karaoke roared to life and ordered another Jack and Coke.

The pit boss approached. "My eyes have not deceived me."

Chase smiled, extending his hand. "Jafari, it's been too long."

"I did not recognize you with the beard." Jafari grinned broadly, shaking Chase's hand with a firm grip. His Brit accent was a result of four years immersed in boarding school. "Your father was a good man, Chase. I miss him greatly."

"He would be proud of all you've accomplished."

Jafari scanned the casino as a slot machine dinged. "Are you staying at the hotel?"

"A house on Lumley Beach." Chase sipped from his glass. "You've been discreet?"

Jafari handed Chase a handwritten note. "I trust you are aware of the risk."

"Definitely aware." Chase slipped a photo from his hoodie pocket, scribbled a phone number on the back, and set it on the counter. "Most likely, he's going under an alias, but his real name is Omar Youssef. He's living somewhere in Hill Station."

Jafari eyed the photo closely. "I will find him."

"Thank you." Chase pointed at the phone number. "Dax will answer when you call."

Leaving the photo and stacked chips on the counter, Chase downed his drink and headed outside. Walking south on Lumley Beach Road, he dug his hands deeper into his pockets, remembering the missionary woman who rescued teenagers living on the streets. She was the one who found Jafari in an alley in Makari starved and beaten. She brought him to her orphanage only days before Chase's dad, the Governor of Indiana at the time, arrived with an American envoy to ascertain the aftermath of Sierra Leone's corrupt President, who fled with millions to Switzerland after claiming political asylum.

At fourteen, Chase stood beside his dad, who took a break from the envoy mission to see the work being done at the orphanage. Most of the afternoon, they shot baskets with the orphans on a homemade hoop as Jafari became an honorary member of the Hardeman clan. Before leaving, Chase's dad pulled the missionary aside with tears in his eyes. Only a handful of times had Chase seen him let down his guard.

On that day, it wasn't only Jafari's life that was changed.

Worlds apart, Chase and Dax partied through their senior year while Jafari excelled with honors at Freetown International School. Shortly after graduation, the missionary was gunned down one block from the orphanage. Chase's father hired the best to search for her killer, but to this day, it remained an unsolved mystery. In the end, the political heavyweight, presidential candidate, and legendary auctioneer crashed in the California desert, not knowing who it was that killed a missionary who impacted his life forever.

Chase snapped out of it and read the note from Jafari again

before ducking into the Baw Baw Bar. Inside, customers lounged around pool tables drinking locally harvested beer. Several others danced to local reggae tunes. Finding a spot at the end of the bar, Chase ordered a shot of whiskey, feeling his head swim a bit more. Ignoring the buzz, he swallowed the hard liquor as it burned his throat and warmed his chest.

A group of Europeans entered in muddy jeans and dirty shirts with the words *Hope House International* imprinted across their chests. Drinks were ordered all around. Chase locked eyes on a woman. Short cropped brunette. Light golden eyes. Fair skin. Slender but strong. She sat next to him and ordered a Star Lager. The bartender slid a bottle across the counter, which she stopped on reflex. Grasping the bottle, she held it up toward Chase, who returned the gesture as a shot glass and bottle clinked.

She took a long drink. "Haven't seen you in here before?"

"Figured I'd start my vacation by drowning my jet lag."

"Ammelie," she said with a disarming smile. "And you are..."

"Chase." He ordered a lager of his own. "How does a woman as beautiful as you end up in a place like this?"

"I see you've had enough liquid courage."

"That ended any chance," Chase chuckled. "Blame it on a lack of sleep."

"Of course, stranger things have happened in Lumley."

"You're saying there's hope for me?"

Ammelie laughed. "I suggest we keep drinking."

"How long have you been with Hope House?"

"Four years. You have heard of us?"

"Started by a Norwegian missionary, right?"

"Agnetha Berget," she said, surprised. "First orphanage

was in Makari."

"I met her once when I was a teenager."

"So, this isn't your first visit to Sierra Leone."

"I've been here a few times with my dad. He worked for the U.S. government. We met Agnetha when we visited the orphanage in Makari. Sad to hear what happened to her. She was one of a kind."

"Sometimes it's those who make the biggest difference who pay the greatest price."

"Amen to that. Here's to Agnetha Berget." Chase held up his bottle. "So, what're you building?"

"Another orphanage and school in Massam." Ammelie nodded to the others. "Some days, I wonder if we'll ever get it finished."

"And on those days, you end up here. Not a bad ritual."

Ammelie finished the bottle. "Do you work for the American government too?"

"No, I've tried to stay out of the political tar pits of Washington." Chase dropped a hundred-dollar bill on the counter, then slipped off the stool, brushing his fingers against her thigh. "The jet lag is kicking my ass. It was nice meeting you, Ammelie."

Her cheeks flushed. "You should visit Massam while you're here."

"Maybe I will."

SIXTEEN

BOUCHARD WINERY—LOS OLIVOS, CA

President Bouchard slowed his quarter horse, Cheyenne, as they crested a rolling hill overlooking acres of grapevines planted in the early spring three years earlier. In a few months cutting vines would commence, followed by a harvest being aged in oak barrels to embolden smooth flavors with hints of raspberry and cocoa.

As the fog drifted towards the ocean, Bouchard breathed in the crisp morning air and thought of how his father's passion captured the attention of wine connoisseurs from all walks of life. At the age of seventy-four, "Pop" Bouchard worked a full day in the vineyard patiently growing, meticulously aging, and precisely tasting in a quest to ensure the perfect glass of cabernet lived up to the family name. Without question, his work ethic rivaled men thirty years younger. That same work ethic was passed down to his children, but the same would not be true of his grandchildren. It was the one conversation a father and son avoided.

Sauntering toward the stables, shadowed by Secret Service riding quads, Bouchard watched as his father shoveled hay into a stall. He dismounted and pulled the reigns guiding Cheyenne into another stall, then unsaddled the horse before picking up a shovel and tossing a pile of hay inside the pen.

"I bet you'll be glad to get this roadshow off your property."

"At least I know where my tax dollars are going," Pop's gravelly voice replied. "Commander in Chief is a privileged responsibility."

"It's a twenty-four-seven news cycle of political debauchery." Bouchard couldn't shake a longing to spend the rest of his days far from the swamp amidst the vines with his hero. "Wish I could stay a few more days, Pop."

"You're making a bigger difference in the world than I ever could."

"Did you know Truman and Johnson never ran for a second term?"

"That's because neither of them won the nomination." Pop stopped working and turned toward his son. "You're the prince of the party, so what's going on?"

"In Athens, Simon was handling a sensitive matter for me." Bouchard weighed his words. "The fact that he's MIA leads me to believe a house of cards is about to fall."

Pop squeezed Bouchard's shoulder. "Then find a way to change the deck, Son."

Leaving Pop in the barn, Bouchard strolled toward the main house. He never left the scopes of sharpshooters perched on the roof or the agents who shadowed only yards away.

A dark SUV drove down the half-mile road from the front gate and pulled up to the craftsman's home. From the backseat, General Benjamin Abbott climbed out. No striped-sleeve uniform. No sign of his Medal of Honor, Distinguished Service Cross, Navy Cross, or Purple Heart. He waited as Bouchard approached, then extended his hand in a sign of respect for the leader of the free world.

"Ben, thanks for getting here so quick."

"You called, so I'm here, Mr. President."

"Come on in." Bouchard motioned toward the front door, fully aware they'd hardly spoken during the Joint Chiefs briefings since Los Angeles. "There's much to discuss."

Heading through the house, White House staffers worked on laptops and around a large dining room table where Avery took charge of drafting an upcoming State of the Union speech. Bouchard greeted each staffer without introducing General Abbott. Both men entered a back study, a far cry from the Situation Room or the Oval Office. Rows of books. Scotch and whiskey on a round corner table. Family photos hung on the walls capturing generations of the Bouchard legacy.

"Have a seat." Bouchard motioned to two leather chairs. He set his Blackberry on a desk, then sat across from one of the most decorated heroes in American history. "I think you know why I asked you here."

"You'll have to be more specific."

"Word is you've agreed to testify in front of the House Intel Committee."

"I swore to serve my country, so I'm simply doing my duty."

"Look, we both have opposing views on my leadership style, but I won't deny you're one of the best war fighters this nation has ever seen." Bouchard leaned in closer, unnerved that Abbott seemed more at ease. "But you need to trust me when I say you're on the wrong side of history here."

"The events of Los Angeles were against protocol. And frankly, troubling, sir."

"If necessary, I will use Executive Privilege."

Abbott leaned back, crossed his arms, and locked a steely glare on Bouchard. "Why am I here, Mr. President?"

"The night Simon disappeared, he was meeting someone." Since leaving Athens, Bouchard rehearsed the story in his mind countless times, but saying it aloud was surreal. He knew what Simon was trying to uncover, including the secrets that were at stake. "He was meeting with Michael Hardeman's son. You knew the governor, didn't you? Well, it seems his son runs in similar circles."

"What do you mean *exactly*?"

"Chase Hardeman is a known associate of the Vihkrovs, whose yacht was blown up on the same night as Simon's disappearance. And he was also under investigation by the Bureau when the attack in LA occurred."

"Why would Simon meet with him?"

"That's the million-dollar question." Bouchard allowed the moment to breathe, knowing the poker face from Abbott was merely the General moving ten steps ahead. "While the Agency searches for Simon, I'm ordering you to locate Hardeman and bring him in. Top Secret mission with your best team."

"I'm not sure I'm comfortable with your request," Abbott pushed back. "Considering—"

"Ben," interrupted Bouchard, "you find Hardeman, and I'll meet with the Intel Committee myself."

SEVENTEEN

LUMLEY BEACH, FREETOWN

A glow from a row of laptops left Dax struggling to keep his bloodshot eyes from closing. Two days without much sleep keeping up with Chase left him wanting to be knocked out cold until this was over. Blowing up the Vihkrovs yacht. Being shot at by a sniper. Leaving Simon Adams' body behind. Escaping on a jet plane with a woman who was playing her own game of roulette. Staying in the fight to protect Chase, no matter the cost, is the way it had always been.

I failed to protect him in Mosul, and nearly lost him again after the attack in Los Angeles. How long will it be before our luck runs out?

Shoulders slumped forward as facial recognition software, courtesy of Silicon Beach entrepreneur Marcus Nicholson, searched the RVG rugged drive for an image match to the headshots snapped aboard the *Midnight Moon*. A second window on the screen scrolled through a list of files comparing screenshots from Laney's abduction with every target they'd neutralized under RVG. Dax was struck by the number of targets they'd gone after in the Middle East.

When you're in the battle, no one keeps score until the dust settles.

It was impossible not to question whether judgment day would lead them to a wide road with those who'd chosen the same path.

Dax stood and stretched his aching bones, feeling years older than his actual age. He limped through the bottom floor of the house and tried to shake an intense pain in his leg. Doctors were optimistic he'd make a full recovery, but as the months passed, the healing stopped with a limp. *If this is as good as it gets, I'll always be a step slower when the sadistic flashbacks accelerate the fear sweeping my mind.* He'd been close to death before, but he'd never been first in line at those gates until the Prodigal. Forcing the past back into a dark corner, he checked his burner for any word from Jafari, then stared at the files as they continued to scroll down the screen. One of which jumped out as the reason why they were in Sierra Leone.

Operation Whirlwind.

Omar Youssef was a mid-level middleman for terrorist cells in Iraq, as well as a collector of black market artifacts in his own right. When they met in Baghdad, no one fully understood how Omar's childhood would introduce them to a network of cells that eventually led to the Prodigal. *All of this mess started with Operation Whirlwind.* To prove themselves to Omar, they smuggled a shipment of gold bars stolen from the Iraqi government's vaults in the back of a truck hidden beneath a pile of manure and two dozen goats. *To say it was down and dirty would be accurate.* It was a plan put into motion within a matter of days ending when the truck crossed the border into Jordan.

Goats: $2,000 Dinar. Manure: $300 Dinar. Gold Bars: $3.2 million, US.

In return for securing Omar's retirement plan, he vouched for them with Akram Kasim. And with one handshake, he turned from asset to liability. Dax remembered the night when Chase put a gun to Omar's head and threatened to pull the trigger unless he agreed to leave his life behind. When he refused, Chase made a call, and the next day, Omar Youssef was gone. In recent weeks, Dax recognized that same look in Chase's eyes. He didn't like what that meant for them both.

The beeping of a horn snatched Dax back to the present. He checked the security cameras and recognized the van with McIntyre behind the wheel. With his SIG slipped into the back of his jeans, he closed his laptop and stepped outside. As he unlocked the gate, he glanced up and down the empty street. Once the van pulled all the way in, he locked the gate and headed inside.

A moment later, McIntyre entered. "Where's Chase?"

"He needed some fresh air."

"It's after midnight."

"Didn't realize we had a curfew."

McIntyre held up a thumb drive. "Well, there's no need to wait."

Dax stepped back as McIntyre logged into her laptops, never mentioning the fact that the cameras, monitors, and computers were already in place. She inserted the thumb drive, clicked on a file name labeled in Hebrew, then played the audio.

"What are the items for sale?"

"There is a wide array, including a remarkable artifact from the Orient."

"How remarkable?"

"Worth a visit, my friend. However, one must be present to

bid."

"Where will the auction occur?"

"An invitation shall be sent very soon."

"Will you be selling the Scepter of Dagobert?"

"My pride and joy," the voice chuckled. "Perhaps it will be on the block."

"Then I will await an invitation."

McIntyre played the audio again. When it stopped, the room fell silent.

"That's Omar asking the questions," Dax pointed out, "but who's the..."

"Brandis." Chase stepped into the room, startling them both. "It's definitely him."

"Freakin' ninja," Dax mumbled, frustrated that Chase had slipped past the cameras without being noticed. "Next time, use the front door."

"Blindspot in the backyard."

"How can you be sure it's him?" McIntyre asked.

Chase replied, "Laney showed me proof that Brandis has the Scepter of Dagobert."

"That was eight months ago," Dax pointed out. "Could be someone else by now."

Chase turned toward McIntyre. "Where'd you get the recording?"

"I tried to fix our issue." She pointed to the Hebrew filename. "Best I could do."

"You're avoiding the question."

McIntyre sighed heavily. "My guess is the call was intercepted by Mossad."

"Israeli intelligence?" Dax asked, knowing the stakes were much higher if Mossad was involved. "Were they tapping

Omar or Brandis?"

"Unicorn intercepted the call," Chase suggested. "Which means it doesn't matter who Mossad was tapping. You can get us intel on both Omar or Brandis. Something you should've told us from the beginning."

"Chase, it's not possible. Not without pissing off a host of governments or exposing who created Unicorn, which will result in innocent deaths. All we can do is ask ourselves what Brandis is selling from Asia. That's our way in."

"First, the mouse is drawn in by a piece of cheese." Dax recognized the fire in Chase's eyes, fearing they were inching ever closer to *those* gates. "Then snap!"

EIGHTEEN

NEXT MORNING

After a restless night, Chase rolled out of bed sweating through his shirt, shaking off a dream he couldn't remember. Half-awake, he slipped on a pair of jeans and headed downstairs, where Dax was sprawled out on a sofa. Grabbing the laptop from a coffee table, he set it on a kitchen counter and logged on. Searching the web, he found an article from the Greek Reporter and read the caption.

MIDNIGHT MOON EXPLODES IN FIERY NIGHT SKY

The luxury mega-yacht *Midnight Moon* owned by Globali Holdings, an import/export company based in London, was left heavily damaged in the Piraeus Marina. At first, sources within the government believed the explosion to be a terrorist attack. However, the Hellenic Police Force has since confirmed an electrical malfunction caused the fire killing four of its crew. With the vessel destroyed, a salvage operation is underway to remove the wreckage from the marina. Attempts to contact Globali Holdings for comment have gone unanswered.

What caught his attention wasn't the story or the fact neither he nor Dax were mentioned—it was the photo above the caption of Elena standing beside someone who looked to be part of the investigation.

The morning she left for London, he nearly told her the truth. No matter the schemes their fathers stirred up, they'd always turned to each other. He loved her for embracing his darkest tendencies in the brokenness they shared. *In another universe, we'd be together with our angel, letting go of the sins that haunt our past. But that's not possible in a harsh, unforgiving, world.* Blowing up the mega-yacht wasn't part of the plan. Betraying Elena's trust, keeping her in the dark, destroyed what bonded them together.

Nothing will be the same. Not after what I've done.

"I want waffles," Dax declared from under the covers, "with maple syrup."

"No IHOP in Lumley." Chase checked the fridge. "No food here either."

"That sucks. Second rate safe house." Dax groaned as he tossed a blanket off of him. "Jafari should hook us up at the Aberdeen."

Chase's eyes were glued to the photo of Elena. "I'll leave that up to you."

"What're you reading, Sherlock?"

"Making sure we sunk with the *Midnight Moon*." Chase pecked at the keys in another search that pulled up a White House X post. "Bouchard issued a statement confirming Adams is still missing, and the Greek government will be taking over lead in the investigation. Both countries will work together, blah, blah, blah..."

"That's cold after all Adams did to cover his shady..."

"Bright side is we're not on Bouchard's hit list, at least not today."

"If this is what freedom smells like, then I'm gonna starve."

"You definitely need waffles."

"Can you imagine what McIntyre's cleaner did to him? Probably cut him up into pieces and burned his flesh and bones."

"I'll be skipping breakfast—and lunch."

"She rode in on a white horse." Dax pushed himself off the sofa. "It ain't right."

Chase closed the laptop, thinking the same. "I'll be back in an hour."

Ducking out the backyard gate, he dug his toes in the sand as waves rolled ashore. A vast blue sky stretched for an eternity, a peaceful canvas amidst a coming storm. His pace quickened into a steady jog, awakening his body from the slumber. He fought the temptation to force McIntyre to take them to Stapha's father, who he'd concluded was the creator of Unicorn and most likely the source for the intel on Bouchard. It didn't matter about the illegal tapping of the conversation or the fact that Mossad was tracking either Omar or Brandis. What mattered most was gaining an advantage with Unicorn to find Brandis and free Laney.

In the same breath, he understood what McIntyre meant about the innocent and stirring the pot for government agencies to strike them off the radar. But he agreed with Dax. White horses were fairytales. McIntyre was playing her own game.

So, which side of the board is she really on?

Half mile down the beach, his muscles and mind fired with each stride. A familiar burn pulsed through his veins. He'd trained for months, anticipating the danger ahead, unsure of whether it would make a difference in the end. Breathing hard, he slowed his pace to a walk and dug his hands into his hips.

Eyes on the prize, Chase.

A voice called out from behind. "How's the jet lag?"

Chase stopped and glanced over his shoulder. "Kicking my ass."

"Looks like you're working hard on your vacation," Ammelie mused.

"Morning ritual. Helps clear the mind and keeps the pounds off."

Ammelie brushed a strand of hair from her eyes. "You know, my invite stands."

"I thought I'd get a head start at Baw Baw."

"Don't worry, they'll leave us a spot at the bar."

Chase took a moment to think it through. *Irresistible.* "First round's on you?"

"You drive a hard bargain, Chase." Ammelie smiled and pointed toward a yellow house with a bright red roof. "Meet at the front gate. Nine o'clock."

Chase chuckled, knowing she caught him checking her out. "Massam, here I come."

"Okay, wonderful." She smiled shyly. "I'll see you then."

Chase watched as she turned and kicked up the sand, hiking toward the beach ridge and the yellow house. *I've caught her eye, now I need to catch her heart.* By the time he reached the safe house his mind was clearer, but his body was worn. He entered the back door and noticed Dax had gained access to McIntyre's laptops.

"She typed her password right in front of me yesterday."

Dax waved Chase over. "Might as well have written it down with a Sharpie."

"Find anything interesting?"

"She's got a bunch of files that have different passwords, but I did get access to the Interpol database." Chase's brows raised as Dax continued. "We've got positive I.D.'s on the shooters at the marina."

"Well, look at you." Chase peered over Dax's shoulder. "Hit me, *Marty*."

"Vadim Zhukov. Alik Vasiliev. Feliks Solovev. Kirill Romanov." Dax lined them up on the screen so Chase could compare their dead shots with their headshots. "All known to be tied to the Kazakstan Bratva."

"You were right all along." Chase shook his head. "Dmitry's behind the bounty."

"He could've taken us out anytime." Dax finished transferring the files to his laptop, then logged out of McIntyre's system. "Why now?"

"When Elena left, it was because Dmitry summoned her to London." Chase scratched his scraggly beard, hearing footsteps crossing above them. He said in a lowered voice, "Whatever he's up to, he wanted us out of the way."

"Told you it'd be easier to dig our own graves."

"Throw a few dice at Aberdeen when you meet up with Jafari. We owe him."

Dax smirked. "Gamble paid off?"

"Half mile down. Red roof. Yellow exterior. Wait until after nine."

"And where will you be?"

"I got a date in Massam," Chase smiled. "With any luck she's the queen bee."

NINETEEN

From a corner bedroom window, McIntyre watched Chase leave through the rear gate and head down the beach. Peering through binoculars, she counted the footprints in the sand until he stopped and waited as a woman approached. *Definitely Chase's type. Laney Kelley. Elena Vihkrov. Sarina Fatima. All captured under the Hardeman spell. All fit a certain profile as well. Surprisingly, beauty is second on his list. At the top is certainty.* Her eyes followed the woman as she trudged toward Chase with no hesitation. McIntyre's curiosity was piqued when the woman walked away and Chase double-timed back to the house.

When she was recruited by Michael Hardeman as RVG's handler, she believed it was for the greater good. Looking in the rearview, a cruel spy game where the pieces were flesh and blood, she wondered if she'd been blinded by the Hardeman spell too. When Chase was taken by Akram Kasim, the following six days were an eternity. She reacted with certainty by threatening sources, shadowing Dax, and urging Michael to tell Bouchard his son was missing. The heavy sigh followed by a long silence still echoed in her ears. She was convinced Chase was surely dead. Even after all this time, she questioned the memories that flooded her mind, ending with Dax carrying Chase's beaten and bloodied body from the backseat of a Land Rover. Weeks later, the RVG operations shifted one final time after a night in Mosul left them exposed.

The Prodigal broke the Hardeman spell, at least for me.

Dismantling a covert operation within a matter of days left her feeling lost in the months that followed. No government nest egg. No medals for democracy. No contact with anyone. She was left with no other choice but to reinvent herself as a dark web arms broker. Black and white morphed into shades of gray. She grew callous to the deals brokered and the deadly aftermath. Then everything shifted on the night she looked into Chase's eyes at the Griffith Observatory in Hollywood. In that moment, she realized what she missed the most was being a guardian angel.

DING.

McIntyre rubbed her eyes and checked a text message on her cell. A photo of a pug hypnotized by an In-N-Out burger appeared on the screen. She opened the image using a stego app. Instead of the pug face appearing, the raw code was visible. A message hidden inside the carrier was simple yet effective. She read it several times before deleting: Espaço Café Belém. 2417.

BUZZ. BUZZ. BUZZ.

An alert flashed on her cell. She switched apps to one that mirrored her laptops downstairs. She enlarged and swiped through a series of headshots. *Vadim Zhukov. Alik Vasiliev. Feliks Solovev. Kirill Romanov.* She packed an extra change of clothes before carrying her luggage downstairs.

"What does Dmitry Vihkrov have to do with any of this?" McIntyre demanded.

Dax glanced up, wide-eyed. "We're on the same team, right?"

"If I entered the password any slower, I'd be a sloth."

Chase noticed McIntyre's luggage. "Where are you going?"

"I have a lead on what Brandis might be selling from Asia."

"And you weren't going to take us with you."

"Seems as though we're still keeping secrets." McIntyre nodded toward Dax, whose fingers hovered over the keyboard. "Until you tell me the plan, this is how it needs to be."

"How long will you be gone?"

"Three days. Maybe four." McIntyre reached into an anvil case and retrieved a burner cell, then handed it over. "My number is already programmed."

Chase held the burner in his palm. "We were ambushed on Dmitry's yacht."

"Should've changed the name of it to the *Midnight Massacre*." Dax pointed to the headshots on the screen. "These were the Russians left behind."

McIntyre crossed her arms, not surprised. "Did Dmitry know what you were up to?"

"We never talked about it onboard," Chase said. "And we never said a word to Elena."

"Strange that Dmitry put a hit out on you two the same night you met with Adams."

"None of us believe in coincidences." Chase leaned against the counter. "What's Dmitry's connection to Brandis?"

"Chase, no one knows what all the Vihkrovs are involved in. If I had to guess, I'd say that Brandis and Dmitry have most likely crossed paths. And if Brandis was behind kidnapping Laney Kelley, then there's a high probability that Dmitry found out about it."

"Figured you'd have them pegged since they're one of your clients."

You're the one sleeping with Elena. "Maybe I should be asking you that question."

"From the very beginning," Dax chimed in, "I told Chase messing around in the Vihkrovs world was a bad idea."

"Elena didn't have a clue what we were planning," Chase bantered. "I'm sure of it."

"The question is, did she know what her father was planning for the two of you?"

"Maybe the *Black Widow of Bratva* sent the hit squad," Dax suggested. "I'm sure you know by now, Chase's love life is more complicated than the last act of Gears of War."

"Chase, have you contacted Elena?" McIntyre asked point blank.

"Not since we blew up Dmitry's boat."

"So, she doesn't know you're alive." McIntyre rolled her luggage towards the door. "Dmitry will want confirmation. He will not stop until Elena brings it to him."

"Are you going to tell us who you're meeting?"

"You'll know if it pans out. Until then, try not to blow up anything or anyone else."

TWENTY

Chase tossed the dossier from Adams onto a rusted barbecue grill. With a squirt of lighter fluid and a match, the dossier ignited and burned to ash. He dropped the rugged drive with the top RVG operations onto the concrete, then smashed a hammer into the center of the metal case leaving the components inside damaged beyond repair.

In the dossier and on the drive were photos and intel on Abu Haji Fatima, Jeric Salem, Najee Azad, Misfirah Jama, Aisha Abed, Raiha Sultana, Marid Abu, Sameer Alli, Karim Salik, and Samara Nasir. A top ten greatest hits of the terrorists they'd left buried in the desert.

He waited until the flames died down, then set the hard drive on the grill and added more lighter fluid. Fire danced toward the sky. Burning the past was freeing, even though he was handcuffed by the present. It was too great a risk if any of the evidence about RVG fell into the wrong hands, especially if they were being hunted by Dmitry.

"Early Christmas present." Dax stepped into the backyard holding a Kevlar face mask. "Found this in McIntyre's toy box. Always wondered what happened to our gear."

Chase recognized the Kevlar mask as soon as Dax slipped it on. He'd only worn his when they entered the homes of targets with children. It was the one rule they'd almost never broken. When their operation went south in Mosul, they'd left everything behind at the apartment in Baghdad and escaped stateside.

"Looks like McIntyre cleaned up after us," Chase said.

"I backed up the hard drive to a USB. Won't let it out of my sight."

"The less footprint, the better."

"You know, I bet McIntyre's a great dancer."

"What makes you say that?"

"She's mastered the sidestep." Dax stared at the fire as if in a trance, then pulled the mask off his face. "You know, she's right. Dmitry will want proof we're dead."

"We knew the possibility when we left. It's why we kept Elena in the dark."

"Do you think she knew what Dmitry was planning?"

"There's no one she'd be more loyal to than him."

"After all you've both gone through, she wouldn't warn you?"

"The devil lives in the still waters." Chase realized Dax didn't follow. "Elena will do Dmitry's bidding, even if that means disrupting the peace. Love has always been secondary to loyalty with Elena."

"That's twisted." Dax held out a quarter-sized coin and a slim device smaller than a thumb drive. With a David Blaine sleight of hand, he separated the coin into two pieces. "Slip the SIM in here, and you're good to go."

"Full of surprises." Chase took the coin and studied the device. "What else is in McIntyre's toy box?"

"You can't open all the Christmas presents at one time." Dax held up the mask. "But I gotta say, this one still has some bad mojo."

Chase couldn't agree more. "Tonight, get in and get out."

"Any idea how many are staying in the house?"

"Eight or nine were at the bar last night, but there could be more." Chase handed Dax the burner cell from McIntyre, then nodded at the second burner next to the laptop. "When Jafari calls…"

"Drop everything and go." Dax held the two burner cells. "Think we really found her?"

"We'll know soon enough." Chase checked his watch. "Don't want to be late."

"Hope you get to second base."

Chase slapped Dax on the back extra hard. "Don't wait up."

With the quarter and cloner in his back pocket, Chase headed down Wilkinson Road before stopping at Basha. Every time he'd been in Freetown, he made a point to stop by the aroma-filled Lebanese bakery. Inhaling the spiced aroma, he ordered two dozen rolls. Each one a mix of cinnamon, black pepper, nutmeg, ground ginger, cumin, ground coriander, and sausage wrapped in pure flavor. By the time he reached the yellow house, he'd eaten two of them. As he arrived, Ammelie and the others were busy loading supplies into a van.

Chase held up the two bags of rolls with a wide smile. "Thought I'd bring breakfast."

"You're timing is perfect." Ammelie wiped the sweat from her forehead. "Everyone, this is my new friend, Chase. He's here on vacation, and well, I recruited him."

"Ammelie brought a Yank," one of them laughed. "Let's see if he'll get his hands dirty."

While the others offered cheery hellos, Chase recognized

the smart ass from the bar. Medium build. Shaggy hair. Piercing eyes. "She was quite persuasive. I couldn't resist."

"You'll have to ignore Wolffie." Ammelie leaned in close and whispered, "He's harmless."

"Let's see if you say that at the end of the day," Wolffie chided.

Chase picked up a twenty-pound bag of rice and loaded it into the van. "Game on."

TWENTY-ONE

HALF MOON ISLAND, NORTH ATLANTIC

A Eurocopter Hermés EC 135 helicopter belonging to Globali Holdings rested its skids on a landing pad near the edge of a cliff. When Elena turned seventeen, she convinced her father to grant permission for her to pursue a pilot license. At the time, she knew he believed it was a teenage phase, but she proved him wrong. With over two thousand flight hours, she was a seasoned pilot and meticulous with every detail of the aircraft. Custom rotors. Modified supercharged engine. Opulent interior with hand-stitched leather and mahogany trim. Globali owned a dozen Eurocopters spread across every continent, and Elena had flown every single one. Being in control of a seven-million-dollar helicopter was the one place she found peace.

From a back compartment, she grabbed a Glock and slipped it into a shoulder holster that wrapped around her back, concealing the weapon once she zipped up her jacket. From the same compartment, she retrieved a Glock 42 and secured it in an ankle holster. Normally carrying one weapon was enough, but being on the island with Brandis left her on guard.

BUZZ.

She checked the caller ID: PAPA.

Ignoring the call, she locked up the Eurocopter and walked a stone path along the edge of the hillside until she reached the main house. Passing the morning shift security, she climbed the steps to the crow's nest. She was hardly inside before she heard his voice.

"Your father is looking for you," Brandis announced.

"What did you tell him?"

"You will be leaving shortly." Brandis paced the room dressed in Bermuda shorts and a silk shirt. "I assume you are taking the American."

Elena steamed a cappuccino and casually eyed the bank of screens monitoring the prisoners being held underground. She sipped her cappuccino and stared at Special Agent Laney Kelley curled up in a fetal position. *Traitor.* Maybe not to her country, but in Elena's mind, there was no doubt. Her actions pushed her father and his associates to the top of Interpol. While that was not unusual, as they'd been watched by Interpol for years, what was unforgivable was that the traitor had betrayed someone she loved deeply. *For that, she must pay.* All night and into the early morning, a question weighed on Elena's mind.

Follow Papa's instructions to interrogate or act on my own instincts?

"I am considering staying a few days longer," Elena said. "I cannot trust you to interrogate the American, so I will oversee the next stage."

"My efforts have been handcuffed," Brandis rebuked. "Loosen the reigns, and she will sing like a nightingale."

"You tortured her because you believe a woman's legs are weak under your spell." Elena finished off the cappuccino. "It is your arrogance that makes you the weak one, Bernhardt."

"You have paid me well," he smirked. "But do not disrespect me, Elena."

"Did my father tell you what he plans to do with the American?"

"I have never questioned Dmitry or his actions. Nor will I betray his trust."

"Trust is a gatekeeper. Loyalty is the linchpin. Where does your loyalty lie?"

"I am not one who needs to be educated in such matters, even though you tempt me."

How had the traitor gained Chase's trust so easily?

That was the other question that haunted Elena. She knew his choice placed her at odds with her father simply because he believed her loyalty was in the wrong hands. She hoped that over time the two men would build the same relationship their fathers had enjoyed. Chase was family, or as close as one could be. He'd been in her life since she could remember, growing up on opposite sides yet still in each other's corner. For a time, Special Agent Kelley had stolen Chase from her, and that enraged her to a boiling point. But realizing her father, who was close to her, no longer felt the same about Chase was disheartening and infuriating.

"My father plans to return her to the Americans."

"The Americans?" Brandis repeated, shocked. "I assure you, I can get much more..."

Elena held up her hand to cut off the barrage of exaggerations she'd heard many times before. "He believes her voice will destroy Bouchard, and fracture their closest allies."

"Dmitry is a sly one," he growled in approval. "Bouchard's mistress? Double agent?"

"For one who locks himself away in his castle, your imagination is lacking creativity." A wave of loss washed over Elena, along with deep disappointment. Both clawed their way to the surface, forcing her to bury them beneath a mound of grief. "My father failed to gain a confession from another, so the American is our last opportunity."

"If she is so valuable to the Americans, why have they not searched for her?"

"President Bouchard is the only one living who shares her secret, and he controlled her until she was taken. She belongs to us now, and we will use her until her last breath."

"Enemies lurk in the jungle outside our fortresses," Brandis quoted the assassin's creed. "And yet we are mostly unaware. If you are suggesting going against your father's wishes..."

"Vengeance is our last defense." Elena approached Brandis and grabbed his hand, allowing him to feel the steady beating in her chest. "You have what I need, Bernhardt."

She gently pushed him away and stepped over to a display case featuring a prized possession, the Scepter of Dagobert. Originally part of the French Crown Jewels, the scepter was created by Saint Eligius dating back to the seventh century, a treasure of the Basilica of Saint-Denis until 1795 when it was stolen, never to be seen again. Filigraned and enameled gold wrapped the priceless treasure in three parts: a rod, a hand grasping the world, and a statue of an eagle carrying a young man.

Elena lured Brandis in deeper. "How did you acquire the scepter?"

"A gift from Dmitry for delivering cargo from Cape Town to Paraguay?"

"Do you know what was inside that precious box of cargo?"

"I knew better than to look inside," he admitted.

"It was a gift for Carlos Espinosa."

She stepped away, allowing Brandis to consider the meaning of her words. She stood in front of the monitors, knowing the name resonated with him. A name she'd first heard when she was thirteen. Carlos Espinosa was head of the Espinosa Cartel, a ruthless competitor to the Bratva in trafficking cocaine and money laundering. Both men had crossed paths in Brooklyn long before she was born, standing on opposite sides in charge of their syndicate's operations in Northern America. During those years, they waged war between the Bratva and the Cartel that started in Little Odessa and erupted into bloodshed across the East coast. Neither side backed down as the casualties mounted. Months before Elena was born, her father and mother left New York for London. But before they left, her father struck one final blow.

"As a little girl, I never thought my father was capable of such things. He killed for the Bratva without limits or mercy. Before my parents departed New York for London, he left a car bomb that killed Espinosa's sister." She was struck again with how the memories of her mother had faded, yet glimpses of what she imagined her father did to protect them flashed in her mind. "When I was a child, Espinosa found us in London and sent his son, Maximiano, to kill my mother. We found her hanging from a tree." She turned and faced Brandis as rage surged through her veins. "You were the gift giver, returning the bones of a son to a coward. Your reward for delivering the message was the scepter and this island. Now I am the one asking for your loyalty once more."

TWENTY-TWO

MASSAM, SIERRA LEONE

From the backseat on a four-hour drive, crammed inside an eight-seater van, Chase watched the locals struck by the simplicity of their lives. Along the Masiaka-Yonibana and Bo-Denema Highways through Waterloo, Taiama, and Gandorhun to the rural farming town in the Southern Provence it seemed family, farming, and food were the glue that bonded Sierra Leoneans.

What a great hiding place if someone ever wanted to drop off the face of the earth. No one will ever find you here. Chase snapped out of his thoughts. "I didn't realize Massam was so far from Lumley."

"Sierra Leone is a beautiful country," Ammelie said. "However, Massam is a special place. Usually, we leave earlier, but don't worry. We'll be off the road before dark."

"I'm not worried at all," Chase smiled. "I'm in your hands today."

On the outskirts of town, lush farmland and muddy roads were a sign of heavy rain. Behind the wheel, Wolffie navigated ditches and spun tires in the dirt. Overhead an African harrier-hawk flew beneath the cloudy skies. Muted grey feathers. Yellow patched eye. Striped chest. Chase was captivated by the hawk's effortlessly smooth flight.

The van lurched forward, and the engine revved and whined, but the momentum stopped, leaving the wheels sunken deeper in the mud.

Wolffie cursed as he slammed his fists on the steering wheel. "Bloody piece of..."

"No worries," Ammelie said, "We'll give it a push."

"I've told you before, we need four-wheel drive," he replied, frustrated.

Chase followed the others as they climbed out. His boots sunk a few inches deeper in the mud while he helped Ammelie keep her balance as she followed. With Wolffie still behind the wheel, Chase and the others pushed the rear of the van with all their strength. Exhaust filled the air, but the van didn't budge.

"Looks like we'll be hiking the rest of the way," Ammelie said to the group. "C'mon Wolffie, no use wasting petrol."

Before leaving, each grabbed a twenty-pound bag of rice. Ammelie led the way as they trudged down the muddy road. Sweat seeped through Chase's shirt as he switched the heavy bag of rice to the opposite shoulder. Pushing forward, he caught up to Ammelie and walked alongside for a while, neither of them saying a word until she reached over and stopped him. In the trees above, a troop of chimpanzees stared back at them with equal curiosity.

"Our welcome party," she whispered. "Harmless unless you provoke them."

Wolffie pushed past, nudging Chase off balance. "Bet you've only seen them in a zoo."

"Wouldn't have seen them at all if you avoided that last ditch," Chase retorted.

"Bloody Yank," Wolffie grumbled.

Chase waved goodbye to the troop of chimpanzees, and they continued on. Another mile deeper into the jungle, they reached a clearing. Beautifully desolate. Acreages untouched by the outside world, except for the barb-wired fencing surrounding a compound with several partially built cinderblock structures. Vegetable gardens were planted in between each of the structures and across the acreage.

Six armed soldiers greeted them at the front gate, none of which were older than their early twenties. Each took a bag of rice and hauled them toward one of the buildings. Chase was glad to be free from the weight on his shoulders, but the burden in his soul remained unchanged.

I'm a sinner, not a saint.

Laughter echoed from the jungle as dozens of children dashed out from the tree line. Even from a distance, Chase couldn't help but grin at the joyous sight. Wolffie seemed to relax with their sincere greeting too. Ammelie was the Pied Piper for sure, as each of the children rushed to hug her first. She was gentle and engaging with each one.

Why does she have to be a modern-day Mother Teresa?

Children called out, "Picture...picture..."

A young girl grabbed Chase's hand and pulled him, snapping her fingers as if trying to shoot an imaginary photo. Ammelie waved her cell in the air, and the children turned their attention to her. She snapped several photos, then faced the screen toward them so they could see themselves. Even more laughter erupted. Wolffie and the others headed for the adults who greeted them warmly. It was like a scene out of a National Geographic documentary where the expedition team emerges from the jungle after a long trek from the industrial world. Ammelie introduced Chase to everyone. He played the part of an American with no clue this world existed.

Most of the afternoon, Chase mixed cement and pushed a wheel barrel between two unfinished structures. All the while, he kept his sights on Ammelie. When she set her cell down on a chair, he knew it was his chance. He set the shovel down and walked across the grassy area with his head on a swivel. Without stopping, he snatched her cell and ducked around the side of the building. He pulled out the quarter-sized coin and the slim cloner device. He popped her sim card out of its slot, pressed it into the cloner along with the blank sim card from the coin's hidden compartment. A few seconds later, a green light on the cloner blinked. Quickly he returned the sim card back into Ammelie's cell, then placed the duplicated sim inside the coin.

As he meandered back toward the cement and wheel barrel, Ammelie broke free from talking with a group of children and caught up to him. No chance to put her cell back.

"Sorry, I abandoned you," she said. "I hope you're not regretting my offer."

"You're still buying the first round, right?

"A deal is a deal," she blushed.

Chase held up her cell. "Looks like you lost something."

"I wondered where I'd left it." Ammelie took the cell and slipped it into her pocket. "Wouldn't be the first time, and I'm sure it won't be the last."

"Looks like they all love you here."

"I've known most of them since they were rescued."

"Rescued?"

"Each one was sold into slavery, and some were trafficked from other parts of Africa." Ammelie waved at several of the children, who waved back. "We aren't a rescue organization, but we do have relationships with nonprofits who know we will take care of and raise anyone they bring to us. As long as we have the space."

"How do you pay for it all?"

"Most of our funding is from private donations."

"Hard to imagine slavery still exists." Chase picked up the shovel and tossed dry cement into the wet wheel barrel. "I bet your parents are proud."

Ammelie paused for a moment. "Honestly, I wouldn't know."

TWENTY-THREE

Late in the afternoon, the children gathered for an early dinner of rice, beans, and cabbage. With Wolffie as the chef, Chase helped Ammelie and the others serve all sixty of the children as well as the ten adults seated around rows of plastic tables and folding chairs. After all were served, Chase and Ammelie slipped out and strolled down to the banks of the Mapandi River, which ran through the acreage owned by Hope House International.

"When I brought up your parents," Chase said cautiously, "it seemed like there was some friction."

"Orphans aren't only those who have lost their parents or been abandoned."

"Which is why you're here, to help those who've been forgotten."

"I suppose it's how I've dealt with the void in my own life. Are you close to yours?"

"Mom died when I was young, and I lost my dad a year ago in a plane crash." Chase itched his scraggly beard, uneasy about diving into the past but knowing he needed to find common ground. "I guess you could say, I've spent the last year running."

"Maybe you're where you're supposed to be." She gently

touched his arm. "In the end, all we can do is hold on to faith."

Chase nearly shot back a rebuttal, but then he noticed a dark plume of smoke rising into the sky, followed by a loud clanging bell. He recognized the panicked look on Ammelie's face before she darted toward the trees. He was on her heels as they reached the community buildings. Smoke drifted near the fence as the children scurried together. Terror struck as gunshots rang out.

Chase grabbed Ammelie's shoulder. "Stay here and lock the gate."

By the time he raced through the front gate, Wolffie was fifty yards ahead, lugging a fire extinguisher. Along the winding dirt road, Chase pumped his arms and legs as his muscles fired on overdrive. When he went through basic training at Pendleton, his fastest mile was six minutes. *I'm definitely not Usain Bolt.* Slugging through the mud, he knew there was a good chance the fire would spread faster than his slowing pace. His heart pounded as he pushed his body harder.

With his sights on the plume of smoke, a beeping horn startled him. One of the guards was behind the wheel of a flatbed truck skidding sideways and kicking up mud in all directions.

Why didn't I think of that?

Barreling down on him, Chase timed it right as the truck drove alongside. He grabbed the side of the vehicle and rolled himself onto the flatbed. Ahead, Wolffie was hunched over out of breath, still holding the fire extinguisher.

"Wolffie!" Chase yelled.

Wolffie stood up and swung the extinguisher in the air as the truck barreled past. Chase caught it squarely in the chest, nearly knocking him off the flatbed. The guard veered to one side, never losing control, as he kept Chase from falling off even as the flatbed gained speed.

An orange glow haloed the flames engulfing the same van they'd left on the side of the road earlier. Surrounding grass and several trees were already burning. It wouldn't be long before an inferno raged through the jungle.

The truck skidded to a stop. Chase jumped off with the extinguisher at the ready. A burst of retardant covered the van then turned toward the trees. He was joined by the guard with two more extinguishers. Within a matter of seconds, most of the flames were out, leaving the truck and surrounding area smoldering in ash and burnt metal.

"That was too close," he exhaled.

Further down the muddy road, four armed men stood next to a pickup truck. One of them raised a semi-automatic and fired several rounds that ricocheted off the charred van. Chase and the guard dove for cover, leaving Wolffie out in the open. Instinctively, Chase reached for his weapon, but he wasn't armed.

He yelled toward Wolffie, who stood like a statue. "Get down!"

When the guard started to move, Chase stopped him. More rounds erupted as Wolffie fell facedown into the grass. Chase kept low and moved towards the flatbed. *Would be nice to have Dax with me right about now.* He used the driver-side door as a shield and looked inside. A Kalashnikov AK-47 was right there on the seat. Not knowing whether Wolffie had been hit or how much longer before the four men advanced, he grabbed the Kalishnikov, flipped the safety off, and pressed the butt against his shoulder.

Moving around the back of the vehicle, he crab-walked toward the front of the passenger side. A barrage of bullets whizzed by his ear. He returned fire then ducked for cover. Moving forward, his next burst shattered the windshield of the pickup truck, sending the men retreating momentarily. Chase dropped to one knee, aimed, and fired again. Blood splattered as one of the men dropped to the dirt. While two of the other men picked up the one Chase hit, a third man climbed behind the wheel, knocking out what was left of the windshield. Chase stayed on one knee with the weapon raised. He heard the ignition whine, but his eyes never left the target. The truck lurched backward before spinning a one-eighty in the mud. He eased his finger off the trigger only after the truck disappeared from sight.

With the situation de-escalated, he turned his attention to Wolffie, who was face down in the grass. Rushing over, flashbacks of seeing Adams' lifeless body at the safe house struck hard. Forcing himself to stay in the moment, he reached Wolffie and turned him over, searching for any bullet wounds.

Wolffie looked back wide-eyed. "That was bloody insane."

"You're one lucky son-of-a…"

"And you're a stark raving mad lunatic. That was some Bourne…"

"Not a word to anyone." Chase handed the Kalishnikov back to the guard, then helped Wolffie to his feet. He slapped him on the back. "Live to fight another day."

"Lips are sealed." Wolffie checked himself to make sure he was alive. "Incredible."

"I'll drive." Chase turned toward the guard. "You're up front with me."

On the drive back to the compound, he gripped the steering wheel tight to stop his hands from shaking. The adrenaline eased, but his body still buzzed from the rush.

Breathe. Breathe. Breathe.

After another guard unlocked the gate, Chase pulled the flatbed up to one of the buildings. Not a soul was outside. He climbed out as Ammelie and the others emerged, trying to wrap his head around what happened.

"We heard gunshots," Ammelie said, worried. "Are you okay?"

"Your Yank's a keeper," Wolffie blurted. "Never seen anything like it."

She asked Chase, "What is he talking about?"

"Four men with guns sending a message," Chase answered.

"It's not the first message," Wolffie added. "Tell him, Ammelie."

"Wolffie," she chastised. "Enough."

Chase didn't need to know more. "You're not safe here, and neither are the others."

"If we leave, we will lose all that we have built." Ammelie glanced over her shoulder toward the children and the adults. "God has protected us this far. He will not fail us."

"Back there, God wasn't the one pulling the trigger," Wolffie mumbled.

"We will hire more security," she answered.

Chase glanced at the young men holding AK-47s. "You're not serious."

"I will file a report with the local authorities."

"A piece of paper isn't going to stop them from returning. Who the hell are they?"

"No one," Ammelie's voice raised a few decibels. "We

should be grateful no one is hurt."

"Van is scorched," Wolffie said. "And we can't walk into town after dark."

"Then we will stay the night." Ammelie faced the children. "Everyone back inside."

Chase stepped forward and pulled her aside. "How many times before?"

"We've never been shot at if that's what you are asking." She checked to make sure no one else was within earshot. "A few months ago, a wealthy family asked to meet with me at the Barmoi Hotel. I thought they were interested in supporting our cause. But it wasn't about a donation to help us build in Massam. Instead, they offered to pay a steep price to purchase the property as long as we agreed to leave Sierra Leone."

Chase ran his filthy fingers through a mop of sweaty hair. "You turned them down."

"One man's greed will not force us to walk away from those in need."

"Taking the high road won't stop people like them from getting what they want."

She shot back with a twinge of sarcasm. "You're an expert in these things, are you?"

"Who did you meet with at the Barmoi?"

"Maliki Dollar." Her brows furrowed. "What did Wolffie mean about you being a *keeper*?

"I have a friend in Lumley who can help with transportation out of here tomorrow."

"I will not leave the children behind or the property vacant."

"Don't worry about the property. It will be here when you

return. You have my word."

"Who are you *really*, Chase?"

"Today, I'd say I'm Wolffie's new best mate."

Chase walked away and dialed on his burner cell. Improvising was part of any operation, but without Dax covering his six, he knew he'd been lucky. A plan they'd set in motion months earlier was veering sideways, and it was up to him to keep it from driving over a cliff.

She's not who I expected, and now I'm not who she expected either.

Dax's voice cut through the static. "Did you get to second base?"

He checked to make sure no one was nearby. "Might as well call this the Coltrane plan."

"Not so fast. We got lucky today. Jafari had a sandblaster sighting. Standby."

Chase waited until his cell dinged. He opened an attached photo. A middle eastern man. Well dressed. Clean-shaven. Standing next to a Mercedes in a residential neighborhood. Even with a new wardrobe and no beard, the eyes were a dead giveaway.

"He found Omar," Chase said in disbelief. "Where is he?"

"One of Jafari's contacts spotted him at Pierre's Beach Bar and followed him to a house in Hill Station. For once, the intel was spot on. He's going by the name Manzur Huq. I was about to head out to keep an eye on the house before you called."

"You've got my GPS coordinates?"

"I've been tracking you all day."

"Send two buses to the main town in the morning and a chopper."

"Two buses *and* a chopper."

"We need a face-to-face with Maliki Dollar. The sooner, the better."

"What the hell happened in Massam?"

TWENTY-FOUR

SÃO BRÁS, BELÉM

McIntyre ordered an espresso at Espaco Cafè and found a table facing the front window. An aroma of freshly ground coffee filled the air. Brazilians huddled around cellphones, tablets, and laptops. Tourists mingled on the sidewalk outside, while others shopped in the high-priced clothing stores across the street in search of the skimpiest dresses for the city's nightlife.

She'd mastered the art of blending in as she nursed her espresso, casually glancing out the window toward the street, then back to her cell. A jolt of caffeine was much needed after rushing to leave Sierra Leone on a private jet. Inhaling deep through her nostrils, she exhaled long as she thought through what she planned to say once he arrived.

To say there was love between them would be—accurate. In Frankfurt, they shared a warehouse apartment as she trudged through the dark swamp of intelligence for the Agency. His visits were a great escape from Rehin-Main Air Base, with weekends spent on the rooftop overlooking the city with a glass of Guaspari Syrah and a block of Queijo Prato cheese.

She'd known him since she learned to crawl. When she turned sixteen, he was the one who taught her to drive. He was also the one who helped her file her first insurance claim when she wrecked her VW bug. *I loved that bug.* He saluted when she stood in cap and gown with a degree in international affairs and linguistics. And he made sure her first assignment for the Agency landed her in Frankfurt where he could keep watch over her. The rest of the world knew him as General Benjamin Abbott, but she'd just always called him Abbott.

I trust him more than anyone, and have kept no secrets from him. Well, only one.

Accepting Michael Hardeman's offer to join the Red Venture Group seemed as if it was for a greater calling. She knew what Abbott would say, knowing his opinion of the flamboyant Governor, so she never told him. Without warning, she resigned from the Agency and disappeared into the Middle East. She'd kept her distance not because of any falling out but because of who she needed to become. He was the most decorated war hero in modern history, and she ended up a broker of weapons to America's enemies. She became an offense to everything Abbott believed in. A family reunion seemed impossible without tarnishing the great General's legacy.

Reaching out to him was a last resort, and yet he replied immediately. She knew why he'd picked the cafe in the heart of Belém. It was the last place they'd seen each other. Before leaving the Agency, she spent a few weeks on R&R and reached out to him at the U.S. Naval base in São Paulo. He insisted on coming to her, as he'd done countless times before. Like he was doing now.

Her eyes locked in on a man standing across the street. Greying hair protruding beneath a Fedora hat. Aviator shades. Broad shoulders. In his right hand, he held a brown paper bag. She finished off her espresso and waited for him to enter. Instead, he stood as still as a statue. Breathing in deep, she wondered if his disappointment caused him to second guess his willingness to meet. When he set the paper bag on the concrete, turned, and walked down the sidewalk, McIntyre was on her feet.

Nudging her way through the crowd and dodging traffic, she kept her sights on Abbott. She picked up the brown paper bag from the sidewalk, reached inside, and removed a red blend bottle of wine labeled *The Prisoner.* Closing her eyes, she settled her mind. *He's not alone.* A quick glance around, then she picked up the pace in the same direction as Abbott. By the time she reached the corner, he was only a half-block ahead. She fought an instinct to run in the opposite direction, fearing she'd placed him in the crosshairs. Jogging down the sidewalk, she reached him as he spun around.

His steel jaw clenched. "I tried to warn you."

She asked urgently, "What's going on?"

Grabbing her arm with a vice grip, he pulled her into a storefront church and motioned to a parishioner who seemed to be expecting them. McIntyre allowed him to guide her into a back office before he closed the door. Rays of light from a single window illuminated the room. In a quick sweep of the space, McIntyre saw nothing out of the ordinary. A bookcase lined with theological texts. An old rusted metal desk and file cabinet. It was sparse, like their conversation so far.

"We don't have much time," he said. "What do you know about Chase Hardeman?"

"Abbott, why would..."

"Don't play games," he barked. "Answer the question, Alison."

"I can't tell you anything about him." A twinge shot up her spine as she stared into his deep blue eyes, recognizing a chink in the hero's armor. *Fear.* She grabbed his shoulder and squeezed it slightly, knowing a confession was her only leverage. "Eight months ago, Special Agent Laney Kelley disappeared. No investigation by the Bureau, and no ransom demands."

"What does she have to do with Hardeman?"

"Everything." McIntyre stepped back to give them both space. She set the brown bag on the desk. "The President and Simon Adams knew who was behind the attack in Los Angeles, and they knew about Agent Kelley's kidnapping. Now Simon Adams is dead. And Hardeman is linked to them all."

His brows raised. "You have proof of this?"

"Adams won't be found." McIntyre retrieved her cell and showed Abbott a photo of Simon Adams dead in a ditch. "I didn't pull the trigger. You have to believe me."

His jaw clenched as he said, "This is a death sentence, Alison."

Tires screeched outside the window, followed by doors opening and slamming shut. McIntyre knew she was out of time when she recognized the look of surrender in Abbott's eyes. Footsteps echoed off the tiled floors. She never had a chance to ask about the Asian artifact. She opened the office door and peered down the hall. Without saying goodbye, she slipped out into the corridor and hurried toward a flight of stairs. Reaching the second floor, the footsteps behind grew louder *and* quicker. At the top of the stairs was a door. Pushing the door open, she stepped out onto the roof as she heard Abbott arguing with whoever it was that was on her heels. Knowing there was no other escape, she darted towards the edge of the building and jumped.

Tumbling onto the roof of the adjacent building, there was a sense she'd escaped. On her knees, she fired off a quick text. As she stood to her feet, a shot rang out. A split second later, a round punched her in the shoulder. Stumbling forward the world closed in around her before she landed face-first on the tarred roof. Arms and legs were paralyzed. Her eyes watched the screen of her cell, begging for the text to go through. Her mind was in a daze. *I wish we could've uncorked The Prisoner.* Abbott tried to protect her, but little did she know the double edged sword that awaited her in the hours ahead.

TWENTY-FIVE

MASSAM, SIERRA LEONE

A cool breeze rustled the trees beneath a cloudy sky as a thick mist rolled through the property. Seated in a folding chair with arms crossed, Chase leaned back and listened to the steady tapping of rain hit the tin roof. He flicked open his eyes and instinctively searched for any sign of a disturbance. Most of the night followed the same routine. Every hour he walked through the dorm where children were asleep on thin mattresses lined across the floor, resting their heads on homemade pillows beneath woven blankets. After checking with the other security guards, he'd return to his chair, doze off, then awaken again the next hour. Each time he swept a beam from a flashlight across the acreage to be sure no one was lurking.

In the stillness of the morning, he thought of Ammelie's words.

"Orphans aren't only those who have lost their parents or been abandoned."

He'd never thought of himself as an orphan, but there was truth to it. He'd never felt abandoned by his mom or dad, but there was no escaping they were gone. Forcing himself off the chair, he set the flashlight on the seat and stretched his aching muscles. Standing on the edge of a concrete slab, as if one more step would send him off a cliff, he knew the only way to stay alive was to push forward.

"You're up early."

He glanced over his shoulder to see Ammelie standing in the doorway. "So are you."

"Welcome to the *real* Sierra Leone." She approached and handed him a cup of black coffee. "There's always someone wanting to take what doesn't belong to them."

"Not sure this place has a corner on that market." Chase sipped a jolt of caffeine from the mug, shaking off the weariness of the night. "You know, when I was eight, I used to get up early on Saturday mornings to go with my dad to auction at local farms across Indiana. He'd sell everything from jars of jelly, tractors, and if we were lucky, we'd find an old rusted car and auction it for a decent price. Some of them we'd get restored, and that's how the family business started before we found ourselves auctioning some of the rarest cars ever made. But even back then, I knew that's all I ever wanted to do."

"You were close to your father?"

"He taught me everything I needed to know about the business *and* life. As a politician he knew how to deal with those in power, and as an auctioneer, he made you feel as if you were getting the deal of a lifetime. But he wasn't bulletproof. When his plane crashed, a part of me died with him. It's been hard to figure out what I'm supposed to do with it all. Mornings like this remind me of how much I miss him."

"Son, you're never lost if you find your own way."

"Finding this place saved me from my father," Ammelie

119

said, subdued. She stepped over next to Chase but kept her eyes focused on the jungle beyond the fence line. "I was thirteen when he murdered my mother."

Chase asked cautiously, "Murdered?"

"Most nights, he'd pass out drunk." She paused for a moment. "But on that night, they argued. Breaking glass. Yelling. And then I heard her scream." She wiped her eyes with the sleeve of her shirt, embarrassed. "When I ran down the hall to their bedroom and pushed the door open, he was on top of her with his hands around her throat."

"Ammelie, you don't have to..."

"I thought he'd stop when he saw me, but he just laughed as I stood there and watched her breathe her last breath."

Chase looked surprised by the revelation. "I'm so sorry, Ammelie."

"He locked me in my room for three days. A housekeeper brought me food and water. On the third day, he unlocked the door and let me out. I remember walking through our house realizing every picture, every piece of clothing, and any memory of my mother was gone as if she never existed."

"Did you tell anyone what happened?"

"My father is not one you betray. He swore he would bury me next to her if I told a soul." Ammelie cleared her throat. "Wolffie and I were close friends at boarding school in Frankfurt. Many times I almost confessed to him, but I was afraid. After graduation, we went our separate ways and lost touch. A few years later, we ran into each other at a party. When I told him the truth, he was determined to help me disappear."

"Makes sense why he's so protective. He left his family behind?"

"That's why I owe him everything," she nodded. "He's the brother I never had."

Chase thought of Dax as he replied, "We all need someone like that."

"One day, my father watched me leave our house, and I never returned."

"Has he ever tried to find you?"

"I'd imagine if he had tried, I'd be dead."

"How'd you end up here?"

"Wolffie had a relative who lived in Amsterdam. We lived there for nearly two years, worked at a local pub, and kept out of sight. He stayed in touch with his parents on and off, so they were assured he was okay, but they never knew our exact location. After Amsterdam, we set off through France and Spain, stayed in hostiles, paid cash for everything, and avoided any electronic trace of our whereabouts. Wolffie was quite adept at keeping us safe. When we reached Barcelona, we met a missionary who worked for the Hope House, and he offered us the opportunity to join the nonprofit. We accepted, rented a car, and drove from Barcelona to Freetown. It took us two weeks to get here, and it has been an adventure ever since."

"I'll admit, I'm liking Wolffie a bit more now."

"Speaking of Wolffie, he told me quite a tale about yesterday."

"Okay, maybe not as much as I thought," Chase mused. "I'm an ex-Marine. That's all."

"He said you shot one of the men."

"Grazed his shoulder. I'm sure he'll survive." Chase redirected the conversation. "Buses should be arriving in town soon. I've made arrangements at the Aberdeen in

Lumley."

"We cannot afford such an expensive hotel."

"It's all been taken care of," he reassured. "Think of it as an adventure for the kids and a mini-vacation for the rest of you. Sounds like you all deserve it."

"Many of the children have never seen the ocean." Ammelie eyed Chase curiously. "You know, so far, you've been full of surprises."

"Don't worry, before long, you'll know all my secrets." Chase's gaze shifted. "I appreciate you opening up to me about your parents. I'm sure that's not an easy memory to share."

"Honestly, I'm not sure why I did," she answered. "Are you sure the property will be safe while we are gone?"

"Men like Maliki Dollar always have an end game. All I need to do is strike a deal."

"You make it sound so easy." She reached out and grabbed Chase's hand, her fingers running across his palm. "I don't trust others easily, but with you..."

One of the children poked her head out from the entryway, the same girl who'd asked Chase for a picture the day before. She giggled as if she'd caught them in the act.

"Mista Chase," she said shyly. "I have a gift for you."

"A gift," he replied, surprised. "What kind of gift?"

She walked closer and held out a sheet of paper. "Ms. Ammelie asked me to draw you."

Chase glanced at Ammelie, then took the paper. A penciled sketch captured him seated in the chair with the moon in the background. One look at the detailed drawing, and he knew she was someone with true talent. "Wow. It's incredible. Thank you."

"Imari is one of our most talented artists," Ammelie pointed out. "Her dream is to one day become an animator, like in the Disney movies."

"Oh yes, I love *Frozen*," Imari said excitedly, "and *Moana*."

"We have movie nights every other weekend," Ammelie added.

Chase kneeled, so they were eye level. "This is the best gift anyone has ever given me."

A whirring noise grew louder, capturing their attention. Off in the distance, a helicopter flew over the tops of the trees before hovering above the Hope House property. Chase stepped out into the open and waved toward an area away from the buildings. When the skids were firmly on the ground, the passenger door popped open, and out climbed Dax.

Ammelie caught up to Chase. "Who is he?"

"You might say, he's *my* Wolffie."

TWENTY-SIX

THURMONT, MARYLAND

"You have leverage."

McIntyre listened to the faint whisper from Abbott as she was pulled from the backseat of an SUV with blacked-out windows. She'd been blindfolded since face planting in a failed escape, but her other senses offered a few clues. The roar of a Rolls Royce jet engine. Smoothness of hand-stitched leather seats. Disembarking to a wave of sticky humidity. She guessed it was all courtesy of the Agency. Climbing out of the SUV with her wrists and ankles cuffed, her muscles ached from the paralytic, but her mind was razor-sharp.

"Take off the blindfold," Abbott ordered. "She's got nowhere to run."

McIntyre felt someone grab her arm before the blindfold was removed. Her eyes adjusted as she was guided down a path deeper into a wooded area. She shuffled along until they reached a dilapidated barn. Inside was a vintage Lincoln Continental. Abbott motioned her forward toward a door. She expected to be locked in a backroom but was surprised when the door led to a stainless steel wall. Abbott swiped a key fob, and the wall slid across, revealing a flight of stairs that descended underground.

One step at a time, the cuffs around her ankles dug a bit deeper. She steadied her breathing and tried to slow her heartbeat. If she was going to get strapped, she needed to be in control of her mind and body.

At the bottom of the stairs, a long corridor lined with LED lights extended thirty yards leading into a larger room. Soundproofed walls. Two chairs faced each other in the center, as well as a lie detector on one side. McIntyre sat where Abbott instructed. The agent who brought up the rear and hadn't said a word connected two pneumographs, a blood-pressure cuff around her upper arm, and two galvanometer finger plates to her right index and middle finger to monitor physiological activity.

"I'm disappointed." McIntyre added, "I was hoping for a cameo from the President."

"You and I both know he's watching," Abbott replied.

"Am I being charged with a crime?"

"Depends on how well you do in the interview."

"Feels like an interrogation." McIntyre glanced around the room. She breathed in through her mouth and exhaled out her nostrils, counting the beats in her chest. "Interrogation without representation is against my rights as an American citizen."

"If you're unwilling to cooperate," Abbott said matter of fact, "you'll be shipped off to ADX in Colorado. The President is aware of your dealings overseas which classify you as an enemy of state. You'll be charged, convicted, and spend the rest of your days in solitary."

"Sounds relaxing."

McIntyre picked up the crumbs left by Abbott. *Overseas. ADX.* She was back on U.S. soil. With the humidity and the thick air, she knew they weren't anywhere near Colorado. And she was in no hurry to be locked away in federal supermax. Being strapped to a lie detector, it didn't matter where she was at that moment. What mattered was guessing how long it would take the techs in the other room to track the pings from her cell forty-eight hours earlier to the house in Lumley.

Staring into Abbott's deadpan steely glare, she tried to decide whether showing him the photo of Adams was a death sentence or a get out of jail free card. At the same time, she wondered if the text message she tried to send on the rooftop in Belém went through.

"You've always said country before self," she said solemnly.

"The global manhunt for Simon Adams has been called off." Abbott held up her cell with the photo of Adams dead in a ditch. "Alison, did you kill him?"

"If you're asking whether I pulled the trigger, the answer is no."

"Were you the one who took the picture?" When she hesitated, Abbott moved on. "Where was the picture taken?"

"Well, I wasn't the photog, and I don't know where it was taken. Standard procedure for a cleaner, which you should know, General." McIntyre glanced toward the lie detector as the needle stayed steady. She'd been truthful. "What I do know is where he was when he died."

"Let's start there then." Abbott was stone cold. "As much detail as possible."

McIntyre looked past Abbott. "Mr. President, is that a story you want told?"

Abbott tilting his head slightly was a dead giveaway for McIntyre. She watched him closely as he stared back as if waiting for instructions. A concealed door opened. President Bouchard entered the room. With his long strides, he reached McIntyre in three steps. She'd never met the President, not in person. *First term has aged him a few extra years.* She recognized the stern look on his face, similar to the third world government leaders she'd sold crates of rocket launchers to who were thirsty for more territory.

"Clear the room," Bouchard ordered. "Ben, that includes you."

As the room emptied, Bouchard stepped closer and turned off the lie detector. McIntyre waited for him to break the ice. He held up a device and showed her which button he pressed. She'd seen an electronic jamming remote used to stop others from intercepting and listening to audio communications.

Bouchard's got his own marked with a Presidential seal.

"You should know your text didn't go through, so no one knows where you are, including whoever it is that was on the other end." Bouchard paused. "Tell me what happened in Athens."

"First, I'd like to discuss the terms of a deal."

"I've got enough to string you up by your ankles for the world to see." Bouchard took a seat opposite of her and leaned forward with elbows on his thighs. "We either find common ground right now, or you and the General will be formally charged with treason."

"He has nothing to do with any of this," she retorted. "You know he's in the dark."

"Aiding and abetting an enemy of state, which he chose to conceal."

"And you've concealed the kidnapping of Special Agent Kelley." She wanted nothing more than to rake Bouchard over the coals, but her options were dwindling the longer she remained shackled. "Charge me, put me in front of a federal judge, and the truth will set me free."

"Chase played the same card in Athens," Bouchard replied dismissively.

"With all due respect, we both know I won't play by the same rules." McIntyre kept her eyes glued to Bouchard, who looked to be weighing the truthfulness of her words. "Mr. President, don't let this be another fumble like Los Angeles."

"We're the last ones standing." Bouchard pursed his lips. "What're you offering?"

"General Abbott walks free and clear, then your hunt for Brandis continues."

Bouchard looked intrigued. He reached into his coat, removed a document, and held it out for McIntyre to read. A quick scan confirmed her request was anticipated. Most of the letter focused on General Abbott's decades of loyal service. She stopped cold at the last paragraph.

"You're forcing him to retire from active duty and resign from the Joint Chiefs?"

"He has agreed to both and will admit no wrongdoing in regards to you. He has also agreed to leave the past where it belongs." Bouchard pointed at the bottom of the page. "My signature seals his legacy in the history books." He paused. "If you cooperate and assist in securing Brandis, you will avoid a life sentence in federal prison."

McIntyre had been in the game long enough to know the negotiations were over. She wasn't sure what else she'd expected other than to step deeper into the swamp.

"I've been shadowing Simon Adams for months up until he entered the house in the Plaka District. No one else knew I was following him. I worked alone."

"Why were you following him?"

"A client offered information that led me to believe there is a mole in your house."

"Who is your client, and who is the mole?"

"My client must remain anonymous as a valuable asset in the bigger picture." McIntyre settled in, knowing it was going to be a long night. She eyed Bouchard, who was like a dog with a bone. "I don't know the name of the mole, but it's safe to say you're the one in the crosshairs."

"Simon expressed the same concern," Bouchard confessed. "I agreed for him to go to the meeting in Athens to confirm his suspicions. We offered Hardeman what he requested in hopes that he would find Brandis and get us the answers we needed." His gaze hardened. "General Abbott showed me the photo you shared with him. That is an unacceptable outcome."

"Brandis is the one you need, Mr. President. Whoever it is that is targeting you from inside our government has crossed paths with him." McIntyre was surprised by Bouchard's candid comments as she eased in a bit more. "But how does Agent Kelley fit into all of this?"

"After the Prodigal, I asked her to approach Hardeman regarding Brandis. I was told he wasn't willing to accept my offer. Agent Kelley requested to hunt Brandis alone, which I refused to endorse. However, it seems she chose to go rogue. Going public with her kidnapping would warn Brandis of our intentions. Until we had a direct link, I issued a complete blackout within the intel community for Agent Kelley's safety."

"It was also leverage to get Chase to step back in the ring."

"Well, that didn't work out so well now, did it."

"He's on the hunt, Mr. President."

Bouchard looked surprised by this revelation. "Brandis is in the line of fire?"

"You succeeded in waking a ghost." McIntyre held up her cuffed wrists. "Rules of engagement are the same as in the past?"

"Considering what's at stake," Bouchard's brows furrowed as his eyes flared, "there are no rules."

TWENTY-SEVEN

KANGBE, SIERRA LEONE

Late in the afternoon, the helicopter hovered over Dollar Farm. Chase looked down on the sprawling ranch tucked between a mountain range and dense jungle. He eyed the jeep bouncing down a dirt road, leaving a dust trail headed toward their landing zone.

"I'm getting a *Yellowstone* vibe," Dax said over the coms.

"If you got a better idea," Chase replied, "I'm all ears."

"Head on. Dead on."

Once the skids hit the ground, they were out and moving toward the inbound jeep. Chase knew Stapha would be the first hurdle. The jeep barely skidded to a stop before Stapha jumped out and stomped toward them.

"You must not be here," he said earnestly. "Father made his wishes known to Mum."

"Well, *Mum* isn't here." Dax grabbed Stapha by the shoulder and shoved the barrel of a SIG in his stomach. "What's the worst that can happen when two alphas meet?"

Chase noticed Stapha flinch. "Give us the grand tour."

Reluctantly, Stapha climbed behind the wheel, turned the ignition, and spun the jeep around. Traveling along the dirt road, Chase took in the surroundings. Rolling hills. Rice and cassava fields. Oil palm trees. Cattle grazing. A vineyard. To Chase, it seemed as if Unicorn was the gift that kept on giving.

Chase remembered riding alongside his dad when they entered Gennaro Santarossa's estate in Florence to deliver a 1962 Ferrari 250 GTO, which sold at one of their private auctions for nearly $5 million. Gennaro Santarossa was an acquaintance of a frequent customer for Hardeman Auctions. An Italian crime family. The hitman lived on a picturesque Italian villa in the countryside as somewhat of a recluse from society. Santarossa seemed humbled and grateful for the gift. So much so that he invited Chase and his dad to stay for dinner. Chase was surprised when his dad declined, insisting they needed to fly back to Los Angeles. It wasn't like Michael Hardeman to turn down an opportunity to add to the Hardeman Auction clientele, hitman or not. On the flight back, his dad confided there was another $5 million hidden inside the engine, and he was convinced they were the targets.

Maliki Dollar wasn't a hitman, but as the creator of Unicorn, there was a good chance he knew the governments who employed their own assassins. *We were ghosts in the Middle East, assassins who targeted anyone who threatened the homeland. But now we can't hide in the desert to escape the aftermath. Still, I won't hesitate to pull the trigger if it means protecting freedom—at least the freedom I believe in.* Chase suspected it was a possibility, but seeing the pain in Stapha's face confirmed where his bullet grazed the day before.

Deliver a message, cut a deal, and leave before dinner without ending up in a box.

By the time they reached the main house, Maliki was waiting on the front porch with a dozen armed men. Chase's look darkened as Dax kept the SIG aimed at Stapha.

"You do not know what you have done," Stapha said under his breath.

"A few inches to the left, and you wouldn't be here," Chase replied. "Today's a bonus."

Chase climbed out of the jeep with a SIG in his right hand and walked slowly toward Maliki, leaving Dax behind with a weapon pointed at the back of Stapha's skull. Maliki didn't look like a programming nerd. He didn't look like a real estate mogul. He didn't even look like a farmer. He was one who disappeared in a crowd. Chase stared into the eyes of the old man, recognizing the look of a father concerned for his son.

He holstered his SIG, then held out his hand. "Chase Hardeman."

"Your presence here has brought this upon us." Maliki stepped off the porch holding a rifle in his grasp, and took a closer look at Chase. "I owe a debt to your father, which is why you will live today. My words are clear, do you understand? Tomorrow you are my enemy."

Chase motioned for Dax to lower his weapon. As soon as he did, Stapha moved away behind the line of armed men. He turned back to Maliki. "I need to talk with you in private."

"Very well." Maliki ordered his men to lower their weapons too. "I will listen."

Chase walked alongside Maliki as they strolled away from the main house. There were so many questions he wanted to ask, but he needed to bridge the gap with Maliki.

"I'm sorry about shooting at your son," Chase said. "But he fired first."

"Stapha acted recklessly without my knowledge," Maliki admitted. "My instructions were to keep watch. Violence has no place in my family." He slowed his pace once they reached the vineyard, then picked a grape from one of the vines and ate it. "Transformation begins at the root."

"That's why you created Unicorn? To transform?"

"I wish my intentions were as pure as this land." Maliki grabbed another grape from the vine. "McIntyre and your father offered an escape from mediocrity. However, the price of Unicorn has been...unexpected."

"Two sides of the same coin." Chase took advantage of the opening. "Who's been listening in on Bernhardt Brandis and Omar Youssef?"

"My trust in McIntyre has kept my anonymity," Maliki said. "But can I trust you?"

"You know who I am. Who I *really* am." Chase pressed a bit harder as he waved his arms around them. "Tell me what I need to know, and your life goes back to the way it's always been."

"I am afraid it is impossible to close Pandora's box." Maliki paused. "Governments believe when we allow access to Unicorn, it is without oversight. In fact, many pay a high price for this guarantee. However, to protect our interests, we created a supervised algorithm to monitor keywords which can be traced back to the source if necessary."

Chase interjected. "Who's the source with Brandis?"

"Mossad." A weight seemed to lift off Maliki's shoulders. "Over the last two years, the Israeli's have been monitoring Omar Youssef and his communication with Bernhardt Brandis. I am sure you are aware, the whereabouts of Brandis is one sought after by many governments."

"Have they been able to pinpoint a location?"

"Not that I am aware," Maliki answered. "However, there

are those who know of the daughter."

"Ammelie," Chase noted. *We're not the only ones.* "Are they watching her too?"

"I do not know who is watching, only what is captured through Unicorn."

"You said there are keywords that are monitored," Chase reiterated. "Is that why you reached out to McIntyre about Bouchard? He's one of those keywords?"

"President Bouchard is on a list within the software along with other world leaders. Several months ago, Mossad monitored a call between Omar Youssef and Bernhardt Brandis discussing a gift to be delivered to the world, one that Brandis referred to as..."

"An artifact from the Orient." Chase knew he caught Maliki off guard. "So, the President isn't the only one Brandis could be after, which explains why Mossad wants to find him?"

"McIntyre expressed to me your resourcefulness and instincts," Maliki noted thoughtfully. "You must know you are playing a game against more than one enemy."

"Is that all you can tell me about Brandis?"

"I have told you what I know," Maliki said firmly. "Now, I must ask a favor of you."

"I'll convince her to leave Sierra Leone. You have my word." Chase wrapped his mind around Mossad being involved, leaving him questioning which other governments were on the hunt too. "All I ask in return is that you complete her work in Massam."

Maliki extended his hand. "I genuinely hope McIntyre is right about you."

"That makes two of us." Chase shook hands. "They'll never see me coming."

Walking alongside Maliki toward the house, he breathed easier knowing he'd closed a deal with the Unicorn. He knew the promise he made would be a hard sell to Ammelie, who he guessed was even more suspicious than ever. His mind rifled through ways to speed up the endgame of Operation Honey Trap.

Easier said than done.

A hundred yards away, he noticed Dax seated on the front porch steps as Stapha and the armed men lingered nearby. What caught his attention, though, were the children playing soccer in front of the main house.

Do they know their inheritance is based on never-ending wars?

As quickly as the question entered Chase's mind, his ears perked to a faint whistling overhead. His eyes glanced upward as a contrail streaked across the sky. In a split second, he realized the strike was imminent. Instead of ducking for cover, he darted toward the house, shouting at the top of his lungs.

"Dax! Incoming!"

Everyone stood confused by his seemingly crazy outburst, except for Dax, who caught sight of the same streak of condensation and was already running for cover while grabbing several children along the way. Chase's voice and the children's piercing screams carried across the valley until...

BOOM!

A wave from the explosion ripped across the ground and punched Chase in the chest, sending him airborne before slamming onto the dirt twenty feet away. A high-pitched tone pierced his ears, splitting through the eery silence. Rolling onto his stomach, Chase glanced over at Dax, whose body covered several of the children. In a daze, the night they hunted the Prodigal flashed in his mind when he feared they wouldn't survive. He shook off the flashback and pulled himself to his feet.

A child's cry cut through the deafening silence. Chase stumbled toward where the house had been only seconds earlier. Rubble was scattered across a deep crater. When he heard the cry again, he turned to see Dax holding two bloodied children in his arms. Glancing past Dax, his eyes locked in on Maliki, who was on his knees hovered over the carnage. An agonizing wailing and weeping echoed across the valley.

A father who loses a son, or a son who loses a father, is never forgotten. How many more will die before the end game?

TWENTY-EIGHT

CASINO ABERDEEN, LUMLEY BEACH

An hour after the missile hit Dollar Farm, Chase and Dax landed on the roof of the hotel. Despite the thunderstruck grief and deadening shock, Maliki urged them to leave before the local police arrived.

Chase tried to shake the sight of limbs and body parts strewn across the crater and blast site. It was impossible to push them aside, especially when he stood over the remains of Stapha's body. He glanced at Dax, and from the look in his eye, Chase knew he was thinking the same.

"There are reports of an explosion at Dollar Farm." Jafari motioned them toward the roof exit door. "Police are closing down all major streets near the property."

"It wasn't an explosion," Dax interjected. "Someone dropped a bomb."

"We need to get to the house," Chase said urgently. "Will you take us?"

"Of course." Jafari led them to a service elevator. "Rooms are ready for your guests."

All three stepped into the elevator as Chase said, "We're at the point of no return."

Walking through the main lobby, guests and workers were

glued to a large flatscreen where several reporters stood at the entrance to Dollar Farm. No one noticed the Americans with their filthy and bloodied clothes. Chase followed Jafari outside to a van with Hotel Aberdeen painted on the side.

No time to take my foot off the gas.

It was less than a five-minute drive to the safe house. As they approached, Jafari cut the headlights and eased in behind another parked car.

Chase eyed the street and neighborhood, knowing there was a good chance they were walking into an ambush. He climbed out of the van and walked briskly down the sidewalk with Dax a few steps behind.

As they approached the exterior gate, he slowly retrieved the SIG from behind his back and flipped the safety off. He'd lost count of the number of times they'd snuck into places they weren't supposed to be. But as he stood in front of the security gate eyeing the lock, there was an extra heaviness deep in his soul.

"Who are you really, Chase?"

Ammelie's voice echoed in his mind as he inserted the key before disappearing behind the gates. Motioning for Dax to move around the side of the house, Chase stepped up to the front door then stopped cold. His heart pounded in his chest when he noticed the door slightly ajar. With his SIG pointed ahead, he gently nudged the door open and entered. He swept the room with one glance, noticing the smashed laptops and open anvil cases.

When Dax entered through the sliding glass door, Chase signaled upstairs. With each step, his index finger inched closer to the trigger.

On the second floor, they split up to clear each room.

Chase entered the bedroom where he'd slept the night before, which looked untouched. On his knees, he stretched his arm underneath the bed frame. His fingers touched the wooden slats holding up the mattress as he searched for what was hidden. He retrieved the leather-bound book and the dented *Speed Racer* tin box, which were banded together. Grabbing his backpack from the dresser, he shoved the treasure inside and covered them with his clothes.

With his backpack slung over one shoulder, he holstered the SIG and met Dax in the hallway. *All clear.* Downstairs he surveyed the damage to McIntyre's gear and Dax's laptop. Everything looked to be destroyed beyond repair.

"Whoever it was, they bashed the hell outta everything." Dax leaned in close and studied the melted plastic on the laptops. "Used some kind of acid. Hard drives may not be salvageable."

Chase glanced inside both anvil cases. "No weapons or ammo left."

"Should we phone a traitor?" Dax held up the burner cell from McIntyre. "She could've called in the airstrike with the help of any one of her shady clients."

"Load up everything. We'll have Jafari help dispose of it all." Chase put his hands on his hips, unnerved by the situation. "Maliki told me he'd written an algorithm that monitored keywords from the intercepted communication between those the governments are spying on. All without their knowledge. It may not have been McIntyre. World powers aren't afraid to launch airstrikes for their own gain. We've seen that firsthand, right?"

"So, Maliki is spying on the spies," Dax reiterated. "Perfect."

"It's possible he wasn't the target," Chase suggested. "It could've been meant for us."

"If that's true, then his family's blood is on our hands."

An unsettled feeling lingered. "We're still in the fight."

"Do you think your cover is blown?" Dax asked. "We bet the house on her."

"She was suspicious in Massam, and she knows I was going to meet with Maliki." Chase ran his fingers through his sweaty hair. "We'll load up what we can and find out when she arrives."

Dax rifled through what was left inside the anvil cases, including grabbing the kevlar face masks. He used a towel from the kitchen to cover the laptops and loaded everything in one case. Chase knew he needed to make a call. *Don't make me regret this, McIntyre.* He took the cell from Dax and dialed the only number programmed into the phone. It rang several times before she answered.

"Where are you?" Chase asked, annoyed.

"I'm chasing down a lead on the Asian artifact."

"Have you heard about Maliki and his family?" When McIntyre didn't reply, he broke the news. "Farm was bombed. A dozen casualties, maybe more. Including Stapha."

"What do you mean it was *bombed*?"

Chase heard the quiver in her voice. "With the size of impact, it was definitely a drone."

"How do you know this?"

"We were there to meet with Maliki when it happened. It's all over the local news."

"Losing Stapha will break him," she lamented. "You shouldn't have gone near him."

"*And* the safe house is compromised," Chase replied dead–

141

pan as he watched Dax wheel the anvil case to the front door. "We need a cleaner within the hour. Can you handle it?"

"I'll make a call," she answered. "Where will you be?"

"Hotel Aberdeen. When will you be back?"

"I'm not certain. Keep this cell on, and I'll be in touch."

TWENTY-NINE

THURMONT, MARYLAND

McIntyre hadn't left the interrogation room since she arrived, but the space had taken on a new look. The entryway that led to the long corridor and to freedom was locked tight. A cot had been rolled in, as well as a folding table and a laptop with no internet access. It was sparse. Bouchard had returned her cell to her before he left the room. When Chase called, she knew someone was monitoring, which is why she kept the call as brief as possible. Hopefully, she hung up before his location was tracked.

She felt unnerved at the thought she wouldn't be seeing the light of day any time soon, but she had secured a far less costly fate than those close to her. *Stapha.* Tears welled up in her eyes on the verge of spilling over her cheeks. Thousands of miles away, she was helpless to retaliate. *I've sold my soul to Bouchard, again.* Slumping down in a chair, she buried her face in her hands and wept.

"Do you go by Alison or McIntyre?"

Her head snapped up as she watched a woman approach. Early thirties. Attractive. She recognized Bouchard's sister from the campaign trail where she stood on stage at the rallies.

"You're Avery Bouchard?"

"I'm here to keep a close watch on you."

"That wasn't part of the deal. Where's the President?"

"He is unavailable. However, I have the authority to speak on his behalf."

"Looking for a promotion from speechwriter? Or maybe you've been stung by the DC fever to step out of your brother's shadow into the swamp. One look at you, and I can tell you're not made out for this."

"I've been briefed on the circumstances of Simon Adams' death," she answered. "I will say, a quick scroll through your cellphone was quite enlightening."

"None of which you can use without me disclosing the truth about RVG."

"I have no knowledge of RVG, and neither does the President."

"So there's not a room full of analysts listening in?" McIntyre itched her right forearm and, for the first time, noticed two small stitches. *Surprise.* Unsure of when that occurred, she assumed it was a tracker of some kind.

"Let me guess, if I try to escape, you'll blow me up?"

"As long as you cooperate, neither of us will have to find out." Avery stepped in close and lowered her voice. "I'll be honest with you, there is no one on the other side of that wall."

"Decrease the circle, decrease the fallout." McIntyre was struck by how skillfully Avery Bouchard deflected. "Do you have any idea of the laws your brother has broken?"

"I'd imagine it's nothing worse than what landed you here. Now that we've got that out of the way, don't you have another call to make?"

McIntyre held her cell, knowing she was about to burn her best cleaner in all of South Africa. With Avery standing guard, there was little choice as she dialed and relayed the address to the Lumley safe house. Once she hung up, she turned her attention back to Avery.

"I'll need a workstation, as well as internet access" McIntyre pushed a bit harder. *Let's see how resourceful you are.* "And intelligence within the last few hours from Sierra Leone."

"I'm afraid you're cleared for the use of your cellphone, which I will be monitoring." She held up a cellphone of her own and played back McIntyre's call. "Nothing more."

"I can't help Chase if I'm stuck in here with my hands tied."

"Alison, this isn't about helping him." Avery smirked. "Hardeman must act alone."

McIntyre pointed to the laptop. "What's that for then?"

"Your confession."

McIntyre felt her words sink into a grave of grief that shoveled a foot deeper.

Maliki, I am sorry.

She lunged forward within inches of Avery. A jolt of electricity shot through her veins, locking her muscles and deadening her nerves. She dropped to the floor and struggled to move. And like on the roof of the building in Belém, she was left paralyzed.

THIRTY

ANDREWS AIR FORCE BASE, WASHINGTON D.C.

Leaning back in a tan leather chair with a Presidential seal stitched into the headrest, Bouchard eyed General Abbott, who was seated across from him. His private office onboard Air Force One was a place of solitude, but on the flight back to DC, it was more of an isolation chamber for his star witness. Wood-paneled walls. An oval AFO emblem hung above where the General was seated. Bouchard wondered if the decorated war hero had stopped breathing since he hadn't blinked in nearly thirty seconds. He appeared more like a statue than flesh and blood.

Wearing a leather bomber jacket with "Bouchard" stitched across the breast, the only uniform he'd ever worn, he dug his elbows into one of two Resolute desks made from the timbers of the HMS Resolute. He was the only President who used both. The other one was in the Oval Office. Seated on his throne as the most powerful leader in the free world, he refused to be intimidated. Abbott was weighed down by medals, but he was more agile to improvise. It was time to change the deck before a house of cards flopped for the world to see.

"Do you know why I appointed you to the Joint Chiefs?"

Bouchard waited for Abbott to respond or to flinch an inch. Instead, Abbott remained stone-faced. "You're one helluva soldier, but every warrior has a chink in the armor. We're fighting a different kind of war, Ben. Leverage replaces threats. Black ops replace boots on the ground or cable news footage of a MOAB. *Mother Of All Bombs.* We must evolve against our adversaries. You know that better than anyone."

"History will uncover every damning detail of your actions, Mr. President."

"From the beginning, I've known about your niece, Alison McIntyre. Don't you think that's something you should've disclosed at some point in your *stellar* career? She's an arms broker to our enemies, for God's sake. Sure, she was once an asset to the Agency, but she has betrayed our country."

"Michael Hardeman. Special Agent Kelley. Simon Adams." Abbott's stern tone commanded attention. "Your casualties are mounting, sir."

"You military dogs are all the same," Bouchard retorted. "You bark at the Commander in Chief, but you don't have the balls to bite."

"Death. Kidnapping. Assassination. A rogue operative unknown to U.S. intelligence." Abbott's steely glare was troubling. "That will be your legacy."

"Script needs work. Major plot holes. It's a B-movie at best." Bouchard knew he was poking the bear, but any sign of backing down would turn the tables. Since the attack on Los Angeles, he'd waited for the right moment to end Abbott's career. "You've rattled off a few names, made a few unsubstantiated claims, and by all accounts, you have zero evidence."

"I've been subpoenaed to testify before the Intel Committee."

"Ben, you go spewing your crazy conspiracy theories, and you might end up in a padded room with no windows." Bouchard slid the letter on White House letterhead across the table. "Don't torpedo your legacy in front of Congress and be laughed out of D.C." He waited until Abbott read the letter then tightened the noose. "I made her an offer, and she accepted to save your skin. In return, you'll agree to retire from active duty and resign from the Joint Chiefs. I'll sing your praises as if you were the next Audie Leon Murphy, and you'll ride off into the sunset to live out the rest of your days on a ranch in Montana."

"What will happen to Alison if I refuse?"

Bouchard stared out the plane window where the press corp were disembarking from the aircraft headed toward a hanger for an impromptu press conference. He had to admit, Avery's idea to leverage McIntyre was a stroke of genius. But he'd asked too much of Avery and pulled her deeper into the RVG coverup, making it difficult to throw in the towel after his first term.

"If you tell your truth, she'll spend the rest of her life in ADX or Gitmo," he said matter of fact. "Not only is she known to be a black market arms broker, but she was in Los Angeles during the attack and in Athens when Simon was killed. She handed you all the evidence I need with that morbid photo. And she was in Sierra Leone two days ago planning to attack a partner of our allies which ended in a drone strike." Bouchard knew at least pieces of his summary were lies, yet he continued. "Put all that together, and I'd say she's the mastermind behind your entire conspiracy theory."

"You promised leniency if I brought her in, and she cooperated in finding Chase Hardeman." Abbott shifted his weight as he stared at the letter. "She's done what you asked."

"She confessed to all of it, Ben." Bouchard enjoyed turning the screws on Abbott. "Now, what we need to agree on in the next sixty seconds is whether that confession gets leaked."

Abbott grabbed a pen from the desk and added his signature to the document. "Executive privilege will cause suspicion with the Intel Committee."

"It's simple, alternative facts. Happens all the time."

A knock at the door interrupted them. Bouchard was ready to leave, so he grabbed the signed document and slipped it into his coat pocket. He motioned for Abbott to join him as a secret service detail led them to the front of the aircraft and down the stairs. Bouchard walked along the tarmac with his shoulders back and a confident stride. He stepped behind a cluster of mics knowing the press core was curious, then directed Abbott to stand off to the side of him.

"Thank you for your patience," Bouchard began. "I was hoping to share the news earlier. However, there was a process to confirm what we now know to be true." He paused and allowed the anticipation to build. "Earlier today, we received an update in our search for Chief of Staff Simon Adams. And I must say..." Bouchard allowed his emotions to show, knowing how it would play to the American people. "From the very beginning, Simon has been a close friend ever since I first met him on the campaign trail. So, it is with the heaviest of hearts for not only his family and our country, but for me personally, that I inform you of his tragic death." He held up his hand to hold off a wave of questions he sensed was about to erupt, then turned toward Abbott. "General Abbott, please say a few words."

Bouchard stepped aside, convinced he'd nailed the headlines and won the battle.

"We have verified evidence that proves Chief of Staff Adams died in Athens. Most likely on the same night he disappeared," Abbott said somberly. "Due to the nature of his death, we will continue the investigation in search of answers. While this is tragic news and not the outcome we hoped for, the President has made it clear that those responsible will be brought to justice."

"Thank you, General." Bouchard stepped up to the clustered mics. "Questions?"

THIRTY-ONE

Chase splashed a handful of water on his face, leaving the soil from Dollar Farm dripping from his scraggly beard into a sink. His fingers gripped the side of the porcelain as he stared at his reflection in a mirror. The Stars and Stripes on his forearm was not only a symbol of patriotism but a reminder of what was hidden beneath. *Death is a chilling blade whose edges cut deep into healed wounds.* Closing his eyes, revenge and retribution seeped into his bones.

When he returned from Mosul, he tried to leave the war behind. Then his enemies hunted him in Los Angeles. Ashes burned in the aftermath. When the dust settled, he faced the ghosts from his past, and not all were demons. His deadliest tendencies left angels caught in the crossfire. Escaping across the Atlantic was an attempt to become who he'd always wanted to be, far from who he was trained to be and who he'd been behind the Kevlar mask. Then Laney was taken. Adams was assassinated. And now, innocence was left shattered in the survivors of Maliki's bloodline.

His eyes narrowed, fixated on the scars that crisscrossed his body. Surviving the interrogation from Akram Kasim gained access to the Prodigal. Scars were a reminder of the strength

151

found in a primal urge to unleash the devil within. He dried his face and pulled on a fresh shirt, then stepped out from the bathroom and entered a main living area of the Penthouse suite.

"Any luck?" Chase asked.

"Above my pay grade." Dax stacked the half-melted hard drives on a coffee table. "We can hang on to them until we find someone who's got better skills."

Chase took in the space. Matching sofa and chairs. Small refrigerator lined with miniature liquor bottles. A kitchenette. Traveling with his dad, he'd been in some of the most luxurious hotels in the world. He rated the Hotel Aberdeen's Penthouse the equivalent of a Best Western.

"What else was in the case?"

"Wires and cables, mostly." Dax pulled himself off the floor and hobbled over to the anvil case. He reached inside a hidden compartment and retrieved two more SIGs. "We've got enough ammo for now, but the way this is going, we should restock."

"What about the security cameras from the safe house?"

"Cloudless. Files are as invisible as the air in this room. Whoever jacked all of this must've gained access to the account."

"Which means they're pros," Chase noted. "McIntyre is the only one who knew we were at the safe house."

"Unplugged." Dax held up the burner cell. "She could've been setting us up from the beginning and hooked us by killing Adams. Explains why she left in a hurry after she'd reeled us in like a 200-pound marlin."

"She didn't stay on the call for very long. And it could be why Bouchard announced proof of Adams' death with General

Abbott confirming the evidence. She could've wiped us clean and given Bouchard what he needed."

"Why would she go to Bouchard?" Dax asked. "She hates him as much as we hate her."

"Scapegoat is the simplest answer," Chase suggested. "Flip the script for a minute. Give her the benefit of the doubt. If she's really helping us, there's a possibility she got caught."

"We dial that number again," Dax held up the cell, "and any advantage we have shifts to the other side—Mossad, Bouchard, or whoever else it might be."

"Brandis is the prize." Chase loaded a mag into one of the SIGs. "Honey Trap is still a go."

Dax picked up the other two SIGs and loaded them. "You don't think she'll cut and run after what happened today? I mean, you're not *that* irresistible."

"We won't know until she arrives." Chase loaded another mag into his second SIG. "What about the surveillance at the Hope House pad?"

"With the breaking news about Omar's location, I never made it over there." Dax hung his head. "I guess now that they'll be staying here, there's no need to do it."

"Jafari will keep eyes on her tonight." Chase was troubled that someone lurked in the shadows. He was even more disturbed the mounting questions produced few answers. *Too many scenarios and threads to know which is the right needle to weave it all together.* "I gave Maliki the cloned SIM card from Ammelie's cell. He'll run it through Unicorn and see if he finds any numbers that match his database. Maybe we'll get lucky." He slipped both SIGs into a custom holster that secured the weapons behind his back, then slipped on a black hoodie. "Ready to go hunting?"

Dax did the same with his SIGs. "I won't lie, I like big bucks."

Both left the room and rode the elevator down. Jafari met them in the lobby and handed over a set of keys and a new burner cell. Walking across the parking lot, a dense humidity seeped through the night. Chase found the Land Cruiser parked near an employee entrance. He climbed behind the wheel while Dax rode shotgun. A quick GPS search on the burner confirmed the destination: Tower Hill.

Cutting through traffic along Aberdeen Road, the Land Cruiser passed the Flaming Evangelical Ministry church, Quincy's Bar, and a row of hotels before turning on Wilkinson Road. A few miles down Wilkinson, the area transitioned into more upper-class neighborhoods.

"Who do you think called in the airstrike?" Dax asked.

"Really? You're asking that question now?"

"Trying to figure out the odds of success for our shifting plan."

"If McIntyre turned on us, then there's one answer."

"Bouchard," Dax noted. "If she got caught?"

"We're dealing with a government who knows Maliki's identity and ours."

"Mossad?" Dax asked. "You said Maliki secretly intercepted their surveillance."

"If that's the case, then the bombing was retribution."

Dax nodded. "Retribution against Maliki, or..."

"From what he said, his fail-safe for Unicorn wasn't limited to the U.S. or Israel. He's using it for all of his clients." Chase kept his eyes on the road ahead, searching for the next street. "So, anyone who discovered his identity as the creator of Unicorn and knew he was listening in could've wanted to silence him."

"I'd still put Bouchard or Mossad at the top of the list. And there's a damn good chance they wanted more than Maliki dead."

"It's possible we were collateral damage," Chase suggested. "Whoever it was left one helluva mess."

"Bouchard is cleaning house," Dax countered. "He reminds me of Horatio Gates."

"Never heard of him."

"He backstabbed Washington after Saratoga because he thought he was the real hero." Dax shifted in his seat. "If that strike was from Bouchard, he's willing to silence anyone who threatens to steal his hero status."

Chase said with a twinge of sarcasm, "You should become a history teacher."

Turning onto Signal Hill, there was only one way in and one way out. Reaching the top of the hill, the road ended in a cul-de-sac. Chase cut the headlights and slowed the Land Cruiser before pulling over to the curb. Properties on the summit of Tower Hill were Freetown's most luxurious estates.

"Whether it's Bouchard, Mossad, or whoever else that's pissed off," Dax said as he unzipped his hoodie and reached inside, retrieving the Kevlar masks. "At least we'll leave them guessing."

"Keep the streak alive." Chase slipped on the mask. "Don't die tonight."

"Good speech, Tony Robbins."

THIRTY-TWO

TOWER HILL, FREETOWN

The Land Cruiser stayed parked a block away as Chase and Dax scaled a cinderblock wall. Following a route Dax mapped out, they crossed through two more properties before landing in the target's backyard.

Chase kept his head on a swivel as he retrieved the SIG from his holster. He'd kicked in doors in Mosul and Baghdad under the guise of a black market smuggler, but if McIntyre was right, his cover, his legend, was blown. He attached a stainless steel suppressor, which housed a titanium tube. Quiet. Durable. Necessary for sneaking into a secured house in Tower Hill. Hard to believe that after all the months of searching and planning, they returned to the hunt.

Two men guarded the rear door, and several more were visible on opposite sides of the backyard. Adrenaline pumped harder with each passing second. It was the same feeling Chase felt right before he stepped out onto the stage and auctioned the rarest collector cars to the roar of a crowd. He motioned for Dax to stay close, and then they moved in step along the back wall. Crouched in a corner, they fired in unison, taking all four guards down.

From the silence that followed, it seemed the security

around front were oblivious to the dead bodies in the rear. Chase moved stealthily to the back door, glancing over his shoulder while Dax picked the lock. Entering into the house, no alarm sounded. Instead, they found themselves in a large chef's kitchen. Imported granite countertops. Stainless steel appliances. A sub-zero fridge. A dark blue Viking Tuscany Range. All top of the line.

Omar spared no expense.

The kitchen opened up to a larger den where a corner lamp illuminated an eighty-inch flatscreen, a fully stocked bar, and a glass showcase. Chase kept the SIG tucked against his chest with an index finger resting on the barrel. From behind the mask, he stared at what was on the other side of the glass. He had forced Omar into an impossible choice, one he couldn't have made. Rather than allowing Omar to stay in Mosul, Chase decided he needed to leave. But it was more than protecting their identities or the covert operation. It was about saving Omar's wife and children from the abuse they suffered under his fist.

The wealth of thieves never equaled honor. Never. And back then in Mosul, there were plenty of thieves who chased the cash from the West. Chase had gained Omar's trust by promising him a big payday. Neither trusted the other, and in the end, Omar wasn't given a choice. Chase wondered whether Omar resisted the temptation to retrieve his property from Mosul—his wife and children.

"Looks like he ended up better than expected," Dax whispered. "You'd think he'd keep all this in a vault considering his security is the C team."

"When you think you're a ghost, you tend to let down your guard."

"Yeah, but how'd he get his hands on all this?" Dax asked. "This is big money."

"Knowing Omar, it wasn't legit, and he probably didn't pay full price."

Behind a wall of glass, priceless artifacts were perfectly lit. A rare Canadian gold coin, snatched from the Bode Museum in Berlin. A Gibson Stradivarius, stolen from the great violinist Sarasate. A Third Imperial Fabergé Egg reported missing from New York's Metropolitan Museum.

"No Scepter of Dagobert," Chase noted. "That would complete his collection."

"Unless we plan on being locked up in his showcase, we better keep this party moving."

Chase led the way into a hallway and said in a lowered voice, "Remember, Omar always flirted with the deadliest of sins."

"Right at home in the dark to feed his twisted ass."

A shadow stepped out into the hallway. Chase reflexively pulled the trigger. A bullet hit the man square in the chest. He slumped to the floor as his eyes stared dead ahead, leaving a streak of crimson on the wall. Chase stepped over the fifth one to die in the last five minutes. He'd never gotten used to taking a life, no matter if they were the lowest of scum. But tonight, his trigger finger was itching. They cleared three bedrooms and made their way to the double doors at the end of the hallway. Gripping the doorknob, Chase heard groaning of pleasure on the other side. He turned the knob and pushed the doors open, pointing the barrel of the SIG in the direction of his target.

"Omar," he whispered loudly. *"Omar."*

In the pitch-black, a voice called out. "Who is there?"

Knowing Omar would keep a weapon nearby, Chase flipped

a switch on the wall and stepped forward with intention. When the lights blinked on, Omar was halfway out of bed, reaching for a Glock on a nightstand. Chase pressed the barrel of his SIG against Omar's skull. To his right, a girl in her late teens who looked to be a local Sierra Leonean pulled the covers over her naked body. Chase held his index finger to his lips, sensing she was on the verge of screaming.

Omar's eyes glared at the Kevlar masks as he hissed, "How dare you enter my home."

"The next few seconds will decide whether you live or die." Chase admitted there was freedom in concealing his face behind the mask. Perhaps that's why he pulled the trigger easier. He stared at Omar's chubby face, double chin, round stomach covered in a mass of black hair, and wondered how much he'd paid for the young girl to end up in his bed. *Some habits never die, even when you're given a second chance.* He turned his attention to the girl who stared back with hazel eyes that had lost their innocence. "You were never here. Get dressed and leave."

Without hesitation, she grabbed the clothes Dax picked up off the floor and dressed under the covers. Dax led her out of the bedroom and closed the door behind. Chase gazed at the man who was once Mosul's most connected herêmî. He was the one who vouched for Chase to Akram Kasim, which led to a face-to-face with the Prodigal, which altered the trajectory of Chase's life. But in Sierra Leone, he was nothing more than a rich Iraqi who thought the past was forgotten.

"What do you want? Money?" Omar demanded. "I have five thousand in a safe."

"Your collection in the other room is worth more than five grand."

"I am a successful businessman with expensive taste."

"That's not who you've always been, Omar."

"How do you know my name?" he asked, bewildered. "Who are you?"

"You have something I need." Chase took a step back, still aiming the SIG at Omar's chest. *Lure him in with a false sense of hope.* Pointing the barrel of his SIG, he waved Omar over to a desk chair near the window. Omar followed his instructions, and once seated, was zip-tied to the armrests. "Tell me when and where the auction will take place, and you'll wake up in the morning a new man."

"You have mistaken me for someone else," Omar objected. "I know nothing about an auction."

"Your memory wasn't always this bad." Chase pressed the suppressor against the side of Omar's neck, feeling the Iraqi swallow hard. "An artifact from the Orient. The Scepter of Dagobert. When and where will they be auctioned by Bernhardt Brandis?"

For a split second, so quick that Chase nearly missed it, Omar's eyes flared, and a reunion was underway. He aimed the suppressor against Omar's right thigh and fired. Before the Iraqi had a chance to wail out in pain, Chase covered his mouth with a gloved palm.

"Tell me about the Asian artifact," Chase said coldly.

"He is not an artifact." Omar gritted his teeth in agony as beads of sweat appeared on his forehead. "Bernhardt captured a scientist recruited by the Chinese."

"What's his name?" Chase pressed.

"Dong Hyun-Ki." Omar looked down at the bloody wound, panicked. "He developed biowarfare at the institute of virology in China." His eyes widened as blood seeped down his leg, dripping onto a white shag carpet. "A shell for Pathogen Level 4. Ebola. Nipah. Crimean-Congo Hemorrhagic Fever." Omar groaned in pain when Chase pressed the barrel of the SIG into his thigh a second time. "Please, I will bleed out if you do not put pressure on the wound."

"We're almost done." Chase steadied himself. "What other artifacts are in his collection?"

Omar's eyes narrowed. "An American he said would fetch a higher price than the others. But she is not for sale. I do not know her name. Please..."

"When and where?"

"One week from now in Monaco." Omar struggled with the restraints. "I know who you are. Show me your face, *tirsonek*." *Coward.*

"This will be over soon." Leaning in close, he whispered, "The invitation."

Omar gripped the armrests as sweat poured down his paling face onto his hairy chest and round stomach. His breathing labored as the blood left his body, seeping deeper into the carpet. He mumbled softly, "The coin."

Dax slipped back into the bedroom and said urgently, "Time to go."

"Grab all three pieces." Chase felt his hand tremble. "I'll be right behind."

"Still a slave to your master." Omar quipped to Dax. "Kûçikê qamçî." *Whipped dog.*

Chase's eyes darkened. "Allowing you to live was more than you deserved."

THIRTY-THREE

HALF MOON ISLAND, NORTH ATLANTIC

On the other side of a one-way mirror, Dong Hyun-Ki worked meticulously inside a white-walled room sealed from the contamination of a contagious world. Wearing a pressure isolated suit, face shield, and gloves, he set a boiling tube down and picked up a syringe. He pulled the plunger, drawing in a clear liquid from the boiling tube after examining it beneath a microscope. With the syringe filled, he injected the hypodermic needle into the stomach of patient zero, who laid unconscious on a gurney.

From the other side of the protective glass inside an observation room, Elena knew her actions were against her father's wishes. *But he chose to do the same against mine.* When Detective Castellanos of the Hellenic Police Force texted her the name Vadim Zhukov, what occurred on board the *Midnight Moon* in Athens blurred into focus.

She'd first met Zhukov in Hong Kong, where he was in charge of their security during meetings in Kowloon with the leaders of the Triads. With China pressing further into Hong Kong's government, it was critical an alliance was strengthened between the two largest crime syndicates to ensure operations within the Golden Triangle remained uninterrupted.

During those meetings, Elena remembered her father mentioning Zhukov was once an enforcer for the SVR, the successor to the KGB, headquartered in Yasenevo District in Moscow. A decorated officer assigned to travel with her father's entourage during the Asia negotiations, courtesy of the Russian president.

She imagined those moments aboard the *Midnight Moon* where Zhukov was killed with Chase or Dax on the other end of the trigger. She grew more convinced there were no survivors. The fact that Zhukov was there in Athens troubled her more than she admitted. Her father had sent an assassin to kill the man she loved. The Vihkrovs and Hardemans were opposites yet loyal allies. She was well aware of the limits when accepting anyone outside of the Bratva, but she was blindsided by the reality.

"He sent me here to do what must be done," Elena said, subdued. With the injection completed, the clock ticked as the virus flowed through Agent Kelley's bloodstream. "It is the only way."

"She will be ready for transport within the hour," Brandis replied, snapping her from her thoughts. "The Englishman will accompany you."

"President Bouchard's allegiance will belong to us very soon." Elena turned toward Brandis. "What will happen to the scientist?"

"He will be the top prize at the auction." Brandis smiled. "As agreed, you will return?"

She leaned in and kissed his cheek. "And I will stay."

Elena left Brandis inhaling her perfume and escaped to the fresh air of the Atlantic. When her father broached her with a scheme to extort Bouchard, she knew it was a death sentence. She urged him to reconsider, knowing it would place Chase in the fray and leave them exposed with the Bratva. If they were going to use Bouchard's involvement in RVG to blackmail him, then she suggested they kidnap Agent Kelley, the traitor, and use her as leverage to expand their global syndicate. She thought her father agreed, but now she was left questioning if he had listened.

Months passed, and the traitor defied Brandis' efforts to torture the truth out of her, which diminished her value. While she hated the traitor for what she'd done, there was a level of respect for standing strong against the German's tactics. Realizing Zhukov was onboard the *Midnight Moon* to kill Chase and Dax meant her father questioned her judgment. *He no longer trusts my decisions.* Her calls to Chase had gone unanswered. She was left with a conclusion that the bodies burned in the fire, the charred victims on the pier, must've included Chase and Dax.

Walking a path across the cliffs, she headed toward the landing pad. When she was with Chase in Monterey, she nearly told him of her father's intentions. But as she gazed out the window of their private cottage in Carmel, seeing him speak with the traitor left her choosing loyalty over love. A wave of guilt washed over her for the secrets she'd kept from him.

My love lost his life. Now it is time for the traitor to lose hers.

An hour later, gunmetal clouds loomed over rough seas. An incoming storm threatened to lockdown the island. Elena finished her pre-flight preparation of the Eurocopter Hermés EC 135, knowing with a kiss she had manipulated Brandis into betraying her father.

Forgiveness was given through retribution.

Even if she paid a steep price with her father, she hoped her decision would avenge Chase's death.

The Englishman approached from the path leading out from the jungle. He nudged the traitor forward as her steps wobbled. A hood was pulled over her head. Noise-canceling headphones wrapped around her ears. Wrists and ankles shackled. The Englishman helped her into the back of the helicopter, buckled her in, and secured the passenger door.

"A shame, really." The Englishman offered a wry grin. "She was quite a treat."

"You have had your fun," Elena replied flatly. "She is a sheep led to slaughter."

Lightning flashed, followed by rumbling thunder. Elena climbed behind the controls while the Englishman buckled into the co-pilot seat. She rifled through a quick checklist, then flipped a switch as the rotors whined. Drops of rain hit the windshield as she worked her hands and feet in harmony, controlling the cycle and collective pitch lever as well as the foot pedals.

The Eurocopter lifted off the landing pad and hovered above Half Moon Island before setting a course west toward Bermuda.

THIRTY-FOUR

HOTEL ABERDEEN, LUMLEY BEACH

"You want to tell me what happened back there?"

Chase heard the question as he parked the Land Cruiser in the same spot in the lot near the employee entrance. Turning off the ignition, he handed over the Kevlar mask, climbed out, and headed for the tour buses at the hotel entrance.

Entering Omar's house, there were two possible outcomes. First, Omar repented for his sins, pledged his loyalty, and led them to Brandis. Second, after being given a second chance, he revealed he was incapable of becoming better. When Chase stared into the eyes of the frightened teenage girl, the choice was made.

Dax shouted, pissed. "Are you going to answer me?"

"The answer is always the same," Chase mumbled. Without weighing his words, he spun around and yelled, "If you're tapping out, I'll ring the bell."

With fiery eyes, Dax hobbled to catch up to Chase before shoving him hard in the back. Chase stumbled forward, managing to stay on his feet. Before he had a chance to defend himself, Dax's fist connected with his jaw sending him to the concrete. Lying on the ground, he wiped the blood from his lip and glared up at Dax.

"You're not in this fight alone," Dax argued. "I've paid as much of a price as you."

"Really?" Chase retorted with a twinge of sarcasm. "Who've you lost?"

"He was a father to me too," Dax retorted. "As close as flesh and blood."

"There is no turning back for me. No surrender. No moral compass pointing the way." Chase calmed his anger, then reached out his hand, knowing Dax was as close as he'd ever get to a brother. "You were a son to Dad too."

"And I made him a promise." Dax pulled Chase to his feet. "I'm with you until the end, so don't keep me in the dark. Got it?"

No apologies. No hugging it out. No pleading to the heavens for forgiveness.

As they walked toward the buses, Chase admitted to himself that Dax had saved his ass far more times than he'd done in return. Questioning his loyalty was out of line, but Chase sensed an edge in his own soul. When he silenced Omar with a bullet to the brain, more of the innocence chipped away. The pronounced limp in Dax's stride was a reminder of the guilt he carried, leaving him wondering if it was right to pull him deeper into the abyss as an executioner.

"One week to Monaco." Chase wiped more blood from his lip. "Reach out to Dario Necci and tell him we've got Sarasate's Stradivarius and the Metropolitan's Fabergé Egg. Ask him to invite a select group of VIPs, including Brandis."

"Smoking him out." Dax nodded. "Enough dancing around."

"With any luck, he'll show up." Chase reached into his pocket and felt the Bode Museum's rare coin. "It's time we bring Ammelie into our world."

"What about McIntyre?"

Chase waved as Ammelie caught sight of them. "We're on our own."

Ammelie quickly approached, leaving the children gathered together as Jafari introduced himself. One look at their wide smiles and faces filled with excitement was a glimmer of hopeful life in a day filled with so much death. Chase adjusted his shirt to cover the back holster and SIGs.

"You finally made it," he called out. "I was about to send a search party."

"There is a fire at the Dollar Farm," she said, concerned, noticing the cut on his lip. "You're bleeding?"

"Banged my mouth against the car door."

"What happened, Chase?"

"We left hours before it started." He gestured for Dax to head out. "Slow down, Silva."

Ammelie met his gaze so intently that he looked away. "What have you done?"

"We met with Maliki Dollar and convinced him you weren't going to abandon the children if your funding ran out," Chase said with a straight face. "You've been here long enough to know there are those who come to rescue the locals, but when the money is gone, so are their promises. I personally guaranteed to cover any expenses needed to keep the orphanage in Massam up and running for years to come. That relieved Maliki's concerns."

"All of this is over money?" Ammelie's lips curled. "You don't know how much it will be to finish the buildings, educational scholarships, and to support the children."

"A promise is a promise," Chase said reassuringly. "We

reached an agreement."

"So, his men shooting at you were..."

"A warning to see if we were serious." Chase sensed Ammelie needed more convincing. "He knows you're not going anywhere, and I'll back you with the cash."

"So, the fire at the farm is a coincidence?"

"I have no idea," Chase shrugged. "Maliki and his family have suffered a tragic loss. His son Stapha was one of the family members killed. But I swear to you we had nothing to do with the fire." Chase gently grabbed Ammelie's shoulder and spun her around so she could see the children. "There's a sight that makes it all worth it." He held out his hand. "Do we have a deal?"

Ammelie seemed to relax a bit as she shook his hand. "I will hold you to it, Chase."

"Wouldn't want it any other way." Chase and Ammelie strolled back toward the hotel lobby. "I told Jafari to take care of whatever you, the children, and the others need. Think of it as an all-expenses paid vacation courtesy of your newest and biggest donor."

Chase and Ammelie entered the lobby and headed for the check-in counter, where Jafari, Dax, Wolffie, and the children were gathered. The clerk behind the counter handed out room keys to the adults who were paired off with a group of children. Jafari blocked out all of the rooms on the top two floors, except for the Penthouse suite. When he announced the swimming pool was open until 10 PM, the children let out a resounding cheer. Guests in the lobby turned to watch the group file toward the elevator.

"You know, on the bus ride here, I Googled you," Ammelie confessed. "Wasn't hard to find your father, Michael Hardeman. He was quite famous."

"Larger than life," Chase said, feeling the night wear on him. "I prefer to fly under the radar. He wanted to build and then steer the radar."

"What you did in Monterey was incredible. It was a world record price."

"We were lucky," Chase admitted. "Now it's time to give some of the windfall back."

"Sorry about..."

"Don't apologize. It's been a memorable twenty-four hours."

Doors opened, and a group of the children boarded the two elevators, along with their chaperones. Dax, Jafari, and Wolffie waited for the next elevator while Chase and Ammelie stood off to the side. Both elevators returned to the lobby, and another group of children boarded along with Dax, Jafari, and Wolffie.

Chase and Ammelie grabbed the next one alone. He took a moment to assess where he stood with Ammelie. His story about the fire was believable, sort of. His offer to finance the orphanage in Massam was a nice touch. He needed one more piece of the alibi to slide into place.

"We'll give Maliki and his family a few weeks, then we'll sit down with him, and the two of you can get to know each other." Chase hit the button for the top floor. "You'll get along fine."

"I bet you are regretting my offer at Baw Baw," Ammelie mused as she leaned against the elevator wall. "Seriously, I'm grateful for what you have done."

"Hold on," Chase smiled, "you're still buying the first round."

"Is that before or after your donation clears?" She bantered. The elevator doors opened, and they headed down the hallway toward her room. "Nice of you to escort me."

"We left the beach house and checked in here." Chase pointed toward the door at the end of the hallway. "Penthouse suite."

"Of course," she laughed. "Trade the beach house for the penthouse."

"I'd rather be closer to you." Chase stopped in front of her room and waited while she inserted the key. "Listen, how'd you like to go to Milan for a few days?"

"Milan? Well, I'm not sure..."

"We're putting on an auction. Thought you'd like to get an inside look."

"A business trip." Her cheeks flushed, embarrassed. She pushed the door open and waited in the doorway. "How many days?"

"Three tops," Chase answered, trying not to be too overt in closing the deal. "Jafari will take good care of everyone while we're gone."

Ammelie paused, considering his offer. "I do miss the chocolate liqueurs."

THIRTY-FIVE

PENTHOUSE SUITE—LATER

Chase flipped through the pages of the leather-bound book he'd kept close ever since Laney surprised him at the cottage in Carmel hours before the Monterey auction. She made him an offer. At the time, he hadn't yet accepted the reality the Prodigal had pulled him back into the fray. He was on the verge of fulfilling a childhood dream to honor his dad and desperately wanted to escape from the wars of the past. He made no apology when he rejected her offer to hunt Bernhardt Brandis. A decision he now regretted, leaving him feeling even more responsible for her disappearance.

I tried to walk away from the sins of my past, and now there's even more scars.

Reading the chicken scratch at the hands of a man he once trusted, he couldn't help but think of how that same man betrayed them all. What was left after the attack on Los Angeles was this book with detailed notes and lists of those who operated in the shadows far from the eyes of Interpol, the Bureau, the Agency, Homeland Security, and other allied government agencies. Each page was a gold mine of intelligence any government would die to have in their possession. And yet, he was the one who was the keeper of secrets.

Katarine Brandis, AKA Ammelie Stroman.

He'd read the pages countless times detailing the death of Brandis' wife and the disappearance of his daughter, who had not been seen in years. Without knowing, Ammelie confirmed most of what was on those pages during their conversation along the river in Massam. His index finger tracked a list of dates and locations earmarking Ammelie's travels over the years until she arrived in Sierra Leone. None of those locations were near Monaco, which was where Omar said the auction would occur.

Ammelie was the honey trap. A long-lost daughter reuniting with her father. Of course, if Chase had to double down, he'd say neither of them wanted to see the other. While the search for Omar offered a smokescreen for McIntyre, he was also the backup plan if Ammelie wasn't willing to go along.

When Chase stared into her eyes that first night at Baw Baw, he knew she was the glimmer of hope he'd been searching for to rescue Laney. In the end, Omar was disposable. But Chase's feelings for Ammelie caught him off guard, leaving him questioning whether he was willing to risk her freedom.

At the same time, a twinge of guilt struck at the thought of using Ammelie, an innocent woman who watched her mother die as a child and escaped the deadly fists of her abusive father.

She's built herself a new life, one of serving others.

As much as Chase tried to think of an alternative, a family reunion was the quickest way to gain Brandis' attention.

"We used the dumpster in the back to get rid of everything," Dax announced as he entered the Penthouse suite. "Jafari said it'll all be dumped tomorrow."

Chase noticed it was after midnight. "I snapped with

173

Omar."

"Tonight was a flash from the past," Dax answered. "We're walking a fine line."

"You still have the thumb drive with the backup files?" When Dax nodded, he asked, "Do you ever wonder how many of the others failed to change?"

"Probably most of them." Dax opened the small refrigerator in the kitchenette and pulled out two bottles of *Founded*. He popped the top with his teeth and handed one to Chase. "No one is innocent in all of this, but we're not judge or jury."

Just executioners.

"Makes you wonder..." Chase took a long drag from the bottle. "Without the RVG missions who or what are we fighting for?"

"Mission has never changed," Dax answered. "Right now, it's finding Laney."

Chase fell deeper in thought. "Is she who you thought she'd be?"

"Laney?" Dax asked, a bit confused.

"Ammelie." Chase slumped down into a chair and propped his feet on a coffee table. "McIntyre. Bouchard. Brandis. Dmitry. Everyone has their own dog in the fight. Ammelie will be an innocent casualty when the dust settles."

"Laney, Elena, and Ammelie all have one thing in common," Dax mused darkly. "They all think you're something special."

"What do you mean? Ammelie hardly knows me."

"Bro, if you don't recognize the look in her eyes, then you're a blind fool."

Dax turned back to the fridge and pulled out a box of Benny cakes, Moorish sesame seed and sugar biscuits. He grabbed a handful then tossed the opened box to Chase, who did the same.

It was late, the night was intense, and he hadn't eaten since the day before. Maybe it was the needed calories to fend off the migraine that pressed against the back of his eye, or maybe it was simply nervous eating, not knowing what was around the corner.

"If Dmitry wanted us six feet under," Dax thought out loud, "he might've known we were planning to go after Brandis and wanted to stop it from happening. Why?"

"It's possible." Chase pondered the question for a moment. "I don't have an answer."

"Even though we didn't tell anyone," Dax added. "He could've been watching us for months without us knowing. Somewhere along the way, he caught on, or maybe Elena knew more than she let on."

Chase joined in the game of twenty questions. "What about Adams at the safe house?"

"Now, I don't have an answer for that one either," Dax admitted. "But stay on Dmitry for a minute. He's the Bratva godfather, so it's likely he crossed paths in some shady ass deal with Brandis sometime within the last eight months. Brandis tells Dmitry he's got Laney locked up."

"Which means Dmitry knew about Laney and saw an opportunity."

"And you don't think he'd connect the dots that you were going after her?"

Chase followed the crumbs from Dax and shook his head. "Elena would've warned me."

"Blood is thicker than love. You know there were battle lines drawn between Elena and Laney in Monterey. Doesn't

175

matter which choice you made. There was a shift between you and the Vihkrovs afterward." Dax stuffed several cookies in his mouth at once, then downed the rest of his beer. With his mouth full, he added, "We're walking right back into Dmitry's line of fire."

"There is a simpler explanation for why Dmitry wants us dead." Chase held up the leather-bound book. "He wants to know the names inside."

THIRTY-SIX

WASHINGTON, D.C.

In a private study across from the Oval Office, President Bouchard leaned back in a high-backed chair peering through the lenses of his reading glasses at a draft of the State of the Union. The small space was cramped with a desk, chair, television, two corner chairs, thick blue curtains, and windows framing a grove of trees outside that guarded the view for security reasons. With a red sharpie, he reviewed the draft and crossed out sentences while notating others. A fifth draft was close, but it wasn't perfect.

The first State of the Union was a rallying cry to his base in the face of the media and opponents who scoffed at any chance of David Bouchard winning the presidential election. An impossible victory proved a monumental feat. Trudging through Washington's swamp, he played the game by strengthening his allies, foreign and domestic. With his tenacious presence on social media, he pushed back against those who used their power against the United States, foreign and domestic. Standing on his convictions, he'd pushed his enemies to critical rage, foreign and domestic.

With his re-election campaign on the verge, the nation was experiencing record unemployment. Record-setting rallies on Wall Street were challenged by an erratic economy resulting in massive selloffs and mergers. An exoneration from the baseless accusations his rivals bombarded across the country that his campaign conspired with the Russians lingered, even though there was no irrefutable evidence.

It's always the Russians.

He counter-punched the rhetoric and placed strict sanctions and tariffs on Russia, Iran, and China, and forged new economic deals with countries that had taken advantage of the United States for far too long. No longer was the nation an endless ATM for the world. He forged partnerships with the private sector to strengthen the country's economy. He forced allied nations to pay their fair share to make the world a safer place.

Decisions made as Commander in Chief are rarely without casualties.

Those who bankrolled his campaign fired back publicly, oftentimes disagreeing with his decisions, claiming they were the ones who helped him win the election and he should show them the respect they deserve. Far too often, those in power believed wealth granted access to the highest office in the land. Reporters spun conspiracies of infighting within the administration and interviewed those who once supported the president yet now opposed his America first mantra. Headlines blasted him for aggressive tactics against the rest of the world, an inability to cross party lines, and blamed him for a general disdain of humanity.

If it's in the headlines, it's true, right?

During his first term, the administration accomplished more than his predecessors. But as he read the conclusion of his speech, he couldn't ignore the fact that the nation had never been more divided, and the words on the page threatened to ignite a civil war.

Bouchard scribbled a note for Avery at the end of the speech while his anger burned against the Speaker of the House, a chameleon to anyone who listened preaching about unity while chiseling a greater divide. Washington was a chasm of division, where there were more cowards than heroes. Find a congressman or senator who stood their ground for what was truly right, and you'd find a man or woman who lost their next election. Popularity was the name of the game. Special interests were the banks. Insider trading from congressmen and senators was the norm. It was a ticking time bomb for the nation. Common ground meant one side was a loser, which was a political death sentence.

During the first campaign, Simon and Avery urged him to run as an independent, which allowed him to target career politicians on both sides from hijacking the country and holding the American people ransom. His message resonated with the marginalized and inspired the powerful from entertainment to economic circles to the middle class regardless of ethnicity. Many supported the change Americans desperately needed, so winning the first election was a referendum on D.C.

When his presidency began, he believed he was the one to deliver the people to the Promised Land. Avery scripted the message. Simon created the playbook. Bouchard was the enforcer. Millions believed the fundamental changes he preached were possible. Intentions were pure, at least as pure as one could be in politics. Now his supporters believed a second term was an absolute certainty, but he was undecided on whether to run, especially with the secrecy of

RVG undetermined. The walls closed in as he was challenged with whether his first term was nothing more than a charade.

The unwritten pages of Simon's playbook were revealed only days after Bouchard stepped into the Oval Office. Along with former Indiana governor Michael Hardeman, he was presented with an extreme proposal to bypass the political swamp and the agencies he was convinced were trying to torpedo his administration. The Red Venture Group was a black ops program to silence those who threatened America's freedom and global influence. While ensuring the country's safety was part of the oath of office, his decision to keep the operation secret within the Oval Office was a criminal act that, if disclosed, threatened the Republic.

Exoneration from a fake Russian crime didn't mean innocence of all crimes.

My decisions saved lives and brought those bastards to judgment.

As quickly as that thought crossed his mind, he admitted he had inhaled the power of the presidency without exhaling the scales of criminality. With Simon dead, the playbook was finished. And like a novel written by a novice, there were too many loose ends. Special Agent Kelley's mysterious disappearance. Alison McIntyre, known as a broker of weapons to the enemy, was RVG's handler. General Abbott's upcoming closed-door questioning with the House Intel Committee. Even though he signed his resignation and agreed to remain silent, Bouchard was far from convinced Abbott's cooperation wouldn't shift if it meant betraying his oath. And there were the wildcards, Chase Hardeman and Dexter Thompson. Freedom's most effective fighters and his greatest threat. They were boots on the ground in the Middle East hunting terrorists without the handcuffs of Washington. But the testimony of their actions would bury him.

Campaigning for a second term with all of these loose ends threatened to amplify the chances of the world peeling back his presidency to peer behind the curtain.

If McIntyre's right, there's a chance I can control the inferno.

A sudden rush of claustrophobia washed over him, followed by a desperate need to open the windows and breath fresh air. He spun the chair around and glared at the bulletproof glass. Breathing in deep, he tried to stop himself from hyperventilating. He cursed his maddening life in a fishbowl and questioned whether four more years were worth it.

Leave the Oval Office with your head held high, or be exposed, and your presidency dies.

Tossing the State of the Union on his desk, he rubbed his palms hard against his face trying to shake himself out of a downward spiral. His presidency launched like a rocket ship, but with Simon's death and the unrest across the nation, his administration was losing altitude like a comet. A global pandemic. A robust economy on the verge of collapse. Tens of millions unemployed. And a volcanic eruption of racial division that threatened to leave a nation forever scarred. One reason why he preferred to work out of the private study was to avoid a view of the thousands of protestors camped outside the White House gates.

"You're looking a little pale." Avery stood in the doorway. "Feeling okay?"

"Simon was the tactician. He navigated the waters. He knew who to leverage and who to put his arm around to push our agenda through. I feel rudderless without his guidance."

"There was no one better," Avery acknowledged as she eyed

the draft. "You have a chance to reset. You're the Commander in Chief. You set the course."

"One more pass." Bouchard handed the speech over. "Ending needs your touch."

"Five drafts, and I'm still trying to stick the landing." Avery stepped into the office and closed the door. From a file folder, she retrieved a document and waved it in front of Bouchard. "Full confession. Confirms her association with a foreign terrorist cell connected to the Prodigal, who she sold weapons to that were used in Los Angeles. And we have her DNA on the laptop."

"She confessed to all of it," Bouchard questioned. "A bit surprising."

"Full confession, not full cooperation. Whatever you said to her in private sealed the deal. It will be solid enough if we need it."

Bouchard scanned the confession, knowing he'd brought Avery deeper into the secrets that haunted him. He couldn't allow her to go any further. Reading the words, she'd matched the tone he'd witnessed sitting across from McIntyre. Her ghostwriting ability translated seamlessly to the political arena.

"I know it was a big ask, one I hope I'll never have to do again."

"David, who is she?" Avery pressed.

"She's precisely who she says she is." Bouchard pointed at the confession. "Nothing more needs to be said."

"I guess I'm trying to understand all the cloak and dagger." Avery paused as she scanned the red markings on the draft copy. "General Abbott's confirmed to go before the House Intelligence Committee the day before the State of the Union.

All of a sudden, Alison McIntyre is captured and brought to a black site. David, tell me what is going on, please?"

"Hand-deliver a copy of the confession." Bouchard felt the claustrophobia subside. "Let Abbott know if he goes after me with the Intel Committee, we'll leak it to the press." He sensed her reluctance as she turned to leave. "Have you decided yet?"

She glanced over her shoulder. "Read Webster's definition of *nepotism*."

"You're the only one I trust."

"Chief of Staff was never part of the deal."

"Avery, I need you to do this for me."

"You know, a diet of Red Bull is not Keto."

"Don't change the..." Bouchard's secure Blackberry buzzed on the desk. He answered, motioning for Avery to wait. He listened intently to his director of national intelligence. "Any idea of the cause? Why was there no indication of this in today's PDB?" *President's Daily Brief.* "Understood. Situation Room in fifteen."

He set his cell on the desk, weighing the sudden development with China's Ministry of State Security. Returning Avery's puzzled gaze, he said, "We've lost cellphone surveillance on all known MSS spies in North America."

THIRTY-SEVEN

MILAN, ITALY

On approach to Malpensa Airport, Chase watched Ammelie closely as she stared out a cabin window of a Praetor 600 Ambraer, a $21 million shuttle courtesy of Dario Necci. An ultra-quiet cabin with Bespoke design. Jet black fully berthing seats. Muted gold carpet beneath turquoise blueish lighting illuminated against stark white paneling. World-class comfort. Industry-exclusive technology. Active turbulence reduction. Proline fusion avionics. Nothing but the best in luxury travel.

"Thanks for coming with me," Chase said, fully aware of the stakes.

"Last night, you said it was a business trip." Ammelie shifted her gaze to him. "I didn't realize it would be only the two of us."

"I asked Dax to stay in Lumley to check on Maliki and his family."

"Quite thoughtful." Ammelie's stare turned curious. "Does this plane belong to you?"

"A friend with more cash than me," Chase grinned. "Once you've flown private..."

"You will never fly commercial again."

Chase and Ammelie laughed together, allowing the moment

to settle. Chase couldn't help but sense the attraction grow stronger.

Dax was right. The look in her eyes is a clear sign.

And he couldn't deny his gaze back at her was the same. There was something special about her, something he desired. She escaped her past, while he was sucked deeper into his own. She found purpose in serving others, while he drifted on a life raft in the Pacific searching for land.

While he barely knew Ammelie, he felt himself being drawn closer to her. He shrugged it off to being caught up in the operation. He'd done the same with Laney and perhaps with Elena too.

Maybe it's a weakness I'll never be able to master.

"Does your friend have a name?" Ammelie asked curiously.

"Dario Necci. Made four hundred million playing for Milan's soccer club. Retired at thirty-four. Invested his money well and pursued his hobby of collecting rare art."

"Is he single?" Ammelie inquired.

"Divorced. Twice."

"Not only a player on the field." Ammelie's cheeks flushed. "Are you a player, Chase?"

He bantered, "I'm not even allowed in the stadium."

"I find that hard to believe. I would say you are a keeper."

"What about you? Anyone pulling your heartstrings?"

"It is hard for me to let anyone close." Ammelie paused. "Well, that's embarrassing."

Chase reached out and grabbed her hand. "We share that much in common."

She gently pulled her hand away. "We are from different worlds."

As the jet banked on its final approach, the cabin grew

quiet as the clouds cleared to reveal a perfect view of the second-most populous city in Italy. Milan was nestled in the northwestern section of the Po Valley between the river Po, the foothills of the Alps with the Great Lakes, the Ticino river, and the Adda to the east. A leading alpha global city of over 8 million with some of the most valuable art galleries in the world featuring major works by Leonardo da Vinci.

Wheels screeched against the runway, and the jet taxied toward a private area of the Malpensa Airport. Chase and Ammelie disembarked and were greeted by an immigration officer holding a tablet. He checked Chase's passport, and the ten grand slipped inside, then welcomed them to Milan.

Chase's smooth sleight of hand kept his forged passport from Ammelie's eyes. He grabbed her hand and reassured her, knowing she couldn't believe they'd slipped through security without revealing her identity.

A chauffeur dressed in a tailored suit stood next to a black Mercedes touring bus. He greeted them in Italian, then grabbed their luggage and loaded it into the rear. From the luggage hold of the jet, he retrieved an anvil case containing Sarasate's Stradivarius and the Metropolitan's Fabergé Egg.

Ammelie climbed inside the Mercedes and slipped onto one of the swivel chairs inside. Chase waited until the chauffeur had loaded the anvil case, then he walked around the side of the Mercedes, digging his hand into his pocket to be sure the Bode coin was still there. He stepped inside the touring van and took a seat next to Ammelie, who was pulling headphones out from her overnight bag. She popped them in each ear, leaving Chase wondering if he'd pushed too hard.

As the driver left Malpensa Airport, the Mercedes headed east toward Via Caprino to a roundabout near Le Robinie Golf

Club & Resort, then continued to Strada Statale in Provincial di Varese. When they reached Villa Olma, the driver turned down Via Cernobbio along the banks of Lake Como set against the foothills of the Alps before turning again on Via Regina.

Several miles down, the driver slowed the vehicle and pulled up to a rod iron gate. After pressing an intercom, and exchanging words in Italian, the gates opened and the Mercedes headed down a long driveway lined with overhanging trees.

An hour after landing, they had arrived at the main residence of the estate. Chase realized he'd never been to Dario's home even though they shared more than one epic adventure hunting treasures.

As the Mercedes stopped in front of the two-story villa, Dario Necci stood on the steps with his round belly hanging over a speedo. Chase glanced over at Ammelie as she removed her headphones and stared out the window at the three-hundred-pound former Italian soccer star.

"Both divorces were rough," Chase said in a lowered voice. "He's a big softy."

Ammelie smirked. "I can see that."

Before the driver opened the door, Dario stepped down the stairs and did it for him.

"My friend," he bellowed in a heavy Italian accent. As he opened the sliding door, his utter shock was as clear as looking at one's reflection in Lake Mashu, the clearest lake in the world. His wide smile disappeared, and his jaw gaped open. "You've brought a guest."

Chase bridged the awkward moment. "Dario, meet Ammelie Stroman."

"A pleasure to meet you," he replied, not knowing how to cover himself.

"Twelve goals in three Intercontinental Cup Finals," she said warmly. "It is an honor to meet the greatest player in A.C. Milan history."

Dario's embarrassment lightened. "Welcome to my home, Ammelie."

THIRTY-EIGHT

LAKE COMO—LATER

Inspired by a traditional asymmetrical Tuscany style, with its tall tower in the center of a stone façade, the lakefront villa boasted twenty bedrooms, ten bathrooms, a thirty-seat movie theater, a fully-equipped fitness wing, dual-level spa including a sauna and massage room, state-of-the-art gaming room, and a dozen more rooms that were never used.

An infinity pool overlooked the lake, while a country house on the property stored a collection of Ferraris. Dario Necci built the estate to raise his family generations deep, but two divorces later and the loss of a court battle over custody of his children turned a home into a mega warehouse to store his accolades and collections.

Throughout the main residence, original oil paintings from da Vinci, Michelangelo, Picasso, van Gogh, Dali, and others were hung along the walls. One of which was Dali's *The Face of War*. While far from the most expensive, it was definitely the most disturbing.

Chase stared at Dali's surreal traumatic premonition of war. "A soccer fan?"

"Wolffie is a Real Madrid *football* Madridistas," Ammelie acknowledged. "When we were living in Spain, we used to buy tickets to the games at Santiago Bernabéu. I remember standing in the last row watching Dario score six goals for Milan."

"I never had a chance to see him play in person." Chase grew more disturbed by the skulls in the painting that seemed to live within themselves in a faded desert. He counted ten in total. Far less than the faces of war he'd left buried. "One of the reasons why Dario retired was because the federation accused him of losing the World Cup twice intentionally."

Ammelie's brows raised. "Is it true?"

"Nothing was ever proven." Chase leaned in close and whispered, "But it's true."

"You can't be serious. He told you this?"

"Secrets never stay buried forever, Ammelie." He held a finger up to his lips with a sly smile. "He'll deny it if you ask. Let's just say at the top of his game, his notoriety brought an unsavory entourage."

"What does that mean, *unsavory*?"

"Losing those two World Cups paid for this place." Chase nodded at *The Face of War* painting. "Milan was the better team in both finals, but instead of dominating, he laid back so he wouldn't end up like one of these guys."

"How did the two of you meet?"

"That's a long story," he chuckled. "Dario tells it much better than me."

"I'm curious." Ammelie faced him and asked warily, "Why did you ask me to come?"

"Honestly, since my dad died, it's been hard to open up to anyone. I don't talk to Dax about it because I know he's still dealing with it too." Chase stepped back from the painting, and the two strolled down a long hallway lined with trophies, medals, rare pieces of art, as well as photos of Dario in action on the field and standing next to A-list celebs. "When we met at the bar, I dropped my guard for the first time in months."

"We hardly know each other, Chase."

"And look at all the adventures we've had already," he laughed.

Ammelie didn't hold back a sheepish grin. "More like misadventures."

For a while, they strolled the halls exploring Dario's castle, waiting for him to return. Shortly after they arrived, Dario had left for a meeting with his lawyer, who filed a request with a judge to reconsider the court's decision to limit visitation with his children. From an upstairs window, Chase noticed the Ferrari barreling down the driveway. By the time they reached the grand living room, the front door burst open. Dressed in jeans and a silk shirt unbuttoned down to the bulge over his belt, Dario entered with a grand announcement.

"Tonight, we celebrate," he bellowed. "Four years of fighting, and I will finally have an opportunity to plead my case to a new judge."

"Well deserved." Chase squeezed Dario's shoulder. "I know it's been a long road."

"Your visit has brought me luck." Dario swung around and snatched Ammelie close before kissing her aggressively on both cheeks. "We need wine!"

As Dario hurried off to his private cellar, Ammelie stood shocked. Chase tried to hold it in, but instead, he burst out laughing. Ammelie punched him in the arm with a swift fist, leaving an ache at the point of impact.

"What can I say," Chase said in defense, "He's a passionate guy."

"Next time, he'll be the one who wakes up with a bruise."

"He's harmless." Chase rubbed his arm, recognizing she packed a punch. "The question is, are you?"

"I'm not sure you want to find out," Ammelie teased.

Within the hour, a table was set outside where a wood-fired pizza oven burned. All three of them raised a glass of Santa Felicità Pinot Noir from Tuscany. Overlooking the glassy lake, the skies darkened into evening, revealing a scattering of diamond stars. Lights from the villas across the water offered a peaceful retreat from the outside world.

Chase and Dario kneaded the dough like pro pizzailis before sliding the pies into the 800-degree pizza oven. Ammelie listened as the two of them reminisced about Dario's rise to fame.

"Dario, how did you two meet?"

"He has not told you?" Dario scooped a fresh pizza from the oven as an aroma from the baked crust wafted in the air. Fresh sausage. Mushrooms. Aged mozzarella. "Of all the stories, it is the best one."

"Give her the bookend version," Chase interrupted as he poured more wine in his glass. "Or else we'll be here until dawn."

"Americans always in a hurry," Dario rebuked. "Ammelie, you deserve the full story."

"Absolutely," she agreed, winking at Chase. "Don't leave anything out."

Chase kneaded and baked two more pizzas and opened another bottle of wine while Dario recounted their first encounter during the Monaco Yacht Show shortly after he and Dax returned from the Middle East. He had yet to dive into the family business, rather he dipped his toes while his dad did the heavy lifting. He remembered being struck by the drastic cavern between Mosul and Monaco. *Two worlds where only the strong survive.* He watched his dad command the room at the Monte-Carlo to auction the Christ by da Vinci. Dario was center stage as the crowd flocked to him, but once the bidding reached forty million, he tapped out. When the gavel slammed, the Christ sold for a record $450 million.

"Damn painting," Dario said as if the pain from the auction was still fresh. "Afterward, Chase helped me drown my sorrows."

"I saw the tear in his eye," Chase added. "He was over-matched."

Dario ignored Chase's sarcasm. "That is the night I heard about *the* legend."

"Sounds intriguing," Ammelie said. "What legend?"

"The Scepter of Dagobert was stolen from the Basilica of Saint-Denis." Chase set the pizzas on the table and found a seat next to Ammelie. "I'd heard the story from my dad as long as I can remember. The Scepter was originally part of the French Crown jewels dating back to the seventh century. Filigraned and enameled gold wrapped in three parts: a rod, a hand grasping the world, and a statue of an eagle carrying a young man."

"But it was stolen in 1795," Dario interrupted.

"You two went on the hunt for a lost treasure?" Ammelie asked.

"Dax, Dario, and me, actually." Chase sipped from his glass. "Dad felt bad that Dario didn't have a chance at the da Vinci painting. So that night while we were at the bar, Dad got all three of us in a frenzy when he gave us a clue to the scepter's location."

"Remember, the scepter was stolen in 1795," Dario repeated.

"During the Civil War, the French breached the Monroe Doctrine to establish a colonial government in Mexico. Lincoln ordered the military in Texas to stop the French. In the Second Battle of Sabine Pass, the Confederates punished the French and sank two of their gunboats."

"Michael believed the scepter was aboard one of them," Dario chimed in.

"You've kept me in suspense long enough," Ammelie said. "Was the scepter there?"

"I don't know if we were naive or suckers," Chase admitted. "Dad gave us an idea of where to look, and the next thing you know, we're diving off the Gulf of Mexico. We found the two gunboats at the bottom, but all that was left was a rusted shell."

"That is not the best part of the story," Dario said. "I insisted I dive with Chase, while Dax was very glad to stay above water." He stood to his feet, acting out each beat. "There we were, diving to the bottom. My heart beat so fast when we find the ships."

"Dad was always making up some crazy scheme," Chase interjected. "So, I didn't think we were going to find anything."

"Ammelie, we are there with the ships, and all of a sudden, a great white shark appeared." Dario widened his arms to show how huge the jaws were, much bigger than in actual life. "Staring into the jaws, I believed my life was over."

"I punched the shark in the nose, and it swam away."

"He punched the shark in the nose," Dario repeated as if no one heard. "Chase saved my life that day, and that is why we are family."

"Wait, what happened to finding the scepter?" Ammelie asked, a bit let down.

"We never found it," Chase answered matter of fact. "Who knows if it was ever there."

"To the one who tamed the great white." Dario raised his glass. "*Saluti*."

"Cheers," Chase echoed, raising his glass to the buzz in his bones.

Ammelie finished off her glass. "With that, I think I'll turn in."

"The night is still young," Dario disputed. "There are more stories to tell."

"Ending on the great white is perfect for me." Ammelie pushed her chair back and stood. "Dario, thank you for a lovely evening."

As Ammelie excused herself, Chase set his glass on the table and crossed his arms. He waited until she was inside the house before shifting the conversation.

"Have you heard back from your people?"

"All have been contacted, including your special guest."

"I know that put you in a bad spot."

Dario shrugged it off. "You paid my debt, so it is a way for me to even the score."

"You don't owe me anything." Chase glanced toward the house. "With any luck, I'll get what I came for."

"Ammelie is *bella donna*," Dario replied. *Beautiful woman.* "Elena will not be pleased."

"Elena thinks I'm dead," he confessed. "And I need to keep it that way."

Chase waited a few minutes before leaving Dario to clean up the mess. He climbed the steps to the second floor and shuffled his feet across the tiles until he reached the guest room. Raising his hand to knock, he braced himself against the wall. He was startled when the door swung open, and Ammelie stood in the doorway wearing shorts and a tank top. Staring at her slender body through bloodshot eyes, he knew his judgment was far from impaired.

"One thing you should know about me," Chase said. "I'm afraid of the dark."

Ammelie left the door open and stepped back into the room. "Me too."

THIRTY-NINE

GOOSE BAY, CANADA

After traveling through the night from Half Moon Island to Newfoundland, Elena tracked a GPS on her cell while the Englishman navigated the Jeep 4X4 along the damp streets before turning down a muddy road. Determined that the traitor would pay the ultimate price, she pointed toward a rustic cabin barely visible in a dense forest, and the Englishman nodded. In the backseat, the traitor's head was covered with a hood, wrists and ankles shackled, and the noise-canceling headphones were still wrapped around her ears. As the Jeep approached the cabin, a Chinese man in his late thirties appeared on the porch holding an AR-15 assault rifle.

The Englishman slowed the Jeep. "What's the rules?"

"Keep us alive." Elena checked her cell. "We have been cleared."

From behind her sunglasses, she eyed the man, knowing her deal with the Triads could end in a double-cross. Without her father's blessing, she leveraged the Bratva's alliance with the Triads to gain access to the PRC. *Peoples Republic of China.* Her impression of the PRC operative was that he appeared more like a college student who studied economics than a spy.

She reached into the glove compartment, retrieved a Glock, and held the weapon close.

As they rolled up to the cabin, the man stepped down from the porch, aiming the AR-15 at the windshield. Elena's grip on the Glock tightened as she climbed out. With her weapon down by her side, the operative stepped forward, shifting his aim toward her. When he reached out to pat her down, she brushed him off while pointing the Glock at his chest.

"We are here to deliver a package," she said coldly.

"I have been given instructions to verify your identity," he replied in fluent English.

Elena glanced back at the Englishman, who was seated behind the wheel. She knew he was itching to engage. "Verification is not necessary. We were never here."

The operative paused as if deciding whether to escalate before lowering his weapon. "Bring the package inside."

Elena motioned for the Englishman to kill the engine. She stepped back and opened the rear door. Grabbing the traitor by the arm, she pulled her out and forced her inside the cabin. The Englishman climbed out of the Jeep and waited near the porch. Inside the sparsely furnished cabin, Elena noticed a satellite monitoring system spread out on the kitchen table. She'd been given a window of time by the Triads to deliver the package and disappear before the PRC changed their minds. But she couldn't leave, not yet.

"A few moments," she said to the operative. "Alone."

The operative checked the screen on the satellite monitoring system. "Only three."

Elena waited until she was alone with the traitor before she removed the noise-canceling headphones. She grabbed Agent Kelley by the arm as a deafening silence weighed heavily in the room.

"Laney," Elena whispered, feeling the traitor's frail body shiver. "Your ransom is paid."

A voice quivered in response, "What have you done to me?"

"It is not what I have done." Elena kept her grip tight. "Bouchard killed Chase and Dax to hide his sins." She felt the traitor's legs buckle, followed by faint weeping. A half-lie culminated eight months of torture. "Hidden secrets are now your message. Do you understand?"

"I never wanted... please Elena..."

Without warning, the traitor pulled herself away, and for a second, she was free. Elena pounced with a striking blow from the butt of her Glock. The traitor crashed to the floor, leaving Elena standing over her. With her finger on the trigger, the temptation to end the traitor's life was nearly too strong to resist.

"Chase's death has set you free," Elena said callously. "Recognize the true enemy."

When the cabin door creaked open, she spun around, expecting to be ambushed. The operative waited in the doorway before walking over to the traitor. He pulled her to her feet and grabbed a syringe from the table before injecting the needle into her neck. Within a matter of seconds, the traitor's body went limp in his arms. Elena watched as he carried her out the back door and laid her inside a wooden cargo crate before sealing the coffin. Satisfied the task was done, she walked around the side of the cabin and stopped cold at the sight of her father standing next to the Englishman.

"You conspire against me," Dmitry scolded. "Elena, this is not acceptable."

"It is what *you* wanted," she disputed. Refusing to back

down, she added, "End Bouchard with the American because..."

"I suggest you both continue this elsewhere," the Englishman interrupted.

Elena's eyes flared as her father's gazed scrutinized her.
"Chase's blood is on your hands, Papa."

"Make sure he stays with the package until it is delivered,"
Dmitry ordered the Englishman, who headed straight for the
back of the cabin. Then Dmitry turned back toward Elena.
"Draw not your bow unless your arrow is pointed."

FORTY

SITUATION ROOM, WHITE HOUSE

In the West Wing basement, Bouchard and Avery greeted those seated around a rectangular table. At the opposite end was a bank of screens monitoring real-time news and intelligence. In one corner stood the Stars and Stripes amidst a dark wood-paneled room that secluded the occupants from the outside world. On the other side of the wall, the Watch Team gathered intelligence and fed the latest to each of the occupant tablets that were in front of them. Bouchard relied on every single person to provide a clear understanding of the intelligence for him to make the right decision. He scanned the room and recognized their veiled curiosity.

"Avery is the new chief of staff," he stated matter of fact. "We'll announce tomorrow."

"Congratulations," Bridget Jacobs, the vice president, said flatly. "Big shoes to fill."

Avery replied gravely, "Feels more like chum to the sharks."

Bouchard pressed forward. "Ross, what's the latest with the blackout?"

"We're still in the dark, sir." As director of national intelligence, Ross Byrd was confirmed by the Senate during Bouchard's first year in office. Three terms in the House of

Representatives to the House Intelligence Judiciary to serving on the Committee on Homeland Security and chairman of the Cybersecurity and Infrastructure Protection Subcommittee. Byrd was the most qualified one in the room. "All cellphone surveillance of known operatives of the Ministry of State Security in North America have gone offline."

"In the past, we've lost surveillance on handfuls of operatives," Albert Skinner, director of Homeland Security, chimed in. He pointed at one half of the walled screen, which showed a map of the U.S. and hundreds of red dots. "When our surveillance is active and engaged, all of those are green. With what's occurred in the last forty minutes, the cyberattack level is heightened. We've mobilized boots on the ground to acquire visuals of these operatives, but that will take time, and there's no guarantee we'll be able to locate all of them."

"Any signs of an actual cyberattack?" Bouchard asked point-blank. He'd pushed hard to get Skinner confirmed as a favor to a mutual friend, but he had yet to decide whether the policymaker was a wise choice. "From the silence, I'm guessing that's a 'no.'"

"Not exactly, Mr. President." Skinner sat up taller in his chair, ready to challenge the Commander in Chief. "Ransomware, data leakage, hacking, and corporate phishing are the norm. However, considering what we are seeing, there is obviously the possibility of a threat from within. Ellsberg to Snowden, it's been an unfortunate facet of our Republic."

"We're monitoring the situation," Morton Pascal, national security advisor, added. He was said friend who requested the favor from Bouchard. A fellow Californian who campaigned hard for the president and had been with the administration since day one. "As of now, what we know is that these operatives have gone dark. If there is a cyberattack of greater magnitude that would mark the PRCs most aggressive action on our soil to date."

Not to be outdone by his peers, Byrd volleyed into the conversation. "Last year, we caught Chinese intelligence officers who recruited hackers from a subcontractor to steal aviation and technology data from Aeronautics."

"It's one thing to poach intellectual property, but it's another to escalate to this level." Bouchard eyed the scattered red dots on the map and harnessed his frustration. *Too much conjecture, not enough fact.* He turned his attention to a videoconference window on the screen where Nancy Frost, U.S. ambassador to China, listened quietly. "Nancy, what's your take on this...are they poking the bear?"

"More likely, they're stabbing the Nine Dragons," she answered. In her early forties, Frost had grown up as an expat in Hong Kong before returning stateside as an entrepreneur who built a Fortune 500 company. Bouchard handpicked her for the task of bridging the relationship between the U.S. and China. In light of the sanctions and tariffs he'd imposed, he needed someone with her pedigree who could close deals, not play political ping pong. She was one of a handful of ambassadors who spoke candidly with him without fear of political fallout. "In recent months, the protests in Hong Kong have dissipated, yet there are thousands of People's Liberation Army at the border. I don't believe any of this is a coincidence."

"China's legislature approved a killer blow to Hong Kong's autonomy," Avery said, ignoring the eyes that locked in on her from around the table. She'd known the ambassador since ghostwriting her NYT bestseller, *The Power of Winning*, shortly after Frost closed a deal to sell her company for an undisclosed price believed to be in the $1 billion range. "National security and anti-sedition laws pave the way for a crackdown against Hong Kongers."

"Absolutely," Frost agreed. "The legislation is aimed at stamping out the protestors' demands to remain one country with two systems. Future actions by Hong Kongers will be deemed as a threat to the PRC national security and will be considered terrorism."

"And the legislation will allow China's security agencies to operate in Hong Kong," Avery noted. "Nancy, how do you think that plays into what's happening here?"

"If China plans to invade Hong Kong, they won't want us to know until it's too late."

Bouchard was struck with brotherly pride for Avery, and at the same time, a growing unease for the situation his ambassador to China described. For three years, he avoided escalating tensions with the communist party, apart from imposing tariffs to level international trade. Crossing his arms, he eyed the room, unable to shake a gut feeling the two powerhouses were on a collision course to a *Battle Royale* on the world's stage.

FORTY-ONE

LAKE COMO, ITALY

Chase rolled out from beneath a thick blanket and sat on the edge of a sofa. He rubbed the sleep from his eyes, recounting how the night ended. A queen-sized bed was left a mess. A foggy morning breeze rolled in through an open glass door. He draped the blanket over him and stepped out onto the balcony where Ammelie was wrapped in a robe, sipping a cup of java.

"I'll give you a hundred bucks for that," he said.

"Two hundred, and you can have half," she mused.

"Didn't see a coffeemaker in the room."

"Got up early. Took a stroll and found the kitchen."

"I don't think I've ever seen it." Chase leaned against a railing breathing in the brisk air, anticipating the awkward morning-after talk. "About last night..."

She sipped more java. "Another bottle, and it might've ended differently."

"Four bottles instead of three." Chase checked off an imaginary list. "Got it."

"Being surrounded by such beauty, it is strange how Dario has the world's wealth, yet he is broken," she pondered. "Makes me think of the children in Massam. I fear their lives will forever be broken no matter how hard I try to help them believe they have a greater purpose."

Chase searched for a way to lighten the mood, still nursing a headache. "I promise you their lives will not end in brokenness but in flight."

"Where'd you hear that one?"

"Fortune cookie from the Poo Ping Palace. Best barbecue pork you'll ever eat."

"You're joking." She laughed, then her smile faded. "How can you be so sure?"

"Because by now Uncle Dax has them dive-bombing at the pool."

Ammelie's lips pursed slightly as she sipped from her mug. "I was the same age as many of them when I escaped. I was so afraid of him—I failed to save her."

"No child is supposed to protect a parent." Chase weighed his words heavily. "After the crash, I struggled to believe my dad was gone. I should've saved him, and the guilt weighs on my shoulders every hour of every day."

"Your father was killed in an accident. My mother was murdered."

"The crash was no accident," he confessed. "It was retribution because of me."

"What do you mean, Chase?" When he didn't respond, Ammelie surmised, "We're strangers imprisoned by the same regret."

"Well, stranger...there's somewhere I want to take you today."

Ammelie eyed him curiously and seemed to lighten up a bit. She handed him the mug and kissed him. Her soft lips left Chase's guarded soul unarmed. He fought a primal urge to go further. Instead, he sipped from the mug, relishing the aroma of the fresh brew.

Ammelie walked back inside as his eyes followed until she dropped her robe. Staring at her naked body, he was struck by the crisscrossed scars on her back. While he'd earned his scars in war, she'd fought her battles as a child. He refused to imagine the torture she endured after her mother was killed.

Deep wounds beneath the scars never heal.

She glanced over her shoulder and caught Chase gawking. He turned around, embarrassed. There was no denying she was stunningly beautiful, but what he hadn't expected was a pure soul.

His mind wandered to Elena and Laney, two women he'd loved in uniquely different ways. Elena captured his heart because she accepted his dark secrets and loved him more for them. Laney brought out the man he hoped to become, yet her betrayal left shattered pieces between them.

So, why risk it all to find her?

He didn't have words to answer, except for a lingering loyalty. The constant urging in his bones kept pushing him to find a way to rid himself of the guilt. Even though he'd only known Ammelie for a blink, he couldn't deny when she peered into his eyes, it was as if she gazed deeper into his soul than anyone he'd met before.

Don't fall in love with a woman you're going to betray.

He stepped back into the bedroom and set the coffee mug on a dresser. Hearing the shower turn on, he was tempted to open the door but thought better of it. Instead, he pressed his ear against the door and listened—then he called out.

"Ammelie, meet me downstairs when you're ready."

Walking out of the room, he wasn't sure she heard him. He

stopped by his room for a quick shower. When he looked into the mirror at his scraggly beard, he picked up a razor and slid the sharp blade over his face. It'd been months since he'd seen his bare skin.

With each stroke, it was as if he was turning back into Chase Hardeman, the one who sold a hidden treasure for a world record price. No longer was he the operative in the deserts of the Middle East. Today at least, he stepped back into the shoes he'd tried to fill since he was eight years old.

Wearing jeans and a t-shirt, he left his room a mess and entered Dario's bedroom at the end of the hall. He headed straight for a walk-in closet larger than most houses. A light blinked on automatically to reveal hundreds of shoes from cross trainers, soccer cleats, Testoni, Louis, Vuitton, Lucchese, and a never-before-worn collection of every Air Jordan ever made. Deeper into the closet were perfectly hung rows of Gucci, Kiton, and Tom Ford suits. All were hand-tailored for Dario before he gained the extra pounds. Chase locked eyes on a unique Vanquish dark grey suit. He grabbed it from the rack, then found a complimentary shirt and tie. On his way out, he picked up a pair of Kitons.

Warriors going into battle must wear the right armor.

Slinging the hung suit, shirt, and tie over his shoulder, he carried the shoes in his left hand and headed downstairs. Once outside, his boots crunched over the gravel as he walked toward an old-world barn with distressed doors and iron window scrollings. At the end of the path, he entered through one of the doors into a vastly more modern interior.

Lined along both sides of the garage, a prized collection reflected iconic shades of red, a signature yellow shield with an Italian flag, and a prancing horse on each one. Not only did the shield signify Enzo Ferrari's birthplace in Modena, but it was inspired by the horse painted on the fuselage of the fighter plane belonging to Francesco Barack, a heroic airman of the First World War. For a moment, Chase took in the $130 million collection, remembering where they found each one globe-trekking with Dario on a whirlwind spending spree over a matter of days.

A Ferrari 250 LM, which won the 1965 Le Mans. A Ferrari 250 GT LWB California Spider Competizione garnered a trophy cabinet of Concours awards. Ferrari 275 GTB-C Speciale featured aluminum bodywork and an extra 70 hp from the 3.0 liter V12. Ferrari 290 MM, driven by five-time champion Juan Manuel Fangio who many believed to be the greatest name in motorsport. And one of Chase's favorites, the Ferrari 335 Sport Scaglietti, which took the crown as the most expensive racing car ever sold when it crossed the Hardeman Auctions stage in Tokyo.

Dario popped up from behind the Ferrari 250 LM. "Good morning."

"Didn't know you were a mechanic," Chase said. "I thought you were just a collector."

"Waxing isn't what do you say, a grease monkey?" Dario chuckled as he tossed a rag on a rolling cart with the rest of his cleaning supplies. "You should drive one while you are here."

"I'd be too afraid to ding the paint. Then I'd owe you more than I can afford."

"I am the one indebted." Dario handed Chase the key fob to the 250 LM. "Your father paid a price I can never repay."

Chase remembered being holed up at the Melian Hotel in Najaf, a city about one hundred miles south of Baghdad.

During that mission, he and Dax were hunting Jeric Salem, the mastermind behind suicide bombings in Kabul, Mogadishu, and Karrada, where militants carried out coordinated attacks in Baghdad, killing 400 civilians.

Omar Youssef was their informant who pointed them in the direction of Najaf, one year before he introduced them to Akram Kasim. Chase paid Omar twenty grand for the lead. It was the first of countless payments. Salem was listed in the top ten of the FBI Most Wanted since attempting to blow up the Lincoln Memorial, which attracted over six million visitors annually. Salem was never caught, leaving his whereabouts unknown.

After nearly two months in Najaf searching for Salem, they wrangled a face-to-face knowing he had possession of the Statue of Farrah, a deity carved into a stone panther stolen during the Battle of Baghdad. Tucked away in a hotel room, counting down the clock, Chase received an unexpected call on his SAT phone from his dad.

Flipping through the channels, he found the World Cup and listened as his dad relayed what was at stake. On the field, Milan was behind by three goals, a total shocker to the hundred thousand fans in the stadium and the tens of millions who watched around the globe. Boos erupted after Dario missed an open shot at goal. But there was a reason why one of the world's greatest soccer players was off his game. His dad relayed the treacherous events leading up to the match ending with Dario's wife and children being kidnapped. If Dario won the game, they died.

In his signature voice, Michael Hardeman recounted how he'd gone to the Cosa Nostra and not only negotiated the family's release but a $100 million payday if Dario held up his end of the deal. Billions were wagered on the World Cup, and even more between the super-rich who built their empires in bloody criminality. Some of them had purchased off-the-books antiquities, rare art, and collector cars from Hardeman Auctions.

Dad was the premier deal maker.

By the end of that afternoon, Milan lost the World Cup 6-2. Chase listened to his dad's voice bellowing in his ear, recounting the moment Dario was reunited with his wife and children. Then after dark on the streets of Najaf, Jeric Salem was assassinated, and the Statue of Farrah vanished.

FORTY-TWO

STONE RIDGE, VIRGINIA

Miles from Washington Dulles International Airport in Loudoun County, population less than 10,000, a red brick two-story house with white double garage doors was as nondescript as the rest of the neighborhood. A large elm tree hung over the shingled roof, shading a front porch with bamboo chairs.

A silver BMW 7 series pulled up to the curb and parked right in front. Avery climbed out from the driver's side and strolled up the concrete walkway to the front door. Bracing herself, she rang the doorbell and peered through the glass as he approached.

Once the door swung open, she said, "May I come in?"

General Abbott paused for a moment before pulling the door open wide. Avery crossed the threshold and followed him into a study off to the left with a view of the street and her Beamer. Hanging on the walls were photos throughout the years of Abbott's wife and children, who were now in their mid-thirties and early forties. Two years had passed since his wife lost her battle against pancreatic cancer. Avery remembered it vividly as she was the one who wrote a private note from her brother to the General. She took in the rest of the room, noticing there were no photos of Alison McIntyre.

"I'm sure you're not here to give me another medal," Abbott said dryly.

"The President asked me to speak with you regarding your testimony."

"I signed the damn paper. What else does he want?"

"Considering the history, we were hoping for more assurance."

She followed Abbott's gaze as he looked past her. For a moment, they stared at a wall-mounted television where reporters were amongst millions of Hong Kongers protesting in the streets, followed by a quick cut to more reporters near the Hong Kong and China border where thousands of PRC military were stationed.

"I heard China's operatives went dark last night," Abbott said gravely.

Avery tried not to be thrown, but her surprise was hard to hide. "I'm not sure..."

"You're the new Chief of Staff, aren't you? You better damn well know about it."

Realizing a mole was in the Situation Room, she stuck to the blanket, "It's classified."

Abbott shook his head, more in disappointment than disgust. "The President is playing with a box of matches, striking each one without considering the inferno that will rage."

"A matter that is no longer your concern." From an early age, Avery learned working in the fields of the family's vineyard with her dad and David that backing down when intimidated was a sign of weakness. Her muscles tensed as she stood a few inches taller and handed over a manila envelope. "A reminder of what is at stake."

Abbott's brows furrowed as he opened the envelope and read Alison McIntyre's confession, ghostwritten by Avery Bouchard. From the smirk on Abbott's face, she knew he wasn't buying the authenticity of the document.

"No one high enough in the Bureau will talk to me about Agent Kelley's disappearance." Abbott nodded toward a stack of files on his desk. "And I've been reading up on Chase Hardeman and Dexter Thompson. Their service at Pendleton was, shall I say, *ordinary*. However, as I remember, Michael Hardeman was quite a character both within Washington and after he left the swamp. Makes me believe what Alison has on the President is nuclear."

"Your niece is the one who poses a clear and present danger."

"She will have her day in court, and the truth will be exposed."

"Or she will be left in a black site prison awaiting trial, *indefinitely*." Avery took advantage of a second of leverage. "Considering you failed to disclose your relationship with Alison McIntyre, there is a possibility this will escalate depending on your testimony."

"I've never left a soldier behind in battle," Abbott countered. "The President assured me that my cooperation would result in Alison being treated fairly. Your overzealous actions coming into my home have caused great pause, Ms. Bouchard."

"General, can the President count on you?"

"The real question here is, can I count on him." Abbott turned off the television and glanced over his shoulder at the files that were spread open on his desk. "The flight from San

Paulo to JFK was, shall we say, enlightening."

"How so?"

"Alison said only three words the entire flight. Red Venture Group."

"What's Red Venture Group?" Avery asked tentatively.

"I suppose whoever answers that question will be the last one standing." Abbott motioned Avery toward the front door. "Let the President know I will go before the Intel Committee and ask them the very question you've asked of me. We each must do what we believe is right to protect the country. No matter the cost, the President's betrayal to the American people must come to an end."

Shell-shocked, Avery recounted the conversation as Abbott closed the door and she headed toward the Beamer. She climbed behind the wheel and immediately sent a text.

GENERAL IS GOING TO WAR.

FORTY-THREE

Along the winding roads from Lake Como to Brera, the Ferrari 250 LM handled the road to perfection as Chase punched the accelerator, shifting through the turns. A ninety-mile drive clocked in at under fifty-seven minutes. As the engine idled through the streets of Brera, part of the Centro Storico district, the artistic quarter known for gourmet restaurants, high-end fashion boutiques, and Italian art spanning centuries, revealed its alluring charm.

Ammelie stared out the window. "Quite an enchanting place."

"Some of the buildings date back to the 16th century." The Plaka District in Athens crossed Chase's mind as they drove through Brera. *Hopefully, this won't end in the same way.* "My parents first met here."

"In Brera?" Ammelie asked, intrigued.

"Mom was an art major at Indiana University and studied here for a semester since it's known for famous artists and poets. Dad was interning for the state governor at the time and got picked to travel with a group from his office to assist at a summit in Milan. Back then, he was younger than I am now, but he already knew where he was headed. It drove him

216

crazy that no one else noticed him. Instead, he was a runner who did whatever task was asked of him. If you had known him, you'd know that wasn't his style." Chase inched forward in traffic, reigning in the Ferrari's 12-cylinder engine, which was desperate to run free. "On the morning the team was to return to the U.S., Dad overslept and missed the flight. No one noticed he wasn't in the shuttle van. And like I said, if you had known him..."

"I'd know that wasn't his style," Ammelie finished.

"He used what cash he had left in the bank to book another flight for the next day. He was a broke intern, so he didn't even have enough to stay at the hotel. So, he packed his suitcase and headed out on a 24-hour sightseeing adventure of Milan."

"He ended up here," she surmised. "I'm sensing a love story is around the bend."

Turning down Via Quintino Sella, Chase pointed at a corner cafe. "Once upon a time."

Ammelie read a brightly scripted sign across a yellow awning. "Vecchia."

"If he hadn't spilled coffee on her sketch, I wouldn't be here." Chase made a left onto Via Cusani, rolling slowly down a cobblestoned alley barely wide enough for the Ferrari. He nodded at an orangish clay stain stoned apartment building ahead and pointed to the top floor balconette with a birds-eye view of the district. "Dad missed the flight the next day and stayed for a month before proposing to my mom right up there."

"Your father was a romantic," Ammelie sighed.

"He said the moment he saw her sitting in that cafe, he was ready to close the deal."

"Like father, like son," she flirted.

Chase's cheeks flushed, knowing she was right. He parked the Ferrari, unlocked the garage door, then pulled the magnificent beast into its stable. As they climbed out of the Ferrari into a space double the size of the garage entrance, Chase counted the years since he'd been back.

Three years, maybe? No, it's been at least four.

Slinging his backpack over his shoulder, carrying the suit, shoes, and Ammelie's luggage, he stepped over to an old slat elevator and pulled the iron gate aside. He waved Ammelie in first as if he were inviting a princess entrance to a castle. Pulling the lever, a motor clanked as the garage disappeared beneath their feet, and the elevator climbed to the top floor.

Daylight streaked across the distressed wood floor as it creaked beneath their steps. The quaint white-walled apartment was decorated with Mid Century furniture and antique artifacts spread throughout, including the Statue of Farrah. While Chase set the luggage down, Ammelie headed straight for the glass doors leading out to the Juliet Balcony. Chase watched as she swung the doors open and leaned out over the railing. He wasn't sure why he'd decided to bring her here of all places. He could've kept her at Dario's estate before the auction, but there was something that was luring him. Maybe it was a moment to exhale, to reminisce on what life could've been if his parents were still alive.

Leaving Ammelie on the balconette, he shuffled down a hallway into the only bedroom. Glancing over his shoulder, he opened the closet and pressed his thumb against one corner of the wall. With a low hiss, a drawer slid open. He unzipped the backpack, retrieved the leather-bound book and the *Speed Racer* tin box, and placed them inside the safe. Pressing his thumb a second time, the drawer sealed itself, leaving no trace of its existence. Reaching into his pocket, he double-checked that the coin was still there.

Walking back into the living room, he noticed Ammelie was still on the balconette. He kicked off his shoes and joined her. "Beautiful view, isn't it?"

"No wonder your mother said yes," Ammelie replied softly. "Why would anyone want to leave?"

Overgrown shrubbery hung off the side of the building. Directly across from the cobblestone alley was a center square with an old church. A bike depot lined one side of the street as a trolly rolled past. Chase remembered being eight years old, standing on the balconette watching his parents cross the road near where the bike depot was now. Early evening enveloped the skies, yet what was left of the day cast a ray of light on the street. He'd never forget the day or the hour. His grip on the railing tightened as flashes of the seconds that followed flooded his mind.

"Chase, are you okay?" Ammelie asked, noticing his white knuckles.

He snapped out of the memory. "Mom was the only one who could tame him."

"What happened to her?"

"They were holding hands, until..." Chase pointed to the street below. "I was standing right here when she was struck by a drunk driver."

"Oh, Chase." Ammelie reached over and touched his forearm. "I'm so sorry."

"A second here, a minute there, and she'd be alive." Chase swallowed a lump lodged in his throat. "She loved it here until it was taken from her—and she loved us until she was gone. Dad never stepped foot in this place again. He gave me the keys the day I was shipped off to boot camp."

"You have carried on their memory." Ammelie leaned in closer, resting her head against his shoulder. "I'd say they raised a remarkable son."

"I'm a sinner, not a saint." Chase shook his head. "With any luck, Mom will sneak me in."

"Perhaps your father has already closed the deal."

Chase smiled half-heartedly. "He's auctioning angel wings as we speak."

After that day on the streets of Brera, Chase struggled with the loss. *Mom might've drawn out the peace that I've tried to find. I'll never know for sure.* From an early age until a year earlier, he followed his dad's lead and did it with lethal force. After the plane crash killed his dad, it seemed the trajectory of life spiraled. When word of Laney's abduction surfaced from a reliable source, he thought rescuing her would cleanse him from the death caused by his hands. He sought shelter aboard the *Midnight Moon* with Elena, the Black Widow of Bratva, and methodically schemed a way to find and rescue Laney.

But Ammelie's innocent in this game. The closer I'm drawn to her, the more I know the end will be damning. When she realizes who I am, who I really am, she'll know I've been playing her since the moment we met. By then, it'll be too late. There'll be no turning back.

FORTY-FOUR

A splendid orange, blue, and purple-hued sunset crossed the skies over Brera. Chase stood in the center of the living room, staring out the window as a wave of thoughts rushed through him. After months of searching for a way to get close to Brandis, he'd found the perfect honey trap. Glancing down at the shiny Kiton shoes, a far cry from the dirty bloodstained boots he'd worn in battle, he wondered if he was no better than the man he hunted. Footsteps echoed off the walls as Ammelie entered wearing a stunning black dress and high heels.

"I found a closet full," she said shyly. "I hope you don't mind."

Chase tried not to stare at her curves. "Absolutely beautiful."

"Your mother had impeccable taste." Ammelie pulled a strand of hair away from her face, picked up a silk tie from the counter, and wrapped it around Chase's neck. Her fingers brushed across his freshly shaven skin before she tied a knot. "When we met at the Baw Baw, I never imagined standing here with you. I cannot decide if it is luck or fate."

"Sometimes life is all about chance."

"You know, you look ten years younger without the beard,"

she teased.

Chase pulled her in close and wrapped his arms around her waist. He kissed her gently on the neck and worked his way to her lips. He felt her body grow weak on the verge of surrendering to his touch, and then she pushed him back gently with a sheepish grin.

"We don't want to be late," she said softly.

Chase half-heartedly protested. "Italians are always late."

"You're not Italian." Ammelie grabbed him by the arm and pulled him toward the slat elevator. "No distractions. I've been waiting to see you in action, Mr. Hardeman."

Chase grabbed two Burberry trench coats. "We'll pick up where we left off?"

"Depends on how well you do," she bantered.

"Challenge accepted."

With the collars of their trench coats turned up, they ventured out into the evening. Holding hands and walking at a brisk pace, the bohemian atmosphere enveloped them. Chase was surprised Ammelie managed to keep up in her heels. With each stride through the artistic heart of the city, he eyed the streets and cars that passed. A few blocks west, they stopped at a crosswalk leading to Largo Cairoli, a roundabout in the center of the district. A twinge struck at the back of his neck, which left him questioning whether they were being followed. In the distance, farther from the red and white "M" signs of the Cairoli Castello metro station, stood the clock tower of Castello Sforzesco Castle.

Taking the escalator below ground to the metro station, Chase found an automated machine and purchased two tickets. Going through the turnstiles, red and white striped trains squealed along the tracks on opposite sides. When the train doors opened, passengers poured out onto the platforms while others stepped on. Chase waited until the trains departed before squeezing Ammelie's hand and heading toward the tunnel leading beneath Via Luca Beltrami.

"Where are we going?" Ammelie asked, confused.

Stopping at the edge of the platform where the tunnel began, he sensed Ammelie's apprehension. *She thinks we're going to jump on the tracks.* He'd thought the same when his dad brought him here for the first time. Along the side of the platform were a set of metal steps leading down to the edge of the rails.

"Ladies first." Chase motioned for Ammelie to step down while he kept his head on a swivel. "Come on, have a little faith."

Her eyes narrowed. "Don't make me regret trusting you."

Stepping down along the tracks, they entered the dark tunnel before Chase grabbed Ammelie's shoulder. He pulled out a titanium card and swiped it against the concrete wall. Seconds passed before the wall slid to one side, revealing an opening to another tunnel within.

"Handed down from generations." Chase held up the titanium card. "Gains you access to the most exclusive events around the world."

Lights beamed from an extended golf cart as it hummed along the tunnel. An elderly man pulled up next to them dressed in a tuxedo. He held a tablet in one hand and asked, "Name?"

"Chase Hardeman."

"Our guest of honor." The elderly man held out the tablet to verify his identity. Chase pressed his thumb against the screen until it flashed green. Before Ammelie was to do the same, he stepped in. "She is not on the list at my discretion. I prefer her anonymity."

"Mr. Hardeman, your guests are eagerly awaiting your arrival. Salire a bordo."

Ammelie's brows raised as Chase motioned her to take a seat. He grabbed her hand and squeezed, attempting to reassure her while reassuring himself. "The night is young."

A short five-minute ride beneath the Piazza Castello led to the underground of Sforza Castle, a towering walled compound built centuries ago turned into the Museo Pietà Rondanni to exhibit the Rondanini Pietà sculpted by Michelangelo from 1552 until his final days in 1564. Chase had seen the sculpture only once before. When he walked around the piece depicting Mary mourning over the dead Christ, he had noticed how each angle offered a unique perspective. While the back of the sculpture seemed unfinished, the front revealed the body of Jesus being sustained by his mother. He always thought of the Rondanini Pietà as nothing more than one artist's interpretation reflected in a work of art. But as the golf cart slowed at the end of the tunnel, what he'd encountered at the orphanage in Massam left him with a deeper appreciation for Michelangelo's last work.

A young woman dressed in an emerald dress greeted them as they climbed off the golf cart. She took their trench coats, waved a security wand over their bodies, then directed them to an arched entryway where *quelli d'élite* was chiseled into the stone.

The Elite Ones.

Pulling a curtain aside, they stepped into a grand room where people mingled as a 15-piece string orchestra played their renditions of Ottorino Respighi. Two giant crystal chandeliers hung overhead, casting a soft golden glow reflecting a wood etched ceiling and smooth concrete floor. On both sides of the room, original writings dating back to the early 1600s were lined up on dark wood shelves. Rows of chairs faced the night's prized artifacts.

"The surprises keep getting better," Ammelie said under her breath.

Chase whispered, "The coach turns into a pumpkin at midnight."

From a passing server Chase snatched tulip glasses of Champagne. *Since I'm bankrolling the night, I might as well indulge a bit.* He handed one glass to Ammelie.

"Did they all arrive the same way?" she asked, curious.

"There is more than one entrance. I thought the subway would build the suspense."

"You were right," Ammelie said, awestruck. "Who are all these people?"

Chase casually nodded down the line of a few who were already seated. "You've got the Keller family who owns the largest big-box retailer in the world. And there's Frank and Olivia Dawson, who built the biggest global manufacturer of food. Let's not forget about the Galindez crew, who control the fastest growing telecommunications company outside of the U.S. or China. Oh, nearly forgot, the guy talking to Dario is Leonzio Beneventi, who founded a pharmaceutical company unrivaled by any other."

"All corners of the global economy covered in the first four rows," she pointed out. "Who are the others?"

"A list of people you're better off not knowing." Chase smirked, slyly. "But everyone here is looking for a steal."

In the center of the grand room were the two prized pieces

up for auction. A Gibson Stradivarius, stolen from the famed violinist Sarasate. Value: $16 million. A Third Imperial Fabergé Egg reported missing from the New York Metropolitan. Value: $15 million.

A bloodied Omar Youssef, tied to a chair bleeding out, flashed in Chase's mind. *I took more than the artifacts from Omar. In the end, the world is a better place for it.* With the egos in the room and the illegal aspect of buying stolen collectibles, Chase was confident the night could net a cool $50 million.

The Elite Ones.

Chase realized there was a covered piece of art that didn't belong to him. A few seconds passed before he realized it must be a painting from Dario's Lake Como estate.

"We have a fabulous turnout," Dario announced as he approached. "You are pleased?"

"You did good, Dario." Chase leaned in close. "Brought one of your own, huh?"

"I have the best auctioneer visiting my country. How can I not take advantage of the opportunity to sell a van Gogh?" Dario's eyes widened at the form-fitting dress that curved around Ammelie's body. "Bellissima!"

Chase's fingers felt the coin in his pocket. "Stay focused, superstar."

"Impossible when you have brought an angel into our presence," he answered.

"Such a charmer," Ammelie smiled. "Please, don't ever stop."

Chase held out his arm as Ammelie slipped hers under his. Leading her through the crowd, he shook hands and kissed cheeks along the way. Thanks to Michael Hardeman, he'd learned how to mingle with the most powerful in society. His dad called it the Hardeman trifecta, not to be confused with the Hardeman mantra: *Live fast. Love hard. Leave 'em wanting more. Play the roulette wheel of life. Tap the blackjack table on fourteen.* The Hardeman trifecta was the art of the deal. First, arrive with a desirable woman by your side. Second, show the rich what it is they desire most. Third, make each one feel as if they are getting the deal of a lifetime.

As the crowd stepped aside, Chase's eyes locked in on one special guest. He pulled Ammelie in close, feeling her body tense. Dario was a few steps ahead as he interrupted the guest, who was surrounded by four broad-shouldered men. Stepping forward, the special guest's gaze fixated on Ammelie.

"Chase," Dario began. "Allow me to introduce you to Bernhardt Brandis."

FORTY-FIVE

With an iron grip, the square-jawed, cauliflower-eared German shook hands. His dead stare shifted to Ammelie. "And you must be Mrs. Hardeman."

"Ammelie Stroman," she replied. "A friend."

"Mr. Brandis, we are honored you are here." Chase was unsure of what response he expected. Shock. Anger. Tears. Rage. Fear. None occurred. Instead, the former MMA fighter and Ammelie seemed undeterred. "I'm sure you'll find the artifacts on the auction block to your taste."

"Ammelie," Dario interrupted politely, "perhaps we should find our seats."

Being face to face with Brandis, the rage burned within. He'd waited months to stand before the man who kidnapped Laney. Now that they were only a few feet apart, he thought of all the ways he'd kill him. Both waited until Ammelie and Dario were out of earshot.

"You have brought a rare selection this evening," Brandis said with his stare locked on Ammelie as she walked away. "When I was first told of the items for auction, I did not believe them to be genuine. Perhaps I was mistaken."

"I assure you they are the real deal, Mr. Brandis."

"You can provide proof of authenticity?"

Chase removed the stolen Bode Museum coin from his pocket and held it in his palm. "One hundred percent genuine."

Brandis studied the coin closely. "You have done business with Omar."

Chase nodded slowly. "Unfortunately, Omar is no longer with us."

"I was in Monterey when you sold the Rossino Otto." Brandis kept his shoulders back as if he were standing at attention. "Remarkable find, and a remarkable price. I am curious to hear how you made such a discovery."

"I've been known to deliver where others fail. I'm sure we can both agree, how you arrive at the treasure is not as important as the prize you keep for yourself." Chase slipped the coin back into his pocket. "I must confess I'm intrigued to see the Scepter of Dagobert up close."

"All with an invitation are given access to bid," Brandis replied deadpan.

Chase nodded toward Ammelie. "Perhaps then I will return what belongs to you."

"You speak in riddles, Mr. Hardeman." Stepping forward until they were inches apart, nose to nose, Brandis added in a lowered voice, "What game are we playing?"

"Omar's invitation will bring me to your exclusive hideaway." Chase noticed Brandis' hands by his sides ball into fists. He braced himself for the German to throw the first blow, knowing he was no match in a brawl. "The Scepter of Dagobert is a remarkable treasure. However, what I'm more interested in is an exchange."

"What kind of exchange?"

"The American for Katarine," Chase said coolly.

"Hotel de Paris Monte-Carlo. Five days from now." Brandis' eyes narrowed as a sly grin pursed his lips. "Mr. Hardeman, bring my dear daughter home."

"Sorry to interrupt," Dario said as he cautiously approached. "Chase, it is time."

"You'll excuse me," Chase said to Brandis. "Showtime."

Chase tugged on his jacket and turned his back, knowing the next stage of the plan was in motion. He glanced at Ammelie who's concerned expression was a dead giveaway that she recognized her murderous father. Following Dario to the front of the grand hall, Chase shook off the excess adrenaline and tried to calm the pounding in his chest.

"I thought Bernhard was going to guillotine you," Dario whispered.

"Me too," Chase replied under his breath. "He's bigger than I thought he'd be."

"Did you get what you wanted from him?"

Chase looked toward Ammelie once more. "We're still negotiating."

"May I suggest you bring Dax to your next pissing contest?"

Chase squeezed Dario's shoulder. "Time to make The Elite fall in love."

The crowd found their seats as Chase stepped to the front and stood beside the Stradivarius and Fabergé egg. Eyeing the room, he noticed Brandis seated in the back row. Out of the corner of his eye, he watched Ammelie glance back several times at the nightmare she'd escaped. Both looked to be on edge, and that's exactly where he needed them.

"Good evening," he said in a raised voice. "My sincere appreciation for all of you being here on such short notice." His cadence quickened slightly. "Many of you knew my father and his antics. He was part genius, part madman, and the greatest deal maker I've ever seen. He would've loved to have been here tonight." With a splattering of applause, he turned toward the big box giant founder. "Mr. Keller, he sold you an island in the Pacific before you realized it was one mile from the Spratly Islands."

"He told me security was included," Randolph Keller shouted in jest.

Playing to the laughter from the crowd, Chase turned toward one of the Galindez brothers. "You bid on a violin from the Titanic's bandleader."

"Your father swore it was waterproof," the eldest, Emilio, shouted.

Laughter grew louder as the others whispered amongst themselves. Each and every one of them related to their own unique story of dealing with the late Michael Hardeman.

Chase sensed the room come more alive as he spun around and pointed at Leonizo Beneventi. "Mr. Beneventi, you bid on the world's largest egg."

"And your father cooked me the world's largest omelet," Beneventi bellowed.

More laughter, and now the room was playing into Chase's hands.

"Yes, he was the best cook," he admitted. "But I'm not here to sell you an island in the line of fire, a waterlogged instrument, or an omelet." He stepped to one side and pointed toward the artifacts. "Tonight, I present to you Sarasote's Stradivarius and the elusive Third Imperial Fabergé Egg. Origins of both unknown. And of course, my good friend Dario was gracious to include one of his most prized paintings, a van Gogh—a surprise to us all."

Dario naturally played along, bowed, then blew a kiss. "Child support and lawyers."

As the crowd applauded and snickered, Chase paced back and forth like a beast on the prowl, leaving the room elec-trified with anticipation. His gaze shifted to Brandis, who glared back stone-faced.

No fear. No surrender.

Battle lines were drawn. A pre-fight stare-down was in effect.

"Let the games begin," Chase's words echoed. On cue, Dario removed the velvet cover from an easel. As soon as the painting was revealed, there was a unified gasp amongst the crowd. Chase was stunned for a few seconds, shocked Dario would part with this one of a kind. "Ladies and gentlemen, van Gogh's *L'homme est en mer.*"

Dating back to 1889, the painting was finished while van Gogh was locked away in an asylum. Bright, strikingly contrasted colors. Vibrant orange and yellow tones captured the fire and straw floor. Cold blues wrapped around a seated woman's dress and a wall behind her. In the woman's arms, a sleeping baby clothed in pure white rested.

Beads of sweat seeped down the back of Chase's neck. "You've heard the story of a woman with a young child worried about her husband away at sea. But if you were to dive deeper into the insanity of van Gogh as he was locked away in an asylum, you'd see a much more disturbing depiction in this priceless work of art." Chase pointed at the painting as the sweat seeped through his shirt. "Van Gogh struggled with mental illness, remained poor, and was an unknown his entire life. So I would suggest to you what is revealed is deeper than what we've believed." Chase continued to pace, allowing the story to linger. "I would suggest to you this woman is troubled, distraught, and fearful her husband will return. She is the protector of her innocent child." Knowing he'd pushed his fairytale far enough, he said boldly, "With the fate of this child in your grasp, which of you will open the bidding at $10 million?"

Immediately a paddle raised from Randolph Keller: $10 million.

"Ten million. Who will give eleven?" Chase's cadence picked up a few beats. As soon as Emilio Galindez raised his paddle, Chase rattled, "Faster than 5G, the Galindez brothers are in at eleven million. Who will give thirteen?" For a moment, the bidding paused. Chase had stood in this exact spot many times before. "If you're not willing to save the child, save the demons in yourself." Randolph Keller raised the paddle a second time, pushing the bid to $13 million. Dario stood off to the side, hoping he hadn't made a mistake in auctioning the painting without a reserve. Chase pushed the room a bit harder as the bid raised millions at a time before hitting $24 million. As he suspected, the main bidders were the economic juggernauts in the first four rows. "$24 million. Who will give twenty-five?"

Know your players, and single out who wants to win the most.

From the back row, Bernhardt Brandis raised his paddle, causing the entire room to look over their shoulders to find the high bidder. Out of the corner of his eye, Chase caught Ammelie doing the same before he acknowledged the bid.

"Twenty-five million dollars!" His voice echoed off the walls as he looked to the first four rows for a counter. When no one raised their paddles, he closed the deal. "Going once. Going twice. Sold for $25 million."

Without delay, Chase moved on to the Gibson Stradivarius and the Fabergé. After improvising to sell the van Gogh on the fly, the remaining pieces sold in record time. By the end of the evening, Dario was $25 million richer, and Chase netted a cool $60 million. What was priceless was the look on Brandis' face when he wired $25 million to Dario, then watched $60 million slip through his fingers from the artifacts owned by Omar Youssef.

Rest in torment, Omar.

As the crowd congratulated Chase on a successful night, Ammelie slipped out from her seat and headed for an exit. Excusing himself, Chase hurried to catch up to her.

He reached out and grabbed her arm. "Ammelie, hold on a minute."

Turning around with tears in her eyes, she said, "He recognized me."

"Who recognized you?"

She whispered in his ear, "My father."

FORTY-SIX

BELL ISLAND, NEWFOUNDLAND

Off the tip of the island, a rock sea stack known as The Clapper jutted toward gunmetal grey skies. A blistering howl screamed across Conception Bay before slamming into sandstone, shale, and red matatie sheer cliffs two hundred feet tall. The harsh climate of the island was far from the lavish amenities the Vihkrovs savored.

Elena dug her hands deeper into the pockets of a North Face jacket as the bitter cold pierced her face and wildly blew her hair in the wind. Staring out on the rough seas, she stood on the edge of the cliff, tempting gravity. Swallowing a lump lodged in her throat, she buried seeds of grief over her loss.

Revenge against the traitor meant she betrayed her father.

Yet, it is his sin that betrayed me.

Loyalty or love was a never-ending battle.

Neither will bring Chase back to me.

Stepping back from the edge, fighting off the urge to take one more step forward, she headed across the grassy acreage toward a modest house on Hiscoks Hill.

Entering the house, she pulled her hair into a ponytail. With the temperature only a few degrees warmer than outside, she kept her jacket on. Grabbing two mugs from a cabinet, she poured freshly brewed coffee. Black. Two spoonfuls of sugar. A peace offering to a man whose retribution for betrayal was swift, except when it came to his only daughter. She found him seated at a dining room table texting.

"I will not ask forgiveness," he stated, glancing up from the screen. "You disobeyed me."

"One day, I will be the one who carries on your legacy." She warmed her hands around the mug, hoping to chisel the coldness between them. "All I have done is to protect you."

"What you set in motion cannot be undone." His somber tone was chilling. "Bernhardt failed to break the American, so I believed you would fail too. Your actions were reckless."

"Do you not see your plan to return her alive will not be enough to end Bouchard?" She protested, trying not to offend him any further. "My actions may have been reckless, but the results will inflict greater pain. Papa, you would have done the same." She paused. "But I will never be able to forgive you..."

"Chase and his father were once an ally, but there is no denying he poses a threat to us. I offered him a chance to prove his allegiance." He pressed his elbows into the slivered table. "He was only loyal to you but a liability to everyone else."

"He planned to search for her," Elena confessed. "You must have known."

"Which left me no other choice to ensure our survival," he barked. "He is dead, Elena."

Pushing the mug aside, she weighed her words. "Then why are you afraid?"

"We are no longer thieves, pimps, and smugglers." He leaned back with arms crossed. "We have been lions amongst our prey, but the animals which surround us now are far more dangerous. Bernhardt made a grave error in speaking of the scientist while others listened."

"Moscow," she surmised, "or the PRC."

"Both." He took a long drag from a cigarette then blew a cloud of smoke that drifted in the air. He sipped from his mug and added, "With their help, we ensured such an error would not occur again for all involved. However, there is a price for such a request."

"What is the price we must pay to erase our debt?" Elena asked matter of factly.

"Same as it has always been."

"Bernhardt lives while Chase is dead." Elena harnessed her anger. "You have not answered my question. You have dealt with both governments in the past. Neither has caused you to react this way."

"There is a new player to the game," he admitted. "One more powerful."

Knowing there was only one other, she suggested, "You presumed my reaction to the American, but you were not expecting my plan for revenge."

"You are my daughter—your actions are beyond anticipation." A cunning expression pursed his lips before he took another long drag from his cigarette. Exhaling the nicotine, he continued. "She will be a match that will spark the world on fire. A pawn who checkmates a king."

Allowing grief to leave her broken was a sign of weakness, one her father recognized. She needed to resign herself from the past and choose loyalty, once again. Staring into her father's eyes, the stone of revenge wrapped around the cracks of a broken heart.

"We are still in control, Papa. What must I do?"

"Go to Washington." Before he said more, the Englishman entered the dining room, leaving their conversation in limbo. "Elena must leave within the hour. Make arrangements with the pilot."

Elena noticed the silent exchange between them, sensing there was more. She pushed her father as far as she needed, knowing any harder would mean being left at Hiscoks Hill. If that were true, her next outing to the cliffs might end differently.

She stepped over and kissed him on the forehead, then left the room.

Once she turned the corner, she stopped and listened.

"Take her to meet with our contact," her father said in a lowered voice.

"Yes, Mr. Vihkrov." The Englishman added, "Seems the bench remains crowded. Mr. Brandis relayed your bloke pulled a blinder. Now he wants to make a trade on Half Moon. Seems the American is of interest. What Mr. Brandis will receive in return is unclear."

"Bernhardt is a first-rate idiot."

"Sorry to say I could not be in two places at once." the Englishman said politely yet assertively. "More difficult target was Simon Adams. You made the right call, sir."

"Tell Bernhardt if he misses Hardeman a second time, there will not be a third." Dmitry paused. "Do what needs to be done."

A shiver rattled Elena's bones as she leaned back against the wall. With her eyes closed, she braced herself from collapsing. Seconds earlier, she had given up the ghost, but if what she heard was true, then the man she loved was very much alive and remained in the crosshairs of her father's rage.

She started to go back into the dining room to confront them both, but her muscles refused to move.

FORTY-SEVEN

CASINO ABERDEEN, LUMLEY BEACH

One day later, the whirlwind trip to Lake Como and Milan was over. Back at the hotel, children raced through the lobby, excited for Ms. Ammelie to return. *No disguising pure unadulterated joy of a child.* Chase noticed the greeting seemed to lighten her spirits. He smiled at Imari as she waved at him, the young artist whose drawing he kept folded up in his back pocket. He waved back as he slipped through the reunion, crossed the tiled lobby, then stepped onto the elevator as the doors closed.

After the auction, The Elite returned to their yachts, villas, castles, and islands. On the way back to the Brera apartment, he was the perfect gentleman, wrapping his coat over Ammelie's shoulders as her body shivered. *Hard to discern between chills and dread.* He gripped her hand tight to reassure her she was safe. On the inside, he relived the rush of selling the van Gogh, Stradivarius, and Fabergé egg. Adrenaline pulsed through his veins as he envisioned the moment he stared into the eyes of Bernhardt Brandis. Nearing the apartment, his senses remained heightened, expecting retaliation from the German for the ambush.

Shortly after returning to the apartment, Ammelie excused

herself to the bedroom, where she stayed until late the next morning. Chase considered pressing the matter of seeing her father that night, but he'd thought better of it. It was after midnight when Dario had arrived to pick up the Ferrari. Neither spoke of Brandis or the millions they pocketed. Both promised to see each other soon, unsure of how much time would pass before that promise was kept.

Once Dario left, Chase found a *Tenuta* cabernet in a dark corner of the garage before settling in a leather chair upstairs. He double-checked between the cushions to ensure the Glock was where he'd left it. He popped the cork and gazed out on the balconette. Being in the apartment was foreign, as if he were invading someone else's space. He thought it would bring him a sense of comfort being surrounded by photos of his parents. Instead, as he gazed at the years of their young lives framed on end tables, hanging on walls, and especially the one he held in his hand of his pregnant mom, he was left empty.

A life I'll never remember.

Snapping back to the present, the elevator doors opened, and Chase stepped out into an empty hallway. His shoes scuffed against the carpet as he dragged himself to the Penthouse suite, beyond exhausted. During the night inside the Brera apartment, he had pulled himself out of the chair every hour to check on Ammelie. He watched her body rise and fall. *Peaceful.* Then he returned to the chair, poured another glass of *Tenuta*, and listened for the slightest disturbance. He dozed off only once before jerking awake, gasping for air as if he were drowning.

Entering the suite, he had yet to shake that sensation. He dropped his backpack on the floor, surprised to see Maliki

Dollar and Dax staring back at him.

"Italian vacation is over," Dax said frankly. "We've got sharks in the water."

"Not sure that's what I'd call it...sharks?"

"Do you want the good news or the bad news?"

Chase greeted Maliki, then slumped into a chair. "Good news."

"There is none," Dax bantered. "Maliki will get you up to speed on the bad news."

"I have not been able to reach McIntyre," Maliki said, concerned. "Have you?"

"She left a few days ago." Chase shook his head and lied, "Haven't heard from her since."

"Like a bat out of hell," Dax added. "No clue where she's gone."

"I am well aware of your relationship with McIntyre," Maliki countered. "There is much you do not know about her or your father. But right now is not the time for a history lesson. When I contacted her with the intelligence gathered through Unicorn, I believed there was an imminent threat against your country. With what has occurred in recent days..." Maliki paused, composing himself. "I am more convinced now than ever."

Chase recognized the anguish on Maliki's face. "What have you found?"

"We recovered fragments of a KAB 1500L precision-guided bomb in the rubble," Maliki said heavyhearted. "I created Unicorn as a tool for governments to keep the peace amongst their enemies. If any are aware they are being monitored, then it is impossible to keep the wars from destroying us all. I have used this safeguard for my own purposes. On the day of the bombing, intelligence sources from your government monitored a Russian drone as it flew across the Indian Ocean from the South Atlantic. From what I have discovered, tracking of the drone occurred after the bombing."

"Don't forget to mention the blackout," Dax interrupted. "Maliki monitored chatter from the Pentagon about all of China's MSS spies in North American going dark."

"Are the Russians and PRC your clients?" *Peoples Republic of China.*

Maliki confessed, "All who pay the price and follow the rules are given access."

"Break the rules, and the world burns," Dax vented.

"Trusting the Russians or the PRC with Unicorn is like pouring gas..." Chase harnessed his anger, knowing Maliki was grieving over his loss. "Apart from Mossad's surveillance, if Russia and China were using Unicorn to monitor Bernhardt Brandis or Omar Yousseff, they might've been able to track Unicorn back to the source?"

Maliki nodded. "If they were using Unicorn, you are correct."

"McIntyre said your identity was unknown."

"No secret is certain." Maliki's eyes narrowed. "As I am sure you are aware."

"He could've been unmasked," Dax suggested. "Happens all the time these days."

"Moscow and Beijing have seen the benefits of strengthening their alliance," Maliki said. "Unicorn has never been about *anatak.*" *Death.* "I believed anonymity was enough."

"Knowing your exact location means someone on the ground also knew your true identity. So, who's missing in this room?" Chase didn't wait for an answer. "McIntyre."

"Not possible," Maliki rebuked. "She has protected my family and yours."

"Everyone's got a price," Chase retorted. "Who else could it be?"

"I told you he'd come to the same conclusion," Dax said to Maliki, then turned back to Chase. "You're going to change your theory after he shows you what else we found."

Maliki spun a laptop around on a coffee table to show a list of numbers on a screen.

"What am I looking at?" Chase asked.

"The SIM card you gave to me," Maliki answered. "All stored numbers."

"Brace yourself," Dax warned. "It's about to get even more twisted."

"Most of the numbers are local, except for one." Maliki pointed to the screen. "Unicorn enabled me to trace the origin of this number to Maksim Popov, Director of the SVR."

"Russia's Foreign Intelligence Service," Chase reiterated. "How can that be?"

"One call to Popov on the same day of the bombing," Dax pointed out. "Wait until you see what's behind door number two."

"The suspense is killing me, literally. Keep going."

"Dax passed along the access codes for your cameras at the Lumley house," Maliki continued. "I was able to recover most of the files from the cloud." Maliki tapped on his trackpad, and the numbers disappeared. Appearing on the screen was a video file. He pressed play. "A lion lurks in the tall yellow grass."

Chase leaned forward as he watched the grainy black and white footage. At first, there was nothing except for a shot of the side of the Lumley house. Dax had hidden one of the cameras high enough that it would have been difficult to notice at night. Leaning forward with elbows dug into his thighs, Chase stopped breathing for a few seconds when a shadow appeared at the side door.

Wolffie.

FORTY-EIGHT

STONE RIDGE, VIRGINIA

Early in the morning, Abbott pecked at the keys one at a time on an old Dell whose trackpad was broken. He worked the mouse to highlight, delete, and copy his thoughts as they took shape in the dossier he'd written for the Intel Committee. In a few hours, he'd recite his opening statement, then present what was spread across his desk. Thanks to friends within the intel community, whose names remained locked in the vault of his mind, he weighed the potential damage to his career.

Quell the storm, and ride the thunder.

Weeks earlier, Abbott negotiated the terms of his interview long before President Bouchard blackmailed him into resigning. At the time, he had little more than speculation and suspicion. But after what had unfolded in the weeks since, his claims within the dossier would ravage the Committee into a feeding frenzy. Bouchard's opponents had searched for a way to not only wound him but put him down permanently. Abbott knew once he presented the dossier, the leaks to the press would follow, and the Administration would suffer a catastrophic blow.

A pair of reading glasses were perched on the bridge of

his nose. He peered through thick lenses at the pages which recounted a deeper dive into his suspicions, knowing it wasn't enough to protect the nation unless he claimed it to be fact. *Best counterpunch, when attacked in the swamp, is to sling mud, no matter whether it's true or false.* What he had witnessed in Bouchard's actions in Los Angeles and the intelligence he gathered from his sources left him with two conclusions which he saved for the final page. While he had yet to find total proof, Abbott was convinced unless President Bouchard was confronted by the Senate, Congress, Bureau, and Agency, he presented a clear and present danger to the Republic.

Stacking the papers neatly together, he flipped the title page over and scanned the opening paragraph, which summarized the FBI's investigation into Hardeman Auctions. What began shortly before the events in Los Angeles, including the fatal plane crash that killed the former governor of Indiana, Michael Hardeman. Abbott remembered Hardeman's failed attempt to run for the presidency before his funding ran dry. Most of the Intel Committee members knew him well, so it was safe to assume they had followed his rise in the auction arena after his political career ended.

Most likely, some owed him a favor or two.

Surprisingly, the Bureau's investigation included targeting Michael Hardeman's son. With the investigation gaining traction, an undercover agent infiltrated the Hardeman circle in an attempt to get close to Dmitry and Elena Vihkrov, the Everest of the Bratva. Abbott meticulously scanned the reports, briefings, and emails documenting the approval of Special Agent Laney Kelley's undercover assignment. Getting his hands on the stack of intel was a result of a favor owed from a soldier who had served under his command in Iraq, someone who'd gone on to be a field agent with the Bureau while Abbott served in the Joint Chiefs.

Access to intelligence is what keeps the world spinning on its axis.

The basis of the investigation was money laundering, which wasn't earth-shattering, and for a politician who'd been in the game as long as Michael Hardeman would've only scratched the surface of what the Bureau could've been investigating. What troubled Abbott was the implications that the Vihkrovs were somehow involved in a possible terrorist threat. Shortly after the operation went dark, the attack in Los Angeles occurred, and the aftermath left more questions than answers. When the dust settled, the Bureau buried the investigation without any resolution.

Adding to his conjecture, he described the unexplained disappearance of Special Agent Laney Kelley, who was not mentioned in any of the Bureau's official documents since. He did find a memo sent to the Los Angeles field office from Kelley asking for extended leave due to personal matters. And there had been no mention publicly or in any internal communication within the last eight months regarding her abduction. Abbott made a point to highlight his conclusion that the more he looked into the matter, the faster the documents seemed to vanish.

Alison's words interrupted his concentration as he replayed Belém.

"What do you know about Chase Hardeman?"

"Abbott, why would…"

"Don't play games. Answer the question, Alison."

"I can't tell you anything about him. Eight months ago, Special Agent Laney Kelley disappeared. No investigation by the Bureau,

and no ransom demands."

"What does she have to do with Hardeman?"

"Everything."

She was the one who exposed the disappearance, but it wasn't enough to accuse the President of being involved. Locked in a bunker during the Los Angeles attack, Abbott remembered hearing the voice of Special Agent Laney Kelly as she relayed the neutralizing of the terrorists. *She was one of the good ones.* Abbott was resolute that her disappearance needed to be brought before the Intel Committee and investigated further.

Turning the pages, the dossier delved into Chief of Staff Simon Adams' mysterious death. As a decorated CIA officer before assuming his role within the White House, the lack of knowledge regarding the circumstances was troubling. Abbott wrote about evidence brought forward proving Simon Adams was left in a shallow grave, the whereabouts unknown. He ended the section by naming a source who could offer much-needed insight. He typed Alison's name a dozen times, reading it over and over, before redacting it. *I'll need leverage with the Intel Committee to gain her freedom.* He continued on and explained how the source was being held in a black site prison by President Bouchard. That was sure to get the Committee's undivided attention, especially when he added the source could offer further information regarding the whereabouts of Special Agent Laney Kelley, the murder of Chief of Staff Simon Adams, as well as the Los Angeles terrorist attack. He recommended the Committee issue a subpoena so the source could be deposed.

Knowing President Bouchard would refuse to testify before the Committee, Abbott relayed his private conversations with the Commander in Chief, knowing he was walking a tight wire with executive privilege. He revealed his interactions with the President during the attack on Los Angeles, Bouchard's intervention at the family vineyard, and his orders to capture a fugitive who knew of a coverup within the Oval Office. Exposing those conversations to the Intel Committee was a risk, but if he played his cards right, the Speaker of the House would pummel the President at the next opportunity. Of course, there'd be pushback for his actions from the other side.

In war you are either the conqueror or the conquered.

Recounting his conversations with the President within the pages of the dossier, he again referred to the source. He detailed how he was ordered by the President to lead a special ops team to capture and return the source to U.S. soil. In that same summary, he reiterated how the President blackmailed him into resigning and threatened repercussions if he sat before the Intel Committee. In fact, Abbott pointed out, he resigned to protect the source.

In the final section of the dossier, Abbott listed terrorists confirmed killed and others who had fallen off the intelligence radar since the President took office. Jeric Salem. Najee Azad. Misfirah Jama. Aisha Abed. Raiha Sultana. Marid Abu. Sameer Alli. Karim Salik. Samara Nasir. Akram Kasim. And the king of them all, Abu Haji Fatima—AKA the Prodigal.

Abbott described the atrocities these men levied on the world. Bombings. Kidnappings. Beheadings. Destruction. Death. He painted a picture of men who were the greatest threat to the nation, and yet there was no clear intelligence of how they died or disappeared, except for Abu Haji Fatima, who the President claimed credit for killing in Mosul.

Abbott exhaled heavily, knowing the next few pages were the greatest leap yet. He brought up the Bureau's investigation, which focused on Chase Hardeman. While enlisted and stationed at Pendleton in California, the soldier's military record was remarkably uneventful. In fact, it was so uneventful the only conclusion the four-star general could surmise was that he had been recruited for black ops. A dozen trips by Michael Hardeman to the Middle East were listed in an effort to tie the father and son together. Details of any black ops involving the Hardemans didn't exist anywhere. In conclusion, efforts to locate Chase Hardeman since the Los Angeles attack resulted in whereabouts unknown.

Removing his reading glasses, Abbott rubbed his eyes. Perching the frames back on the bridge of his nose, he stared at surveillance photos of Chase Hardeman boarding Air Force One at Los Angeles International Airport the morning after the attack. From what Abbott had found, it was the only direct connection between Hardeman and the President. In a scathing rebuke, Abbott called Bouchard's actions unprecedented, unethical, and dangerous. Then he rattled off a list of questions for the Intel Committee to answer.

What was Bouchard's knowledge regarding the attack on Los Angeles?

What led to Chief of Staff Simon Adams' death? Who was responsible?

Did Simon Adams use his experience as a previous Central Intelligence Agency officer to cross the line on President Bouchard's behalf?

What involvement did Bouchard have in the deaths of the terrorists listed? If he was involved, how did he keep the intel community in the dark?

What did he currently know about the disappearance of Special Agent Kelley?

Where was Chase Hardeman, and what answers could he provide?

Were there any current unsanctioned military operations in motion without Congressional oversight?

Finally, Abbott eluded back to the beginning of the dossier. As a warrior who fought on the frontlines in battle against the nation's fiercest enemies, it was his firm belief the President was using the Oval Office and black op agents such as Chase Hardeman without Congressional or military oversight to fight in the shadows. With those assumptions, limited evidence, and a reliable source willing to testify, he was left with only two conclusions: impeachment or treason.

Closing the dossier, Abbott gathered his files and glanced at a whiteboard detailing a roadmap to his assumptions, accusations, and his version of events. His scribbled markings were the only way to hit back at the President and negotiate Alison's release.

A doorbell rang.

Glancing out the study window, a man dressed in a dark suit walked up the path. Abbott noticed the unmarked black suburban with tinted windows parked at the curb. He'd been told the Intel Committee had arranged for an escort to bring him to the Capitol. Checking his watch, he gathered the dossier and files, then slipped everything into a briefcase. On the way out of the study, he grabbed a coat from a rack and opened the front door.

"General Abbott?"

"The one and only," Abbott replied. "You're early."

From his coat, the Englishman removed a SIG with a

silencer and pulled the trigger in three rapid successions. Two shots to the chest. One shot to the center of Abbott's skull. Abbott fell backward and hit the floor with a thud.

The Englishman stepped over the dead body and entered the study. Out of the corner of his eye, he caught sight of the whiteboard. For a moment, he took in all of the scribbled markings, not fully understanding what it all meant. With gloved hands, he picked up an eraser and wiped the board clean. He grabbed the laptop off the desk, slipped it into the briefcase on the floor, then picked up the briefcase and walked out the front door.

FORTY-NINE

After finishing a six-mile run on a treadmill, President Bouchard broke his daily routine of three Red Bulls and opted for a throwback. He finished off a stack of pancakes, eggs over easy, extra crispy bacon, and a pile of hash browns courtesy of the executive chef hidden somewhere in the basement of the White House. Being raised on a divided plate and loving Salisbury steak TV dinners as a kid, the habit hadn't changed in the years since. But there was something about breakfast that tossed the rules. Broken yolk over the top of buttermilk pancakes, crispy bacon, and hash browns took him back to a simpler time growing up on the vineyard.

Nearly four years in the bubble left him questioning if a lasting change was possible or if it would be erased by Congress and the Senate. Most mornings, he fought off the nightmares from the lines he'd crossed to keep America safe. He guessed no more than any other who'd sat behind the Resolute.

On this morning, he dragged himself across the living room with the responsibility of Commander in Chief weighing on his shoulders. Closing his eyes, he pictured the pride in his father's face when he announced his bid for the presidency and the bear hug that followed when he shocked the world and won. A nod of approval from a father never failed to boost a son's ambition.

Slumping deeper into a plush sofa, most likely purchased by his predecessor's spouse, he downed a glass of freshly squeezed orange juice and cracked open the first Red Bull of the day. Living alone in the White House was like being locked in a historical museum. He imagined what it would be like if Nadia, Ryan, and Sadie were there with him. Dinner around the table. Helping Ryan and Sadie with homework. Movie night. Bowling in the Nixon alley. And sharing his deepest concerns with Nadia. He was the leader of the free world, but as he opened his eyes, his reality reminded him of a loneliness he'd carried since that fateful day. Maybe he'd find solace if they were still alive instead of the constant torment that ached in his soul.

Bouchard is in bed with Russia. Bouchard is weak on trade against China. Bouchard's finger rests on the button with Iran. Bouchard is a puppet for the Saudis. Bouchard is ignoring the millions who are streaming across the border. Bouchard's popularity has dropped thirty points in the last six months. He's not the leader Americans voted for to drain the swamp.

Grabbing a remote from a glass table, he turned on a flatscreen mounted above a brick fireplace dating back to when the Kennedy's remodeled the space. Flipping through the channels, he stopped on a network's daily segment of burning him at the stake.

Anti-Bouchard propaganda.

His jaw clenched as the cable hack vomited an array of false accusations, none of which would ever be proven in a court of law. But that wasn't the point of the mud-slinging. If a story stuck and gained traction for one or two days on social, it was deemed a success. Actual proof was a luxury.

The point of the 24-7 barrage of accusations, insinuations, and flat-out lies was meant to keep the world guessing as to whether a second term under the same president was the right choice on Election Day less than a year away. *Anarchist tactics handed down from political insiders desperate to snatch the keys to Camelot.* He fired off a dozen social posts ranging from shots at the Speaker of the House to reposting from those in his base who were gloved in his corner.

That'll drive them insane today.

"David?" Avery's voice called out.

"In here watching the abuse of free speech."

She appeared in the doorway. "Abbott is dead."

Bouchard's brows raised as he pulled himself up. "You're fooling with me."

"Shot three times." Avery shook her head. "Feds arrived at his house an hour ago."

"Any suspects?"

"So far, no fingerprints or DNA. No witnesses yet, either. Feds are checking the house and neighborhood security cameras, but that will take a while." Avery stepped deeper into the room. "He was scheduled to testify before the Committee this morning."

Bouchard nodded at the flatscreen. "Vultures will know before lunch."

"Feds have blocked off the street, so we can get ahead of it."

Taking a long drag of Red Bull, the rush of sugar spiked his senses. "You could've texted me the news. What'd they find?"

"A laptop charger was plugged into a wall, but no laptop." Avery grabbed the remote and turned off the television. "No time to torture yourself. We need to know what Abbott was planning to spill. Starting with what you haven't told me."

Bouchard weighed the truth, knowing Avery's forged confession from Alison McIntyre left her complicit. He ran his fingers through a mop of hair with more strands of grey than on his first day in office. "We're treading on razor-thin ice. One wrong step, and it's over."

"Alison McIntyre won't sing like a bird to us," Avery pointed out. "David, let me reach out to the Bureau and request they keep us in the loop. That's the best we can do unless you're ready to tell me what's really going on."

Bouchard nearly confessed but stopped. "As long as I stay ten steps ahead, we're good."

"Well, you're forty minutes behind schedule."

With that, Avery left as abruptly as she arrived. Alone, Bouchard picked up the final draft of his State of the Union speech and stepped over to an arched window that perfectly framed the Washington Monument. With the speech in his grasp, he thought of how the founding father's legacy was under attack hundreds of years after George Washington became the Father of His Country. Those in the shadows hidden behind masks of secrecy wished to burn the country to the ground. Rediscover a better America meant to erase the nation's history. Even though he had his doubts about running for a second term, he'd been in Washington long enough to know if he stepped aside, the socialists would steal the people's freedom without them even knowing.

RVG defended democracy and the nation. But they'll never accept my abuse of power.

Reading through the first paragraph of the speech, his mind drifted to the soldiers who followed Washington into battle. Going to war against his adversaries, there was no tougher soldier by his side than Avery. While that might win a few battles, it wasn't enough to win the war. *McIntyre better be right about Hardemen. If not, I'll lynch her myself.*

FIFTY

LUMLEY BEACH, SIERRA LEONE

After nightfall, the Aberdeen Casino buzzed with locals and tourists dropping chips and flipping cards for a chance to get rich. Chase tossed another stack of chips on a green felt table and watched as a roulette wheel spun. Checking his watch, he realized he'd been in the casino for nearly two hours and was ten grand in the hole.

Since the meeting with Maliki in the Penthouse, the operation shifted to Wolffie.

Who is he, exactly? How much does Ammelie know about him? What does he want from her?

For most of the afternoon, Chase and Dax tag teamed surveillance down by the pool, where the children were having the time of their lives, oblivious to the dangerous adults who surrounded them.

When Dax followed Wolffie into the hotel bar, Chase slipped downstairs as not to attract unwanted suspicion. A white ball bounced unpredictably around the wheel until it rested on red seven. Another two grand in chips were scooped up. Strangely, he didn't care. There was a time when money was a driving force, even while they were hunting terrorists in the Middle East and hiding the spoils of war for themselves.

259

Money was power, and without it, they never would've gotten close to the world's most dangerous men. In the months since the plane crash, it all seemed less significant.

Wealth loses its luster when you're worth more than you could spend in one lifetime.

A text buzzed from Dax: WOLFPACK IS ROAMING.

Chase stepped away from the roulette table and nodded at Jafari as he exited out the back. His mind methodically ran through the twists since arriving in Sierra Leone. Omar's confirmation of an American being held captive by Brandis. Dong Hyun-Ki, an expert in biowarfare. McIntyre's sudden departure and the calls that followed. His decision to cut off all communication before exposing Ammelie to the beast in Milan.

He could still feel Ammelie's body uncontrollably shake on the walk back to the apartment in Brera. The following morning she had kept quiet and subdued, which lasted during the flight back to Freetown. On the drive to Lumley Beach, he gave her space, but now that he knew who had broken into the safe house, the suspicions about Wolffie forced the timeline.

Lurking between cars in the parking lot, he steadied himself. Dax was adamant about being the one to tail Wolffie if he left the hotel. Chase figured it was because he'd been cooped up in the hotel too long, or he was pissed he was left out of the drama in Milan. Someone needed to stay close to Ammelie, and Chase's decision was final.

Wolffie emerged from the hotel at a brisk pace headed down a sidewalk toward Baw Baw. Chase ducked between the cars and closed to within fifty yards. Knowing fragments of a Russian missile were recovered by Maliki on his farm and a call was placed hours earlier from Ammelie's cellphone to the

Director of the SVR left little doubt in Chase's mind. *Wolffie's tied to the Russians.* He had plenty of opportunities to snatch her cellphone. Anyone who'd fought in war recognized those beside them who'd done the same. Chase's response in the jungle of Massam must've triggered Wolffie to make the call. Keeping Wolffie in his sights, he knew it could very well be one reason why Maliki had lost those he loved.

Chase lowered his head as Wolffie glanced briefly over his shoulder. *What doesn't make sense is why Wolffie infiltrated Ammelie's world for so long? He's a pro if he's kept his real identity a secret without exposing what he's really after. Maybe Brandis is holding one of the Kremlin's own. Nothing else makes sense.* Closing the gap to thirty yards, the pace quickened as Wolffie turned down a residential street leading away from the beach. By the time Chase reached the corner, he'd lost visual.

Reaching behind his back, Chase retrieved his SIG and held it by his side. He moved cautiously down the sidewalk with his head on a swivel. Out of the corner of his eye, he caught movement. A shadow lunged forward, knocking him off balance. He stumbled backward, keeping a tight grip on his weapon. Another blow knocked the wind out of him. Dropping the SIG to the ground, he bent over as pain rifled through his body. Before he could recover, a fist connected squarely against his jaw. His body hit the concrete with a thud, and for a few seconds, white stars flickered in front of him. Rolling onto this knees, he struggled to catch his breath as he reached for his gun.

Wolffie's boot kicked the SIG away as he stood over Chase, pointing a Grach pistol at his chest. "I've been told you are a legend, but your actions prove you are a coward."

"I should've shot you in Massam." On his knees, Chase glanced around. "Does she know who you are? Does she know the SVR is watching her?"

"I have seen the livestream from London." Wolffie nodded toward the Stars and Stripes tattoo on Chase's forearm. "We both know what is hidden beneath."

Chase's hands clenched into fists. "Innocent blood is on your hands."

Wolffie shook his head as a warning. "You made a mistake following me alone."

"That's where you're wrong." Chase's eyes narrowed in on a red dot hovering over Wolffie's chest. "If you pull the trigger, we'll both die tonight."

Wolffie stepped in closer, noticing the red laser tracking him. He pressed the Grach against Chase's skull. Chase closed his eyes, ready for his fate to be decided while hoping for one more breath. He felt the barrel of the Grach ease off his temple.

"Trade," Wolffie said in Russian, then again in English. "Trade for information."

Chase opened his eyes to see Wolffie lowering the Grach with the red laser still pointed at his chest. Pulling himself to his feet, Chase grabbed his SIG then held out his hand for Wolffie to surrender the Grach. Once he complied, the red laser dot disappeared.

"Why is the SVR so interested in Ammelie?"

"Hiding her from Bernhardt was our way to keep him cooperative. Her safety allowed us to gain important intelligence from his captives. The intelligence and access to his prisoners kept the operation in play longer than anyone expected, and it has kept Ammelie alive."

"Why'd you bomb the Dollar Farm?"

"We know who you are and what you've done," Wolffie admitted. "You are a threat."

From the shadows, Maliki emerged holding a red laser pointer pen. Wolffie hung his head, realizing he'd been duped. Headlights from a van appeared from around a corner and pulled up next to them. A side door slid open. Two men jumped out with semi-automatics at the ready as they zip-tied Wolffie's wrists while Maliki glared into the eyes of the man who killed his son.

"I have told you the truth," Wolffie said to Chase. "Now I must walk away."

One of the men wrapped duct tape over Wolffie's mouth and pulled him inside the van as the Russian struggled. With a strike from the butt of the semi-automatic cracking against the back of his skull, Wolffie was out cold. Maliki pulled the van door closed, then turned and faced Chase.

"Leave Sierra Leone," Maliki said. "I will care for the children as agreed."

"$60 million has been transferred into the account." Chase knew the money would never make up for the loss. "Maliki..."

"Your father offered me freedom once. Now I will do the same."

FIFTY-ONE

CASINO ABERDEEN—LATER

Chase and Dax cleared the penthouse after loading luggage and the anvil case into one of the hotel vans. Dax was on his cell confirming a private jet be on the tarmac at Lungi International Airport within the next two hours. Wolffie's disappearance wouldn't remain unnoticed for long. Authorities would lock down the airport as soon as they discovered a foreigner had disappeared on their soil.

"How're you going to convince her to leave?" Dax asked.

"I'll tell her the truth."

"Her best friend since childhood is a Russian agent?"

"I'm not going to lead with that," Chase answered. "Too subtle."

"So, you're gonna tell her you want to kill her father." Dax's sarcasm was unrelenting. "After you freaked her out in Milan, she'll be dying to go with us to Monaco."

Chase's burner cell rang. *Jafari.* He answered and listened intently, then hung up. "Truck pulled up to the entrance downstairs. Four European bruisers are in the lobby." He grabbed his SIG and checked the mag as Dax did the same. "Time to go to work."

Before stepping out into the hallway, Chase waited in the

264

Penthouse doorway for a few seconds and listened. Depending on whether the men downstairs were looking for Wolffie or them left only a matter of minutes to escape. Chase led the way down the hall until he reached Ammelie's door and knocked. The door swung open, and they were greeted by Imari.

"Mistah Chase," she said. "Brotha Dax."

"What a surprise to see you here," Chase said lightheartedly. "Can we come in?"

Imari smiled wide as he and Dax casually entered the room. Imari wasn't the only one there. A half dozen other children were lounging on the bed watching the *Disney* channel. Ammelie was seated with her feet up, staring in their direction.

"We need a minute," Chase said urgently. "Please."

Ammelie rolled off the bed and walked over to them. "What's wrong?"

Chase answered in a hushed voice, "Which room belongs to Wolffie?"

Looking over his shoulder, she replied, "He's across the hall, why?"

Chase noticed the adjoining door. "Take the children into the next room and lock the door."

"Chase, you're frightening me."

"Good reason." Dax turned to Chase and added, "Go for it, Shakespeare."

"Your father knows where you are," Chase lied. "You're not safe here."

"What does that have to do with Wolffie?" Ammelie asked, confused.

"No time to explain." From the hallway, Chase heard the ding of an elevator so he pushed the room door closed until it

265

was only cracked slightly open. "We need to move."

Dax didn't waste another second as he gathered the children and ushered them into the adjoining room. "Everyone needs to be very quiet." Once they were all safely inside, he closed the door between the rooms and turned the deadbolt.

Ammelie said, "I'm not going anywhere until..."

Chase held his index finger up to his lips. Voices were heard in the hallway, followed by knocking. He stepped over and pressed his ear against the door. He wasn't a linguist but recognized the voices as Russian. All three jumped at the sound of splintering wood.

Ammelie asked in a hushed voice. "Where is Wolffie?"

"We can't wait them out," Dax pressed. "They'll keep knocking down doors."

"We're cornered in here." Chase locked eyes with Ammelie. "You trust me, right?"

"Yes, I trust you."

"Then stay close."

Chase retrieved his SIG from behind his back and flipped off the safety. Grabbing the doorknob, he glanced back and said, "Once we're in the hallway, don't look back."

Opening the door, the adrenaline pulsed as he poked his head out. Scattered across the carpeted floor were shards of wood. Chase motioned to Dax, and they moved in unison, keeping Ammelie between them. Heading away from Wolffie's room and the elevators, they were near the stairwell exit when a voice shouted in Russian.

Pushing the exit door open, gunfire erupted. Bullets ricocheted off the walls. Dax pushed Ammelie forward and up the stairs. Chase returned fire, sending the Russians scrambling for cover. Reaching the next floor, he burst through the door trailing behind Dax and Ammelie. Hearing the footsteps in the stairwell, he feared they weren't moving quick enough. Dax reached the elevator first and punched the button, keeping Ammelie protected behind him. The Russians entered the hallway in tactical formation. Chase fired more rounds, attempting to hold them back.

As soon as the elevator doors opened, Dax pulled Ammelie inside and returned fire, giving cover for Chase, who emptied his mag on his way to the elevator. Seconds ticked like hours before the doors closed. Chase reloaded his SIG on the ride down, ignoring the terrified gaze in Ammelie's eyes. Reaching the ground floor, the second elevator was a few floors behind. Racing through the lobby, the second elevator doors opened, and the four Russians stepped out with guns raised. Chase fired rounds in the air, sending guests in the lobby scattering.

Reaching the outside, he slipped behind the wheel of Jafari's van. Dax fired off more rounds leaving the Russians truck with two flat tires. Ammelie climbed into the back as Dax jumped into the front passenger seat. Turning the ignition, Chase punched the accelerator. With tires screeching, the van lurched forward and swerved onto the street. Shots rang out, shattering the back windshield. In the rearview, the four Russians disappeared into the night.

"Everyone okay?" Chase asked.

Dax patted himself down. "Still breathing."

"Ammelie, are you hurt?"

"We must go back." She looked up with tears in her eyes. "The children."

"They'll be safe." Chase was responsible for shattering the world she'd known, but he'd never been more determined to bring the fight to her estranged father. "You have my word."

"I'm on it." Dax dialed his cellphone. "Jafari, we're on the run."

Shortly after midnight, the van was left abandoned at Lungi International Airport.

FIFTY-TWO

WASHINGTON, D.C.

Inscribed on the temple walls of the Great Emancipator's memorial was Lincoln's Second Inaugural Address. A message to heal a once-divided nation. A nation that found itself once again facing cavernous divides from racial injustice, an economic downturn, and a civil war against anarchists threatening to destroy the freedoms of the American people. Lincoln's speech was remembered throughout history as one of his finest, delivered forty-one days before his assassination.

Avery admired the prose and courage of the nation's 16th president: *With malice toward none with charity for all with firmness in the right as God gives us to see the right let us strive on to finish the work we are in to bind up the nation's wounds, to care for him who shall have borne the battle and for his widow and his orphan—to do all which may achieve and cherish a just and lasting peace among ourselves and with all nations.*

Lincoln captured the heart and soul of a nation that struggled for freedom and equality for all. After reading countless speeches during her time as speechwriter, Avery hoped the State of the Union would live up to the legacies of those who had gone before.

Walking up the steps to the memorial was Louise Higgins, CEO of The Lincoln Initiative, one of the most powerful and influential political strategists in Washington. Late forties. Fiery red hair. Thick black-rimmed glasses. Dark pantsuit. Three-inch heels. She had consulted for the top Silicon Valley and Silicon Beach companies who navigated the turbulent waters of D.C. With an air of confidence and arrogance, her stride covered the distance between them effortlessly.

"Chief of Staff." Higgins smiled cordially. "A wise choice."

"Poetic place to meet," Avery noted. "Do you bring all your clients here?"

"When the world around me gets fuzzy, this is where I find my center." Higgins reached out and shook hands. "While the President and I don't always agree on policy, I've stood at the ready if my services were needed."

"Well, that day may have arrived."

"Death of a knight means trouble in Camelot."

"Feds are working off the theory it was a homicide."

"I would think that would resolve your concern." Higgins motioned for Avery to walk with her. "What occurred in Los Angeles peaked the interests of the hierarchy in both parties. I'll admit I was quite curious myself to hear what General Abbott had to say to the Intel Committee."

"That makes two of us," Avery admitted. "I'm afraid there might be more coming."

"Any idea what that might be?" Higgins asked curiously.

Avery shook her head. "Whatever it is involves Alison McIntyre."

"Ex-CIA. Blacklisted." Higgins continued down the steps. "Whereabouts unknown."

"Not anymore," Avery replied as she kept stride. "She's

being held at Camp David."

"Well, that changes things."

"I was afraid you were going to say that."

Strolling along the National Mall beside the Reflecting Pool, Avery questioned her decision to reach out. Within the White House, it was widely known that Louise Higgins wielded ruthless tactics to build a lucrative war chest of wealth paid by one party to expose the darkest secrets of the other side. Twenty-four-hour news cycles with unverified headlines from anonymous sources. And with her influence in big tech, she was ruthless in wielding that sword. Hit jobs from whistleblowers were a glancing blow. But when The Lincoln Initiative stepped into the ring, it was for nothing less than a knockout.

"A few days before the President's entourage left for Athens, Simon Adams reached out to me," Higgins stated. "He asked if there was a way to reason with General Abbott. I told him Abbott is a man of conviction. There is no reasoning against one's convictions."

"What does Alison McIntyre have to do with General Abbott and my brother?"

Higgins stopped halfway down the Reflecting Pool and gazed across Constitution Garden to the Declaration of Independence Memorial on a small island set in a lake. "Does the President plan to run for a second term?"

Avery was thrown by the question. "He's undecided, actually."

Higgins headed toward the World War II Memorial. Fifty-six granite pillars, seventeen feet tall, in a semi-circle with forty-three-foot triumphal arches on opposite sides. Two inconspicuous engravings of "Kilroy was here," a symbol of American soldiers whose presence protected where it was inscribed during World War II. On the west side of the memorial, etched into Freedom Wall, were over four thousand gold stars and the message, "Here we mark the price of freedom."

Higgins asked genuinely, "Would you vote for him?"

"If he chooses to run again, of course. No one has fought harder for this country."

"Hundreds of millions are invested in him, and yet he's lost the confidence of strategic allies, including his donors in Silicon Beach." Higgins paused, then turned toward Avery. "A scandal of any kind will cause the dam to break."

"You're the Washington whisperer," Avery bantered. "What can be done?"

"Several years ago, a governor sought my expertise to squelch a rumor within the halls of Congress regarding a supposed black ops initiative signed off by the President." Higgins kept her eyes on the World War II Memorial. "Before the rumor ignited a firestorm, I reminded the Speaker of the House of an encounter he'd kept hidden with an underage victim and the two hundred grand he'd paid out to make it all go away. Within an hour of our conversation, the rumor was debunked as baseless." Higgins smiled coyly. "In the end, it actually solidified the Speaker's position in Congress because he was seen as a leader willing to work with both sides. A twisted world we live in when you think about it." Higgins hesitated. "Have you heard of the Red Venture Group?"

"Never." Butterflies fluttered in Avery's stomach as she remembered Abbott's words. "What is it?"

"Depends on who you ask, I suppose. Better you don't know the particulars. What is important is the Red Venture Group has been disbanded. Hopefully, it will remain unwritten in the history books. However, the black ops initiative existed during the President's term, and was signed off without oversight. If it were exposed while he is in office or in the midst of a re-election campaign, it would bring him to his knees before the American people."

"If the Red Venture Group is what Abbott was going to expose, then we need to know whether he told anyone else before it goes nuclear."

"Avery, I won't let your brother fall on his sword." Higgins paused. "I'll reach out to my contacts on the social side to ensure if anything posts, they'll be able to censor the content immediately."

FIFTY-THREE

At the intersection of Pennsylvania Avenue and First Street, located on the Capitol grounds adjacent to the Reflection Pool, was Peace Circle. And in the center of the traffic roundabout was the Peace Monument, erected in 1878. Facing west, two classically robed sculptured female figures signified Grief, who held her covered face against the shoulder of History and wept in mourning. History held a tablet inscribed with the words: *They died that their country might live.*

Stopped in front of the Peace Monument, a black cargo van idled across from the Capitol. Behind the wheel, the PRC operative from Goose Bay was leaned backward. His lifeless eyes stared blankly out the front windshield at an empty street.

Beneath Grief and History was a third female figure, who represented Victory as she held a laurel wreath and carried an oak branch signifying strength. Below Victory were infants who captured Mars, the god of war, and Neptune, the god of the sea. Facing the Capitol was a final figure draped from the waist down holding an olive sprig—Peace.

From the cargo hold, Laney pressed her cheek against inch thick glass, attempting to gain a better vantage point. She'd woken minutes earlier free from the wooden coffin, which was gone. Nothing else was in the cargo hold. Separated by inch thick glass, she slammed her fists, unable to gain access to the cab. She struggled to keep her balance with barely enough strength to hold herself up. Sweat seeped through the stained grey sweatshirt and blue scrubs, the same clothes she'd worn seated across from Elena Vihkrov.

Throughout the ages, grief was the aftermath of humanity's battle against the endless epidemics of disease, poverty, injustice, and anarchy. While countries embraced a cancel-culture to erase the sins of history, nations warred against enemies and allies in the ultimate quest for supreme victory. An endless circle captured through soundbites of global leaders, senators, congressmen, governors, mayors, and anyone with a social megaphone whose rallying cry was their interpretation of peace—a definition which evolved depending on elusive criteria skewed to one's audience.

Laney's nostrils filled with a pungent odor of urine and vomit. With no sense of time or place, she tried desperately to catch her breath as her heart skipped every other beat.

When the engine revved, she braced herself as the memory of begging Elena to spare her life flashed in her mind. Suddenly, tires screeched, and the van lurched forward. She tumbled backward, slamming against the side of the van and rolling over several times. Once the van veered to the left and accelerated straight ahead, she managed to scramble back on her knees and returned to the glass window. Peering out the front windshield, she recognized Pennsylvania Avenue, only a few blocks away from the White House.

Panicked, she pounded on the window several more times before heading to the rear of the van. She tried to pull the latch down on the rear doors, but they were welded shut. Gasping for her next breath, her muscles blazed like an inferno. Instead of her heartbeat quickening, she felt it drastically slow, leaving her struggling to breathe. Scrambling back to the window, she groaned in agony as pain ripped through her insides. Tears dripped down her cheeks, mixing in with the sweat that drenched her body. Fear paralyzed her as she stared out the front windshield at red and blue flashing lights.

Crashing through a police barricade at the corner of Pennsylvania Avenue and 15th Street NW, the cargo van veered right and plowed into protestors near the South Lawn. Muffled screams faded as bullets pinged off the metal. Laney knew there was no way to control what was happening, so she braced herself. Several rounds punched through the metal and whizzed by her ear. A searing pain pulsed behind her eyes, leaving her vision blurred. At high speed, the van slammed into the round concrete barricades of the White House south entrance.

Gravity forced Laney's body airborne for several seconds before slamming hard against the floor of the cargo area. Barely conscious, she heard screaming and shouting outside followed by pounding on the windows of the cab in front. Curling up on the floor, the chaos faded with each gasp of air. Voices called out, but the words were muffled. A highlight reel of life didn't flash before her eyes. No loved ones reached out from the grave. Instead, a fog of peace in the midst of an endless war wrapped around her as she surrendered.

Beat. Beat. Beat. Silence.

A jolt of electricity slammed through her body. Her eyes bulged open as she snatched a massive breath, grabbing oxygen from the air. Electrical activity spread through the walls of the atria, forcing blood into the ventricles, steadying the rate and rhythm of her beating heart. She tried to lift her arm and realized she was strapped down with her wrists handcuffed to a gurney. Dazed, she turned her head and locked eyes on the smoke billowing from the van and paramedics removing someone from the driver's side before covering him on the concrete. Nearby a half dozen ambulances were lined up as police officers forced the massive crowd back so they could tend to those who'd been struck by the out-of-control van.

A paramedic leaned over and strapped an oxygen mask over Laney's mouth while another inserted a needle into her forearm. As one held up an IV bag of fluid, the other pushed the gurney toward a waiting ambulance.

She was numb, maybe more from the realization her nightmare was over than the drugs that flowed through her veins. Being handcuffed to the gurney was not a shock. She knew it was standard procedure. Once they realized who she was, she'd be set free. Her body was thrashed, more so than she realized. As the gurney was lifted into the back of the ambulance, the sedative eased the pain, but she knew the wounds would still be there when she woke.

The aftermath of a presumed terrorist attack left the streets in the surrounding area shut down as thousands of protestors were forced to abandon their cause. On a hotel rooftop two miles away, the Englishman worked the remote and guided the drone vehicle from Peace Circle until it crashed into the gates of the White House grounds. Finally, he was back on the hunt.

Weeks would pass before investigators found a pin-sized camera hidden alongside the radiator and realized what was built into the engine allowed the van to be controlled remotely.

But it would only take a matter of hours before the PRC operative and the missing FBI agent were identified. One would be labeled an enemy of state, and the other a hero.

Injuring or killing the innocent was collateral damage when waging war in search of peace. After all, history would agree they died so that freedom might live.

FIFTY-FOUR

KENILWORTH PARK—LATER

Near the border of D.C. and Maryland, less than a mile from the Washington Times headquarters, the park was surrounded by oak trees behind an apartment complex. Elena grasped General Abbott's briefcase as she walked a path between the buildings, which was secluded enough not to attract unwanted attention.

Breaking news had already reported an unidentified driver smashing through police barricades and running down protestors outside the gates of the White House. Cellphone footage was broadcasting on network channels and trending on social platforms. Shaky and grainy video captured a man being pulled from the driver's side of the van by law enforcement before being laid on the ground. Another clip showed paramedics covering the man with a sheet. And another bystander filmed paramedics performing CPR on a disheveled white woman strapped to a gurney. Amidst the chaos, a voice was heard shouting on video, "She's breathing."

Elena left the Englishman hours earlier and had monitored the trending story while she waited in a rental car before heading to the park. She found a bench facing the Anacostia

River and set the briefcase between them. Both women gazed on a starry night as a full moon lit the dark sky.

"My father sends his regards," Elena said.

"There were to be no survivors."

"We needed to send a message."

"You have made a grave mistake."

Elena nudged the briefcase over with one foot. "She will not survive."

"You don't know that for sure," the woman protested. "Don't play me for a fool."

"We understand what is at stake."

"The headlines will read: *Special Agent Laney Kelley Resurrects After Unexplained Disappearance.*" The woman pulled the briefcase close. "What will she say to the world when she wakes?"

"If she wakes, we have taken the necessary precautions." Elena harnessed her anger. "I am curious, what have you promised my father in return?"

"I've always admired his tenacity as a predator amongst his prey. Rarely have I encountered anyone as ruthless as Dmitry. Unfortunately, he has reached the end of his reign, a dinosaur on the verge of extinction. I offered him an opportunity to evolve, as we have all been forced to do."

"You underestimate him," Elena warned. *And you underestimate me.* "My father is king of the Bratva."

"He hid his intentions from you, then lied to your face." The woman shifted her weight and pointed her index finger toward Elena. "Blind loyalty is a sign of weakness."

"When the day arrives, he will offer his blessing, and I will inherit my rightful place."

The woman seemed undeterred. "You sailed the ocean blue,

while he betrayed you."

"You know my father better than me?" Elena retorted. "Blood loyalty *is* strength."

"The interesting thing about bullies in a sandbox..." She paused. "There is always someone bigger, badder, and more brutal waiting to step in."

"We will honor our agreement. However, if you betray us, there will be no mercy."

"Your words are hollow." The woman grabbed the brief-case. "Time is running out."

Elena remained seated as the woman stood and walked away. Her first instinct was to pounce and strangle the life out of her, but her father had warned against it. She'd recognized the fear in his eyes on Bell Island, which confirmed there was more she didn't know. Since she was young, her father had taught her animals with a loud bark were harmless until they sunk their teeth into your flesh. She'd threatened the woman, and yet as she stood and walked in the opposite direction, she couldn't help but sense the woman was the very predator her father had warned about.

She climbed into the rental car, realizing it was only a matter of time before Chase knew the traitor was alive. *Why did he leave without telling me? Why is he not answering my calls?* Before she asked herself even more questions, she already knew the answers. *After all we have been through, he would rather me believe he is dead than trust me to protect him from Papa.* She left the apartment complex and pulled out onto Quarles Street headed southeast to the Anacostia Freeway.

As she fought against the fracture within, she punched the accelerator and the rental car accelerated on the onramp, then cut across several lanes nearing an overpass. A split second later, a bullet pierced through the windshield and the car careened across traffic before plunging over the shoulder. After rolling multiple times, the rental landed in a ditch.

From the rear, a fire erupted, sending flames and thick smoke into the air. Hanging upside down, Elena was light-headed as blood oozed from a bullet that pierced her chest. She struggled to free herself as her body grew cold. Her mind flooded with a memory of herself at six years old, running across the grounds of Wicker Castle toward *the* tree.

Then in a blink, mother and daughter were reunited once more.

FIFTY-FIVE

OVER THE NORTH ATLANTIC

Shortly after takeoff, turbulence rocked the Gulfstream for ninety minutes as Chase, Dax, and Ammelie were buckled in tight. While the jet wrestled with the atmosphere, lightning flashed outside the oval windows. Chase eyed Ammelie until the pilot found a smoother route, then he unbuckled his seatbelt and switched seats. He glanced over her shoulder at a screen mapping their route to Nice as Dax disappeared into the cockpit.

"I'll tell you what I know, but you may not want to hear it."

Ammelie asked point-blank, "Where is Wolffie?"

"I don't know where he is, but I do know he's not who you believe him to be."

"We've been in each other's lives since we were children," she retorted.

"Dax and I were at the Dollar Farm when the explosion occurred. It wasn't an accident." He paused. "It was a drone strike."

"A drone strike?" Ammelie said in disbelief. "By who?"

"Maliki has solid evidence that points in one direction," Chase said solemnly.

"I don't understand what that has to do with Wolffie."

No turning back now. "He was the one who called in the coordinates."

"That's not possible." Teary-eyed, Ammelie held up her cell. "If he doesn't answer when I call, then I'm going straight to the authorities when we land."

"You're holding the proof." Chase reached out his hand. "Unlock your cell."

Ammelie reluctantly obliged, then handed over her cell. Chase scrolled through her call log and stopped on the number Maliki rattled off in the Penthouse. He flipped the cell around, so the screen was facing Ammelie and pointed.

"Do you recognize this number?"

A bit confused, she studied the digits and shook her head. "No."

"If you dial that number, the person who will answer is the Director of Russia's foreign intelligence." Chase allowed his words to sink in. "Wolffie's a Russian agent."

"There must be a mistake." Tears spilled over her eyelids. "I need to speak with him."

"I'm afraid that's not going to happen." Chase leaned forward, knowing if she dialed the number, then the Russians would have a tracker on their ass within seconds. He retrieved his burner cell from his pocket and set it on the armrest before hitting the speaker. He played back the recording and kept his gaze on Ammelie as she listened.

"Trade for information."

"Why is the SVR so interested in Ammelie?"

"Hiding her from Bernhardt was our way to keep him coopera-tive. Her safety allowed us to gain important intelligence from his captives. The intelligence and access to his prisoners kept the operation in play longer than anyone expected, and it has kept

Ammelie alive."

"Why'd you bomb the Dollar Farm?"

"We know who you are and what you've done. You are a threat."

Burying her face in the palms of her hands, Ammelie wept softly. Chase stopped the recording before it played what happened next. That would remain between him and Maliki. *Message delivered loud and clear.* He started to reach over but stopped, unsure of whether to console her or join Dax in the cockpit to give her space. *Whenever I've tried to get close, she backs away as if she's protecting herself from being hurt, again.* He was caught off guard by a sudden urge to tell her everything—beginning with the day he was recruited into the Red Venture Group.

"I'm the reason Maliki lost his son, and his family is broken," Chase confessed. "I'll have to live with that the rest of my life."

Lifting her head, tears rolled down her cheeks. "Is that why you are a *threat*?"

"One of many, I'm afraid." Chase's cell buzzed, but he ignored it. "Ammelie..."

Dax cleared his throat loudly. "Pilot needs you for a minute."

Chase's eyes flared before he realized the text was from Dax. Tapping the screen, he read the Washington Times headlines: *Democracy Under Attack.* He excused himself from Ammelie and stepped down the aisle until he was inches from Dax.

"You're not going to believe it," Dax whispered. "I'll keep an eye on her."

Chase entered the cockpit and slumped into a jump seat. Tapping on the link, he waited for the page to load. Scanning the first paragraph of the article, he caught the main gist of it. An unidentified driver crashed into protestors near the White House. He tapped on the embedded video, his nose whistling as his jaw clenched. Shaky cellphone footage captured a woman strapped to a gurney outside the White House gates. He blinked several times to be sure he wasn't imagining what was on the screen.

She's frail, but there's no doubt. Laney's alive.

Months of planning had gone into the covert operation searching for Ammelie Stroman, who had escaped the trauma of being Katarine Brandis. She was the leverage needed to bargain with Bernhardt in exchange for Laney's freedom. He rubbed his eyes in disbelief, and his gaze remained fixed on the screen. Stepping out from the cockpit, he returned to the seat across from Ammelie, stunned the rescue operation was abruptly over.

"All these years, you've been bait for the Russians to keep your father in their pocket. Wolffie was their way in as your protector. You said it yourself, you reunited with him several years after not seeing each other. That's plenty of time for him to be recruited." Chase caught sight of Dax's raised brows, knowing his brother in war knew where he was headed. "Now your father has seen you alive, which means you'll never be safe unless he is no longer an asset to the Kremlin." Chase weighed his next words with caution. "Katarine, it's time to stop running from the past once and for all."

"How..." Ammelie wiped tears from her eyes. "It's been many years since I have heard that name spoken aloud."

"You've asked me who I am...who we are?" Chase glanced at Dax, who was already nodding in agreement. "We're the ones who bury evil in the graveyards of sin."

Ammelie didn't respond at first, then whispered, "I need time to think."

"If you want to be free..." Chase checked the flight route, then his watch. "We'll need an answer before we land."

FIFTY-SIX

BELL ISLAND, NEWFOUNDLAND

A biting wind howled and rumbled against the house on Hiscoks Hill. A single light was visible around the back of the darkened house. Spread out on a dining room table were five cellphones, a laptop, and a Glock. Dmitry's empire was laid out in front of him. He paced back and forth, dialing each cellphone one at a time to reach his top lieutenants. There was no signal or connection. Then he tried going online using the laptop, but that was pointless. It wasn't unusual for dropped cell service or intermittent internet on the island, especially with the bitter weather.

Returning to Hiscoks Hill for a few days after so many years away left Dmitry reminiscing. The first visit to the island was with his bride, Olivia. From the streets of Dagestan to the nightclubs of London to the alleyways of major global hubs, the orphan who bloodied his fists to build an empire was now envied by those within the Bratva and beyond. It was in this very house where an ex-MI6 analyst and a Bratva enforcer schemed a path to wealth and power.

I never imagined returning to this place without Olivia by my side.

Walking through the bottom floor, he pondered his decision. He'd been offered an opportunity to evolve the Bratva beyond trafficking, drug dealing, money laundering, and prostitution. Billions were at stake. Without a doubt, those within the Bratva would bristle at his actions because they had their own kingdoms to protect. Those who opposed the Bratva, including the Triads, would pounce on an opportunity to take over what was left behind. Both alternatives left him open to retaliation.

The noose tightened. He'd lost Olivia to his enemies, and with tensions mounting within the Bratva decades later, he refused for his daughter to suffer the same fate.

Stepping into the living room, he wondered why Elena had not called after her meeting in Washington. He'd kept the truth about Chase being alive from her, but that was to protect her and the endgame. When she returned, he would take the time to explain his actions. Whether she believed him or not, it needed to be said if she was to use her Cambridge education and assume her role atop Globali Holdings.

Peering out the living room window, he noticed the Range Rovers parked on the street were gone. He pulled the blinds closed a bit more and moved back into the dining room. Realizing his security detail had disappeared, he grabbed the Glock from the table and turned off the light. Checking the back windows, it was clear the only escape was out the front door.

The wind howled, and the walls rumbled. Aiming the Glock with his index finger resting on the trigger, Dmitry ducked into a dark corner. He'd been hunted before, and still, the pounding in his chest intensified. *Fear shovels the grave.* Stepping gingerly from the dining room through the kitchen into the living room, Dmitry kept his sights on the front door.

In a blink, a shadow appeared out of nowhere. Dmitry reacted by firing his weapon. The shadow disappeared. At first, he thought it was an illusion. Maybe his mind was playing tricks. Then from behind, a forearm wrapped around his throat. Instinctively, he fired the Glock again, but as the pressure increased around his trachea, he was left losing consciousness. Bright stars hovered as his muscles weakened. Flailing his arms, desperate to grab hold of his attacker, he barely heard the Glock thud against the floor.

The Englishman's voice whispered, "She didn't suffer, Mr. Vihkrov."

When Dmitry regained consciousness, he was facedown on the grass. Blinking several times, he realized he was no longer inside the house. Pulling himself to his knees, the blistering wind nearly knocked him over. Forcing himself onto his feet, he locked eyes on the shadow in front of him then glanced behind at the cliff's edge. Before he spoke, a boot slammed into his chest, sending him stumbling backward. He tried to regain his footing, but there was not enough earth left beneath his feet.

Before slamming into the rocks two hundred feet below, Dmitry swore eternal fire from the gates of Hell as vengeance against the king of the night and the Judas in D.C.

FIFTY-SEVEN

BETHESDA, MARYLAND

Along the eight-mile stretch from the White House to Walter Reed AMC, blue lights flashed along a route mapped out by the Secret Service. The unplanned order from President Bouchard was given only hours before the State of the Union.

Blacked-out windowed SUVs drove in the lead and rear of the Beast—a heavy-duty chassis rolling fortress with five-inch-thick bulletproof windows. Equipped with Kevlar-reinforced run-flats, gas cannons, and night-vision cameras, the military-grade armored vehicle weighed an estimated 20,000 pounds.

The Beast rolled across Bethesda with Walter Reed in the distance. Since the early forties, the prominent medical center in the U.S. had served presidents from one administration to another. One of the most notable occurrences within its walls was the Kennedy autopsy.

Bouchard thought about this as he gazed out the bulletproof window. Kennedy's life was an inspiration to him at an early age, and even more so now that he was Commander in Chief. He better understood the man who hid his sins for the greater good. Since Kennedy's assassination, it seemed the fight for freedom had remained an endless battle.

Earlier in the evening, Bouchard watched from the residence of the White House as protestors chanted, waved signs, and held up bright glowing red umbrellas in a sign of solidarity with Hong Kongers who were struggling to keep their autonomy. The message was to stop the People's Republic of China from its reign of aggression against anyone who opposed them. Bouchard was front and center as the most powerful leader in the world, and the time had arrived when he needed to make his stance policy.

Is it right for the U.S. to remain the world's law enforcement? Whose freedoms am I sworn to uphold and protect?

America First was a mantra hated by half the country. While all men were created equal, the nation had never been more divisive. Equality was in the eye of the beholder. And no matter what choice he made, there would be more protests marching for social justice, cancel culture, and the countless challenges facing the planet.

Never let a good crisis go to waste.

Bouchard exhaled deep in an attempt to rid himself of the responsibility. In a matter of hours, the world would tune in to hear his State of the Union. A speech many believed would define his presidency and set the course for his re-election campaign.

Am I ready to go through all of it again?

During his first term, he was a maverick who confronted both parties. For a while, it was enough to keep the American people rallying on his side. Since the attack on Los Angeles and the media's anticipation of General Abbott's testimony before the Intel Committee, he had lost the confidence of those on Wall Street *and* Main Street.

No time to reminisce.

Anarchists waged a civil war. Politicians fought to keep their constituents on their side at the ballot box. People around the globe who faced an uncertain future begged for America's intervention. And the Deep State, whoever they were, lingered in the swamp ready to drown his presidency. He thought of General Abbott's secrets buried in the grave, which left him searching for a ghost who might bring down the castle.

Kennedy united a country. His assassination altered history.

"Do we know how the hell he got through the barricades?" Bouchard asked.

"With the protestors spread out, the area was not yet secured." Albert Skinner, director of Homeland Security, was seated beside Bouchard. "We have identified the driver as Tao Weimin. Intel confirms he was a decorated military operative for the PRC. We believe he was instrumental in placing dozens of other operatives within the tech and pharmaceutical industries to steal intellectual property and trade secrets. While we had him on our radar, we were never able to catch him in the act. We're still confirming the exact cause of death."

"Why do something so reckless? No way the PRC green-lighted it."

"We're working on that answer, Mr. President."

"You're sure it's her?"

"Fingerprints match."

The Beast pulled up to the rear entrance at Walter Reed. Bouchard's thoughts returned to a wish that Nadia and the kids were still alive. *Nadia would know how to advise me. She never lied to me, loved me with my flaws, and her insight is still the missing piece of my presidency.* For so long, he'd repeated that wish to himself, but each time it fell deeper into an abyss of hopelessness. He'd lost the life he dreamed of living and instead found himself the most powerful man in the free world.

As the door opened, Avery stood waiting. Bouchard climbed out and slipped on a PPE mask with the Presidential Seal stitched on one side. Shadowed by his Secret Service detail, he followed Avery down a long white-walled corridor with Skinner a few steps behind.

"She's in a private room," Avery said in a lowered voice. "Doesn't look good."

"Al said there were fourteen others injured. Two dead."

"Six of the fourteen are in critical condition. Law enforcement. Paramedics. Protestors." Avery glanced over her shoulder. "Nothing more on General Abbott, but I'm working on it."

"Mr. President," Skinner's voice interrupted. "A moment, please."

Bouchard turned and recognized the look on Skinner's face. "What is it, Al?"

Skinner held up his cellphone. "Agents on the ground near Kenilworth confirmed the identity of a deceased gunshot victim as Elena Vihkrov. She was found along the south side of the Anacostia Freeway. It appears to be a single round penetrated the windshield of a rental car, striking her in the upper chest. To be clear, this was not one of our operations, Mr. President."

"Do we have a location on Dmitry Vihkrov?"

"At this time, we don't believe he is within our borders."

"When he gets word, he'll retaliate." Bouchard paused. "For now..."

"She's a Jane Doe," Skinner agreed.

Dr. Bradford, the President's physician, met them in the corridor and ushered Bouchard and Avery through a secured door into a private wing, leaving Skinner behind. Footsteps echoed off the tiled floors as they passed one empty room after another. At the end of the hallway, two Secret Service agents from Bouchard's detail guarded the only occupied room.

"She's been in a coma since she arrived," Dr. Bradford said matter of fact. "We're running tests to determine why her organs are failing. Right now, the ventilator is her lifeline."

From behind his mask, Bouchard replied, "You need to keep her alive."

FIFTY-EIGHT

Avery waited in the hallway while her brother opened the door and entered the room alone. As the door closed, she breathed in the antiseptic and took in her surroundings. Walls, floors, and glass were spotless. No dirt. No grime. No dust. No germs. It was as sterile a place as she'd ever seen. But step outside the solitary secured wing, and one was exposed to it all.

Her mind shifted to news of the Bratva King's assassinated daughter. Shaking off the old habits of a daydreaming ghostwriter, she forced the Hollywood plots back into the treasure chest of creativity. She knew her brother would adamantly order a visit to Walter Reed once he knew it was Special Agent Laney Kelley. Nothing else he valued more than loyalty to family, friends, and fellow patriots. With tubes shoved down her throat, Agent Kelley had earned a high degree of respect. Witnessing the respect shown by her brother, Avery second-guessed the deal she struck with Louise Higgins.

You're now baptized in the swamp.

She remembered the night in an emergency room alongside David. Hours earlier off the coast of Monterey, her sister-in-law, Nadia, and nephew, Ryan, were brought ashore in body bags. Avery grit her teeth as a wave of memories washed over her. Torment was too simple a word to explain the aftermath of that day. Death was complicated, infuriating, and relentless.

Merciful on those who have passed. Merciless on those of us left behind.

In the emergency room, she stood beside her brother. A deep ache tore through her as she gazed upon her niece, Sadie, hooked up to a ventilator. As machines pumped oxygen and morphine into her frail body, her soul was already gone. Nothing prepares a parent for the moment when they are forced to choose to end their child's life on this side.

From that day, penance was Avery's expression of remorse. She'd been drinking from a sports bottle mixed with vodka and orange juice, and yet she begged Nadia to let her drive the boat on open waters. Slamming into the waves was a rush until she lost control, and the boat capsized. Flotation vests didn't protect them from the impact of the crash.

A day on the ocean with family turned into unspeakable devastation.

Avery was in a daze when she was rescued and brought ashore. David and Pop waited alongside the press and authorities, who were eager to get to the truth. It was David who shielded her from being exposed and from prosecution.

The hum of a ventilator brought her back to the present. Staring at her brother, she watched as he stood silent next to Agent Kelley's bed. From the other side of the window, she noticed he had grasped Kelley's hand. *Keep her alive.* It wasn't the words. It was the sorrow in his eyes. That's what struck Avery as a chill shot down her spine.

A voice echoed off the walls. "The President needs to get out of there, now!"

Spinning around at the same time as both secret service agents, all three were in a defensive stance. A group of doctors, including Dr. Bradford, sprinted toward them, pulling on PPE gear without losing stride. Avery turned back to David, who still held Kelley's hand. He looked up at Avery with a peaceful gaze. Then his eyes rolled back, and his body collapsed to the floor.

Grabbing the door latch, Avery yelled at the agents. "Help him."

"Stay where you are," Dr. Bradford called out. "Do not enter."

"Hollywood is down," one of the agents relayed into his coms. "Hollywood is down."

The doctors reached them before Avery had a chance to open the door. Dr. Bradford nudged her aside and asked urgently, "Did any of you go inside that room?" When all three shook their heads, he added, "We need to quarantine immediately."

At the word *quarantine*, Avery demanded, "Get my brother out of there."

"We can't help him until you're clear of this area."

"Not happening," one of the agents retorted. "Eyes on POTUS at all times."

"I'm not leaving either." Avery pushed Dr. Bradford, who didn't budge an inch. More secret service agents appeared in the hallway. She found herself standing between the agents and doctors with both sides ready to go in. Pointing to her brother's closest agent, she said, "Hank stays, the rest of us will go."

Hank nodded. "He won't leave my sight, ma'am."

Avery squared off with Dr. Bradford. "That's the best you'll get."

"Put this on," Dr. Bradford said as he handed Hank an extra hazmat suit, gloves, and a shielded helmet. "Do exactly as we tell you."

Avery moved quickly alongside the other agents in the opposite direction, knowing the doctors were waiting valuable seconds until they were on the other side. Fear struck as she burst through the security doors into a hallway that was in the fray of being locked down. Avery pressed her cheek against the small square glass panel on the door with only one thought racing through her mind.

"Keep him alive."

FIFTY-NINE

NICE, FRANCE

Beneath an overcast sky, the Gulfstream's final approach piloted along the southeast coast of France. During the flight, Chase searched for more than the grainy footage of Laney's unexpected reappearance in D.C. Nothing trended on social. No media named her publicly. No government official had confirmed her identity. After disappearing nine months earlier, the response so far when one of their own resurfaced was mute.

He noticed there were fewer posts online than he'd expected about what occurred outside the gates of the White House. Reports of the bullet-ridden van that drove into protestors before crashing into the south gate of the White House were interrupted by breaking news. The State of the Union to be delivered by President Bouchard had suddenly been postponed. Cable news was on fire with conspiracy theories, conjecture, and innuendo, but as the hours passed, it seemed the footage that proved Laney was alive had disappeared from all channels.

Chase turned off the tablet and slipped it into his backpack. His fingers touched the coin in his pocket. Out of the corner of his eye, he watched Ammelie staring out the window. Four months aboard the *Midnight Moon* searching for Katarine Brandis resulted in one of The Elite narrowing the search to Sierra Leone. *Thank you, Leonzio.* Before blowing up the *Midnight Moon*, Chase contacted Jafari with the name Ammelie Stroman, and Operation *Honey Trap* was in full motion.

What troubled Chase was finding Omar Youssef's location on Adams' thumb drive. In Mosul and Baghdad, when they hunted the Prodigal, Omar was the one who bragged about his connections which included the elusive Bernhardt Brandis. Knowing Omar had placed himself miles from Brandis' daughter was beyond disturbing. Thinking through what it meant, he concluded Omar was playing the same game as the Russians.

Keep her close, and you have Brandis in the palm of your hand.

Wheels screeched against the runway at Cote D' Azur airport. The Gulfstream taxied across the tarmac, passing the spaceship-designed glass-windowed passenger terminal. Reaching the private area, the pilot shut down the Rolls Royce engines, and the cabin lights blinked on. Dax unbuckled his seatbelt, then gathered his backpack and gear. Chase remained seated with his eyes fixed on Ammelie.

She turned her attention to him. "How did you find me?"

"One of the people you saw in Milan helped narrow down the search," Chase admitted. "Sierra Leone was all we knew before Jafari was able to track you down."

"Do you work for the American government?"

"We don't work for anyone. Dax and I are caught in a web, just like you."

"You invited me to Milan, knowing my father would be there." Ammelie shifted uncomfortably. "So, nothing between us is real. I cannot trust you, Chase."

"Wolffie is the one who watched over you for the Russians as leverage against your father," Chase pointed out. "Which means your father has known you are alive the entire time. Now he's seen you face to face. He'll hunt you, Ammelie. And don't think for a minute when the Kremlin finds out Wolffie's exposed that they'll forget about you."

Dax headed for the cabin door as the pilot unlatched the lever, then stepped out.

"I have never taken a life," she said in a solemn voice. "Can the same be said of you?"

"Wolffie's fate is out of my hands. But yours..."

Dax's voice called out. "Chase, trouble on the Riviera."

Chase left Ammelie in her seat and headed down the aisle. He reached the cabin door and peered down. At the bottom of the steps stood an elderly man dressed in a dark suit and overcoat in front of a black Mercedes. Chase stepped down onto the tarmac.

"Finally, our journeys have crossed, Mr. Hardeman," the elderly man said.

"You know who I am," Chase replied, frankly. "And you are?"

"Nathaniel Fineberg, director of Tzaekah." The elderly man peered over dark-rimmed glasses as the chilly night grew a few degrees colder. "I have been watching you since before London."

Dax joined them and barged through the politeness. "What the hell is Tzadekah?"

"We've been watching you as well, Dexter."

"Name is Dax." He spoke louder in case the old man was hard of hearing. "D.A.X."

Chase held up his hand to keep Dax from picking a fight with a senior citizen and possibly facing the embarrassment of getting his ass kicked. *Tzadekah*. Chase didn't remember hearing that name before, but whoever this man was, he knew enough about them to be waiting when they landed.

"Mr. Fineberg, what is it you want from us?" Chase asked.

"I represent an organization of individuals who believe a righteous life is committed to acts of goodwill." Fineberg tugged at this overcoat to cover the belly bulge that hung over his belt. "All be it, our acts of goodwill take on a rather darker tone. I believe we share that in common, wouldn't you agree?"

"I'm afraid you have us confused with someone else," Chase answered.

"Jeric Salem. Najee Azad. Misfirah Jama. Aisha Abed. Raiha Sultana. Marid Abu. Sameer Alli. Karim Salik. Samara Nasir. Akram Kasim. *And* the Prodigal." Fineberg removed a hankie from his overcoat and blew his nose. "An impressive resume has garnered an invitation for you both to join us."

"Sounds like a pyramid scheme," Dax blurted. "I'll pass."

"We share common enemies and interests," Fineberg countered. "Our allegiance is not to a country, a government, or a leader. And, we happen to share a mutual interest in Bernhardt Brandis."

"What's your interest in him?" Chase asked, a bit more intrigued.

"We believe the Bratva are on the verge of a regime change, one orchestrated from within Washington. Our intelligence suggests Brandis is involved and has aspirations to be crowned king of the Bratva."

"Dmitry will never allow that to happen, and neither will

Elena."

"The Bratva, Vihkrovs, and Brandis are mice in the jungle." Fineberg's spidery brows furrowed. "We are hunting the lions who lurk in the grass."

"Mr. Fineberg, we appreciate the invitation, but we operate better alone."

Chase noticed Fineberg glance past them toward the interior of the Gulfstream. When Ammelie appeared in the entryway, he watched Fineberg's expression shift as deep ridges appeared on his forehead. He barely heard the elderly man's voice as he whispered in Hebrew.

"Child."

SIXTY

Vice President Bridget Jacobs placed her palm on the George Washington Inaugural Bible held by Chief Justice of the Supreme Court. "I do solemnly swear I will faithfully execute the Office of President of the United States and will to the best of my ability, preserve, protect, and defend the Constitution of the United States."

With the backdrop being two 747's in the Air Force One hangar, Acting President Jacobs had landed ten minutes earlier from a fundraising trip to California. Avery waited off to the side until the acting president's own chief of staff stepped away.

"Avery, I'm so sorry." Jacobs embraced her. "What are the doctors saying?"

"He's in a coma. The virus is attacking his internal organs. Kidneys are functioning at twenty percent. Lungs are deteriorating rapidly. His gestational diabetes has made the virus extremely aggressive. Right now, a ventilator is all that's keeping him alive."

"He's a fighter. Never met anyone tougher than him."

Avery wiped tears from her eyes and tried to compose herself. "Tests have determined the virus is a mutated strain

305

of Covid, but initial results are hinting it's synthetic."

"If that turns out to be true, the PRC has declared war."

Behind Avery and Jacobs, a small crew began setting up a microphone and podium with the presidential seal on the front. A few feet away, a single camera was secured to a tripod.

"I've been told there are others from the protests who are infected, including several officers and paramedics." Jacobs' brows furrowed. "How could the PRC know Tao Weimin would cross paths with your brother?"

"Agent Kelley was on the ground during the attack in Los Angeles. She disappeared nine months ago. Then she reappeared outside the gates. Doctors confirmed she's infected with the same virus." Avery's voice quavered. "Bridget..."

"David will pull through." Jacobs grabbed her by the shoulders. "If you're up for it, I need your help to address the nation. We can't keep the press locked out much longer. I'm going live as soon as possible."

"Whatever you need, I'm here."

"Keep it short and to the point."

As military and intel officials hovered, Avery stepped away and found a spot in the hangar where she started working on her tablet. She stopped every so often and listened to the conversations between Jacobs and the experts. Decisions made within the hour would alter U.S. policy, relationships with allies, and a brewing tornado with the PRC.

Separate emotion. Stick to the facts, Avery.

She tried to keep the tone steady, but as the words evolved, anger seeped into the message. And when breaking news escalated, the tense situation turned razor-sharp.

First, cellphone video shot from a Houston apartment overlooking the Chinese Consulate-General showed what looked to be fires burning in the courtyard. Second, BBC broke the news that China had expanded Hong Kong's National Security Law in the late-night hours to broaden Beijing's wide-reaching power to prosecute and punish. *One document erodes Hong Kong's democratic and political autonomy.* Bypassing Hong Kong's elected legislative council, the stringent law established its own law enforcement presence in Hong Kong, as well as empowering a secretive national security committee.

One country, two systems is dead.

Avery thought about the State of the Union she'd written. She knew firsthand the message her brother planned to deliver, but she needed to condense it down. Proofing the words one last time, she approached the acting president, handed over her tablet, then waited in anticipation.

"You've captured David's voice," Jacobs said under her breath. "Definitely provoking."

"Fire across the bow, Madam President."

Jacobs turned to her chief of staff. "I'm ready."

While the military and intel officials gathered on one side, Jacobs checked her pantsuit and pulled a strand of hair over her ear. David Bouchard had selected her because of her appeal to the flyover states and her bullish commitment to push his agenda through. Most Vice Presidents were seen on the campaign trail, then invisible during a president's term. But Jacobs' Texas roots engrained in pride, stubbornness, charm, and bootstrapped resilience proved a perfect counterbalance to the east coast tactics of Simon Adams.

Joining the group of staffers, military, and intel officials, Avery questioned if the acting president was ready to step into David's shoes. Then she recognized the steely glare in

Jacobs' eyes as she stepped behind the podium and focused on the camera.

Three. Two. One.

"I come to you from Joint Base Andrews after being sworn in as acting president." Jacobs kept a somber yet deliberate tone. "Yesterday, we witnessed a calculated attack on our democracy. While most have seen reports of the terrorist attack near the south entrance of the White House, what has been uncovered by our intelligence community in the hours since will enrage every American."

Jacobs paused exactly where Avery noted.

"We have confirmed the identity of the man behind the wheel of the van as Tao Weimin, a decorated military oper-ative of the People's Republic of China. His presence within our borders as an asset of the China government has resulted in an assassination attempt against President Bouchard. As I stand here, the man you elected into office, my dear friend, is fighting for his life."

As scripted, Avery approached and joined the president-elect behind the podium, knowing the nation was watching in real-time.

Jacobs wrapped her arm around Avery and gazed into her eyes for a long moment, then spoke loud enough for the microphone to pick it up. "An entire nation and the world is praying for your brother." Then she turned back to the camera as Avery stepped aside, still in frame of the lens. "Within the last hour, we have seen China's blatant disregard for their actions. Even now, the Chinese Consulate-General in Houston is burning documents, and we are witnessing the dismantling of Hong Kong right before our eyes. Our nation's approach to China's continued threats and aggression against freedom and sovereignty has been measured diplomacy. But diplomacy is no longer enough."

Jacobs grabbed the podium and fortified herself.

"As the acting president, I have sworn an oath to every citizen of this great country to go to the ends of the earth to protect against any adversary who declares war on our soil. We are not looking for a fight, yet we face a moment in history where we must once again prove our resolve. From the day President Bouchard stepped into office, this has been his message, and I intend to keep his promises. The People's Republic of China's actions will be met with a measured and decisive response, beginning with an executive order to close designated Chinese embassies and consulate-generals across the country effective immediately. Our message to China is clear, an attack on one American is an attack on us all."

SIXTY-ONE

MONTE-CARLO, MONACO

The convertible Rolls Royce cruised Avenue de Monte-Carlo on a perfect sunny afternoon. An exclusive fairytale paradise on the French Riviera, nestled between France and Italy with the picturesque Alps as a backdrop. The second smallest sovereign state in the world, after the Vatican, was known by the locals as "the Rock." A waterfront city regarded as the premier destination of privilege and indulgence. Five-star luxury hotels. An iconic casino. Private jets. Chartered yachts. Stunning supercars rumbled through the streets. It was an international hotspot where real-world problems were left behind.

"Does that occur often?" Ammelie asked.

"Getting propositioned to join a secret league?" Chase paused. "Only one other time."

"I wonder what Tzadekah means," Dax said.

"*Righteousness* in Hebrew," Ammelie replied. "A spontaneous act of goodwill."

"How'd you know that one?"

"Studied religion as part of the orientation process for the Hope House."

"Should've called it the mousetrap or the lion slayer." Dax

raised his arms and stretched them out as if he were on top of a rollercoaster about to fly straight down. "One thing is for sure, this city is definitely righteous."

"You two have been here before?"

"A few times," Chase answered. "We auctioned a Mongolian dinosaur skull once."

"Seriously," Ammelie laughed. "A real one?"

"As real as an extinct dinosaur can be," Dax bantered. "Sucker was massive."

"A fossil smuggler was on the run from Interpol and brought it to Monaco to unload it. We were here with my dad closing a deal for a collection of Bugattis. Got lucky and sold the skull for $4 million."

"Then we played Texas Hold'Em until dawn with the buyer," Dax added. "Interpol caught the smuggler when he tried to steal a yacht from the dock."

"We got stiffed on our commission." Chase slowed the Rolls Royce and pulled into the Hotel de Paris Monte-Carlo next to a valet. "I'll be right back."

"The smuggler was the *real* fossil." Dax chuckled at his own dark humor. "One day, someone might dig him up."

Entering the lobby, Chase smirked at Dax's bluntness in the midst of the situation. Most of the time, his words ended with a foot in his mouth or a boot in his ass. *There's no one else I'd go into battle with, and that'll never change.* Again, he felt the coin in his front pocket, paranoid that it might disappear. A key he'd carried since that night in Omar's house, the night he'd crossed the line. He tried to stay focused on the prize, but there was no stopping the flashes that flickered in his mind.

Is there anything righteous about ending a life?

311

A bright ray of light shone down through a domed glass ceiling sparkling off a teardrop chandelier. Marble floors reflected the sunlight across the lobby, offering a magical touch to the textured white walls and smooth arches of the classic European architecture. The lobby bustled with business and pleasure. Europeans. Americans. Asians. Brits. Indians. Africans. A virtual melting pot of the human race— the elite race. Discrimination in Monaco wasn't about skin color, it was about the size of one's fortune.

Chase cut between a long row of matching sofas, crossing over an oval carpet of equal size to the dome above. He approached the front desk, well aware of his surroundings. *A normal day in paradise.* No one seemed the least bit concerned about the unfolding tensions between the U.S. and China.

Shortly after landing and leaving Fineberg standing on the tarmac, the news pinged on his burner cell of what transpired in Washington over the previous 24-hours. He listened to Acting President Jacobs deliver a scathing and condemning threat to the Chinese, struck with a feeling that something wasn't right.

If Bouchard is fighting for his life, who else knows we're hunting Brandis?

His fingers tapped against a marble countertop as he thought of the only time he'd been in Bouchard's presence aboard Air Force One on the runway at Los Angeles International Airport. Bouchard had backed him into a corner, one where there was no escape. *Chase, you are my boots on the ground...I'm giving you a second chance.* While he never trusted Bouchard, there was no denying the most powerful man in the free world. In the days since Simon Adams was killed and with Laney reappearing, he wondered again why Bouchard wanted Brandis alive.

Did Bouchard know the Chinese were coming for him?

As the question lingered, Chase weighed the reasons for being in Monaco. He was there to unleash justice for Ammelie— and retribution for whatever Laney endured.

Brandis doesn't seem like someone who goes gently on his captives. What does he know that's got Bouchard so adamant about his capture? Maybe that's why Fineberg approached us. The old man knows the dangers and pitfalls better than we do. Ammelie still hasn't given an answer, but that's not going to stop us from doing what must be done.

A young woman stepped over wearing a Hotel de Paris uniform. "May I help you?"

He removed the coin from his pocket and slid it across the marble. "Chase Hardeman."

"Mr. Hardeman." She punched the keys on the screen. "I am afraid I do not see you as a guest in our system. Are you checking in?"

Chase shook his head. "I believe someone left something for me."

The woman checked behind the desk, asked a co-worker, then turned back to Chase, a bit confused. "I am afraid nothing has been left for you."

He retrieved the coin from the counter and stepped away. *I guess it's not a Bond movie.* He surveyed the lobby, searching for anyone out of place. At first, no one blipped on his radar. Then he noticed a bellhop wheeling a cart filled with Brunello Cucinelli luggage. His eyes were locked on Chase as he wheeled the cart next to him before slipping a keycard from his pocket. With a sleight of hand, Chase seamlessly exchanged the coin for the keycard.

On one side of the keycard was the Le Grill Terrace emblem, and on the other side, a number. Chase walked briskly through the lobby, noticing two stocky men moving at the same pace. He texted on his cell before entering a stairwell: CUSTARD. Bounding up two steps at a time, he heard the footsteps behind. Reaching the top floor, he stepped out onto a panoramic view of the Mediterranean. Entering the Le Grill Terrace restaurant, he weaved his way around the waiters and guests. Glancing over his shoulder, the two men were closing in. He reached the glass door to a private room and swiped the keycard.

Slipping into the coppered ceiling room with its emerald floor, he was surrounded by a continuous wall of glass displaying the most expensive wines in the world. In the center of the room, an ancient tree trunk was the base of a titanium topped table. He checked the number and searched for a match with one of the wine bottles. When he didn't find a match, he knew he'd been lured into a dead end.

No invite to the party, Bernhardt?

Spinning around, he peered between the bottles through the glass to see the two men raising semi-automatic weapons. Chase dove beneath the table as glass shattered and bottles exploded. Outside of the room, screams shrieked and panic erupted. Shards of glass rained down, slicing into his arm. Ducking behind the tree trunk, he braced himself for the two men to breach. Grabbing his SIG from behind his back, he tucked it against his chest. More rounds punched into the trunk while others whizzed past his ears. A few seconds later, the gunfire stopped.

Reloading.

Blood dripped down his arm and smeared against the floor

beneath his boots. He fired several rounds in an attempt to keep them on defense. Crawling toward an opening in the shattered glass wall, he was halfway out when more bullets ricocheted around him. One slug hit him in the shoulder. Another pierced his upper thigh. Grimacing in agony, the adrenaline surged through his veins. *Move or die.* Scrambling out in the open, he slid on his knees behind a marble statue. Blood seeped through his shirt and pants. A crimson stain left a trail on the marble floor. Peering around the side of the statue, he saw bodies scattered and terrified guests in tears crouched beneath tables.

Jump six stories or empty your mag.

In an attempt to hold them off a few more seconds, he fired until there were no bullets left. Closing his eyes, he surrendered. *It'll be over soon. Death is a welcomed escape from my sins.* His breathing was labored. His body shivered from shock as he heard muffled voices amidst the wailing and screams. His instincts were triggered at the distinct sound of a SIG. Peering around the side of the statue, he watched Dax flank the attackers, firing until they were both down.

Dax knelt beside him and immediately checked the gunshot wounds.

"Shoulder is through and through," he said calmly. "Can you walk?"

"Won't beat Usain Bolt in a hundred yards, but I'm not staying here to bleed out."

Grabbing Chase under his good shoulder, Dax pulled him to his feet. Guests reappeared from their hiding places, stunned. Chase leaned against Dax as he limped out of the restaurant, grabbing a stack of white cloth napkins along the way. Reaching the stairwell, he gritted his teeth and pushed through the pain one step at a time. He stopped for a few seconds as Dax ripped the napkins into strips and helped tourniquet his leg and bandage his arms. Chase kept pressure on his shoulder to slow the blood loss. Reaching the bottom floor, an alarm blared as they joined hundreds of guests who poured through the main lobby onto the streets.

Real-world problems had struck mayhem in the hearts of the elite.

Sirens wailing in the distance grew louder as they turned the corner. Ammelie was behind the wheel of the Rolls Royce. Dax jumped over the side into the backseat as Chase slumped in the front passenger seat, barely conscious. He ripped fresh strips from the napkins, tied a tighter tourniquet around his leg, and grimaced as he forced more pressure against his shoulder.

Wide-eyed, Ammelie punched the accelerator, and the Rolls Royce lunged forward. Tires screeched as she narrowly missed side-swiping a Lamborghini before being swallowed up by traffic headed away from the hotel.

SIXTY-TWO

PORT HERCULES—LATER

At the end of Jetée Lucciano, the iconic Stars and Stripes flew from the stern of a $40 million 165 foot mega yacht. Docked at the deep-water port, substantial enough to provide anchorage for hundreds of vessels, the jet matte black and metallic silvered *Winning Bid* encompassed a bold sleekness. A crew of three waited on the dock. Captain. First Officer. A medic turned chef. Handpicked by Chase and vetted by Dax. All were ex-military who traded endless wars for the more lucrative private sector. After Milan, he requested the maiden voyage bring the *Winning Bid* to Monaco, where the crew had waited since.

Chase grew weaker as Dax and Ammelie helped him down the dock, keeping him wedged between them. During the day, the port was less congested, as most were in the city. It was after dark that Port Hercules roared to life. Once the crew realized their employer was in trouble, they sprang into action. Chase was brought aboard and taken directly below deck to a custom-designed state-of-the-art mobile medical room. Dax and the first officer raced to the abandoned Rolls to grab all of their luggage.

Leaning back against the bed, Chase felt the prick of a

needle in his arm. As the pain eased, he opened his eyes and glanced around the room, impressed by the advanced tech built into every inch of the space. He didn't know what any of it did. But he'd paid a steep price to ensure all of it provided the best chance to survive.

With the IV started, the medic turned his attention to the bullet wounds. He peeled back the bloodied tourniquets from Chase's shoulder and leg. He methodically cut off the shirt and pants, leaving Chase wearing only his boxers. Ammelie stood quietly as the medic waved a portable scanner over Chase's body. A flatscreen captured a 3-D visual of his internal organs and skeletal structure, confirming the bullet entered and exited his shoulder with no visible fragments left inside. Dax reappeared in the doorway as the medic injected a sedative then went straight to work with a scalpel.

"Whoa," he said in a lowered voice. "I think I'm gonna puke."

Chase glared at Dax, then turned his face so he didn't see the blade slice into the wound on his leg. With precision, the medic retrieved the compressed slug.

"You were lucky, sir." The medic grabbed a needle. "I'll stitch you up, and after a few drinks, you'll be ready to win big at the roulette wheel."

As the morphine flowed, Chase lifted his head and mumbled, "Girolata."

The captain motioned to his first officer. "Topside."

"Dax, you need to clean up the mess."

"I'll make the call," Dax replied. "You good?"

"Yeah, never better." *Actually, I've never felt worse.*

After the medic stitched up the wounds, a peripheral intravenous catheter was hooked up to administer AB-negative blood. Chase knew he'd left a trail from Hotel de Paris to Port Hercules, including the bloody interior of the Rolls Royce. He also knew Dax would make a call to a trusted cleaner of their own in Monte-Carlo, and all the evidence would disappear. Once Chase's vitals were stable, the medic excused himself.

"You'd get the checkered flag in the Grand Prix," Chase said as his body relaxed.

"I don't even have a driver's license." Ammelie offered a halfhearted smile. "You nearly died."

Chase pointed at the heart monitor. "Still kicking."

"Excuse me." Ammelie wiped her eyes as she glanced away from the scars that crisscrossed Chase's chest. "Our worlds are not the same. I don't know how..."

"You never get used to it." Chase heard the engines rumble and felt the vessel reverse. "You only hope you survive to fight another day."

"Why would he try to kill you now? I am with you. Isn't that what he wants?"

"In Milan, he was willing to make the trade." Chase grabbed his burner cell from a metal table lined with scalpels. He watched Ammelie closely as he played the video of Laney outside the White House gates. "Your father believes he's lost his edge to get you back. But if he kills me, there'll be no one left to protect you."

Ammelie stared at the screen. "Who is she?"

His eyes grew heavy as he answered, "The past."

Across the seas on the opposite side of the world, troops assembled along the border of Mainland China and Hong Kong. Acting President Jacobs delivered a stern message to the PRC. In solidarity, the streets of Hong Kong overflowed with millions who marched in protest against China's controversial security laws, denials, accusations, and claims the assassination attempt of President Bouchard was American propaganda. Thousands of American flags waved across Hong Kong Island and Kowloon as a symbol of unified freedom.

As Chase dozed off to the steady beeping of the heart monitor, the *Winning Bid* cleared the Bay of Cannes, entered open waters of the Ligurian, and sailed south toward the Gulf of Girolata.

SIXTY-THREE

BETHESDA | THURMONT, MARYLAND

Lost amongst the acreage of vines, she dropped to her knees and sobbed. She'd been lost for hours wandering in the summer heat. At six years old, the family vineyard was a world unto its own. Blue skies dissolved into vibrant hues of orange, violet, and crimson. A soft haze drifted in the air. She wiped her dirty hands on her muddy clothes.

Frightened, she was convinced she'd be lost forever. All she wanted was to escape her father. Then she heard a voice calling out her name. David appeared between the vines. She leaped to her feet and raced into his arms. He had searched all day, refusing to give up until she was found. Returning to the house in time for supper, he kept her secret.

Memories from that day were vivid in Avery's mind as she stared through the glass, wondering if she'd ever hear his voice again. Since leaving Andrews Air Force Base, she received word Dr. Bradford planned to move David to the presidential suite. By the time she arrived, he was still quarantined and hooked up to a ventilator. Tubes. Wires. Medication. It was hard to comprehend how the ashen-faced patient was the same person who found her in the vineyard before capturing a nation and the world.

Hank stood inside the room wearing full protective gear. He had been with them since the start of the presidential campaign, shadowing David every step of the way.

No doubt he'd keep his promise.

Another dozen Secret Service agents lined the corridor, and dozens more were spread throughout the hospital. So far, the virus at Walter Reed was contained to the isolated wing. But there were reports of new patients being admitted to emergency rooms across the city.

Sneakers squeaked against the tiled floor.

"Ms. Bouchard." Dr. Bradford approached. "Sorry to keep you waiting."

"Have you found out anything more?"

"We are running tests, but from the initial results, the specialists still believe it's a possible strain of Covid. However, based on their expertise, they don't believe it's one we've treated before. Possibly it's a variant of some kind, or it might be something more. Homeland has taken samples. As you can imagine, the best of the best are on the team."

"I was tested," Avery said. "Results were negative."

"A dozen positive cases are being treated at WHC, but there have been no deaths reported, other than those who were struck by the van." Dr. Bradford checked his cellphone. "Without knowing the length of exposure for everyone, it's difficult to predict whether to expect the patients to become more critical. While we don't have a definite handle on what we're dealing with yet, we feel we can safely move him to the presidential suite within the hour."

"Understood." Avery stared at David, willing him to rise. "So, there's no treatment to stop what's killing him."

"I've seen miracles happen in the direst of situations. For

now, we'll continue to keep him in a medically induced coma and allow the ventilator to do its job." Dr. Bradford paused. "If there are other family or friends…"

"Secret Service is waiting for my dad to land at Andrews and will bring him straight here." Avery held a thumbs up to Hank, who returned the gesture. "Without a vaccine, how long does he have?"

"If he doesn't respond to treatment, you're looking at a matter of days."

"You are to tell no one," Avery instructed. "Including anyone in the administration."

Dr. Bradford acknowledged her direction. "Your brother is a great man."

"Be sure you tell him when he wakes up."

Avery stepped away and walked down the hallway, exiting out of the isolated wing. She never stopped to look in the opposite room where Special Agent Kelley faced the same fate. Leaving through the ER entrance, she climbed into a black SUV with government plates.

The SUV left Walter Reed, passing a mini media village that had begun to establish a mile away from the hospital. News vans. Portable satellites. Cameramen. Audio engineers. Reporters from major networks and local affiliates. All walked a thin line between breaking news and op-ed on the latest developments with President Bouchard. So far, the details remained contained, which in DC was the biggest miracle of all.

Avery gazed out the tinted window and couldn't help but wonder what she would've done if David hadn't found her that day. It wasn't the first or the last time she ran away, and somehow he had always been the one to bring her home.

After the accident, and against her father's wishes, she escaped for the bright lights of Hollywood. She thought of it as a disappearing act. Years passed before David asked her to help him during the first campaign. She knew his intentions were more about returning her to the family than his need for a speechwriter. She'd done her best behind the scenes. She crafted his message, and to an extent, his presidency.

Reluctantly, she accepted his offer as Chief of Staff. A role Acting President Jacobs suggested she step away from until her brother regained consciousness.

My team will step in. Your brother needs you. That's all that matters, Avery.

During the hour ride from Walter Reed to Camp David, she quietly allowed the tears to spill over like a waterfall. Rolling down the window, she flashed her identification at the gate. Along the winding road to the main cabin, there were military and Secret Service who saluted as she passed. No media. No cameras. She wasn't a military brat or a four-star general. She took it as a sign of respect and loyalty from those who served the country with the utmost dedication.

Entering the main cabin, she was escorted to a solid steel door hidden behind a painting of Reagan riding his Arabian horse El Alamein at Rancho del Cielo. A pin-sized camera performed a retinal scan, and the door hissed open. She was the only one who proceeded to the underground black site.

In the underbelly of Camp David, a maze of tunnels led to secured rooms. One of which was a room within a room encased in bulletproof glass. Built in the aftermath of 9/11, the space was used sparingly, with access granted only by the Commander in Chief.

Avery sidestepped informing Jacobs at JB Andrews. Instead,

she called in a favor through Hank to the agent in charge at Camp David. It wouldn't take long before her visit was leaked to Jacobs or someone on her staff.

Standing in the room, she admitted her arrogance had gotten the best of her when she forged McIntyre's confession. Now that she had returned, a piece of her regretted it.

"I thought you were my legal team." Wearing an orange jumpsuit, McIntyre sat on a metal chair with her heels perched on the edge of a barrack-sized cot. A toilet and sink were in the opposite corner, but nothing else was inside the ten-by-ten box. "Oh wait, screw due process and the Sixth Amendment."

Avery stepped closer to the bulletproof glass. "I was wrong for what I did."

"Typical D.C. playbook." McIntyre's eyes narrowed. "I'm not a priest."

"We're under attack." Avery steadied herself. "I can't trust anyone in the White House."

"Ask the General for help. Your brother trusted him enough to bring me in."

"That's not possible."

McIntyre pulled herself up and stepped toward the glass. "Why isn't the President here?"

"He's fighting for his life," Avery bantered. "If you don't help me, he'll die."

McIntyre glanced around. "Not much I can do from inside this aquarium."

Avery punched a red button on the side of the wall. The glass cell began to lift off the cement. She feared McIntyre would even the score. Instead, McIntyre waited in the exact same spot until Avery tossed her fresh clothes along with her cellphone. Then McIntyre stripped right in front of her, leaving the orange jumpsuit in a pile on the floor.

"With all the tax hikes, the government should spring for a privacy screen in here." McIntyre slipped on her boots. "Point me to the nearest toilet, and then we'll save the world."

SIXTY-FOUR

GULF OF GIROLATA, CORSICA

Turquoise waters slapped against the hull of the *Winning Bid* while it was anchored in an inlet to the island. A lower deck featured guest cabins, state-of-the-art medical, engine room, crew quarters, and a swimming platform at the stern. A muted yet sleek design flowed seamlessly through the main deck between the saloon, dining room, galley, owner's suite, a second stateroom, wheelhouse, and a secured room only accessible by unique thumbprint. Outdoor dining was on the exterior of the upper deck, along with a sky lounge and captain's bridge. On the uppermost deck was a hot tub and a glass-enclosed gym.

Chase's body ached as he limped into the owner's suite. With the morphine wearing off, his shoulder and thigh throbbed. Stitches on his arms itched. Dust-sized pieces of glass seemed to move beneath his skin. He'd been shot, banged up, interrogated, and beaten, but lying on the floor at Le Grill, there was a moment he was certain it was over.

Sliding the closet open, he grabbed a t-shirt and shorts from a shelf. Gingerly he pulled the clothes over his bandages. Slipping on flip-flops, he picked up his backpack from the bed and carried it with him out of the owner's suite a few strides to another door. Pressing his palm against a digital panel, he entered the secured room.

A black-walled room was illuminated with a soft white glow that wrapped around the ceiling and floor, displaying the lethal weapons mounted on the walls. Some were new, while others like the AR-15 bore the remnants of the RVG ops. Stories concealed in the optical scope of the AR-15 would turn the heads of those in the free world.

He noticed the Barska industrial safe built into the wall. Setting the backpack on an island in the center, he retrieved the contents and set them inside the safe one at a time.

The leather-bound book with scribbled secrets had become a hit list of sorts with Bernhardt Brandis at the top. The *Speed Racer* tin box was a time capsule to remember how close he'd come to the other side. Closing the safe, he pulled out the last two items from the backpack. A SIG and the Kevlar mask. He hung both on the wall of weapons.

After the auction in Monterey that literally changed the course of his life, he had commissioned the custom build of the mega yacht. He planned to give Elena the grand tour when it was finished. Glancing around, he knew she'd be more impressed with this room than any other. She hadn't garnered Dax's nickname as the Black Widow of Bratva for no reason. She was capable of wielding any of the weapons on the wall.

Tossing the empty backpack on the floor, his ears rang with Elena's laughter, knowing she'd be shocked he finally spent a fraction of his Monterey bounty. He had dreamed that together they'd sail away and escape the darkness.

Then Laney disappeared.

Yes, she put the Vihkrovs in her crosshairs and I blame her for

Dad's death. But after Los Angeles, the truth left all of us balancing on a tightrope, swaying violently in the midst of a typhoon. I fell in love with two women. One betrayed me, and the other protected me. Neither deserves to die because of me.

Keeping his intentions to rescue Laney from Elena was for her protection. He knew the plan to lure Brandis into a trap threatened the Bratva and the Vihkrovs. Dax warned him about putting himself in the line of fire. His unwillingness to appease Dmitry's requests to extort President Bouchard with the evidence of RVG's black ops caused a divide between them. One that had only been bridged by their mutual love for Elena. Knowing Dmitry tried to kill them aboard the *Midnight Moon* meant Elena's stabilizing force was no more.

How do you let go of a past you believe defines your future?

Chase was too tired and too sore to dig into his soul for an answer. He left the room and found Dax in the galley, stirring a pot of his famous bolognese sauce. Butter. Onion. Celery. Carrot. Ground chuck. One part pork. Two parts beef. Salt. Pepper. Milk. White wine. And the secret ingredient—whole nutmeg. Chase inhaled the sweet aroma as he grabbed the wine bottle and added another douse.

"You're messing with greatness," Dax said. "I'm surprised you're on your feet."

"Feels like I went five rounds with Jean Claude St. Pierre."

"In case you were wondering..." Dax dropped the pasta in a boiling pot. "You lost."

"Never landed a punch," Chase chuckled. "Next time, you're in the octagon."

"Those days are over." Dax stirred the sauce. "I'm thinking of a new career."

"Chef BoyarDax."

"It's a global brand." Dax tasted one of the noodles. "You can be my angel investor."

Chase dipped into the sauce. "Thanks for covering my ass today."

"Six flights of stairs in Olympic time with an old man's limp." Dax used tongs to pull the boiled bucatini out of the pot and mix it in with the sauce. "A few more seconds, and you wouldn't be here enjoying this five-star cuisine."

"Brandis could've told Dmitry we were alive," Chase suggested. "Which means those men were Bratva sent to stop us once we arrived in Monte-Carlo before the auction."

"Either way you slice it..." Dax ran a knife through the bread. "Honey Trap is a bust."

"We watched Laney with our own eyes, but that doesn't mean Brandis shouldn't pay."

"Chase, she's alive. She's back on U.S. soil. Going after Brandis will get us all killed."

"Ammelie deserves retribution for what he did to her and her mother."

"First, it was Laney, and now it's Ammelie. Are you a contestant on Dare Dates?" Dax picked up a large serving dish piled with bolognese and bucatini. "Upper deck."

"I hear what you're saying," Chase reassured Dax.

"Be sure you tell the Black Widow it was all your idea."

Chase returned to his suite and grabbed his cellphone, the same one that hadn't been turned on since that night aboard the *Midnight Moon*. When he powered it on the cell pinged with dozens of voicemails and text messages

On his way to the lower deck swimming platform, he scanned the call log, read texts, and listened to Elena's concerned voice pleading for him to return her call. Away from earshot, he gazed out on the stillness of the bay, knowing she was his stabilizing force.

SIXTY-FIVE

WASHINGTON, D.C.—EARLIER

With a privacy shield raised inside the SUV, McIntyre listened to Avery recount all that occurred since she'd been held underground at the Camp David black site. She swallowed a lump lodged in her throat when she was told about Abbott. Harnessing her rage, she knew Avery Bouchard was the only reason why she was breathing fresh air, but there was a temptation to inflict pain against the president's naive sister.

"Any suspects?" McIntyre asked frankly.

"No DNA matches in the Bureau, Homeland, or Agency databases, except for General Abbott. Ring footage is being gathered from neighbors, and agents are also searching through street camera footage in the area. Honestly, right now everyone's efforts are focused on figuring out what led up to the crash outside the White House grounds." Avery paused. "Special Agent Kelley resurfacing has left everyone stunned. There's no record she was missing, only a memo documenting her request for an extended leave of absence."

"Especially when she reappears with a PRC military operative who spied on U.S. tech and pharmaceutical intellectual property, days after the government experiences a full blackout of China's operatives in North America." McIntyre shook her head. "What a cluster. I think it's safe to say that the memo you're referring to is a coverup."

"Agent Kelley is in the isolated wing at Walter Reed. Doctors are considering her to be patient zero. Ninety percent sure the virus was airborne and transmitted to my brother during their brief encounter." Avery handed over medical records. "Tests confirm they are both infected with a synthetic virus in the same strain as Covid—but extremely more aggressive to a level classified as biowarfare."

"PRC is known for its bioweapons program. For years they've recruited from around the world and offered big paydays for scientists who delivered the most lethal outcomes." McIntyre scanned the test results. "Agent Kelley wasn't a scientist, so why would she be kidnapped on our soil, held captive for months, then delivered to your brother's doorstep?"

"Honestly..." Avery shrugged. "I was hoping you might know the answer."

"Not yet anyway." McIntyre eyed her closely. "What else?"

"Minutes before the president entered Kelley's room, he was briefed about Elena Vihkrov's death." Avery handed over another file with the Bureau's field report. "She was found inside a rental car upside down in a ditch off Anacostia. A single shot to the chest. High powered rifle."

McIntyre's brows raised at the deadly photos. "Dmitry will retaliate."

"No confirmed sightings." Avery paused. "Alison, what do you have over my brother?"

"History." McIntyre flipped through the medical results and Bureau reports, remembering the Asian artifact conversation intercepted by Unicorn between Brandis and Omar. *If*

Chase finds out about Elena, he'll scorch the earth. "Have you talked with anyone else about this?"

"After General Abbott was found in his house, I met with Louise Higgins."

"Louise is a piece of work," McIntyre chided. "She slices with a thousand cuts."

"She asked if I'd heard of the Red Venture Group."

"Fairytales, mostly." McIntyre exhaled. *Without a happily ever after for most.* "She told you about the Speaker?"

"And that she protected a governor and my brother in the process. I believe she told me the truth." Avery's brows furrowed. "How were you involved?"

"The governor she mentioned recruited me." McIntyre knew there was no point in holding back. "Under the protection and anonymity of the Oval Office, we sidestepped the political swamp and protected our country. All with the blessing of your brother."

"Who else was part of it?" When McIntyre remained quiet, Avery asked another question. "Is the Red Venture Group what all of this is about?"

"If the PRC is involved, then I'd say this isn't about the sins caused by RVG." McIntyre closed the files and set them on the seat between them. "It's about gaining the upper hand after your brother crippled their economy."

"If you're right, how do we save him before it's too late."

"You're asking me into bed without taking me out for dinner and a movie." McIntyre leaned in closer. "A few days ago, the president betrayed me, and you were willing to lynch me in front of the world."

"You have my word, the confession disappears, and you will be granted full immunity. I know that won't even the score for General Abbott, but that's the best I can do."

"Presidential pardon in writing, and we have a deal." McIntyre nodded out the window as the SUV pulled up to the 4th Street Field Office. "You're up, Chief of Staff."

Avery climbed out of the SUV and slammed the passenger door. McIntyre pulled out her cell and powered it on. She dialed a series of numbers. Each one rang to voicemail. Realizing Chase had dumped the burners, which is what she would've done, she dialed another number. She was still coming to grips with Abbott's death when Maliki answered.

"You are too late."

"Maliki, I ran into a roadblock in D.C." McIntyre kept her eyes glued to the Field Office entrance. *Don't mention Stapha.* "No choice but to go underground. What's wrong?"

One question unleashed an emotionally charged story of a Russian drone strike, Stapha's death, and Chase locating and capturing a Russian spy who infiltrated Katarina Brandis' new life.

"I'm so sorry, my friend." *Katarina Brandis?*

"You refused to listen," Maliki argued. "Yet you call me *friend*."

"Maliki, there was no way I could've..."

"We treated you as one of our own." Maliki's voice quivered. "No more."

With that, the line went dead. McIntyre was left shaken. Her first impulse was to redial and keep Maliki in the game. She had burned one of her best assets and a close friend. Knowing it was pointless, she tried calling the burner cells again anyway. If what Avery said was true, the only other ones left alive from the RVG ops were Chase, Dax, and Bouchard. Her mind lingered on the Asian artifact while she waited for

Avery to return.

Forty minutes later, Avery knocked on the front passenger door and relayed a message to the driver. Then she climbed into the backseat with her hands full. First, she gave McIntyre a pardon on official White House letterhead signed by Acting President Jacobs. Second, she set a small box on top of the file folders between them. Third, she removed a black box device from her jacket pocket.

"In exchange, you'll agree not to go public." Avery kept her hand on the box. "One word to anyone, and the deal is off."

"Wouldn't have it any other way," McIntyre replied. "What'd you tell Jacobs?"

"You're the best chance to save my brother."

"That's all it took?"

"She owes her career to him." Avery pointed at the pardon. "That's worth something."

As the SUV headed down 4th Street, McIntyre removed the lid from the small box and peered inside. A cellphone. Ten grand. Counterfeit American passport. That's all that was left of Elena Vihkrov. She studied the cellphone for a moment then grabbed the black box device, which had two lightning plugs protruding from it. Plugging her cellphone into one and Elena's into the other, the gateway hacker began a process of cracking Elena's password.

Within a matter of minutes, Elena's cellphone unlocked the home screen. McIntyre searched text messages and call logs. She didn't want to appear too interested with Avery watching, but she intended to go through the cellphone meticulously when there was more time. She scrolled through the call logs where true identities were swapped with the top mobsters of the past century. One name matched the date Simon Adams was killed and the *Midnight Moon* exploded.

Meyer Lansky.

Dialing the number, she waited until she heard his voice.

"Chase...it's McIntyre."

SIXTY-SIX

GULF OF GIROLATA, CORSICA | PORT DE FONTVIEILLE, MONACO

Words failed to soothe an ache deeper than a sob, a groan, a wail, a yell, or a scream. McIntyre delivered the news straight, leaving Chase paralyzed once the call ended. Staring out on the peaceful waters, a war waging within exploded into a towering inferno. A set of rules in the fight separated him from those who threatened the innocent. Those rules had been broken. Omar was a breaking point. Hold on too long, and those who were too close died.

Despair shot through him as he fought an urge to drop to his knees, curse the heavens, then dive into the water and sink to the bottom. Steadying himself, new rules of engagement emerged. *No mercy, no surrender. No peril, no glory. No death, no life. No darkness, no light.* While it wasn't eloquent, it was damn sure the truth.

Reaching the upper deck, he found Dax, Ammelie, and the crew relaxed around a table digging into Dax's famous bolognese bucatini and a bottle of Insignia Pinot Noir. He wanted to sound the alarm: Elena's dead! But his voice refused to utter the words.

Not yet. Not now. Not ever.

With his jaw clenched, his eyes caught Dax's attention when he glanced up with a mouthful of pasta. The captain and first officer noticed the exchange, and the three of them pushed their chairs back and excused themselves. Ammelie and the medic watched as they headed below.

Peeling away from the others, Chase and Dax entered the secured room.

Dax's eyes widened as he took it all in. "Badass doesn't do this justice."

Chase opened a closet hidden seamlessly within the walls. Jeans, shirts, and suits were hung on hangars. Boots and shoes lined the floor. Each was equipped with a lining of Kevlar developed by the Israelis that was more durable and thinner than the standard vest.

"Could've used these earlier today." Dax inspected the clothing. "Spill it, Chase."

"I spoke to McIntyre. Bouchard and Laney are infected with a synthetic virus, along with dozens of others from the protest. And they identified the dead operative, which she believes confirms an attack from the PRC."

"Did you tell her about Dong Hyun-Ki being *the* Asian artifact?"

"I told her what Omar told us and that we believe he's being held by Brandis." Chase slipped out of his t-shirt and shorts into the armored clothing. Dax did the same. "She's convinced someone in Washington is pulling the strings. But no one is going to launch a global manhunt until Bouchard either wakes up or dies. Doesn't matter if the virus was a direct attack on him or a way for the Chinese to stir the pot before his re-election. What matters is we need to find the scientist before more people die, including Laney."

"Makes sense why Bouchard wanted Brandis back alive." Dax handed Chase a shoulder holster custom-fitted to conceal two handguns behind the back and extra mags of ammo. "Brandis has the Korean mastermind who creates deadly viruses for a living. If Brandis isn't behind it, he'll sure as hell know who is."

Chase grabbed two SIGs from the wall. "Either way, he's dead."

Dax holstered several of his own. "How'd you know where to call McIntyre?"

"She called me from..." Chase's stare hardened. "She's gone because of me."

Dax realized who Chase meant as his voice trailed off. "Oh sh..."

Chase pulled two dark-colored Kevlar hoodies off the hangers, each stitched with a matching-colored Mongoose emblem on one sleeve. In a world slithering with snakes it was a fitting salute to the men who helped even the score. And to the soldier who made the ultimate sacrifice when they hunted the Prodigal.

Gingerly pulling on the hoodie, he whispered, "Never out of the fight."

On the lower deck, the captain and first officer maneuvered a 25-foot speedboat using hydraulics to remove it from a portion of the mega yacht's hull. With skilled precision, the lift swung the vessel across the stern before lowering it into the glassy water. *Deal Maker* was a 4-engine speedboat with a 424-horsepower supercharged V-10 at a top speed of 80 MPH.

Ammelie appeared on the stairs with her hands on her hips. "Where are you two going?"

"Beer run," Dax answered. "We'll be back in an hour."

Chase climbed aboard with Dax right behind. Flipping a switch, the engine drowned out Ammelie's objection. He pushed a remote lever forward, and the engine roared. Cutting across the open water, the glow of lights from *Winning Bid* faded into blackness. As *Deal Maker* accelerated, the bow gradually rose, slicing through the current with ease.

Twenty minutes later, the speedboat docked at Port de Fontvieille, a few miles southwest of Port Hercules. Chase pressed a button on a remote, and the cockpit sealed. Walking down Quai Jean-Charles Rey, they crossed Avenue Albert II in the direction of Jardein Animalier de Monaco—Zoological Garden of Monaco. Before reaching the traffic tunnels, there was a dilapidated storefront with dingy blinds covering the windows directly across from the zoo entrance.

Chase removed the titanium card from his wallet, the one that gained access to The Elite. He swiped the card across the door and heard a lock disengage. Traffic sped by as they slipped into the storefront, knowing a secret passageway was hidden inside.

"For what you're paying, you'd think they'd send a limo," Dax said.

Chase knew it was Dax's subtle way of empathy. "All part of the game."

"Remember London?" Dax ran his hand over a wall expecting it to open. "We were a modern-day Sherlock and Watson." With a frown, Chase held up his forearm where the Stars and Stripes tattoo was hidden beneath the Kevlar. "My bad. Sherlock would've figured out the clues before that happened."

"Smartass." Chase stepped on a loose board, and a wall slid

open. "You were saying?"

"You're a leprechaun," Dax snickered. "Now where's the pot of gold?"

On the other side of the wall was a tunnel that led underneath the street to stairs circling upward inside a castle tower. On their way to the top, a rhythmic pulse vibrated the stones. When they reached an iron door, Chase pushed it open to reveal a sprawling grassy lawn on the edge of a sheer rock cliff overlooking the Port de Fontvieille. Hundreds of twenty- and thirty-somethings were packed on the grass, dancing in sync to flashing lights from a portable stage where a scantily dressed woman DJ acted as ringleader to her animals.

Pushing and nudging their way through the crowd, they headed for a brick building with a terracotta roof. Chase brushed off a few drunkards who were lost to their drugs of choice while others dove into a packed swimming pool. Chase and Dax were the same age as most of them, yet they'd spent more time in the trenches than puking over the side of a castle tower.

"Sure this is a good idea?" Dax asked under his breath.

Chase shook his head. "It's a terrible idea."

A human wall of Italian muscle guarded a door to the brick building. Heavyweight security tatted from head to toe in allegiance to the Cosa Nostra. It wasn't the first option, it was the last.

"We need to speak to Luigino." Chase slipped the titanium card from his pocket and flashed it in front of them. "Rules dictate our request must be granted."

One of the Italians grunted to another and motioned them aside. Chase and Dax were escorted inside a spacious room with vaulted ceilings. Sculptures were scattered throughout the space. A theater-sized screen covered an entire wall broadcasting football matches across Europe.

In front of the wall of sports, smoking a stogie with a glass of scotch, was Luigino Sagese—the Cosa Nostra's golden boy who was a younger and more brutal version of the Bratva's Dmitry Vihkrov. Chase knew Luigino assumed the throne a year earlier after a car bomb killed his father in Rome. No one knew for sure who had taken such a brazen act, but if an identity ever surfaced there was no doubt Luigino would be the executioner.

"Thank you for meeting with us."

"What choice do I have?" Sagese mused. "A perk of being one of The Elite."

Chase extended a hand. "Our fathers crossed paths on occasion, Luigino."

"I remember your father." Sagese glanced at the screen, his attention divided. Then he cursed at Club Milan for allowing another goal. His slick blonde hair, silk shirt, golden chains, and rings were a sign of someone who tried too hard to prove they were more powerful than their predecessor. *True power is subtle.* He shook Chase's hand with an extra firm grip. "Dario was an exceptional player who retired too soon. But I am sure he is enjoying life on the lake."

"I suspect he put a few million in your pocket." Chase paused. "We would not have come unless it was urgent. We are in need of information we hope you can provide."

"You left a mess at Hotel de Paris."

Chase's brows raised. "There is a bounty on our heads."

Sagese poured three glasses of scotch, and then his attention turned razor-sharp. "Why have you not gone to the Vihkrovs for this information?"

"We've been unable to reach them."

"Dmitry and my father shared a mutual respect to ensure the survival of our families." Sagese muted the games, and the room fell eerily quiet. No sound from the hundreds of partiers who danced to the DJ's tracks either. "If one were to cross the other, there would be bloodshed. So, when necessary, each side has stepped in to remind the other of our commitment."

In one swig, Chase finished the scotch. "Respect is what has kept us all alive."

"Elena was two years ahead of me at Cambridge. Top of her class." Sagese drew from his glass. "I have always thought of her as a *bellezza pericolos*." *Dangerous beauty.* "As I remember, she was quite fond of you." Sagese paused. "Out of respect for Elena, I have ensured all cameras from the hotel to Port Hercules were erased. You have no concerns, my friend."

"We are grateful and will return the gesture. But that is not the information we seek."

"So we are clear..." Sagese set the scotch down. "The men were not Cosa Nostra."

"We don't think they were Bratva either," Dax chimed in. "No branding."

Sagese's quizzical stare dissolved into a realization. "Then it is true."

"What's true?" Chase asked, a bit unnerved.

"A coup d'état."

SIXTY-SEVEN

HALF MOON ISLAND, NORTH ATLANTIC

Bernhardt Brandis walked the grounds of his eighty-acre island, ensuring security was tight for his guests' arrival. After inspecting the bungalows, he sent coordinates on behalf of Dmitry Vihkrov to the twelve members of the Bratva Council.

Most of the morning, he tracked the escalating tensions between the United States and China, knowing his opportunity to showcase his paradise needed to be postponed. Tech billionaires. Blockbuster celebrities. The one percent. Most knew him as Bernhardt, a reclusive millionaire who never left his paradise. Those who stepped foot on Half Moon lost themselves in their darkest tendencies, leaving their secrets buried on the island.

With his feet in the sand, he launched a bidding war.

By early afternoon the dark web app pinged with coded messages on his cellphone from counterintelligence agencies bidding on their most prized assets. Once the clock counted down to zero, the funds would be transferred, and a delivery location would be confirmed. No government knew who was the mastermind. Global intelligence agencies had failed to locate the underground prison hidden beneath his paradise in the Atlantic.

Beijing's Ministry was at the top of the bidding for the Korean scientist. Brandis caught them once already attempting to breach the firewall protecting his customized app. Russia's Foreign Bureau and Israel's Mossad were in the running for a computer hacker who sold Israeli intelligence to the SVR. While more were slated on the auction block, the two he watched most closely reached into the tens of millions.

Why deal in millions when billions are at stake?

Trudging through the sand he knew he was playing a most dangerous game, one more lethal than the web he'd weaved his empire upon. He set the trap and lured Dmitry into a game to beat all games by introducing the Bratva Kingpin to the Washington power player. Billions more were in play for the Vihkrov war chest, and his reward from Dmitry had been threats and disrespect. When his men failed to kill Chase Hardeman in Athens, he was left vulnerable and at the mercy of Dmitry's wrath. But if the Englishman succeeded, retribution was an impossibility. He'd turned the tables on Dmitry, and the bastard never saw it coming.

Revenge, well, revenge is best served once Elena stands by my side.

His mind wandered to the moment he caught sight of Katarine in Milan. She was his little girl. Flesh and blood who belonged to only him. He never forgave her for running away. In time she would see his actions were justified. His anger boiled at the second failed attempt to kill Hardeman in Monte-Carlo, but he wanted Katarine more than ever. Once the Englishman returned, he would unleash the assassin's skills to finish the task. Then it would only be a matter of time before father and daughter were reunited again.

In the distance, the Eurocopter Hermés EC 135 helicopter belonging to Globali Holdings flew over the ocean as dark clouds rolled in behind. Brandis climbed the rocks, a shortcut to the landing pad. He reached the edge of the cliff as the skids from the Eurocopter touched down.

The Englishman climbed out from the pilot's seat. "Storms brewing about ten miles east."

"Guests won't arrive until morning." Brandis glanced past the Englishman. "Why is Elena not with you?"

"She stayed in Washington to meet with your contact. As promised, she plans to return to Monte-Carlo sometime before the end of the week." The Englishman retrieved a hard case from the rear passenger seat. "Call her in a few days and greet her when she arrives. By then, grief will be your way into her stone-cold heart."

"Does she know the truth...about Dmitry?"

"No one knows the truth, including me."

Brandis couldn't escape his voyeurism. "Tell me how he died."

"He's bait for the sharks." The Englishman handed over the case. "Laptop. Cellphones. As requested. Should be good enough for your meeting with the Council. My job is done."

"Chase Hardeman is still alive, and I need him dead."

"Afraid that's not possible. New contract. I'm sure there are others who can get it done for you at a less expensive price."

"Double. Triple. Name your contract."

"Golden rule is to never stay with one client for too long. It's been a pleasure, Mr. Brandis."

"My offer stands if you change your mind. Where should I wire the funds?"

The Englishman smiled slyly and pointed to the helicopter. "Consider it wired."

Brandis stood back while the Englishman performed a quick pre-flight check of the Eurocopter. He had to admit, the Englishman was a true professional. Holding the treasure chest to his future, Brandis waited until the Eurocopter lifted off before he headed toward the Peak House perched at the highest point of his private oasis.

Climbing the steps leading to the crow's nest, the clouds loomed overhead. Entering the open-air living space, he imagined the Bratva Council being awed by his ace-high straight flush. Glancing over at the bank of screens where cameras monitored his underground prisoners, he thought of how good it would feel when those cells were empty one last time. Setting the case on a desk, he flipped the latch bolt and opened it. Brandis blinked several times before his eyes locked in on a gold compass pendant covered in dried blood.

SIXTY-EIGHT

MONTE-CARLO, MONACO

Shortly after midnight, a tank-like Mercedes G63 rolled out of the gates of Luigino Sagese's cliffside castle. Toting six 37-inch wheels on three rigid axles, the tenacious off-roader weighed in at over 8,000 pounds with a top speed of 100 MPH.

Behind the wheel, Chase barreled down the hill, making his first call to an emergency number Elena had given him a year earlier for Dmitry. *Strange to warn someone who wants you dead.* Each time he dialed, the call disconnected. He moved on to the next one.

McIntyre's voice cut through the Burmester audio system. "What've you got?"

"Luigino's never dealt with Brandis directly." Chase swerved in and out of traffic before pulling a tight right turn onto Avenue Pasteur. Accelerating through the winding road, the Mercedes handled like it was in the Grand Prix. "He gave us a lead, so we're chasing it down."

"What'd you promise him in return?"

Dax mumbled loud enough for her to hear. "A winter home in Siberia."

"Everyone has a price. We'll deal with it later." Chase merged onto Avenue du 3 September. "What about Bouchard

349

and Laney?"

"President's vitals are deteriorating. The same is true for Laney."

Chase hoped for better news. "What about retaliation against the Chinese?"

"I'm assuming all options are on the table. With Jacobs, who knows how strongly she'll respond until there's a definite outcome with Bouchard. But if you get me a solid location on Brandis, I'll run it up the chain of command."

"Always pictured you with a broomstick, not a magic wand." Dax chimed in again. "Since when do you have enough pull in the White House to *run it up the chain*?"

McIntyre said in a lowered voice, "I'm standing in the same room as Avery Bouchard."

Exchanging raised eyebrows with Dax, Chase asked, "How'd that happen?"

"We've all experienced loss in the chaos," McIntyre replied. "Differences and indiscretions are being set aside. But when this is over, the ghosts who've caused the madness will show themselves, and the wolves will hunt them down."

"We're here." Chase slowed the Mercedes and looked for an open spot. "What about..."

"I'm working on narrowing it down. Call me back when you've got a location."

Parking the Mercedes across the street from a stonewalled estate, Chase shut off the headlights. For a moment, he attempted to clear his mind. *We've all experienced loss in the chaos.* If he let down his guard, then he'd be left broken forever. He'd lost those he loved before, but coming to grips with Elena was unthinkable. With each breath, darkness seeped deeper into his bones.

"McIntyre goes MIA, then reappears on the other end of Elena's cell." Dax shifted in his seat as if he were about to jump out of the Mercedes. "And now she's with Bouchard's sister? Something ain't right, Chase."

"We're on one side of the battle." Chase eyed the estate entrance. "No telling how long she stays on Bouchard's good side. We can't trust anyone but ourselves."

For the next hour, they watched and waited. Parked between Winston Churchill Avenue and Avenue du 3 September, both split their attention between the gates, side mirror, and rearview. In any other city, the rugged but sleek Mercedes G63 would stick out like a lighthouse beacon. But in Monte-Carlo, it was just another million-dollar trophy, camouflaged amongst dozens of more luxurious trophies.

High on the hillside of the estate, lights flickered between the trees. Chase turned the ignition and waited until three Range Rovers appeared at the gates. Once they pulled out on Avenue du 3 September, he turned on the headlights and followed the caravan at a distance.

"Operation Thunder," Chase said. "Hard and fast."

"I was afraid you'd say that." Dax tightened his seatbelt. "Remember how that ended?"

"Last time, we didn't have a tank."

"You do know those Range Rovers are bulletproof."

Switching lanes into oncoming traffic, Chase punched the pedal, and the Mercedes rumbled ahead. Closing in fast, he swerved the Mercedes into the back bumper of the last Range Rover, sending it skidding sideways. He never let off the gas as the Mercedes slammed into the driver's side, sending smoke billowing and sparks spraying across the windshield as tire tread screeched against the concrete. Chase let off the gas for a few seconds, then rammed the Range Rover a second time, forcing the vehicle to crash into the barricades.

"You're up next," Chase said to Dax.

Dax unbuckled his seatbelt, then opened the passenger door wide enough to slip out onto a foot rail. Chase glanced in the rearview to see him climb around into the bed of the Mercedes. He accelerated, swerving into oncoming traffic, gaining speed until the Mercedes was parallel to the second Range Rover. The back window of the Range Rover lowered, giving Chase a split-second view of an elderly man in between two other men. When a semi-automatic rifle pointed out the window, he slammed on the brakes as multiple rounds pierced the body of the Mercedes.

Staying on the attack, he accelerated alongside the Range Rover again, then passed it, going 80 MPH. *Time to improvise.* Chase set his sights on the lead vehicle. He glanced in the rearview as more rounds pinged off the Mercedes. He couldn't see Dax, but he could definitely hear him even in the midst of the engines, bullets, and screeching tires of oncoming cars left swerving out of the way.

"Déjà vu Operation Thunder, my ass." Dax shouted.

Chase cut in between the Range Rovers before ramming into the back bumper of the lead vehicle. He accelerated again, reaching speeds of 90 MPH, forcing the vehicle to skid out of control before flipping end over end and ramming into oncoming traffic.

Tonight, we're leaving our mark on Monaco.

With the wreckage burning behind them and traffic slamming on the brakes in the opposite lane, there was nowhere for the target vehicle to escape. Chase slowed the Mercedes as Dax appeared in the rearview and tossed a metal hook that was connected to a tow hitch.

While Chase couldn't see whether the hook caught the Range Rover's bumper, he could feel it in the tension on the steering wheel. Flipping a switch on the console, he began reeling in the Range Rover as they neared the Zoological Garden of Monaco and the one-way tunnel from earlier in the evening. Swerving from side to side, he kept his eyes on the rearview as the Range Rover attempted to counter maneuver hooked like a great white.

Reaching the tunnel, Chase veered once more, sending the Range Rover careening into the entrance wall. Slamming on the brakes, the axles screamed, and tires howled. Chase hopped out from the driver's side with his SIG at the ready. Dax was on the other side as they flanked the vehicle. Dax shot the driver, who was barely out of the Range Rover, then Chase hit the front passenger in the chest, dropping him on the road.

Moving in unison, as they'd done countless times before, they stayed on the attack. When the back doors opened, automatic gunfire erupted sending them sliding toward the front bumper of the Range Rover. Chase looked underneath and fired three rounds. The first hit one of the men in the leg, then the second and third hit the other man in the ankle and foot. Dax swung around the front bumper as one of the men stumbled backward, shooting him between the eyes. Chase rounded the other side pulling the trigger, leaving the other man dead on the street.

Bystanders and drivers emerged, shocked by the crash and massive wreckage. Chase and Dax approached the backseat of the Range Rover. On both sides, they pointed their SIGs at the wide-eyed elderly man who was still buckled in. While Dax unhooked the tow chain, Chase pressed his weapon against the elderly man's chest.

"Live or die?"

SIXTY-NINE

GULF OF GIROLATA, CORSICA

By early morning, Monte-Carlo's Police Chief issued a statement regarding the unsettling events of the previous twenty-four hours. From the shooting at Hotel de Paris to the major wreck and crime scene near the Zoological Garden, he assured Monaco's citizens the investigations were his top priority. Of course, there was no mention of the deleted security footage from inside the hotel or the streets nearby. And when he showed the press and viewers footage of a Mercedes G63 reversing out of the tunnel at high speed, no one knew the 8,000-pound battering ram was already sunk at the bottom of Port de Fontvieille.

Cutting across the open waters aboard *Deal Maker*, Chase kept watch over the hooded, gagged, and zip-tied prisoner. Luigino Sagese had pointed them to the one Bratva Council member who could turn the tide. While Dax captained the speedboat, Chase held on as a strong wind blew against him. His body thrashed. His mind drained. His spirit shattered.

What else can I do but press into the pain?

Chase remembered the summers spent at the Vihkrov Montecito estate along the California coast, including the frequent visits from a man Elena referred to as Uncle Vasiliy.

He always arrived unannounced without a security detail, spending a few days at a time. Elena told Chase it was her father's way of checking on her since he refused to step foot back in the States after he departed New York decades earlier.

Hours were spent in a grand kitchen cooking dumplings, crêpes, borscht, pelmeni, and beef stroganoff. Uncle Vasiliy's presence kept Elena at ease as she laughed at his stories about her father, which led to drinking another vintage bottle of wine. During those summer days, Chase learned Vasiliy Stepanov was not a blood relative of the Vihkrovs, but he was Dmitry's most trusted lieutenant.

She trusted him. He was one of her guardians. And now she's dead.

He texted McIntyre: ELENA. NEED PROOF.

As the *Deal Maker* reached the inlet to the island, Dax maneuvered the speedboat toward the stern of the anchored *Winning Bid*. The captain and first officer readied the hydraulic lift and lowered it into the water deep enough for the speedboat to lock into position.

Chase grabbed Vasiliy Stepanov under his arm and pulled him onto the lower deck. The captain, first officer, and Dax continued securing the speedboat by returning the vessel inside the hull of the mega yacht. Chase's cell pinged as he removed the hood and gag from Stepanov.

"Where is Dmitry?" He asked point-blank. "I know he wants me dead."

"Attack me, kill my men, then ask me this?" Stepanov growled, defiant. "You are the one who dishonored the Bratva by choosing loyalty to Bouchard. Of course, Dmitry wants you dead."

"My loyalty has always been to Elena." Chase met

Stepanov's glare with equal intensity. *Don't show him any weakness. He'll smell an ounce of fear.* "Which is the only reason you're alive. Now, I need a face-to-face with Dmitry."

"I am the one who said to Elena, 'you will never be one of us.'"

Removing his cellphone from his pocket, Chase unlocked the screen and tapped on McIntyre's text. Before seeing the attachment for himself, he turned the screen to Stepanov.

"It is one of you who has betrayed the Vihkrovs."

Stepanov's icy stare hardened. "What is this?"

"The King will be overthrown." Chase swallowed hard as he cut the zip ties, allowing Stepanov to be free. "Unless we warn him."

"Elena..." Stepanov lowered his head, distraught. "Dmitry has summoned the Council."

"When?" Chase pressed. "Where?"

"We are to arrive today." Stepanov retrieved a note from his shirt pocket and handed it over. "Half Moon Island."

"Take me to Dmitry." Chase squeezed Stepanov's shoulder. "And I will find whoever is responsible and kill them myself."

Once the anchor was raised, the mega yacht set sail with the latitude and longitude programmed into the navigation. Dax escorted Stepanov to the sky lounge while Chase slipped away to the exterior deck and relayed the coordinates to McIntyre.

"Bratva Council has been summoned to Half Moon," Chase said. "We've got a way to get on the island, and if I can talk to Dmitry, then there's a chance we will leave with the scientist."

"You and Dax can't take on the Bratva and Brandis at the same time."

"Well, you can't drop a bomb and expect to find the scientist

357

alive." Chase weighed her words for a moment. *She's right, but we're cornered.* "Mongoose is the team I'd trust to pull off the recovery."

"Avery will relay the location to Jacobs." McIntyre paused. "Don't count on Mongoose."

Chase disconnected the call. "I don't intend to."

The *Winning Bid* sailed across a vast ocean headed for the North Atlantic. From the exterior deck, Chase gripped the cellphone tight, fighting an urge to see for himself. He closed his eyes, breathed in deep, then unlocked the screen. Opening his eyes, he tapped on the message icon and opened McIntyre's text. He stared hard at the photo of Elena on a gurney with a white sheet pulled down far enough to show only her ashen face. *A shell without a soul.* He avoided reading Elena's text messages. Instead, he switched screens and scrolled through dozens of photos of them aboard *Midnight Moon* sailing across the globe—it was the only way he wished to remember.

Sensing he wasn't alone, Chase locked his cellphone. "What happens after you die?"

"Some believe in spirits, afterlife, and reincarnation to be reborn again." Ammelie inched closer. "Others believe in a heaven-like paradise, or even Purgatory where the dead must be purified for their sins before entering Heaven."

Turning around, he asked, "What if your sins are unforgivable?"

"No sin is beyond forgiveness, Chase."

Yeah, well, my sins are buried a mile deep and I'm nowhere near finished.

SEVENTY

WASHINGTON, D.C.

A subterranean tunnel zig-zagged from the Treasury Building to the East Wing of the White House, allowing for the evacuation of the president in the event of an emergency. Throughout the years, the tunnel was used by Presidents to sneak in girlfriends, mistresses, and to avoid protestors when leaving the grounds.

At various checkpoints in the tunnel, Secret Service monitored security cameras, alarms, and guarded cipher locks.

Near the end of the 700-foot long tunnel, Avery punched in a code on a cipher lock, and the door opened to a staircase. McIntyre followed her lead and climbed the steps until they reached the top.

When Avery opened the second door, McIntyre found herself standing in a short hallway next to the president's private restroom. She had heard about the tunnels during her stint at the Agency, but actually seeing where the tunnels led made it more than folklore.

"I'll do the talking," Avery whispered to McIntyre.

A few steps from the secret stairway that led to the secret tunnel was yet another door. McIntyre peered over Avery's shoulder as the door cracked open. Seated behind the Resolute desk was Acting President Bridget Jacobs. Until that moment, McIntyre had never been inside the Oval Office.

"Madam President," Avery announced. "We've got a lead on the scientist we believe originated the virus and who could hold an antidote."

"Then a full pardon was worth it." Acting President Jacobs stepped around the front of the Resolute, her eyes focused on McIntyre. "What've you got?"

"Dong Hyun-Ki specializes in viruses, chemical agents, and global pandemics." McIntyre ignored Avery's instructions from moments earlier. "He created a vaccine for H1N1 and has been regarded as a national treasure for the Korean people. Sources believe he was abducted by the Chinese years ago. We're tracking his location to an island owned by Bernhardt Brandis."

"Bernhardt Brandis," Jacobs said. "What ties him to the Chinese?"

"I can't answer that for sure, Madam President. But it's the best lead we've got."

"Who are your sources?" Jacobs asked pointedly.

"Chase Hardeman," Avery chimed in. "And Dexter Thompson."

From the blank stare on Jacob's face, McIntyre knew the conversation had turned murky. *How am I going to explain the Red Venture Group without incriminating Bouchard, Chase, Dax, or myself?* Now that the names were out in the open, she needed Jacobs to stay engaged with the possibility of saving Bouchard and the others who were infected.

"If he were conscious, President Bouchard would personally vouch for Hardeman and Thompson," McIntyre assured. "Both are valuable assets to the United States government."

"What agency or branch are they operating under?" When McIntyre didn't answer, Jacobs took a step back and turned her attention to Avery. "Sounds a little deep state."

"Deep state is General Abbott being shot to death hours before he was scheduled to testify before the Intel Committee." McIntyre's patience ran thin. "Deep state is the disappearance nine months ago of Special Agent Laney Kelley without any acknowledgment from the Bureau or this administration. Not to mention her reappearance outside these gates with an operative of the PRC. With all due respect, President Bouchard's death will be on your hands if you hesitate to act."

Avery stepped in and tried to calm the escalation. "This is a chance to save lives."

"Wouldn't be the first time a president operated out of bounds." Jacobs crossed her arms and pursed her lips. McIntyre knew she hit a nerve. *Never let a crisis go to waste.* She remained quiet until Jacobs continued. "I'll assume the three of us in this room know that better than most."

"You can trust Hardeman and Thompson," McIntyre urged. "They've sacrificed before, and they will do it again."

"Where is the island?" Jacobs asked.

"North Atlantic." McIntyre reached into her coat pocket and retrieved a printout of a map. "Hardeman is requesting Seal Team Mongoose rendezvous at these coordinates."

The main door to the Oval Office opened with three individuals standing in the doorway. Jacobs motioned them inside to a sofa and chairs.

"Madam President..." Avery began.

"You'll have my decision within the hour." Jacobs waved a Secret Service agent over. "Please escort Ms. Bouchard and her guest to the residence."

McIntyre and Avery were ushered out of the Oval Office as discreetly as they had arrived. Following the Secret Service down a long corridor, McIntyre admitted she'd hoped for a more decisive outcome, but she anticipated the pause. She'd served her country, but in the eyes of Jacobs, she was a threat to national security. And Chase and Dax were total unknowns, whose military records would verify nothing more than they were enlisted at Pendleton.

Is Jacobs willing to walk a tightrope to save Bouchard and the others if one wrong step means political suicide? We'll know in the next sixty minutes.

"Did you see who entered the room?" Avery asked in a hushed voice.

"Pascall, national security advisor. Who were the others?"

"Albert Skinner, director of Homeland, and Nancy Frost, U.S. ambassador to China."

The Secret Service agent left them at the bottom of a red-carpeted grand staircase that led up to the second floor, the private living quarters for the president.

On the second floor, McIntyre followed Avery into the Yellow Oval room. Gold curtains framed the tall windows. Hanging from the ceiling was a gold and crystal chandelier. Bright-colored velvet furniture brought the sense of a historical museum, not a residence. Paintings hung from the walls as a reminder of those who had gone before. McIntyre admitted it was a better prison than the one she'd been kept in at Camp David, but it was still a prison.

From behind bulletproof glass, she stared out the window beyond the Truman balcony overlooking the South Lawn. On the other side of the gates, the protestors had thinned out considerably. She imagined the route the van had taken with Tao Weimin and Agent Kelley. While it was a deliberate attack, it was out of character for the Chinese.

Why lose one of their operatives? How'd the PRC know Bouchard would cross paths with Weimin or Kelley? Why would Brandis kidnap Kelley, then release her to the PRC? Who killed General Abbott and Elena Vihkrov? Is there a thread that weaves this all together?

McIntyre snapped out of her thoughts as Marine One approached and landed on the South Lawn. Walking across the grass, Acting President Jacobs, Albert Skinner, and Nancy Frost headed for the Sikorsky VH-60N "White Hawk." All three disappeared aboard Marine One before it lifted off headed in the direction of the Washington Monument.

Avery stood next to her at the window. "She said within the hour."

"And then what?"

McIntyre turned around and headed toward the grand staircase. Avery was on her heels. Reaching the staircase, they were stopped by two Secret Service agents.

"I'm sorry, Ms. Bouchard. You are to remain here."

Avery dialed Jacobs' private number. No answer. She turned back to the agents on the staircase. "I'm the Chief of Staff."

"Looks like you've been ghosted." McIntyre pulled Avery back, knowing that provoking the agents wasn't going to get them anywhere. She led Avery into the Treaty Room, which was slightly less gaudy than the Yellow Oval. "Get someone with enough clout to spring us loose."

On her cellphone, Avery stepped into a corner of the room near Chartran's painting commemorating the peace treaty signed by William McKinley in 1898 to end the Spanish-American war.

McIntyre turned off Elena's cellphone which she'd been carrying. Then she walked over to the Treaty Table, a magnificent Victorian desk piled with stacks of documents and a laptop. Hanging on a wall across from the Treaty Table was *The Peacemaker*, depicting Lincoln conferring with his advisors at the end of the Civil War.

Peace was only achieved when the bloodshed was over.

McIntyre pointed at the laptop on the Treaty Table. "I need to access this."

"What for?"

"Siprnet."

"You're not poking around in there." Avery set her cellphone on the table and slipped into the seat. "Fine. I'll do it."

McIntyre knew the gravity of accessing the government's secret internet protocol router. She watched Avery hit the space bar and enter a password, one she wasn't able to decipher. A few more clicks, and Siprnet launched. McIntyre relayed an IP address to Avery, which bypassed the dark web to a landing page with an icon of a Unicorn.

"Let me get in there." McIntyre recognized Avery's hesitation. "You can babysit."

Avery stepped away but peered over McIntyre's shoulder. "What program is that?"

"Trade secret."

McIntyre entered a passcode, and another screen appeared. Her fingers flew across the keys, and she entered Chase's burner cell number into a blank box.

A map appeared with a red flashing light, which moved

slowly across the screen.

She clicked on the red icon, and a pop-up screen appeared listing the call log and text messages from the burner. Knowing the odds were stacked against them with Jacobs, she typed only two words.

SEVENTY-ONE

NORTH ATLANTIC

From the Alboran Sea to the Strait of Gibraltar, the *Winning Bid* rose and fell as waves crashed against the hull. Since leaving Girolata, gloomy weather turned nasty. Charging at 50 knots, the captain navigated the Atlantic to outrace thunder and lightning while dodging twenty-five-foot waves that slammed over the sides of the vessel.

As a precaution, Vasiliy Stepanov was confined to the saloon where Dax kept first watch. He wasn't restrained since he was outnumbered and had nowhere to run. Chase had taken the Russian's cellphone and locked it in the safe in the artillery room. Once they hit rough waters, Ammelie had excused herself nauseous from an unending roller coaster ride. Entering the saloon Chase's cell pinged. He glanced at the screen, bewildered by the message originating from his own burner to himself.

Tapping on the screen, he read the message.

PLAN B.

He texted himself back.

PLAN Z.

Chase knew the request for Mongoose support wasn't an easy ask, but it was possible. McIntyre should've been able to convince Acting President Jacobs to make the right decision. And the fact that she wasn't communicating using Elena's cell meant something had gone wrong. He'd seen it before with politicians weighing risk, fallout, and reward. *Operation Honey Trap was a bust the moment Simon Adams was killed in Athens.* Chase knew it then, but he couldn't stop himself. As the mega yacht threaded the eye of the storm, it felt as if the mission was headed to the ends of the earth.

Dax broke the silence. "What's the good word?"

"No cavalry." Chase eyed Stepanov. "We stay the course."

"Dmitry must be told about Elena," Stepanov interrupted. "Allow me to call."

"I must be the one." Chase stepped toward Stepanov. "He won't believe it any other way."

"Thirty years I have been his most trusted friend."

"I'm the one who was in love with his daughter."

"I have eyes. I have seen. Who would do this to her?"

"Vasiliy, I swear to you I don't know." Chase grabbed a railing as the mega yacht lurched forward, then climbed a twenty-foot white-capped wave before cresting over the top. "When we arrive, you will take me to Dmitry, and we will tell him together."

Dax mumbled, "Hope this boat floats as good as the ark."

"We'll be there by tonight." Chase turned his attention back to Stepanov. "In the meantime, you'll tell Dax what you know about the island."

Chase left Dax guarding Stepanov and went to the lower deck to check on Ammelie. He knocked before opening the door. He found her curled up on the bed, hugging a pillow.

"Did you take Dramamine?"

Ammelie opened her eyes. "Stopped me from puking pasta."

"Well, that's a good sign." Chase stepped inside and sat on the edge of the bed. "You'll stay aboard while we go to the island. Safer that way."

"You've brought me this far, why not use me?" Ammelie pulled herself up, still hugging the pillow. "I'll be a good distraction if nothing else."

He considered her offer, knowing she had a point. "I don't want you in the line of fire."

"Who else are you after on the island?"

"A scientist who can help President Bouchard and the others who've been infected."

"How do you know this?" When he didn't answer, Ammelie surrendered, "Probably better if I stop asking questions."

"Less you know, the better." Chase smirked. "Have you ever fired a weapon?"

Ammelie shook her head. "I'm not a believer..."

"Point and shoot. Reload. It's pretty straightforward."

Ammelie's eyes softened. "I could never take a life."

"Since you're the only religious one aboard..." Chase stood and started to leave before turning back. "Say a prayer we make it out of this alive."

He left Ammelie and headed back to the main deck, where he unlocked the artillery room. As the door closed, he was struck by how this was the one room where he felt the most at home. Not the owner's suite. Not the bridge. It was here surrounded by lethal weapons and a safe that guarded his past. He set the SIGs and the holster on the center countertop, then changed out of the clothes he'd worn all night. Flipping on a flatscreen, he tuned into world news as the fuzzy signal cut in and out. News anchors were on standby at the Capitol waiting for a statement from Acting President Jacobs.

Chase picked up one of the SIGs and took it apart.

Remove the magazine, pull the slide, check ammo, allow the slide to spring forward, pull the trigger. Pull the slide an eighth inch, fire to release the hammer, pull the slide down, push the slide forward, remove it from the receiver.

Five seconds flat. He did the same with the second one, then grabbed more ammo from a compartment in the wall before turning his attention back to the flatscreen.

Acting President Jacobs stepped behind a cluster of mics with Albert Skinner, Nancy Frost, and the Senate Majority Leader standing on each side.

"Good evening, everyone. By now, the world is aware of the actions of the People's Republic of China in its attempt to assassinate a sitting United States president. As of an hour ago, we have confirmed thirty citizens at the protests are now showing signs of the virus. Unfortunately, six have died. We are working with the CDC to determine possible treatment options as we believe it is a synthetic strain of Covid, untreated by any of our hospitals nationwide. Moments ago, the medical team at Walter Reed informed me that President Bouchard's condition has worsened. Our prayers will continue to be with his family and all the other families affected by this blatant attack on our democracy."

Chase watched Jacobs closely. She was well prepped and delivered the message clearly. *She's not a stone cold killer like Bouchard.* Knowing the inroads the China government had made into the very fabric of the nation and the politicians it kept in its pockets, the question remained whether Jacobs was going to throw down the gauntlet.

"I've seen news reports, and those within the administration have been monitoring social media. Citizens are concerned China will unleash this virus in other cities. We have not received reports of this occurring, but that does not mean we are clear of this invisible enemy. I want to assure each and every one of you that we are mobilizing all resources to contain the virus. With that said, we will be implementing a curfew within the D.C area beginning tonight at 9 P.M.

"The world is witnessing the People's Republic of China's feeble attempt to deny their actions, even spreading conspiracy theories to avoid responsibility. As I stand here as a fellow citizen, there is no doubt one of their operatives brought this virus into our country, and if we do not respond, there will be further aggression. The executive order I signed a few days ago will be expanded effective immediately to include all Chinese embassies and consulate-generals. We will also be placing sanctions on any corporation dealing directly with the China government. Senators from across the aisle have offered their support. For too long, we have allowed the communist party to infiltrate our nation, and that stops now.

"No matter where you are in our great nation, I'm asking every American to unite, regardless of party lines, and say a prayer for President Bouchard. Thank you."

Jacobs stepped away from the microphones without taking any questions. The broadcast switched back to the anchors in a studio before cutting to a reporter outside of Walter Reed amidst a portable media city filled with network news vans, reporters, and onlookers.

Chase zoned out the reporter as his attention was focused on the cutaway footage showing thousands of Americans of all races and walks of life marching in the streets to protest against China. Thousands more carried red, white, and blue flags holding cellphones with white lights shining in the night from D.C. to New York to Austin to Los Angeles, spreading to cities and towns across the nation. Turning off the broadcast, Chase realized he was the gauntlet.

SEVENTY-TWO

HALF MOON ISLAND, NORTH ATLANTIC

By evening they'd passed through the torrential storm and were anchored off the coast of the island beneath a splendid moon and scattered stars. About fifty yards apart were four other mega yachts illuminated by exterior lights reflecting off the glassy water. Windowed frames on each vessel revealed those who traveled in opulent luxury as part of the council's entourage.

On the upper deck, Chase peered through night vision binoculars. He eyed the armed men aboard each of the mega yachts, then turned his attention to the island. The binoculars showed three helicopters on a landing pad. From his vantage point, none looked to be the Sikorskys flown by the Vihkrovs. Sweeping down toward the dock, he counted a dozen armed men scattered along the hillside and on the beach. The binoculars steadied when he locked in on Brandis with his feet in the sand dressed for the island life. Even in the dark, the night vision offered a clear view of the German's broad shoulders and biceps that stretched the fabric of his shirt. The former MMA fighter had created the perfect hideaway in Half Moon, a paradise fortress unknown to the outside world.

A crisp breeze chilled the air, dropping the night a few

degrees. Chase tugged at the Kevlar vest that wrapped over his black fatigues. His shoulder and leg throbbed, cuts and bruises ached, but he refused to allow his pain to slow the freight train. Before any operation, the anticipation simmered in adrenaline—which is what kept fighters and warriors alive.

I've tried to escape it, but the truth is I'll always be a fighter.

Surviving the RVG operations was a rush of pure instinct, not from any kind of special ops training. Going after Brandis, he needed warriors. It was one reason why he requested Mongoose, the most badass SEAL Team the government ever assembled led by Commander Norm "The Bear" McDonnell. He'd been with them in the slums of the Philippines and had seen firsthand the difference between a fighter and a warrior. But McIntyre's message was clear. Request denied.

No mercy, no surrender. No peril, no glory. No death, no life. No darkness, no light. Allow rage, retribution, or revenge to control you, and you're a dead man walking. Cast the rage, retribution, and revenge into every Remington, and you'll live to tell the tale.

Through the binoculars, he followed Brandis down the dock. For a moment, the earth stopped spinning as he settled his mind and eyed the target. Lowering the binoculars, he locked the memories of Elena in a place where those he loved and lost lived on.

By the time he reached the lower deck, the captain and first officer had readied the tender, a smaller watercraft than the speedboat, with Stepanov aboard.

"Drop off and head straight back," he said to the first mate.

From inside the lower deck, Dax stepped out wearing the same gear. A Kevlar vest, black fatigues, and a holstered Sig Sauer. He held an AR-15 in each hand. Right behind, Ammelie followed, dressed in hiking pants, a dark flannel shirt, hooded fleece jacket, and the same muddied boots she'd worn since the night Chase laid eyes on her at Baw Baw. He noticed her pale complexion from earlier had regained most of its color.

Chase asked, "Feeling better?"

"Much, thanks."

"I'm feeling a little bloated," Dax cut in. "Thanks for asking."

The first mate started the tender and pulled away from the stern, headed for the beach. Chase stepped over to the side and peered through the night vision binoculars. He followed the wake of the tender until it reached the dock. From a pin mic hidden in Stepanov's shirt button, Chase listened through his in-ear coms.

Brandis greeted with a cordial handshake. "You are the last to arrive, Vasiliy."

"Leave it to Dmitry to pick such a place so far from civilization," Stepanov grumbled. "Speaking of Dmitry, I must see him regarding an urgent matter."

"Unfortunately, he has been delayed and will not arrive until morning."

"Why has he been out of reach for so long, Bernhardt?"

"You understand Dmitry better than anyone. Perhaps he has a big announcement. You know how he appreciates the flair for the dramatic."

Stepanov paused. Chase held his breath.

"Please, you have traveled a long journey." Brandis pointed toward a Thai bamboo building at the top of the hill that Stepanov had referred to as the Peak House. "The rest of the Council are enjoying a wonderful dinner. Come, let us drink the night away with friends."

"I could use a shot of Grey Goose," Stepanov relented.

Exhaling, Chase watched Brandis and Stepanov shuffle down the dock and trudge up a flight of stairs leading straight up the hillside. The first mate cut the engine as the tender drifted alongside the *Winning Bid* before switching spots with Dax.

"You hear anything that raises a red flag," Chase said to Ammelie as he handed her a walkie-talkie. "Sound the alarm." He turned his attention to the captain. "Rendezvous in one hour at the north point. If we're late, disappear."

Chase climbed aboard the tender carrying the burden on his shoulders. He gripped the side of the boat as Dax started the engine and spun the watercraft around. Headed away from the island, they kept out of sight of the other mega yachts. The cold hit him in the face as he double-checked the AR-15 before slipping a pair of optics on the bridge of his nose. He'd commissioned Marcus Nicholson, who built a social media startup into the fastest growing tech empire on Wall Street, to amplify the technology used on military goggles. Silicon Swindler, as he'd been nicknamed by Dax, had delivered two pairs of state-of-the-art night vision with sharper thermal imaging, red beam reduction, live compass navigation, and a real-time distance gauge to a target. All built into the lenses.

"I'm gonna enroll in Le Cordon Bleu," Dax said matter of fact.

"Trading in an AR-15 for a chef's knife?"

"Rather chop off my finger than get my head blown off." Dax steered the tender toward the shoreline. "I'm looking for a sponsor. Can I count on your support?"

"Tell you what, we get out of this, and you've got a full ride."

"Paris, France. Not Paris, Arkansas."

"Deal."

Cutting the engine, the tender dragged itself against the sandy bottom. Chase and Dax jumped out, splashing into the knee-high water. Wearing the optic glasses, their surroundings were crystal clear. Pressing the butt of the AR-15 against his shoulder, Chase led the way with Dax a few paces behind. Following the GPS navigation built into the lens, they climbed the rocks to the top then gradually made their way through a dense jungle.

Twenty minutes into the trek, they were drenched in sweat, even though the night was brisk. At the summit, they emerged from the jungle on the outskirts of an open area, revealing a row of ocean view bungalows. Crouched in the shrubs, Chase eyed the men who stood guard. Without having to backtrack to find an alternate route, the best option was straight ahead. He was about to move when the captain's voice cut through the coms.

"Ammelie's MIA."

SEVENTY-THREE

Chase didn't know what to think.

Hovering in the shrubs, he aimed the AR-15 point-blank at armed men lounging outside of the bungalows smoking unfiltered cigarettes. A decision needed to be made. Retreat and search for Ammelie, or stay on mission. *It's a 160-foot mega-yacht. Maybe she's still onboard.* He motioned for Dax to circle around to the oceanfront. Then he turned his attention to the one bungalow where thermal images on the lens lit up like Christmas.

Dax's voice cut through the coms. "Geared up."

The limbic system of his brain governing his emotions and memories went blank.

He whispered, "Say goodnight."

Moving swiftly through the shrubs, he fired suppressive rounds, hitting one target after another. *Whock. Whock. Whock.* Around the corner of the last bungalow, Dax appeared, pulling the trigger with cruel intent. Suppressors didn't get rid of all the noise, but the sound was limited enough to catch the men flat-footed. Not one returned fire. With all targets down, a peaceful night resumed.

Reaching the bungalow at the same time as Dax, Chase turned the knob and pushed the bamboo door open. Leading with the M4 barrel of his AR-15, he saw movement but hesitated to fire. Pressing his index finger against his lips, he stepped closer and kneeled in front of a woman and three children huddled on the floor.

"Everything is okay," he said in a lowered voice.

"Please," the woman pleaded. "My children are afraid."

"We're not here to hurt you."

Dax zip-tied the woman and children's wrists together, then looped another zip-tie to the leg of the bed frame. Far from a perfect scenario, but the innocent were to be left unharmed. Chase weighed whether to gag them, knowing the ruckus they could cause would draw unwanted attention. He pulled four spit hoods from Dax's backpack and pulled them over their heads.

Leaning in close, he whispered, "Don't leave this room."

"Spasibo," the woman replied. *Thank you.*

Keeping in the shadows they followed a path along the ridge of the island until they reached the landing pad. Chase knew it was a gamble leaving the woman and children loosely constrained with the ability to scream at the top of her lungs. So far, there wasn't a sound. But it wouldn't take long before someone noticed the dead bodies.

"Checked every crevice. She's overboard."

"We're in a frickin' Carr novel," Dax mumbled. "Which one of us dies next?"

"All three of us agree, three to one odds, you're the first to go."

"Good to know we left Larry, Curly, and Mo aboard our getaway boat."

"Way to keep it real, fellas." Chase checked the helicopters for the Globali Holdings insignia. *Seems Brandis told Stepanov the truth—Dmitry hasn't arrived yet. Good and bad. Good that*

Dmitry isn't hunting us on the island. Bad because we'll need him to spare our lives if all else fails. He turned toward Dax, who was checking the photo on his cellphone of a crude map Stepanov had drawn. "Lead the way, Columbus."

Winding up and down crisscrossing paths, they reached the northwest side of the island. Chase kept his eyes on the digital navigation displayed on the lens, amazed Marcus built such an advanced piece of equipment without bragging about it to the rest of the world. Silicon Swindler never missed a chance at a headline with his name in bold letters. He'd make billions if he ever sold the blueprint. But they had an agreement to keep the technology secret, amongst the other projects Chase was bankrolling. Keeping his head on a swivel, he waited for Dax to retrieve molded explosives from his backpack. Slapping one C-4 brick on the door, Chase grabbed several more from Dax as they took cover.

"We're gonna wake the dead," Dax warned.

A scream shrieked from somewhere above them in the direction of the Peak House. Chase's heart pounded through his chest a split second before semi-automatic gunfire erupted in the distance. *Was McIntyre wrong about Mongoose? Who was the woman who screamed?* No time for reconnaissance in the middle of an active op with an extraction countdown.

Chase looked over at Dax. "Part the Red Sea, Moses."

Dax detonated the explosive, and a concussive blast ripped the iron door from its bolted hinges. Moving through the smoke and dust, they found themselves inside an underground prison. Each slapped C-4 on cell doors all the way to the end of the corridor. *It's gonna leave a mark. Better to blast all at once than one at a time.* Crouching at the end of the corridor, they triggered the C-4, and the doors exploded.

Chase entered the first cell to find a frail elderly African man lying on the floor, barely conscious. He moved to the next cell as Dax did the same on the other side. He checked two more before he found the Korean chained to a bed.

"Dong Hyun-Ki?" As the scientist nodded, Chase retrieved bolt cutters from his backpack and cut through the chains. "We're here to take you home."

His voice quivered. "Is she dead?"

"She's still alive." Chase pressed. "Is there an antidote?"

"L65ZA82U83."

Chase pulled him to his feet. "Is the antidote here, on the island?"

"Yes." His voice grew stronger, but his legs were shaky. "The German..."

"Six others." Dax stood in the doorway. "No way we get them all to the tender."

"The antidote is on the island." Chase pulled Dax into the corridor. "Worth the risk."

"We've got the mad scientist," Dax objected. "He can brew up another batch."

"Who knows how long that will take."

"Don't say it, Chase. It's not gonna happen."

Knowing the captain was monitoring coms, he said, "Extraction northwest side."

"Copy that. Anchor's up. Heading there now."

Four consecutive blasts shook the underground prison. Chase braced himself against the wall as fear shot down his spine. The prisoners stumbled out from their cells, unsure of whether they were being rescued or the island was being bombed. Four men. Three women. Varying nationalities. All wore soiled and stained clothes. A stench permeated the air.

No idea who they were, why they were kidnapped, or which government was desperate for their return. It didn't matter, all of them deserved to be rescued from this hell hole.

"Boats in the bay exploded. We're sweeping the vessel for IEDs."

"Get them to the extraction," Chase urged Dax. "I'll find the antidote."

Dax surrendered without a fight. "Then I'm coming back for you."

All of the commotion outside left Chase wondering who else was on the island. If Mongoose had been given the green light, then this battle would be over quickly. The fact that no one had confronted them in the underground prison after they breached the doors meant there was a greater threat topside.

Dax ushered the prisoners down the corridor, then disappeared out into the night. Chase hesitated for a moment, then entered an empty cell at the end of the corridor. Stepping deeper into the room, a sadness washed over him as he studied dozens of hash marks etched into the moss-covered stone.

As long as I know you'll come back for me.

SEVENTY-FOUR

MOMENTS EARLIER

Brandis heard Stepanov's muttered criticisms and accusations as he mingled amongst the council. He harnessed his anger, knowing he'd been screwed by them all. His loyalty to the Bratva had gone unnoticed and unrewarded, something he would no longer accept. He thought he'd be more furious when he found the bloodied pendant, but his infatuation with Elena ceased once the case was opened. He was enraged by the betrayal of the Americans and swore to even the score with the Englishman. All failed to deliver keys to the Vihkrov kingdom. Amidst the council he was merely a servant to the Bratva.

In the octagon, he always had a strategy. Strike. Clinch. Grapple. Punch. Elbow. Kick. Takedown. Ground and pound. Know your opponent's weakness. Prepare for the worst. And don't rely too much on a game plan. Those had been his rules in battle.

As he eyed each of the council, he thought of his strategy and how the game plan had been tossed from the ring. He knew their greatest weakness—loyalty to Dmitry. That's what brought them to the island. That's what enabled him to gain control.

"My friends." He raised a glass of champagne. "And Vasiliy."

The Bratva twelve were seated around a long table overlooking the ocean with a five-star spread of world-class cuisine and bottles of expensive wine. Not one responded cordially to Brandis' toast or his swipe at Dmitry's top lieutenant. Instead, each carried an expression of disgust and indifference.

"You are a roach on a spec of sand," Stepanov rebuked. "A traitor."

"Seems Vasiliy drowned the Goose." Brandis smiled coyly as he stood at the head of the table. His gaze shifted from one council member to the next. "You have eaten my food, drank my wine, and taken advantage of my kindness. Now you dare question my loyalty?"

"Why are you the only one who has spoken to Dmitry?" Stepanov stood to his feet, slightly hunched over, and pointed to each person. "None have been able to reach him."

"You are his most loyal servant, and yet his absence leaves you doubting your position." Brandis placed his palms on the table, then leaned in. "Why does he trust me more than all of you?"

"We know Elena was here," Stepanov seethed. "Now she is dead."

Brandis' brows furrowed. "Her death was not by my hands."

"And Dmitry?"

His stare darkened. "The king has suffered an unfortunate end to his reign."

The council gasped as each began to push away from the table. Reaching down, Brandis retrieved a Glock hidden underneath his seat, then shot Vasiliy Stepanov between the eyes. One of the women screamed as the old Russian collapsed into his chair. Brandis barked orders to his men lingering around the open patio, and each opened fire leaving the Bratva council forever crimson stained.

A few seconds later, an explosion shook the island. Brandis was startled as if he'd been struck in the face with a round-house. *Counterpunch.* Another sequence of explosions kept him on the attack.

"Find them and kill them," he shouted.

While his security raced toward a billowing cloud of smoke, Brandis studied the dead. Reaching into his pocket, he retrieved a detonator. With a flip of a switch, the mega-yachts near the shore exploded into a fiery inferno. Only then did he crown himself king of the night.

SEVENTY-FIVE

McIntyre paced across the Treaty Room and checked Bouchard's laptop for any messages on Unicorn. While Avery kept a watchful eye, she took a moment to stare out the window.

On the other side of the White House gates, a sea of glowing white lights spread far and wide, a drastic shift from earlier in the day. For the last several hours, scenes like this were broadcast from cities across the nation. People pushed pause on the rhetoric of division, disagreement, and protest to find common ground. Who knew how long it would last, but as she eyed the masses, there was a sense of patriotism that struck the right chord. A foreign power launched an unprecedented attack on the leader of the free world. Like him, or not. Agree with his policies, or not. All bets were off when party lines and allies linked arms to stand for a cause greater than their own prejudice and bias.

"No one is answering my calls," Avery complained. "I've been getting texts from world leaders, but I can't reach anyone within the White House."

"Should've left me at Camp David. I'm no use locked up here."

"Are you sure you can trust Hardeman and Thompson to see this through?"

"If you knew them like I do, you'd never ask that question."

McIntyre turned her attention toward the laptop, knowing being secluded in the President's private residence left her powerless to protect them. Gazing at the screen, she willed a response, but the cursor continued to blink.

"What *exactly* did they do under the Red Venture Group?" Avery asked.

"They fought the battles you'll never read about in the history books." McIntyre was tempted to rattle off the terrorists they'd killed, but boasting about what any of them had done never felt right. *True patriots find refuge in the silence.* "Not too many like them left."

McIntyre stepped away from the laptop and returned to the window. Years shadowing Chase and Dax across the Middle East, she'd grown adept at the mental battle of being holed up in a room waiting for them to resurface. She remembered the day Chase disappeared in Baghdad. When she called Michael Hardeman with news his son was missing, he calmly reminded her of the Red Venture Group's golden rule: remain a ghost. For days she didn't sleep. She didn't eat. Visualizing the moment she surveilled Dax pulling Chase out of a vehicle badly wounded still left a pit in her stomach. Weeks later, her intelligence confirmed it was Akram Kasim who tortured and left him to die in the desert.

Ping.

McIntyre spun around at the same time as Avery. Both stared hard at the message.

PACKAGE SECURED. MAYDAY.

A smile pursed McIntyre's lips. She snatched Avery's cell-phone and dialed.

Dax's staticky voice yelled, "God, I hope you're not a telemarketer."

"It's McIntyre," she shouted back. "What the hell is going on?"

"Party of seven. VIP is alive and well."

"Extraction point?"

"Northwest beachside." A burst of gunfire caused Avery to jump back, while McIntyre leaned in. "We need eagle eyes, or the show is curtains."

"There's a way," Avery blurted. "But it's a long shot."

"Better than dying on Gilligan's Island," Dax called back.

Avery grabbed the laptop and slipped it under her arm. "Come on then."

Leaving the Treaty Room, McIntyre stayed on the line as she hurried alongside Avery into the Lincoln Bedroom. Avery pushed a hidden wall open to reveal a private elevator.

McIntyre heard Dax's breathing grow labored. "Is Chase with you?"

"Negative." Muffled voices cut through. "Mac, you get us out of this...clean slate."

McIntyre sensed the dire situation unraveling as the elevator descended. When the doors opened, she stepped out and realized they were standing in the Situation Room. Avery hurried over to the rectangular table and plugged in the laptop. Bringing cellphones or laptops into the Situation Room was against policy, but nothing about what was unfolding was in a national security handbook. Another door opened, and an officer from the Watch Team entered.

"Ms. Bouchard, no one is scheduled to be in here."

"You can report me, or you can help save the President."

The officer hesitated. "What do you need, ma'am?"

"Access to AFSPC's mainframe and a predator drone."

"We're in a war, soldier." McIntyre relayed the coordinates. "No time to think it through."

The officer took the coordinates and returned to the Watch Team center on the other side of the wall. McIntyre set the cellphone on the table and hit the speakerphone. She knew it was better to remain quiet unless her words moved the operation forward.

Dax's voice broke up, but she caught the last two words. "Stay down!"

Precious seconds passed before the bank of screens at the opposite end of the Situation Room blinked on to reveal an aerial view of blackness.

The officer poked his head into the room. "ETA. Four minutes."

"Dax, four minutes," McIntyre relayed. "Copy?"

"Four minutes before we meet the Reaper. Got it." A rustling sound broke up the staticky connection before his voice was clearer. "Heads down. Asses ready."

Avery slumped into a chair and dug her elbows into the table. McIntyre remained standing with her arms crossed, inching closer to the screens. She counted down the seconds before the predator reached the island. Night vision captured a cluster of thermal images on the northwest side with four others approaching from above.

"Dax, you've got four TIC's double-timing topside."

"Heading downhill," Dax replied. "Hit me if we're quicksand."

"Copy that."

One look and McIntyre knew the cluster was moving too slow. She forced herself to stay locked in on Dax and not worry about Chase's whereabouts. Four combatants on-screen closed in as more rounds echoed through the speakers.

"I'm hit," Dax grunted. "Last magazine, then I'm out."

"Twenty yards and closing." A chill shot through McIntyre as a vessel on the screen moved swiftly toward the shoreline. She feared the worst. "You're being flanked from the beach."

"Perfect," Dax groaned. "We're in a trash compactor."

McIntyre stopped breathing and watched the combatants from the top and the three who were heading up the hillside from below. A barrage of bullets and shouting so intense she flinched and stepped back. Holding her breath, she didn't exhale until the four from the top stopped only feet away, and the other three merged with the cluster.

"Status?" McIntyre ordered.

"Friendlies." Dax's voice was calmer but pained. "Moving to extraction."

"Copy that." McIntyre ran her fingers through her hair, not knowing who the friendlies were but grateful they were in time. "We'll search for Chase."

"Check the big house," Dax groaned.

McIntyre glanced over her shoulder at Avery, who was a statue. She turned back to the screen to see one of the heat signatures on the night vision headed up the hill.

"Dax, where are you going?"

"Never leave a brother behind." Dax paused. "Thanks for having my..."

All of a sudden, the call disconnected. McIntyre dialed back but no signal.

"Now what?" Avery asked, stunned.

Acting President Jacobs stormed into the Situation Room with a razor-sharp glare. She marched up to Avery, who pushed back from the table and stood.

"Under what authority do you demand a predator?"

"Madam President," McIntyre interrupted. "We have Dong Hyun-Ki."

Jacobs snapped her head toward McIntyre, dumbstruck. "Visual?"

"Yes, ma'am." McIntyre held her ground, knowing she was on the verge of a long vacation in Rikers. "Operation is still hot."

Jacobs shot a look at the drone feed, then her Secret Service detail. "Recovery only."

"CSAR at minimum." *Combat Search and Rescue.*

"You said they have Dong Hyun-Ki." Jacobs pointed to the screen. "Looks to me like they are boarding a vessel away from the island."

The Watch Team officer poked his head in the room, avoiding eye contact with McIntyre or Avery. "Madam President, what are your orders?"

"Disengage the predator."

"That's a mistake." McIntyre looked to Avery for support. "Hardeman and Thompson are still on the island."

Jacobs held up her hand before another word was spoken. "I'm in command."

McIntyre watched Dax on the screen before the predator feed cut out. She weighed the consequences, but without the drone overhead, it was pointless. *What the hell.* McIntyre lunged forward and grabbed Jacobs by the shoulders, pinning her up against the wall. As she reached back to strike, she was tackled by Secret Service agents who wrestled her to the floor.

"Attacking a president is treasonous." Jacobs brushed off her fiery response, regained her composure, then motioned to the agents. "Your pardon is revoked. You're under arrest."

"You're a coward," McIntyre seethed. "Just like Bouchard."

"Take her out of my sight," Jacobs ordered.

As McIntyre was escorted from the Situation Room, Jacobs dialed on a secured line and conferenced in General Bert Goodman, secretary of defense, and Admiral Myra Gutierrez, chief of naval operations. She ordered the Sixth Fleet to the predator's coordinates, then hung up the phone and locked eyes with Avery.

SEVENTY-SIX

MOMENTS EARLIER

The Crow's Nest offered a bird's-eye view of the island. On the screen, Brandis watched his men race down a path toward the underground prison. His grip tightened on the Glock when he realized the prisoners were gone from their cells while the bidding for each continued to rise on the monitors.

The smoke cleared in the corridor, revealing the rubble caused by the explosions.

He stepped closer when someone appeared on the screen. His jaw clenched once he recognized Chase Hardeman in the same cell where he'd tortured and raped the American.

He tracked his men until they disappeared into an overgrown jungle leading down the hillside. Semi-automatic gunfire echoed. Instincts as a fighter kicked in. He couldn't allow his prisoners to escape the island. Each had a price on their head and a government willing to pay a premium for their return.

Out of the corner of his eye, he noticed the double doors to the balcony were ajar. He flinched as cold metal pressed against the back of his neck.

"Drop your weapon. Slowly."

At the sound of a woman's voice, Brandis kneeled and set

the Glock on the floor. Rising up, he felt the barrel of a gun release the pressure on his neck. He was in the octagon, and his opponent had just made a mistake. He slowly turned and faced the intruder who stood drenched from head to toe.

She'd never been more beautiful as she aimed a weapon at his barrel chest.

"My prodigal daughter has returned home."

"One chance to ask forgiveness for your sins."

His shoulders tensed. "Your mother deserved to die."

"She begged for her life." Her steely glare narrowed. "And you killed her."

"You were too young to remember."

She said in barely a whisper, "Run, Katarine, run."

He eyed her index finger as it twitched on the trigger.

With a loud roar, he swept his arm upward, and in one swift move, grabbed the weapon. Twisting it quickly away from his body, his iron grip allowed him leverage to push his weight forward. Punching her hard in the face, he grabbed the butt of the weapon and forced it free.

Stumbling backward, blood poured from her nose and dripped down her chin. Instead of backing down, she lunged forward and struck two blows that knocked him backward. He hadn't expected such a forceful retaliation as she dug her knee into his side.

Absorbing the blows, he caught her leg before she could pull it back and lifted her off the floor. Spinning around, he smashed her against the bank of monitors as she wailed out in pain. Keeping her in a tight grasp, he body-slammed her to the floor, then pounded her ribs until she coughed up blood.

Leaving her sprawled on the floor, barely conscious, he retrieved his Glock and her weapon. Grabbing a handful of hair, he forced her to her feet, then stared into the dazed eyes of his beaten and broken bloodline.

SEVENTY-SEVEN

Chaos unfolded in Chase's ear as he moved stealthily down a hallway. His night vision lenses adjusted to the fluorescent lights. Clearing several interrogation rooms, he listened to one side of the bantering between Dax and McIntyre. He heard enough to know the *Winning Bid* crew had broken his one rule and engaged in the operation.

Raises all around.

Dax's winded voice cut in. "Remind me to lay off the pasta."

"How bad are you?" Chase whispered.

"I'll never be Baryshnikov." Dax breathed hard. "Where you at?"

"Underground."

With the AR-15 tucked against his shoulder, he turned the corner and crept down another concrete hallway. Footsteps echoed. Chase ducked low and peered through the scope while slipping a flashbang from his belt. He waited until the footsteps were closer, then he tossed the stun grenade. A blinding flash and intense decibels from the concussive blast stunned the armed men. Impaired, they fired blindly with rounds ricocheting off the concrete. Chase moved from his position and downed the targets, then stepped over their lifeless bodies.

"Halfway up," Dax exhaled, breathless. "You owe me a Peloton."

"Copy that, *chef*."

Further down the hallway, Chase stopped next to a large window framing a room. He waited a beat, peered inside, then tried the door. *Locked.* To conserve what ammo he had left, he pulled the bolt cutters from his backpack. With a swing like Bond's, the glass shattered. Climbing through the opening, lights blinked on to reveal state-of-the-art medical equipment. A gurney. Arterial Line. Triple Lumen. Endotracheal Tube. Intracranial Pressure Monitor. IV lines and pumps. Heart monitor. Ventilator. Pressure suits. Face shields. Gloves. Syringes. And restraints.

Brandis' own mad scientist lair.

He opened a refrigerator, scanned the clear vials that lined the shelves, and recounted the alphanumeric sequence. *L65ZA82U83.* Halfway down, he found a single vial that matched.

"Blackjack," he whispered. "Heading out."

"See you at the top."

Everyone's aboard, boss. Dax, two to one odds.

With the vial in his hand, Chase acknowledged the captain. As he turned to leave, shots rang out, hammering him squarely in the chest. Falling against the ventilator, he landed on his back on the tiled floor. The force of the bullets knocked the wind out of him. Opening his eyes, stars flashed in front of him. Drawing in a deep breath, he reached for his Kevlar and felt the slugs lodged in his body armor. *No blood.* He searched for his AR-15.

From the hallway, footsteps entered the room. Chase reached across the floor and picked up a syringe. With a tight grip, he waited until the attacker stepped around the gurney before sweeping his leg across, knocking the attacker off his feet. Rolling onto his knees, he landed a punch squarely in the groin before thrusting forward and plunging the syringe into the attacker's neck multiple times. Blood spurt across the walls and tile as Chase wrapped his arms around the neck and twisted with all his strength. The attacker flailed wildly, stumbling across the room, but Chase refused to let go. With a sudden jerk, he broke the attacker's neck, and both tumbled to the floor.

"Chase?" *Boss?*

Catching his breath, he found his AR-15 underneath the gurney. "Still alive."

"Tried McIntyre back. No answer."

He picked up the vile off the floor. "Let's get clear of the island and deal with it."

"You're the one holding up the Uber," Dax grunted.

Chase tucked the vial into his vest and headed down the corridor at a full sprint, leaving bloody bootprints behind. He reached the end, bounded up a flight of stairs, and exited out a door similar to the one they'd blown earlier. It took a few seconds to get his bearings. With his AR-15 at the ready, he stayed close to the wall and moved toward the front of the Peak House. His heart pounded. His muscles fired on all cylinders. Poking his head around the corner, he was stunned by the bloodshed amidst the flaming torches. Then he noticed the mega yachts offshore ablaze.

Snap.

A heat signature in the brush lit up his lens. Firing quick bursts, a shadow rolled out from the bushes. Bullets whizzed past, grazing his side. A searing pain ripped through him as he returned fire dead ahead. Finding cover, he tried to reload the magazine but the AR-15 jammed. He struggled as the muzzle flashes moved within twenty yards.

Whock. Whock. Whock.

"Man down," Dax said as he stepped over the dead body. "Stand down."

Chase leaned back and breathed easier. "It's about time."

"I'd say that was an epic entrance." Dax limped over and helped Chase to his feet. Bloodied gauze was crudely wrapped around his leg. He pointed over his shoulder. "That's some sick..."

Chase wiped the blood from his hands onto his pants, feeling the open wounds bleeding out beneath his clothes. "You okay to walk the hill?"

"With an island like this, there's gotta be a golf cart."

"You know we can't leave them behind."

"We'll stop by the bungalows on the way down."

Chase paused. "Where's Brandis?"

Dax nodded toward the Peak House. "Only one place left."

Sweeping the bottom floor of the main house only confirmed it was empty. But inside, they found a private staircase leading upstairs. Shoulder to shoulder, they climbed the steps and entered an open-air living space. While no one was to be found, it was clear there had been a struggle. Monitors smashed. Splattered blood on the floor. Balcony doors were left ajar.

On a desk, a case was opened. Chase reached inside and picked up a pendant. Eyeing it closely, he rubbed his thumb against the dried blood. Slipping the pendant in his pocket, there was no doubt it was the one he'd given Elena in Carmel. No longer able to control the limbic system of his brain, he felt the pain open the floodgates of rage.

"Dude..." Dax picked up a torn piece of flannel. "Ammelie was here."

Chase tossed the AR-15 as he rushed out onto the balcony, his lenses switching to night vision. Thermal imaging lit up as the distance gauge counted: 300 feet. Without looking back, he climbed over the railing and dropped to the patio below.

In a full sprint, he darted down the path, retrieving his SIG from its holster. Two rounds fired overhead. Dax had seen what he'd seen. Neither shot found its mark but instead warned Brandis that he was in the crosshairs. Chase was shredded as he pumped his arms and legs faster and faster. Agony tore through every muscle and tendon. Blood pumping through his veins escaped from every open wound, leaving him struggling to stay sharp.

Adrenaline of the hunt leaves me more alive than a thousand peaceful days.

Chase pushed the pace and cut across the hillside, losing sight of Brandis for a moment. He climbed up the rocky ridge and pulled himself onto the landing pad. He stopped cold as Brandis slipped Ammelie off his broad shoulders, wrapped his thick arm around her limp body, and pressed a gun against the side of her skull.

With the landing pad lit up, Chase was struck by how badly she was beaten. He aimed the SIG at Brandis and looked for a clear shot.

"That's close enough." Brandis inched toward the pilot door of a helicopter. "Have you ever asked yourself why the women in your life end up tortured or dead?"

Chase followed Brandis with the barrel of his weapon. "Let

her go."

"You refused to prove your loyalty to Dmitry, and you forced Elena to prove her love to you. Both are dead, and the American will be soon." Brandis kept his dark eyes locked in on Chase as he unlatched the door. "You're one selfish bastard."

"The game is over." Chase ignored the bait and looked for a shot. "We've both lost."

"You don't even know the rules or the game master." Brandis started the engine and sneered. "Checkmate."

Rotors began to spin, and the engine whined, muffling the sound of the ocean waves. Chase shifted his gaze to Ammelie, who lifted her head and opened her eyes. *No fear.* He exhaled, and the moment slowed as his index finger applied pressure to the trigger. The world returned to full speed when Ammelie, with her wrists and ankles bound, lunged backward and head-butted Brandis squarely in his crooked nose. Chase fired the shot, striking Brandis in the cheek. While the German dropped his weapon, he refused to go down.

On the attack, Brandis picked up Ammelie and charged forward like a freight train crashing at close range. A vicious collision. Chase lost his grip on his SIG, then tried desperately to guard himself against Brandis' brutal ground and pound. He deflected several blows, but the German had kept his skills sharp. A loud ringing pierced his ears. Tunnel vision left him on the verge of losing consciousness.

One shot rang out.

Chase shook off the haze and stared up at Brandis' stunned expression. Blood seeped through the German's shirt as Ammelie held the SIG in both hands and fired again. Afraid the bullets might only slow Brandis down, or piss him off even more, Chase rolled onto his knees and lunged at the German. As Brandis swung aimlessly, Chase grabbed the beasts shoulders and dug his knee deep into the German's ribs. Expending all of his strength in a matter of seconds left Chase gasping for air as his lungs burned.

Still, Brandis remained on his feet, but he was unsteady.

Chase knew Ammelie might fire another shot, but there was a darkness within desperate to be the one. He charged again and this time launched himself into Brandis' chest before tumbling to the ground. Brandis groggily stumbled backward with a fiery glare of defiance—until the helicopter's tail rotor sliced into his spine, leaving his dead body mangled in a pile of flesh.

Shakily, Chase got to his feet and shut down the helicopter engine. Reaching beneath his vest, he felt the shattered vial and liquid. He stepped over to Ammelie as she dropped the SIG, catching her as she collapsed. Slipping one arm under her legs and the other around her back, he picked her up and carried her along the path toward the Peak House.

She leaned into his chest and said in a hushed voice, "Katarine is free now."

At the opposite end of the stone path, a six-seater golf cart approached with Dax behind the wheel. Chase eased at the sight of his best friend, his brother, once again saving the day.

The golf cart screeched to a stop, and Dax hobbled over. As they laid Ammelie carefully on the second row of seats, Chase couldn't help but notice what was in the front: a rod, a hand grasping the world, and a statue of an eagle carrying a young man.

Even though he was bloodied and beaten he had to ask, "Is

that what I think it is?"

"Scepter of Dagobert, baby!" Dax slipped behind the wheel. "Spoils of war, right?"

"Spoils of war."

Chase climbed in, feeling the wave of adrenaline subside into a puddle. Heading toward the bungalows to free the woman and her children, Chase reached in his pocket and retrieved the pendant. Holding it in the palm of his hand, he knew the only way forward was to lock the pain and rage away.

Time never healed.

Dax reached beneath his Kevlar vest and handed Chase a snapshot. "Found this too."

He didn't recognize the group in the photo. Then he looked beyond, toward the background, and it all made sense.

SEVENTY-EIGHT

BETHESDA, MARYLAND

By late morning, the SH-60 Seahawk helicopter hovered over Walter Reed.

During the flight over the Atlantic, a text message confirmed Ammelie was stable with two broken ribs and a dozen stitches. Dax was patched up and itching to collect his winnings from the crew for beating the odds. And the *Winning Bid* was headed east. Destination: Portugal.

Being the first to get stitched up after Monte Carlo, Chase knew he'd left them in skilled hands. He'd hired true pros who earned every nickel. Seasoned warriors who were invisible when the Six Fleet's assault ship arrived at Half Moon Island shortly before daybreak.

Chase stared out the window of the Seahawk at the hospital below, where a heavy military presence guarded the grounds. A makeshift media village was near the gates with portable satellite dishes, vans, and anchors anxiously waiting for their ten seconds of history. Beyond the gates, thousands more gathered, many of whom had camped out for several days. Witnessing it in person, the mass of humanity seemed larger than the reports twelve hours earlier.

Taking it all in left Chase speechless. *Tick. Tock.*

As soon as he was aboard the *Winning Bid*, he was tended to by the medic before he changed out of his bloodied clothes, showered, and washed the dead away. In a shot to being ignored, he wore jeans and a fresh hoodie with the Mongoose emblem embroidered on the sleeve. He was numb and his body was shredded as he packed enough clothes for a week, unsure of how long he'd actually be gone. Before the Six Fleet arrived, he stored the Kevlar and weapons in the artillery room.

When he boarded the assault ship, the captain isolated him and Dong Hyun-Ki from the others and escorted them directly to the Seahawk. Within minutes they were buckled in and airborne, leaving the hostages and the Bratva woman and her children in the hands of the U.S.Navy. A steady vibration and turbulence during the flight left him between a wakeful state and deep sleep. He dozed off only to jerk awake with flashes of what had occurred on the island.

Have you ever asked yourself why the women in your life end up tortured or dead?

Perhaps the most damning question of all—one he'd asked himself a thousand times.

In the end, Ammelie—Katarine—got her revenge and now she's free.

Sunlight pierced through the helicopter windows snapping him back to the present. Once the landing skids hit the rooftop, he climbed out, ducked his head, and shuffled his aching body alongside Dong Hyun-Ki. Neither had spoken since he unchained the scientist from his prison. Aboard the assault ship, Chase had heard the heated exchange between the Korean and the Six Fleet captain when asked to hand over the formula for the antidote. Dong Hyun-Ki insisted he was the only one who could replicate and administer it. Clearly, a bargaining chip for when he was questioned by the Agency regarding his dealings with the China government.

Chase had mixed feelings about the Korean. He'd infected the innocent to save his own blood. *Would I have done the same? Maybe. But he was unwilling to sacrifice himself so others could live. That's unforgivable.* He fought off the urge to strike as he thought of Laney being injected with the virus at the Korean's hands.

Secret Service led them down a stairwell guarded by more agents. Tensions were thick as they entered the isolated floor and were greeted by a medical team huddled together. Chase watched as they whisked the scientist away, disappearing on the other side of a glass door. He'd delivered the best chance at saving Laney, Bouchard, and the others who were infected.

If the Korean strikes a deal for immunity, then that's the price to pay.

When Simon Adams was killed in Athens and McIntyre appeared, it left him wondering if he'd find Laney in time or if they'd die trying. He'd expected McIntyre to be there when he arrived. *She won't miss seeing this through to the end.* While he didn't trust her completely, she'd proven her loyalty when it counted.

An agent directed him into an empty room, where he found a hazmat suit, gloves, and a shielded helmet. It took him a few extra minutes to pull them on, careful not to aggravate the bandaged wounds spread across his body. Suited up, he entered a secured wing while the agent waited in the hallway near the elevator. His shoes squeaked against the tiled floor at a slow pace that turned the corridor into what felt more like the length of a football field.

The rooms were empty, except for only one with the fluorescent lights on. Peering through the glass window, she was barely recognizable. A ventilator mask covered most of her face, but he could tell she was skin and bones. Entering the room, he heard the machines pump and the monitor beep to a steady rhythm. *Laney.* His jaw clenched as the guilt weighed heavily at the dire state she was in.

In Carmel, she asked him to hunt Bernhardt Brandis. He was on the verge of auctioning one of the most significant works of art for a world record price. So, he turned her down. He couldn't imagine what Brandis had done to her, and in the end, he hunted the bastard anyway.

Grabbing a chair from the corner, he set it in front of the bed and slumped into the seat. For a long time, he watched the machines work with no change. Ammelie's faith must've rubbed off as he whispered a prayer, unsure of whether his words reached a higher power. He checked a clock on the wall and wondered how long before the Korean was done mixing a dose of the antidote.

As the hours passed, his thoughts turned to memories of Laney from their weekends in Coronado to relaxing nights at his Bird Street home in the Hollywood Hills. *Everything changed when she betrayed me. But that doesn't matter now.* Anger only left him broken. And the thought her life was on the verge of the other side brought a heaviness of grief.

Late in the afternoon, he stretched his aching muscles and headed down the hallway. Reaching the end of the secured wing, he peered through the glass and watched the Secret Service agents who guarded the elevator, access to the stairwell, and the secured wing. Silence rang in his ears as he shuffled back down the hallway, his mind shifting to Elena and Dmitry.

Who will take over the Bratva? Where was Dmitry killed? Who killed them? Bouchard? Brandis? Who is left to honor Elena's memory?

BEEP. BEEP. BEEP.

Chase darted into the room to the ringing of alerts and alarms. In desperation, he slammed his palm against a red button. He heard the double doors of the wing hit the walls. Hurried footsteps grew louder. A medical team wearing protective equipment entered the room and went straight to work on Laney. One of the nurses pushed Chase out into the hallway. He watched as they injected needles and checked vitals before pulling the sheet away from her emaciated body. When they opened up her gown, revealing raw bruises and scars, Chase couldn't help but glance away.

A doctor pulled the automated external defibrillator and used the paddles. "Clear!"

Laney's chest arched upward toward the ceiling, then dropped back onto the bed. When the doctor repeated the order, Chase darted down the hallway. *I'm not going to stand here and watch her die.* Bursting into the corridor, he caught the Secret Service agents off guard as he plowed through the glass doors leading to the opposite wing.

Frantically he searched the rooms, surprised each one was empty. He spun around as agents surrounded him. Looking past them, he started to attack. Prongs from a taser pierced through the hazmat suit and struck him in the chest. Muscles seized as he dropped and flopped like a fish. His blurred vision focused across the tile toward the opposite wing, helpless to stop another soul from leaving him behind.

Minutes passed before his legs were steady enough to stand.

He never felt the agent remove the prongs. He never felt anything, actually. Agents gave him space as he walked solemnly down the hallway, passing the doctors who avoided eye contact. He reached the room as a nurse shut off the medical equipment and covered Laney's body with a sheet. Then Chase was left alone, and for a long time, he stood frozen.

No tears. No curses. No miracles.

Only regret...and revenge.

SEVENTY-NINE

WALTER REED—TWO DAYS LATER

Inside the presidential suite, a nurse checked vitals on Bouchard while his closest agent, Hank, stood guard in a corner. Hank had barely slept in days, only leaving the President's side for minutes at a time. The six-room suite included an ICU unit, living room, conference room, bedrooms, dining room, and a kitchen. All of which were outfitted with protective devices and secured communication equipment. Bouchard was moved to make him more comfortable during treatment and to keep him isolated. Agents canvassed the floor on rotating shifts which only elevated since the Seahawk landed a few days earlier. The nurse smiled at Avery and Higgins as she passed them in the hallway.

"I've persuaded the Speaker to bury the Abbott inquiry as long as there is no lingering evidence that could trace back to the President," Higgins said. "Is there any evidence?"

"Not that I know of, but I can't be certain," Avery replied in a hushed voice. "I've gone through his laptop and haven't found anything that connects to RVG. If something is brought to light, you'll be my first call."

"There is talk in Congress about considering the 25th Amendment."

"You just said the Speaker is backing off."

"Can't keep all the jackals in the pack." Higgins checked her cellphone and returned a text. "Well, we can both agree I've held up my end."

"And that won't be forgotten, Louise."

Avery sensed a renewed hope after Dong Hyun-Ki's arrival, even with the uncertainty about how everything would play out. Twenty hours passed since the antidote was injected into her brother. Since then, it had been a waiting game. She breathed easier after the ventilator was removed and she caught a few hours of sleep in a bedroom.

"No one knows the condition he'll be in if he wakes." Higgins brushed a few strands of her fiery red hair away from her thick black-rimmed glasses. "People will question the origins of the virus and the vaccine, especially since there are others who are being treated without FDA approval. Of course, the blame will fall on the PRC."

"The Agency is debriefing the scientist, but they won't authorize his identity to be public. He's officially our best asset against the China government. And I'm sure he's set the terms and conditions to cooperate." Avery glanced toward her brother, who was in a medically induced coma. "Jacobs is still in charge, which means it's up to her to decide what to tell the world."

"Who led the operation to rescue Dong Hyun-Ki? How was he located? Where was he found? What intelligence agency provided proof he was behind the virus? I've spoken to my sources within the intel community, and no one has a clue."

"Alison McIntyre."

"McIntyre's always been a fire starter." Higgins exhaled deep. "Where is she now?"

"San Quentin." Avery grew uneasy with the casual inter-rogation. "Jacobs called the shots when it counted, and she made the right decisions."

"She also started a cluster with our allies *and* within the party. Signing off on closing all China embassies? I under-stand one or two to make a point, but her actions will bring retaliation. And I don't need to tell you, leaving McIntyre in San Quentin is a loose end."

"The PRC attempted to kill my brother, and now he has a fighting chance to live."

"You have to admit even for the Chinese, the attempt was amateurish." Higgins studied Avery, and when there was no response, she added, "Are you back in the inner sanctum?"

"I am the Chief of Staff if that's what you're asking."

"Kumbayah between parties is a facade. Battle lines will be drawn. Get ready."

"I will do what is necessary to protect the President." Avery grew tired of the political jockeying. "David was undecided about a second term."

"For the first time in years, our nation is unified. If he wakes, he wins."

Pop Bouchard's gravelly voice interrupted as he ap-proached, "Strategizing already?"

"Mr. Bouchard, have you considered speaking to the press on your son's behalf?"

"Why the hell would I do that?"

"The country needs to hear from one of you," Higgins bantered. "It'll go a long way."

"We'll think about it." Avery leaned into Pop. "Excuse us, Louise."

Avery and Pop entered Bouchard's room as Hank stepped

out into the hallway. When Avery glanced over her shoulder, Higgins had slithered back to the swamp. She regretted meeting with Higgins at the Lincoln Memorial, but it was a necessity. At that point, she feared David was on the verge of being skewered by his adversaries, especially if General Abbott turned whistleblower. Now Higgins had a part to play in the presidency, no matter how dirty and nasty she might be.

"She's a slippery one, isn't she?" Pop pointed out.

Avery stepped over to David and touched his arm. "She's the best at what she does."

"You've always been the stronger one, Avery." Pop crossed his arms. "Proud of you."

"He's the leader this world needs, Pop."

"That's the nicest thing anyone's ever said about me," Bouchard's weakened voice mumbled as he opened his eyes and squinted at the bright light. "But Pop's right, though."

Tears spilled over Avery's lids as she dove on top of him. "David..."

Bouchard grunted then flinched. "I made it this far. Don't suffocate me."

Pop stepped over to the other side of the bed. "That was quite a nap you took there."

"The last thing I remember...Agent Kelley..."

"You were infected with a virus." Avery released her embrace, thrilled beyond words. "Agent Kelley died two days ago. No living relatives to notify. We'll release the news at the appropriate time. I wasn't sure what you'd want me to do."

"A virus?" Bouchard asked, confused. "How long..."

"Avery can fill you in later," Pop chimed in. "All that

matters is you're alive."

"And you're the Commander in Chief." She stepped out of the room and kissed Hank on his stubbly cheek. "Thank you."

Hank blushed.   "I'll notify Acting President Jacobs, ma'am."

Avery wiped tears from her eyes as she turned to see her dad lean in and hug his son. Then she retrieved her cellphone and sent a text to Nancy Frost.

HOLLYWOOD IS BACK.

EIGHTY

SAN QUENTIN, CALIFORNIA—ONE MONTH LATER

Four hundred and thirty-two acres of desirable waterfront real estate, large enough to have its own zip code, overlooked the north side of the San Francisco Bay. With a 130-percent occupancy rate, San Quentin was maximum security where the guilty lingered within barbwire fences that surrounded the yard. Whites. Blacks. Mexicans. Asians. Survival rested on keeping with your own kind.

Uniformed guards watched over the population, including seven hundred inmates in the Condemned Unit. Headshots of inmates were posted on a wall in each block—the ones incarcerated on death row, condemned to die for the sins they inflicted on the innocent. Their only form of grace was a lethal injection instead of the gas chamber.

In socks and rubber slippers, DCDR #701 shuffled down the corridors in an orange jumpsuit as ankle chains dragged along the concrete. Her fifty-five-year-old frame was strong, but the time in solitary showed her age, leaving her dyed hair with streaks of white. She was one of only a few women on the block—and the only one who hadn't been convicted of a crime. There was a list of charges that could be levied, and the one that found her in solitary was treason. But there had been no lawyers, no trial, and no verdict. Only a guard who shoved three meals a day through a slot in her cell door.

Thirty days had passed, and she hadn't spoken to a soul.

Her career as an Agency analyst, a covert handler for the Red Venture Group, and an arms broker to enemies of the United States left her as a noose for Bouchard. It's one reason why he'd left the tracker in her arm to remind her there was no escape. She followed three guards into a stark white-walled room, where she was led into a steel cage large enough to turn and stand in one spot. She eyed the floor as the guards stepped off to one side.

Chase watched through the vertical glass as the cage door locked. Then he entered and motioned for the guards to leave. He stood only feet away wearing a full beard, faded jeans, a t-shirt, and steel-toed boots. He had added to the ink on his forearm of the Stars and Stripes that covered up the demons of his past. Wrapped around his arm was a monotoned cobra and mongoose battling before disappearing beneath his sleeve.

He took a moment to gather himself. "It's good to see you, Alison."

"Damn." She grinned slyly. "You know my first name."

"Took the fate of the world to uncover the greatest mystery." He glanced around the room out of habit, fully aware the cameras were turned off. "You shouldn't be in here."

"I've been in worse places," she mused. "At least I've got my own room."

"Dax misses you."

"Then my dreams have come true."

Chase locked eyes with McIntyre. "This is not how it's supposed to end."

"Bouchard's got a forged confession." Her gaze softened.

"How about Agent Kelley?"

"Laney died before she could get the antidote. And I can't shake a haunting feeling that I'm the one who got Elena and Dmitry killed."

McIntyre's brows raised. "Dmitry Vihkrov is dead too?"

"Security footage found on Half Moon by the Bratva confirms Brandis admitted it to the council the night they were executed. A new regime believes I avenged the Vihkrovs death, so that's how I got in here to see you. Seems there's a few guards on the payroll."

"The dust settles, and the President is the one accepting a Nobel Peace Prize." McIntyre's gaze shifted as her sarcasm hung in the air. "None of it makes sense."

Chase's gaze darkened. "Brandis said there's a game master."

McIntyre eyed the room. "So, there *is* someone on the inside."

"Brandis had his own contingency plan in case it went sideways." Chase stepped closer to the cage and retrieved the snapshot from his pocket. "Dax found this on the island."

Holding the snapshot close to his chest, he watched McIntyre's reaction. Her curious stare turned to genuine surprise. He knew the second she looked past the group of twenty-somethings strolling along a sandy beach with oil rigs offshore in the distance and recognized the four people who stood on the balcony of a beachfront home.

One was dead, but the others were alive.

"Question is..." McIntyre whispered. "Which of them is the game master?"

"We had the street camera footage from Laney's kidnapping enhanced, which shows the same man on scene. And we got our hands on state highway cameras outside of D.C. that captured the moment Elena was shot. A few minutes after her car rolled and landed in a ditch, another vehicle pulled up and the same man climbed out. He walked over and reached through the driver's side window." Chase pulled at a chain around his neck until the gold compass pendant appeared from beneath his shirt. He held it close for McIntyre to see. "He took this as a trophy from Elena, and we found it on Half Moon." Chase slipped the chain and pendant back underneath his shirt, then tapped the snapshot with his finger. "Do you recognize him?"

"He's known as the Englishman." She stared at the snapshot and muttered, "Ex-MI6. A highly trained killer contracted by the Bratva, Cosa Nostra, Triads, and God knows who else. Dmitry introduced him to us when we began planning the RVG operation. He had been selected by MI6 for a similar program reporting directly to the Prime Minister. But he disappeared after a source accused him of slaughtering women and children in Sudan. We considered having him train you and Dax, but in the end your father determined he was too unstable. It was a brief interaction, and he was gone."

"How do I find him?"

"He's not someone who can be found."

Chase slipped the snapshot back into his pocket. "I'll get you out of here, Alison."

"And ruin the only vacation I've had in ten years?" McIntyre's brief smile faded. "Chase, remember, you're never lost if you find your own way."

EIGHTY-ONE

MASSAM, SIERRA LEONE

A rusty green Land Rover skidded and swerved down a muddy road surrounded by lush farmland. Behind the wheel, Ammelie itched the deep scar along her jawline. Overhead an African harrier-hawk welcomed her beneath a striking sky and pillowy clouds. Since leaving the village, she'd noticed the new power lines paralleling the road amidst the cotton trees.

A mile deeper into the jungle, she reached the clearing where the barb-wired fencing for the compound began. Pulling up to the gate, the guards greeted her with wide smiles as the children charged across the grass from the cinderblock structures.

Ammelie stopped the Land Rover and climbed out surrounded by the children. Kneeling, she hugged each one with a warm embrace. *No place like home.* Imari nudged her way through, holding a piece of paper in the air.

"Ms. Ammelie," she called out. "Mistah Chase sent me a lettah."

Ammelie took the piece of paper and read a handwritten note.

Imari,
You are a gifted young girl.
And that gift must be shared with the world.
Your friend,
Chase

A lump lodged in her throat as she scanned the official letter-head attached to the handwritten note. It was a letter from Ron Levowitz, CEO of Destined Studios, inviting Imari to join an apprenticeship through a foreign exchange educational scholarship that was fully funded.

"Imari, congratulations."

"I am going to America." Imari grinned wide. "Will you go with me, Ms. Ammelie?"

"Sounds like a grand adventure."

The other children pulled at Ammelie in the direction of the cinderblock structures that had been only partially finished when she'd left and were now completed buildings painted canary yellow with dark blue trim. She felt as if she was seeing everything for the first time.

Entering one of the buildings, the children's excitement was electric as they showed her the new kitchen appliances, dining hall, and the custom mangrove community tables. Then she chased them up the stairs to the dorm rooms. Brand-new bunk beds, mattresses, blankets, pillows, and storage for their belongings. Candid photos of the children hung on the walls in each room. Bright smiles. Renewed hope. It was almost too much to take in.

"There is more to see, Ms. Ammelie." Imari waved eagerly. "Come."

Passing the vegetable gardens, which had only grown fuller

with the rains, she was the Pied Piper as they raced toward the second building. Her eyes were drawn to a beautiful bronze plaque bolted to the wall. Imari hushed the other children as Ammelie read the dedication:

TO THE SELFLESS SACRIFICE OF SISTER AGNETHA BERGET AND TO THE SON OF FREETOWN, STAPHA DOLLAR. MAY ALL WHO PASS THROUGH THE KING'S GATES OF HOPE FOREVER BE FREE.

Stepping inside, Ammelie gazed toward the opposite end of the room, where a large whiteboard had the week's lesson plans. Each desk was lined up perfectly, equipped with its own tablet and notebooks. Shaking her head in disbelief, she brushed tears from her cheeks knowing Chase had lived up to his promise.

A bell rang out, and the children went running toward the dining hall. For a moment, Ammelie stood in the classroom alone, astonished. She inhaled the fresh aroma of barbecue chicken as she walked across the acreage, escaping down to the banks of the Mapandi River. Breathing in the silence, she exhaled the chaos.

"Maliki did an incredible job, and in record time."

Ammelie turned toward the voice, her lips pushing together into a smile. Nathaniel Fineberg, director of Tzedakah, wiped the sweat from his forehead and stepped down the side of the hill, balancing the bulge that hung over his belt with his boney legs. In his late sixties, the former head of the Kidon embraced Ammelie warmly.

"Your journey has been far too long, my child."

Ammelie stared into her mentor's eyes. "I thought it was

over in Nice."

"When you went dark, we feared the worst." Fineberg sat on an ironwood tree trunk that had fallen centuries earlier. "Chase Hardeman smoked out Wolffie as the Russian spy. Remarkable."

"We missed that one from the start," Ammelie admitted. "Wolffie was...convincing."

"Explains why we were never able to get close." Fineberg's spidery eyebrows furrowed. "Ammelie, is Hardeman the one?"

"I am not convinced he is recruitable. He does not believe as we do." Ammelie sat beside Fineberg and dug her elbows into her thighs. "I failed to gain his trust, and there is a side of him we cannot control."

"His relationship with the Vihkrovs is no longer an issue." Fineberg glanced at Ammelie, troubled. "However, he re-mains a flashpoint to President Bouchard."

Fineberg recruited Ammelie when she was a teenager. He mentored and trained her using the skills he mastered as one of an elite group of assassins who operated under the Caesarea. There was no one she trusted more within the Tzedakah. His warnings were rooted in wisdom.

"They will come for him, Nathaniel." Ammelie gazed out onto the river, pondering the meaning behind her words. "However, if we are hunting Jericho, he is the only one."

"Then I will leave the rest to you." Fineberg slapped his thighs and pushed himself to his feet with a low groan. "Now, how about we join the others. I'm starving."

"You're always starving." Her laughter trailed off as she whispered, "Maybe I'm the only one who can tame him."

EIGHTY-TWO

PHOENIX, ARIZONA

Bouchard adjusted his silk tie in front of a full-length mirror, then downed a handful of pain killers along with the rest of a Red Bull. Doctors warned about the accelerated progression of his diabetes and the permanent deterioration in his lungs due to the effects of the virus, but he'd always been in charge of his own destiny, and that wasn't going to change. Staring at the deep lines in his forehead, weariness in his eyes, a more frail frame, and the streaks of gray in his thick hair, he wondered what could've been.

"When I looked at you in that room, I was ready to see Nadia, Ryan, and Sadie."

"I know—it was all over your face." Avery remained solemn. "But I'm grateful you're still here, and so is Pop."

Bouchard stepped over to his desk and tossed the empty can in a trash bin. He picked up an American flag pin and secured it to the lapel of his jacket. "Simon warned me there was someone within the administration who wanted me dead. Before Athens, he'd only been able to narrow it down to someone connected to Bernhardt Brandis." Bouchard glanced out the oval window at the thousands who were gathered at Deer Valley. "We can't trust anyone, Avery."

"Higgins said the Speaker called off the truce and is threatening to go nuclear. House Intelligence Committee is investigating General Abbott's death with the intent to uncover what he planned to testify at the hearing. Congress is moving ahead with a committee to review the 25th Amendment to determine your fitness to remain in office. With Brandis dead, how are we going to find the mole lurking among us?"

"As long as I'm the president, I'll be a target on all sides. We need to play the long game, especially now. Whoever the mole is within our circle will try again, and when that happens, we will bury them. As for the speaker, no evidence has surfaced to accuse me of anything. And Congress is beating a dead horse if they think they're going to take me out. If that changes, then Higgins knows what needs to be done."

"Intel community has been unable to locate Hardeman or Thompson."

"Both were ghosts when this all began, but they remain a threat that must be neutralized when the time is right." Bouchard checked his watch, knowing he was thirty minutes behind schedule. "What about Alison McIntyre?"

"As far as we know, there have been no visitors to San Quentin."

"Then she stays where she is until Hardeman surfaces." Bouchard buttoned his jacket and turned toward the door. Clearing his throat, he rehearsed a line from his speech. "With great power comes great responsibility."

When Bouchard stepped out from the cabin of Air Force One, the crowd roared. He stood on the stairs and waved with his Hollywood smile. Walking across the tarmac, he reached out and shook the hands of his supporters, being sure to look each one in the eye. Cellphones captured every second, and it didn't take long before President Bouchard trended online with the hashtag: #BouchardIsBack. Twenty thousand stood shoulder to shoulder on the tarmac surrounding a stage lined with American flags. Posters waved with Bouchard's campaign slogan: FREEDOM ISN'T FREE. UNITED WE STAND.

Air Force One was the perfect patriotic backdrop as Bouchard climbed the steps to the stage. He clapped his hands, waved, and smiled, which garnered a raucous response. Stepping behind the podium with the presidential seal on the front, he looked out on a sea of people and steadied himself.

The crowd chanted, "We love you...we love you..."

Bouchard stepped back from the podium and pointed across the massive crowd—a fist waving in the air was a sign that he was fighting for each one of them. He waited until the cheers died down, then grabbed the podium with his trembling hands. "You don't know how much that means to me. It's been a rough stretch, but I'm back."

More chants erupted. "Four more years...four more years..."

"I'll never get to the speech, but that's okay." His voice echoed through the speakers. "I had this incredible speech ready to go for the State of the Union, and then you know what happened. I got knocked on my ass, that's what happened." Laughter cut through the air, then raucous applause. "I'll tell you it was touch and go there for a minute. I didn't see a bright light, so I guess that means there's still more I need to do. You know I was going to give this speech to Congress. But you've seen the fake news and the Speaker accusing me of some nasty things with the tragic events that happened in Los Angeles last year. None of which they have a shred of proof, by the way. Russia. Russia. No, wait. Iran. Iran. No, wait. North Korea. I wish they would make up their minds. How quickly they go back to their old ways to protect their power. You're all smart enough to know it's always about the power. Honestly, I've never been around so many crooks in my life. And that's why I boarded Air Force One to escape the swamp and be with you!"

"Drain the swamp...drain the swamp..."

"You've all seen the polls. People are unified in our country for the first time in decades while the Speaker and his cronies are grasping at conspiracies." Bouchard chuckled to himself, knowing Avery was freaking out. She'd written the perfect speech, but he'd decided to brush off the prompter. "In the coming weeks, my administration will be releasing a full report regarding the assassination attempt on my life by the Chinese. And by the way, it ties back to Los Angeles too. Chief of Staff Simon Adams and General Benjamin Abbott were killed in their effort to get to the bottom of what happened. True heroes who sacrificed themselves for all of us."

"We have a full confession from a very bad actor that ties it all together. But we wouldn't have found out about any of it if it weren't for the bravery of one of our fallen FBI agents who went undercover and brought down one of the largest crime syndicates in the world with ties to Russia *and* China. While her identity will remain classified for national security, she was one of the greatest unsung heroes in our nation's history. She must be honored, and I will make certain that it is done. Every citizen of this country will see the report at the same time as Congress and the Senate. No leakers!"

Bouchard grabbed the mic, stepped away from the podium, and paced across the stage like an evangelist ready to give an altar call. "In recent months, the world has seen the brazen acts of the People's Republic of China. I've spoken at length with our allies regarding China's viruses continuing to escape from their borders—killing millions and devastating millions more through the global economy. China lied to the world, and not just about Covid. The virus they unleashed on me and others who were innocent was no accident." Bouchard paused. "In the past, my administration has placed strong sanctions and tariffs on China and other countries, and I've worked through diplomacy with China's leaders." He stepped to the edge of the stage. "And where has that gotten our country or the rest of the world?"

The crowd shouted angry and fiery responses.

"China's Ministry of State approved devastating legislature against the Hong Kong people that destroys their autonomy. While protestors march in the streets to desperately protect the freedoms of their society, the China government has labeled them all terrorists." Bouchard looked toward the cameras. "To the people of Hong Kong, we see you, and we hear you. Your voices will not be silenced. We understand without a doubt who are the true terrorists."

Bouchard crossed to the other end of the stage as the crowd applauded and shouted their support. "Our nation was attacked in Los Angeles, and then only a month ago those attacks reached the White House. We cannot allow these acts of war to go unanswered. Vice President Jacobs made the tough decision to close all China embassies within our borders. I supported her decision, but we will not stop there. Today, I'm putting our enemies on notice that we will protect our freedom at all costs. And we will not allow them to control our destiny. Attack one of our own, and we will unleash the full might of our fury."

Taking a breath, Bouchard peered over to the side of the stage at Avery. There was more he wanted to say, but he knew the message had been delivered. Turning back to the crowd, he picked up his speech from the prompter. Breezing through the words Avery had written, he closed with an emphatic, "God bless America."

Stepping off the stage, he waved his fist at the crowd in another sign of solidarity. Walking across the tarmac, sweat dripped down the back of his neck and seeped through his shirt as he clenched his fingers into fists to stop them from shaking.

"Not exactly how I'd written it," Avery mused.

"I thought I'd freestyle." Bouchard loosened his tie, his stride a step slower. "So, how was it?"

"Looks like we've found our villain to win a second term."

EIGHTY-THREE

SUMMERLAND, CA

A metallic silver Triumph Bonneville cruised down Highway 101 through San Jose, Monterey, Pismo Beach, then Montecito before exiting at a small beach town. Founded in 1888 by H.L. Williams, Summerland was once known as a spiritualist hideaway. Population: 2,025. Over the years, the oil derricks that were once on the beach and piers stretching into the ocean were replaced with oil rigs off the coast pumping the natural resource from the earth.

Chase's nostrils filled with a burnt fuel odor of natural oil seeping from the surrounding area as he parked the Triumph outside of *The Nugget*, known for the best T-Bone steaks in the Golden State. From the old western saloon exterior to the red leather booths, animal heads mounted on the walls, and the framed photos of celebrities and politicians who visited over the years, it was an iconic spot in a forgotten town.

By late afternoon, the saloon bustled with locals.

Slipping into a booth with a direct view of a flatscreen mounted on a wall, Chase ordered a T-Bone medium-rare, steak fries, and a Clooney Mule. While checking his cellphone for any notifications, he watched President Bouchard in Phoenix. A bartender turned up the volume, and the locals cheered as if Bouchard was their hometown hero. A mix of tequila, ginger beer, and lime only heightened the rage that seeped deeper at the lies that were rallying a nation.

On the five-hour, 342-mile ride down the coast, his mind was troubled after seeing McIntyre in San Quentin. His brain rattled the odds. Even though money was not an issue, the outcome folded the cards on every hand.

The game master is still playing, and there's only one move left.

A waitress dropped the piping hot plate on the table and rushed off to another customer. He inhaled the smoky aroma of the 16-ounce T-Bone and sliced along one side. He finished off the Clooney Mule, then ordered a house cabernet. It felt like an eternity since he'd stopped to breathe, knowing the devastation he'd left in his wake. *Elena. Laney. Dmitry. Abbott. Adams.* He'd failed to save them all. The buzz grew stronger, so he ordered a second glass and ravaged the steak and fries. His mind wandered to Ammelie, who he hadn't seen since that night on Half Moon. *Katarine is free now.* He took solace in knowing he'd helped rid herself of her demon. Finishing off the second glass of cab, he paid the bill in cash and left a hundred dollar tip.

He shuffled down Ortega Hill Road, passing Summerland Beach Cafe, before ducking into Sandpiper Liquors, where he bought a six-pack. Ducking down the stairs on the side of the liquor store, he retrieved a key from his pocket, cut across a parking lot, then unlocked a door that led to a sparsely furnished apartment on the second floor.

Slipping into the short-term rental, he bolted the door and set the six-pack on a coffee table before slumping onto the sofa. He grabbed a tablet next to him and swiped. On the screen was a live video feed of a beach house less than two blocks away. He opened the first beer in hour one, and by the time he'd finished the sixth, the color feed had turned green and black.

For the next week, it was the same routine. Early dinner at *The Nugget.* Another six-pack from Sandpiper. Another day and night without any sign of life from the beach house. *Patience wins the prize.* That was his mantra as time passed slowly.

On the seventh day, he switched up the routine and ordered breakfast from the Summerland Beach Cafe for pickup. It took him five minutes to run next door and back. He flipped on the television and spread out the to-go boxes of eggs over easy, bacon, hash browns, sausage, and pancakes. He never had a chance to take a bite once breaking news interrupted all channels.

He watched in shock as people on the streets of Hong Kong were brutally beaten, chased, and arrested. As the afternoon and night progressed, reporters on the ground relayed unsettling rumors the China government had issued orders for its troops on the border to begin an invasion of the once autonomous city. Hour by hour reports and footage escalated, until it all stopped.

No news. No social media posts. Hong Kong was shut off from the rest of the world.

Chase's cell buzzed. He answered on the first ring.

Dax's face filled the screen. "Are you seeing all of this?"

"It's hard to believe." Chase leaned back on the sofa with his heels on the coffee table. "Bouchard threw down, and China isn't surrendering without a fight."

"They're escalating because of his crazy speeches!" Dax

paused. "Haven't heard from you in a week. You good?"

"Yeah, sorry about that. I guess I needed some space."

"Any ideas of how we're gonna spring McIntyre?"

"Nothing solid." Chase's cell buzzed again. He checked the notification on the screen while Dax was distracted. "Hey, I'm gonna crash."

"Sounds like you've got a hot date."

"I'll call you tomorrow."

Chase disconnected the video call and grabbed his tablet. On the screen, he watched the green and black hue of the beach house. Headlights flashed at a private gated entrance near Lookout Park before the vehicle disappeared down a long driveway.

EIGHTY-FOUR

LATE NIGHT

Walking briskly beneath the underpass of the 101 Freeway, he pulled his hoodie over his head, slipped on a pair of gloves, and crossed the train tracks. It was long after sundown when he entered Lookout Park at the same time as the historical invasion of Hong Kong continued. Heading down a concrete path from the park to the sand, flashes from Half Moon struck with each wave that crashed against the shore. His heart pounded to a steady rhythm as he focused on finishing the mission.

Inhaling the burnt odor of oil, he stuck close to the cliff as he retrieved his SIG and screwed on a suppressor. He'd imagined this moment since leaving Walter Reed. But even though he gripped the SIG in his right hand, he'd yet to decide the manner to impose justice.

No mercy, no surrender. No peril, no glory. No death, no life. No darkness, no light.

Glancing over his shoulder, he ensured no one was following. He scaled a ten-foot sea wall, digging the steel-toed boots into cracks between the cliff and concrete. Pulling himself over the top, he crept beneath the secluded house on a remote part of the shore.

Hiding behind a pillar, he listened intently, then moved to the end of the driveway before climbing onto an ocean view deck. He kept his body pressed against the exterior, then cautiously poked his head around the corner to get a look inside.

She's alone.

With the sliding door opened, he slipped into the house and stood in the living room as a record player scratched needle against vinyl, reverberating Coltraine's Chain the Trane. In one corner, a wood-burning fireplace was ablaze, and behind him was the blackness of night. She was pouring herself a scotch, oblivious to his presence. Wet hair draped over her shoulders, and a white cotton robe wrapped around her slender figure. Chase aimed the SIG at the back of her skull, tempted to pull the trigger and disappear. Picking up the glass, she casually turned around. Gasping in shock, she dropped the scotch, leaving pieces of glass shattered on the oak floor.

"What are *you* doing here?" Avery asked.

Chase kept his weapon aimed at the center of her forehead. "You were so close."

"I don't know what you're talking about." Avery started to reach for her cellphone. "If you don't leave right now, I'm calling the police."

"One more step, and this ends." Chase motioned toward a sofa with the barrel of his SIG. He pulled the snapshot from his pocket and tossed it on her lap. He watched her closely as she studied the photo of her standing beside Dmitry Vihkrov, the Englishman, and Nancy Frost on the deck right outside. "You're responsible for the deaths of Simon Adams, General Abbott, Laney Kelley, as well as Elena and Dmitry Vihkrov.

Deny it, and I'll put a bullet in your brain."

After a long moment, Avery hung her head. "Nancy made the introduction. No one was supposed to die."

Retrieving his cellphone, Chase pointed the camera and hit record. "Confession time."

"Have you ever gone against everything you believe to protect someone you love?" Avery shifted uncomfortably and locked her eyes on the suppressor. Glancing at the snapshot again, she stared into the lens. "We made Dmitry Vihkrov a once in a lifetime offer. In exchange for silencing those involved with Red Venture Group, he would receive $2 billion from the China government to Globali Holdings."

"What do you know about the Red Venture Group?"

"At the time, I didn't know anything except my brother was in serious trouble, and knowing the Vihkrovs were targeted in Los Angeles meant they might know the whole story. Nancy offered to help, and I trusted her to negotiate the deal. Dmitry agreed to our terms and said he knew how to handle it. You have to see, it was necessary to protect the presidency."

"You were played by the PRC from the beginning because you owed them something in return." Chase glanced around the room at the photos of Avery with her brother on the campaign trail and in the Oval Office. He recognized the celebrities captured in candid photos with the Bouchard family. A row of awards lined the mantle, and a writing desk was piled with papers and a laptop. *In a million years, I never would've guessed Avery Bouchard is the ring master. She's definitely a storyteller, so it's hard to know whether she's spewing fiction or fact.* "You and the ambassador gave the Chinese an excuse to invade Hong Kong. Were you taking orders from the President?"

"David is in the dark on this one, I swear. I wasn't even aware of you or Dexter Thompson until Elena Vihkrov entered into the equation. Nancy reassured me that was necessary for me to have plausible deniability." Avery nodded toward the glowing flames in the fireplace. "Then Elena brought me the dossier from General Abbott."

"You had her executed," Chase shot back. "Dmitry would never have..."

"It was out of my control—especially after Alison McIntyre was captured."

Chase struggled to resist a temptation to take one life for another. "And you made sure McIntyre ended up in San Quentin."

"Honestly, I'm not sure how she fits into the Red Venture Group, except that she trusted you without question—and she's the General's niece."

Chase was surprised by the revelation but stayed focused. "What about the General?"

"Dmitry must've issued the orders." Avery started to hyperventilate, and he knew she was keeping even more secrets. "I don't know any details. But you're right, he wasn't involved with what happened to his daughter."

"Agent Kelley?"

"She was supposed to be returned unharmed once the Red Venture Group was buried."

"Not good enough," Chase barked. "She was kidnapped, tortured, and stripped of her dignity as bait to lure me out. Her death is on your hands because of what you've done."

"Dmitry assured us that she would be set free at the right time." Avery exhaled deeply as her lips quivered. "When the plans changed, she was supposed to transmit the virus to

David, then spend a week in the hospital before the vaccine was administered. Blame would be placed on the PRC, and in return the assassination attempt would cause a greater rift between our countries. But you have to believe me, my knowledge about the Red Venture Group was limited."

"Your actions allowed the PRC to send troops into Hong Kong to gain greater control."

"I wasn't involved in those discussions," Avery confessed. "Nancy was in charge."

He aimed the suppressor toward Avery's temple. "Laney wasn't given a vaccine."

"Dmitry guaranteed us there was one, and said he confirmed with the PRC that one existed. He told Nancy that he knew where it was being stored."

"She died alone." Chase shook his head slowly. "To keep your brother in office."

"Don't you see, I nearly killed my own brother to protect our country." Avery wiped beads of sweat from her forehead. *And to give him a boost for a second term.* "I never thought the Chinese would retaliate, or that Agent Kelley would die."

"You're too blind to see the ambassador was limiting the collateral damage," Chase seethed, disgusted. "Both of you are traitors." He redirected his questions, realizing she had revealed the plan changed. "How'd you get tied to Brandis?"

"He sent me the same photo to my private email account." Her body trembled, and her hands shook as she grasped the snapshot. "He demanded a new deal of his own, a regime change in the Bratva. If we didn't coerce that to happen, he'd expose everyone involved and end David's presidency."

"So you ordered Elena and Dmitry killed." When Avery didn't respond, he pressed the suppressor against her skull.

Sorting out the actions of Elena and Dmitry was something he'd have to do later, or maybe never. "You're out of lies, and I'm out of time."

"Please, don't kill me," she begged, nodding toward a briefcase next to the fireplace. "Dmitry's cellphones and laptop are inside. Take them, control the Bratva, and the Red Venture Group remains buried."

"You're trying to bribe someone with nothing left to lose. You stole those I love from me, and now you face the consequences." Eyes flared as his index finger itched on the trigger. He stopped recording. It wasn't a full confession, but he'd heard enough to see how the puzzle pieces fit together. "I'm not a priest, so you won't hear words of forgiveness from my lips." As if playing a game of cat and mouse, he pulled the SIG back long enough for her to take another breath. "One last question...who is the Englishman?"

Cheeks flushed as her stare shifted. "Who?"

"No more lies." Chase stabbed at the snapshot. "What's his name?"

"I thought he was Dmitry's bodyguard, that's all."

"He kidnapped Agent Kelley, and assassinated Elena Vihkrov. That much I know for sure. And I'm betting he killed Dmitry, General Abbott, *and* Simon Adams." Chase kept the SIG aimed with precision. "I'll ask you again, what's his name?"

"Nancy called him..." Avery's mouth gaped open, struggling to respond. "Jacob...Jacob Thomas."

Chase wasn't going to torture her for the whole truth and nothing but the truth. In the end, it wouldn't change the outcome. She'd given him what he came for—*Jacob Thomas*. He'd sealed her fate and knew there would come a day when

Nancy Frost paid for her sins as well.

"Stand up and turn around." Chase grabbed her arm. "Do as I say, and you'll live."

Avery kicked her legs out, but he pushed them aside, pounced, and straddled her while pressing the suppressor against her forehead. With his other hand, he retrieved a syringe from his hoodie. He stabbed the needle into her skin, pushing the plunger all the way until the full dosage was gone. Avery grabbed her throat, glared wide-eyed, then her arms dropped to her sides.

Chase whispered in her ear, "You will greet your brother at the fiery gates."

Avery's eyelids fluttered, and her pupils rolled back, revealing only the whites of her eyes. A black market drug flowed through her veins, designed to stop blood from pumping through the mitral, tricuspid, aortic, and pulmonary valves. He climbed off of her as her head tilted backward. Checking his watch, he listened to her labored breathing.

Stepping over to the briefcase, he picked it up and shot a glance at the flames in the fire. He stared at the charred shreds of paper and assumed it was in fact the Abbott dossier, which would've exposed them all. *I'm not here for evidence, I'm here to settle the score.* Counting down the seconds, he waited until Avery breathed one last breath.

Reaching the Triumph Bonneville he'd left parked underneath the overpass, he tucked the SIG and suppressor into his backpack and secured the briefcase to the back of the leather seat. He slipped on a helmet and kickstarted the motorcycle. Then he watched a clip of Avery's confession on the screen of his cellphone, scrolled through the rest, and with one tap, he sent it to Bouchard's private number.

Tucking his cellphone away, he flipped the visor of his helmet down and revved the engine before riding the Triumph onto the on-ramp of the 101 South. Swerving between traffic, the motorcycle sped along the coast toward Los Angeles and a Gulfstream waiting to take him home.

Deep in the shadows where darkness lingered, a secret disrupted a delicate balance within the hallowed halls of freedom. A secret the powerful kept hidden from the world. A secret the game maker ensured protected one man's reign. A secret that sparked a treacherous war with no end. Avery couldn't have scripted it better, except this wasn't fiction. There were consequences for ending a life. Chase knew that better than anyone.

EIGHTY-FIVE

BRERA, ITALY—MONTHS LATER

A blender sounded off as an alarm clock.

Rolling out of bed, Chase rubbed his eyes hard and glanced briefly at the closet where the safe was hidden. He hadn't opened it since placing Elena's pendant inside. He'd decided to keep the past locked away for now where it belonged.

Since he arrived in Brera, he'd unplugged from the rest of the world.

After his text to Bouchard went unanswered, he determined it was a stalemate. When the world mourned Avery Bouchard's death at her memorial, he spent the night kneading dough with Dax, testing out the new pizza oven on the roof.

The continued blackout from Hong Kong, where the only news was rumors, as well as the mounting rhetoric between the U.S. and China regarding the American citizens caught within its borders left him content to stay hidden in the apartment.

Before leaving Los Angeles, he'd made arrangements with the help of Silicon Swindler to bury Laney beside his dad at Forest Lawn in Hollywood Hills. It was the least he could do and the most without stepping back on U.S. soil. While the situation with McIntyre ground to a halt, he woke every morning consumed with finding another way.

As the weeks passed, he realized how weary he was from war. And with the breaking news of Nancy Frost resigning as U.S. ambassador to China, his lack of determination to even the score meant he was too damaged to hunt Jacob Thomas—the Englishman.

The distressed wood floor creaked beneath his bare feet as he shuffled down the hall. More whining from the blender before it turned to a steady hum. Yawning wide, he ran his fingers through his mop of hair and stretched his muscles. *Less pain today.* Some scars healed over time, while others remained scabs to be picked. Daylight streaked across the living room, brightening up the kitchen where Dax was busy mixing a concoction.

"You couldn't wait until eight?" Chase grumbled.

"Rise and shine, lazy ass." Dax poured a dark green liquid from the blender into two glasses, then handed Chase one. "I'm calling it the Gut Punch."

Chase winced as if he'd been offended. "What is it?"

"Kale, spinach, arugula, broccoli, peanut butter, pineapple, cucumber, banana, protein powder, almond milk, and dates."

"What is this, a cleanse?"

Dax slapped him on the back. "Guaranteed to go right through you."

"Perfect." Chase downed the glass and tried not to gag. "Tastes...terrible."

"Yeah, you better stay close to the porcelain throne just in case."

Chase and Dax burst out laughing. It was the first time since Chase returned to Brera that his lips had broken more than a smile. He shuffled across the quaint white-walled apartment decorated with Mid Century furniture and antique artifacts spread throughout. The Scepter of Dagobert had found a perfect spot next to the Statue of Farrah. He stopped to look at the framed photos of his parents when they were young, in love, and the world was a glorious adventure.

Opening the glass door leading out to the Juliet Balcony, he held his arms above his head and arched his spine. The balconette offered a bird's-eye view of the district, and at this time of the morning, the city glowed. Leaning out on the iron rod, he noticed how the overgrown shrubbery creeping down the orangish clay-stained walls was thicker than the week before. When he turned his gaze toward the alley, a woman appeared walking down the cobblestone alley. Her sundress flowed with each stride until she stopped beneath the balconette and looked up from below.

"I waited at Baw Baw, but you never showed." Ammelie removed her dark sunglasses and perched them on the top of her head. Her short-cropped brunette hair had grown past her shoulders. With a shy grin, she added, "I still owe you a beer, remember?"

Dax stepped out next to Chase and said casually, "What's up, Ammelie?"

"I'm trying to ask Chase out on a date," she winked. "You are looking good, Dax."

"Stay right where you are," Chase called out. "Don't go anywhere."

He hustled across the apartment as Dax mumbled, "Damn, always the third wheel."

Darting into his bedroom, Chase slipped out of his wrinkled clothes and grabbed a pair of jeans and a fresh shirt. He didn't think twice about leaving Dax behind in his test kitchen. Pulling on his jeans and shirt, he hurried down the hall before stepping onto the old slat elevator and closing the iron gate. Butterflies attacked the green juice. Reaching the garage, he passed by the 1962 Ferrari 250 GTO, a gift from Luigino Sagese after Chase hand-delivered the briefcase with Dmitry's cellphones and laptop to the Cosa Nostra's golden boy.

Slipping out from the garage, their eyes met, and time slowed. Chase had thought about what he'd say if he ever saw her again. Now that she was standing there in front of him, he was tongue-tied.

"Don't come home after curfew," Dax shouted from above. "Chase...you're welcome."

"Thanks, Dax," Chase answered with a three-finger salute, then turned to Ammelie. "So, where do you want to go?"

She grabbed his hand. "I know the perfect place."

Walking down the alley toward the center square, he didn't know where they were headed, and he didn't care. With their fingers perfectly intertwined, he followed her lead.

"I never had a chance to thank you," she said. "For everything."

"I can say the same to you, Ammelie. You were the one who ended your nightmare. I guess we should talk about..."

"We will bare our souls later."

Chase lightened the conversation. "How's Imari?"

Ammelie grinned. "You've changed that young girl's life."

"Levowitz is one of the good guys in Hollywood. He'll see how talented she is."

"Maliki found a chaperone to go with her." Ammelie paused. "Why didn't..."

"I'm a big chicken," Chase bantered. "And I don't take rejection well."

Ammelie leaned in close and kissed him on the cheek. "So much to learn about you."

He felt the heat on his face. "Buy me that beer, and I'll tell you all you want to know."

She gripped Chase's hand and led him down Via Quintino Sella. Only then did he realize where they were headed. *Vecchia*. Memories of his parents rolled as if playing on vintage film. At the same time, he hoped the butterflies would turn into killer hornets and fight off the Gut Punch.

Reaching the bright yellow awning of the corner cafe, he followed Ammelie toward a sidewalk table. He was a perfect gentleman as he pulled out a chair and waited for her to be seated. Then he slipped into the chair across from her and relaxed. Staring into her eyes for a moment, life was simple. He never anticipated the other woman who joined them at the table.

His gaze darted between them, astonished. Similar brunette hair. Equally fair skin. Both with slender and strong figures. But it was the glint in Ammelie's light golden eyes that separated them from a mirrored reflection. His brows raised as he waited for someone to speak. On the edge of his seat, Ammelie grabbed his hand and smiled warmly.

"Chase, allow me to introduce you to Katarine."

About the Author

With the DNA of a world traveler, D.J. Williams was born and raised in Hong Kong, igniting an adventurous spirit as he ventured into the jungles of the Amazon, the bush of Africa, and the slums of the Far East. His global travels submerged him in a myriad of cultures, providing a unique perspective that fuels his creativity.

As a fresh voice in mystery, suspense, and YA fantasy, his novels have climbed the charts ranking as high as #1 on Amazon Hot New Releases. His books *The Auctioneer* and *Hunt For Eden's Star* have received stellar reviews from *Kirkus Reviews*, the most trusted voice in book discovery. Williams has also been featured in Publishers Weekly and Writer's Digest, as well as being an executive producer and director on over 500 episodes of broadcast television.

You can connect with me on:

🌐 https://www.djwilliamsbooks.com

🐦 https://twitter.com/djwilliamsbooks

🔗 https://www.instagram.com/djwilliamsbooks

Subscribe to my newsletter:

✉️ https://www.djwilliamsbooks.com

Also by D.J. WILLIAMS

Author of mystery, suspense, international thrillers, and YA supernatural fantasy.

THE AUCTIONEER (Book One, Chase Hardeman)
"An exciting, well-executed thriller . . . the danger is palpable . . . a highly recommended read that will make readers hope for a sequel." *Kirkus Reviews*

Chase Hardeman, a former special ops veteran, is left questioning whether his past covert missions in the Middle East are the cause of the chaos that's erupted in his life. Dreams of leaving a clandestine war behind and becoming a legend like his father in the auction arena teeter on the brink once he implements a contingency plan amidst an FBI investigation. Captivated by an old flame, Chase navigates the dark corridors of the collector car world in search of a myth. He believes finding this hidden treasure will reveal answers to a ghost buried in the desert of Mosul known to US intelligence as the Prodigal. On this perilous quest, Chase is drawn closer to a deadly threat as he leverages the criminal underworld to prevent a global terrorist attack. With the clock ticking, Chase is forced to relive the past in an imminent showdown and discovers the truth is not as it seems.

HUNT FOR EDEN'S STAR (Book One, Beacon Hill)
Discover the story of an intrepid, globe-trotting teen and a motley group of friends in a world where choices have epic consequences.

In this new coming-of-age YA fantasy novel full of action-packed adventure, Williams tells the tale of a teen who is thrown into a world of ancient secrets when he discovers a supernatural artifact that protects a weapon of mass destruction. With the help of a diverse group of friends, he embarks on a global adventure, seeking the truth about his sister's death. He uncovers two clandestine, supernatural societies waging an epic, hidden war that threatens the future of civilization.

As Jack races to collect ancient artifacts critical to the survival of the world, readers are transported to incredible international locales across Asia, including the lush jungles of the Philippines and the high-energy streets of Hong Kong. Themes of addiction, revenge, faith, and friendship emerge as Jack battles literal and psychological demons, and even his own friends and family members, on his quest to thwart the forces of evil.

SECRETS OF THE HIGHLANDS (Book Two, Beacon Hill)
Jack Reynolds has uncovered ancient secrets at a great cost. Now he must unleash the truth with the help of his crew: Vince, Tim, Amina, and the chosen one, Emma.

Jack is the only one who can wield the power of Eden's Star, but can he control it before it destroys him? Badly weakened by the compass and hunted by powerful dark forces across international cities and secret realms, Jack and his crew are desperate to find him a healer. But when new enemies emerge to test the team's loyalties, the search for the Cherub's ancient artifacts intensifies.

Fighting against her own heartbreak, Emma struggles to stop the Merikh from capturing innocent Cherub and stealing their powers for their own sinister schemes. As the truth of a haunting prophecy is revealed, and an ally turns to the dark side, Jack and Emma must decide together if trusting a narrow path is worth the sacrifice.

25772368R00278